WAKING UP

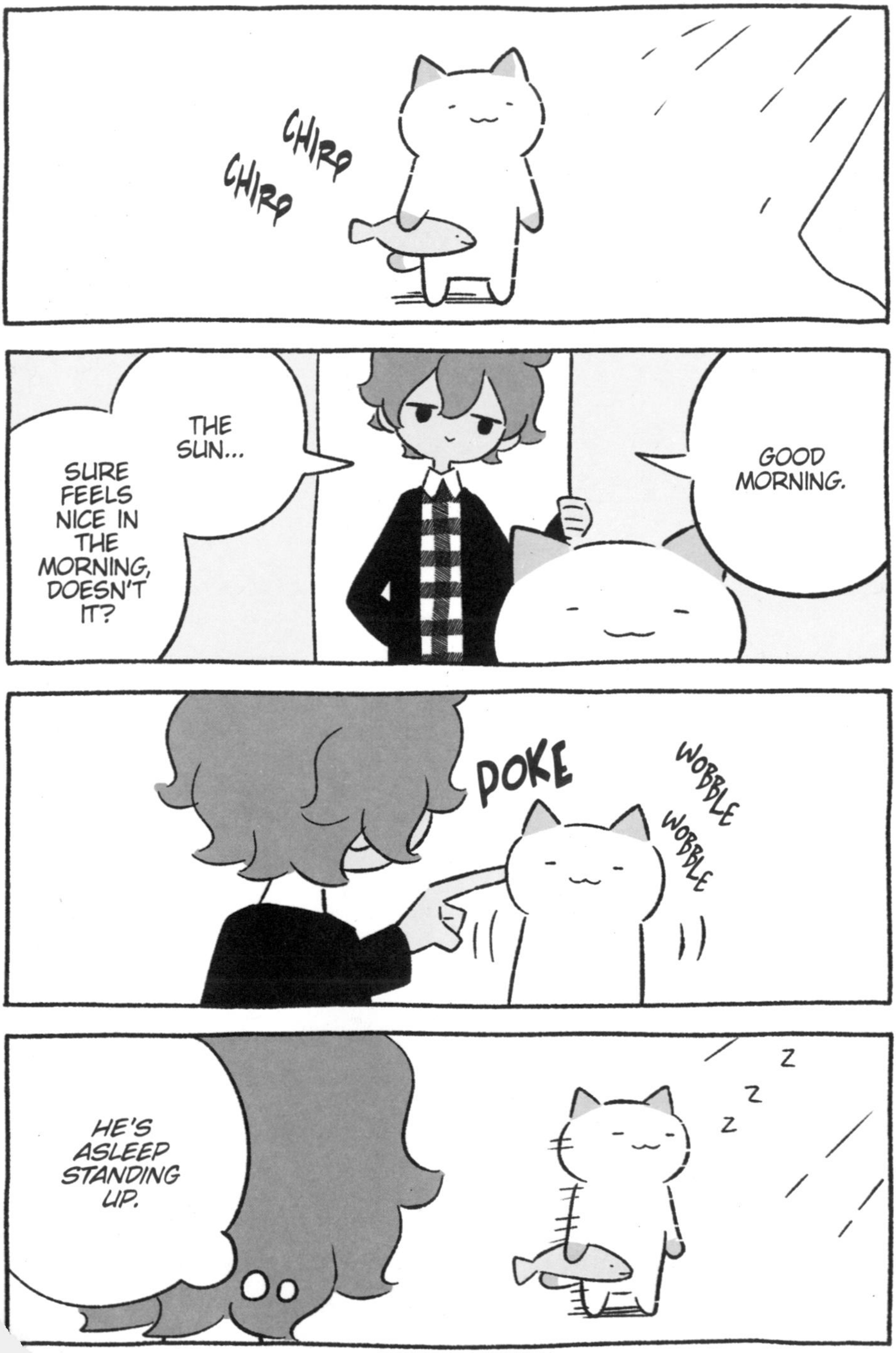
CHIRP
CHIRP
GOOD MORNING.
THE SUN...
SURE FEELS NICE IN THE MORNING, DOESN'T IT?
WOBBLE
POKE
WOBBLE
Z
Z
Z
HE'S ASLEEP STANDING UP.

TOPPINGS

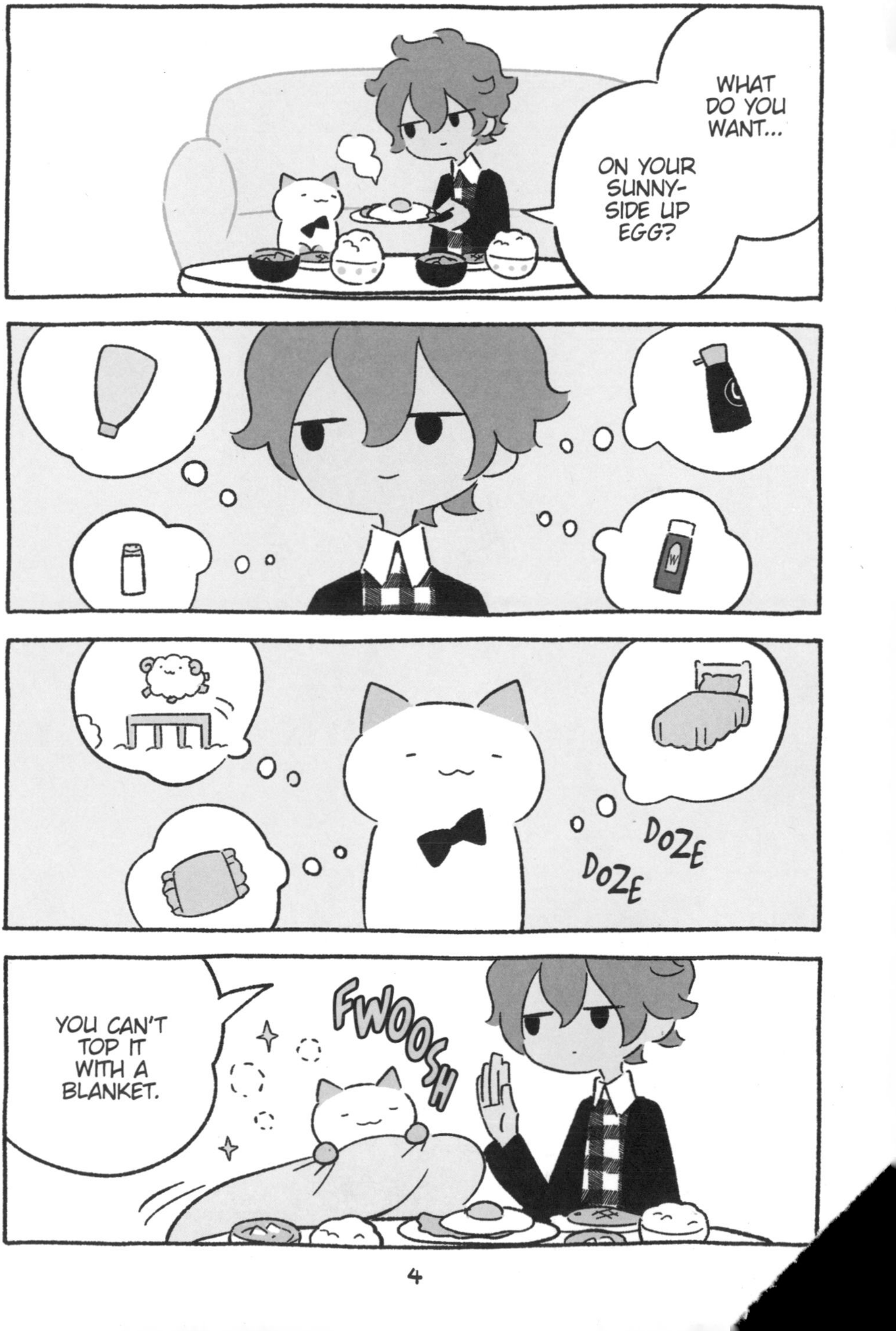
WHAT DO YOU WANT...
ON YOUR SUNNY-SIDE UP EGG?
DOZE
DOZE
FWOOSH
YOU CAN'T TOP IT WITH A BLANKET.

NEST

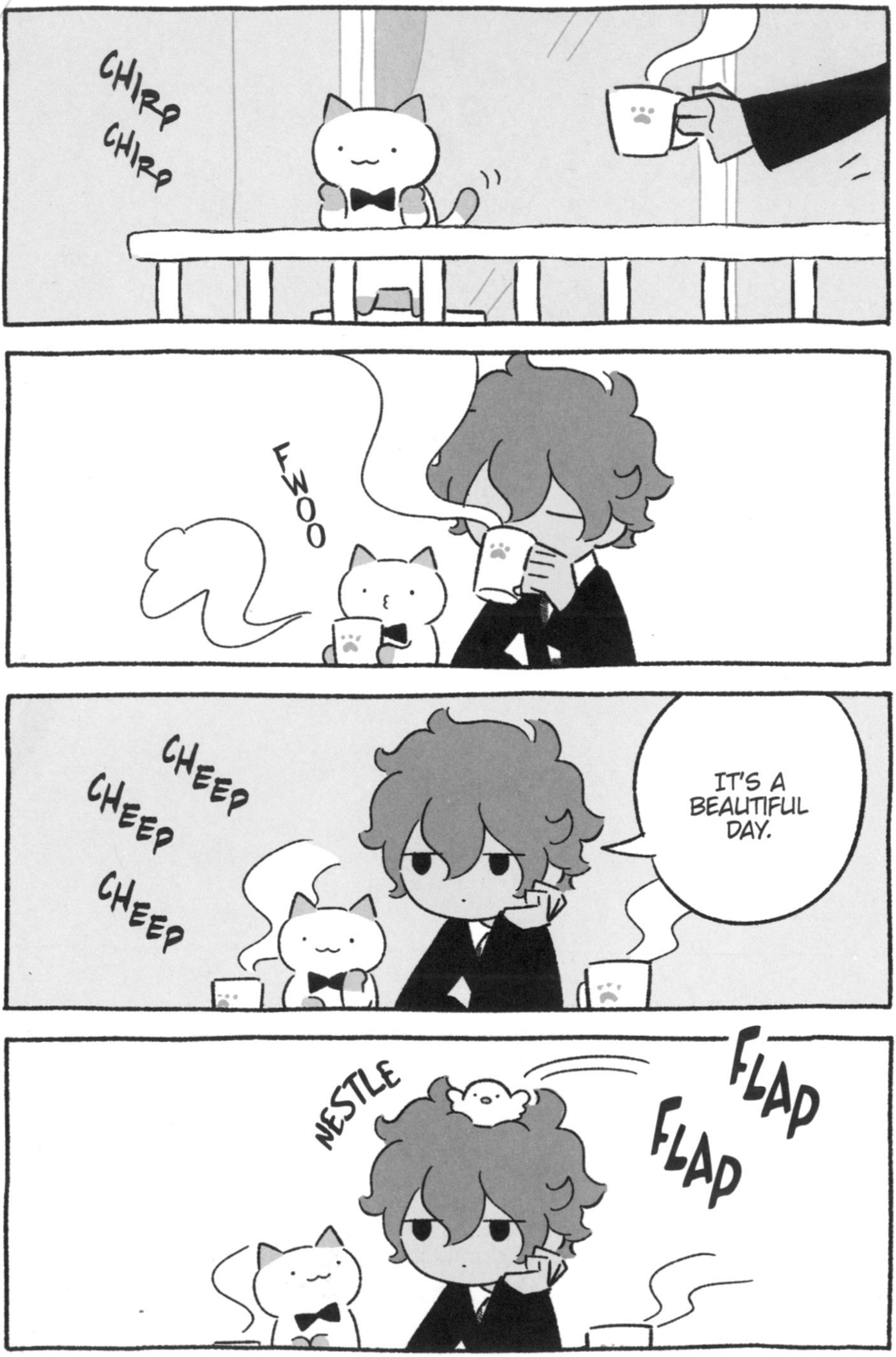
CHIRP
CHIRP
FWOO
IT'S A BEAUTIFUL DAY.
CHEEP
CHEEP
CHEEP
FLAP
FLAP
NESTLE

BIRD

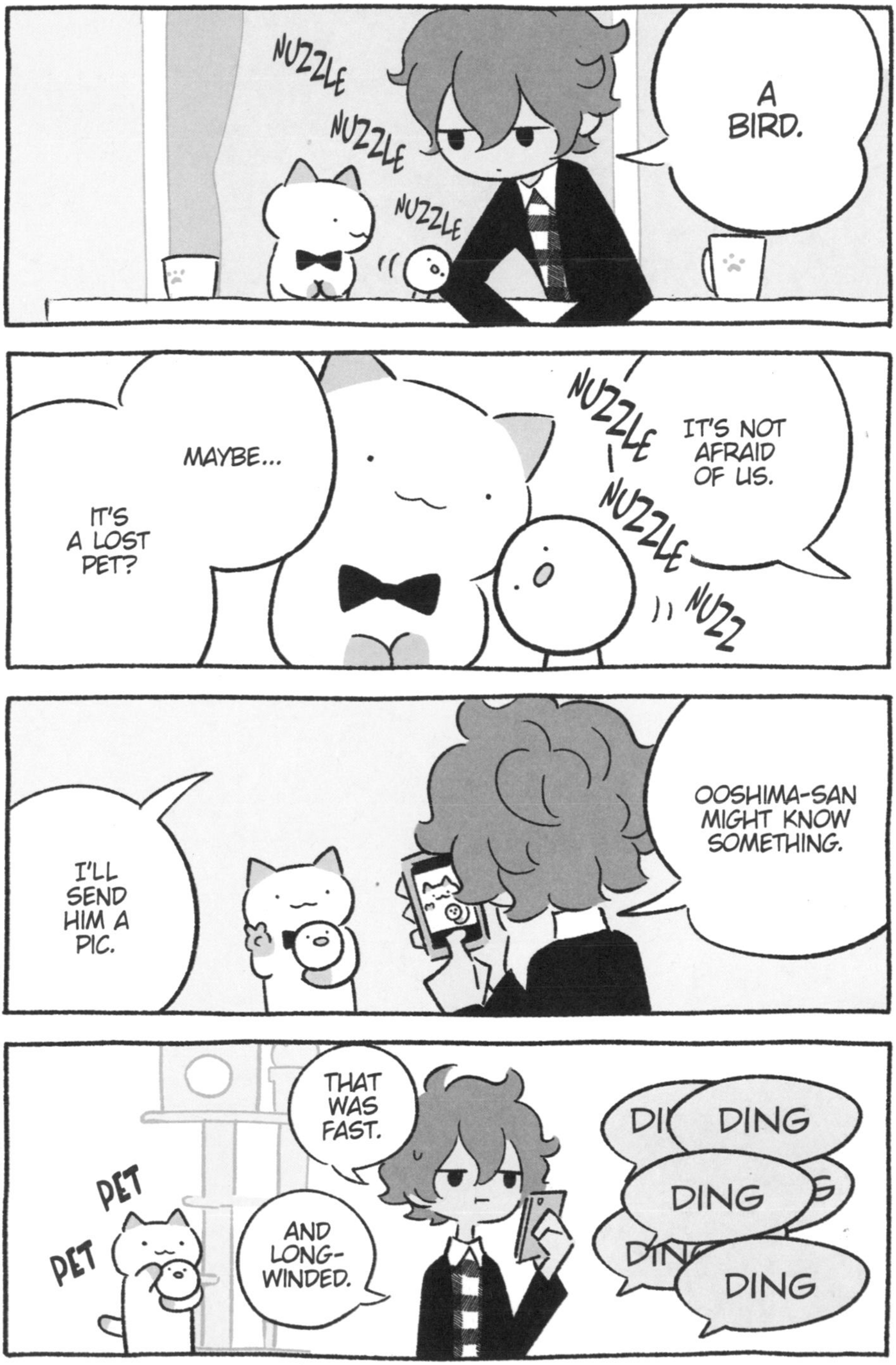
A BIRD.
NUZZLE
NUZZLE
NUZZLE
IT'S NOT AFRAID OF US.
NUZZLE
NUZZLE
NUZZ
MAYBE... IT'S A LOST PET?
OOSHIMA-SAN MIGHT KNOW SOMETHING.
I'LL SEND HIM A PIC.
DING
DING
DING
THAT WAS FAST.
AND LONG-WINDED.
PET
PET

COMPANIONSHIP

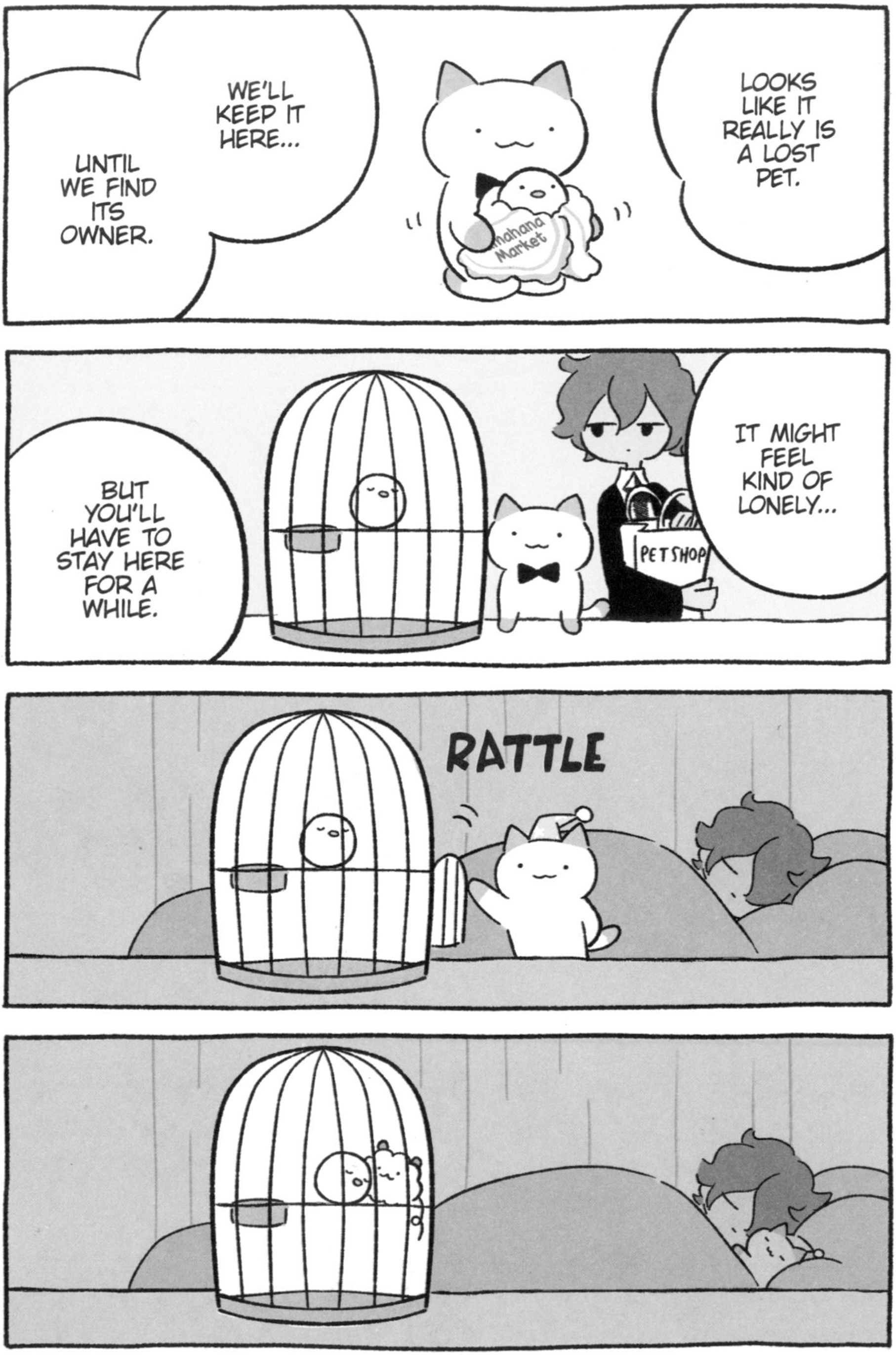
LOOKS LIKE IT REALLY IS A LOST PET.
WE'LL KEEP IT HERE...
UNTIL WE FIND ITS OWNER.
IT MIGHT FEEL KIND OF LONELY...
PETSHOP
BUT YOU'LL HAVE TO STAY HERE FOR A WHILE.
RATTLE

REACHING OUT

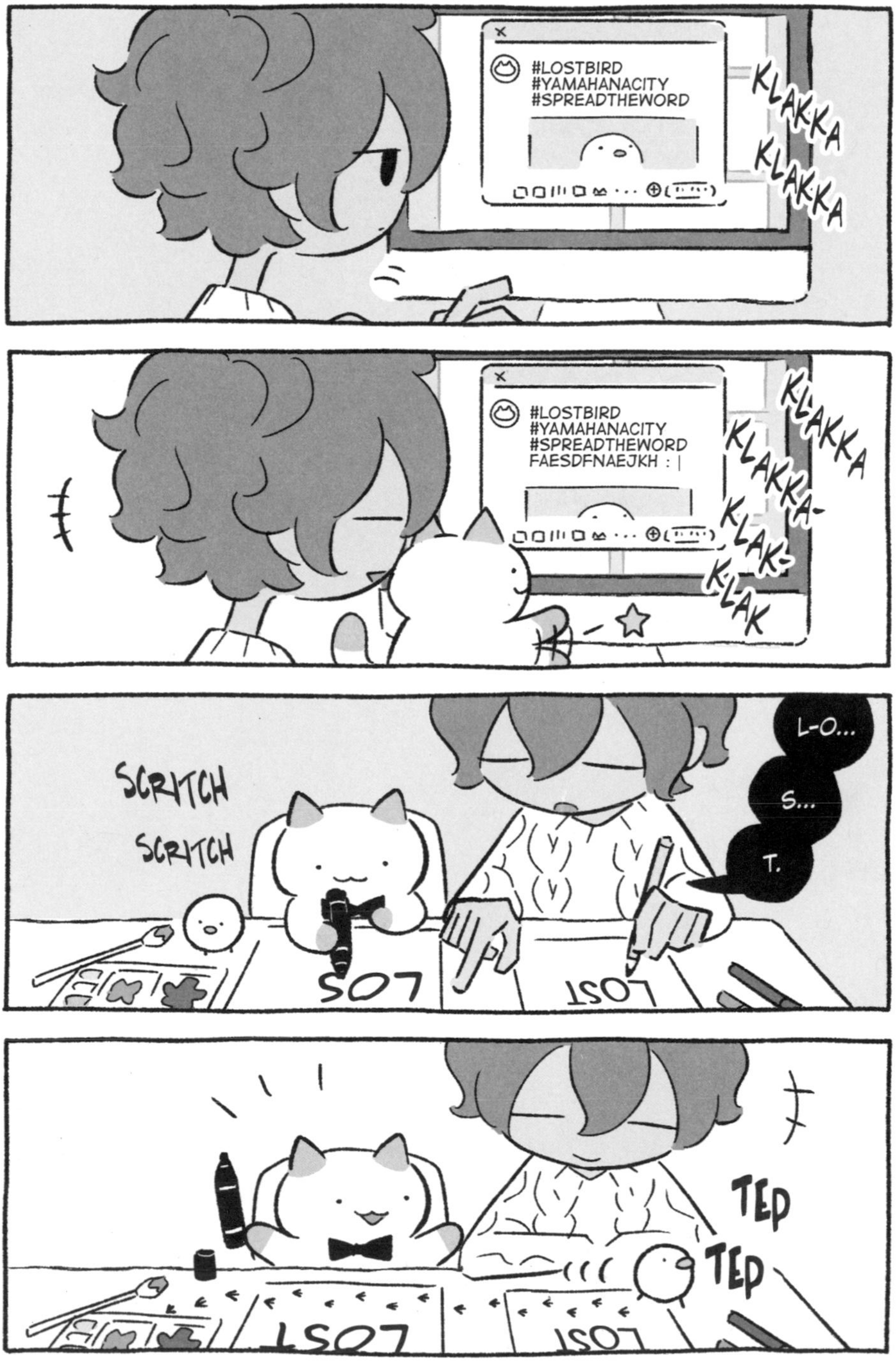
#LOSTBIRD
#YAMAHANACITY
#SPREADTHEWORD
KLAKKA
KLAKKA
#LOSTBIRD
#YAMAHANACITY
#SPREADTHEWORD
FAESDFNAEJKH : |
KLAKKA
KLAKKA-
KLAK-
KLAK
L-O...
S...
T.
SCRITCH
SCRITCH
LOST
LOS
TEP
TEP
LOST
LOST

BUDDIES

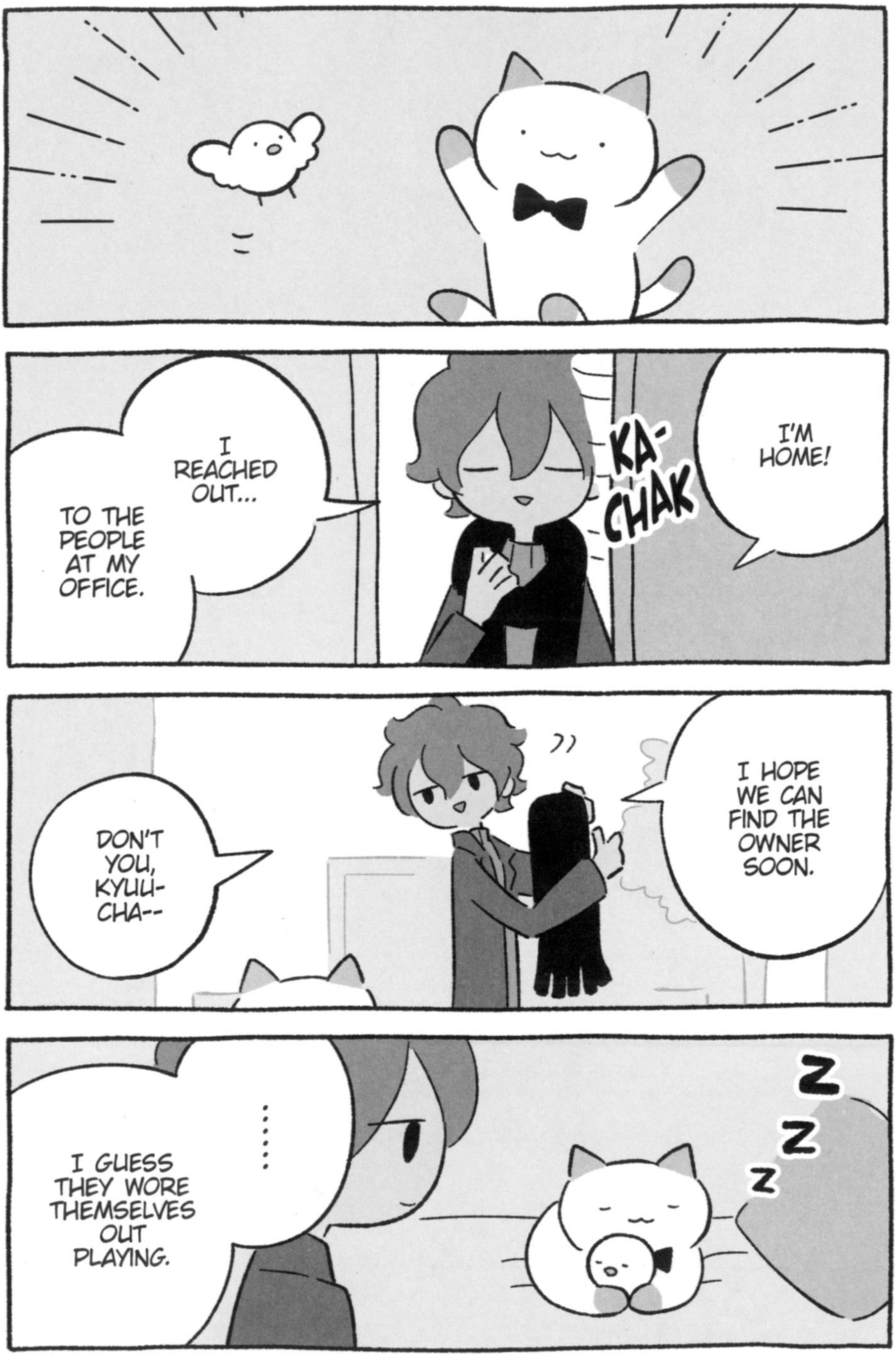
I'M HOME!
KA-CHAK
I REACHED OUT...
TO THE PEOPLE AT MY OFFICE.
I HOPE WE CAN FIND THE OWNER SOON.
DON'T YOU, KYUU-CHA--
Z Z Z
......
I GUESS THEY WORE THEMSELVES OUT PLAYING.

LEAVING THE NEST

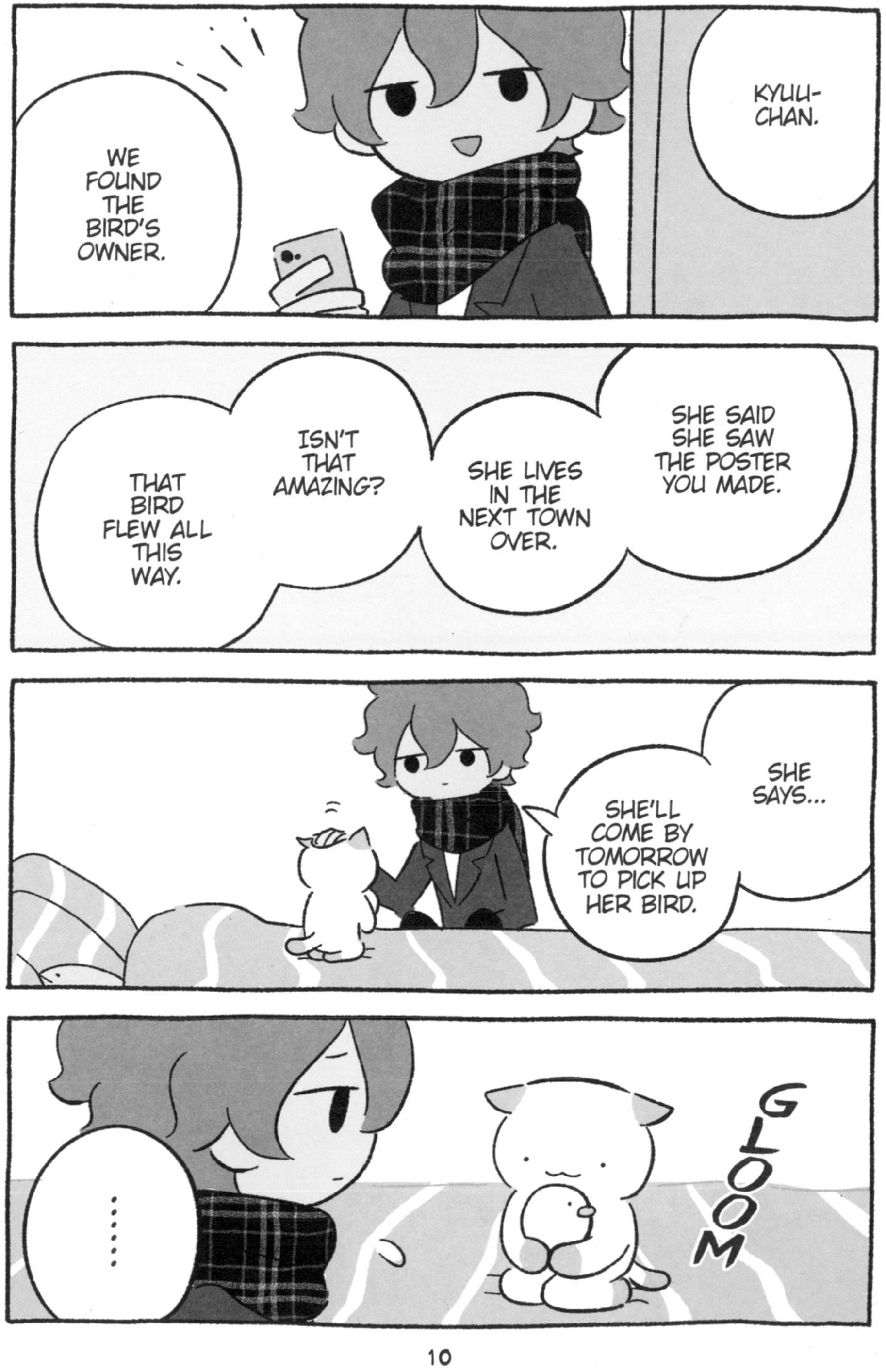
KYUU-CHAN.
WE FOUND THE BIRD'S OWNER.
SHE SAID SHE SAW THE POSTER YOU MADE.
SHE LIVES IN THE NEXT TOWN OVER.
ISN'T THAT AMAZING?
THAT BIRD FLEW ALL THIS WAY.
SHE SAYS...
SHE'LL COME BY TOMORROW TO PICK UP HER BIRD.
GLOOM
......

GOODBYE

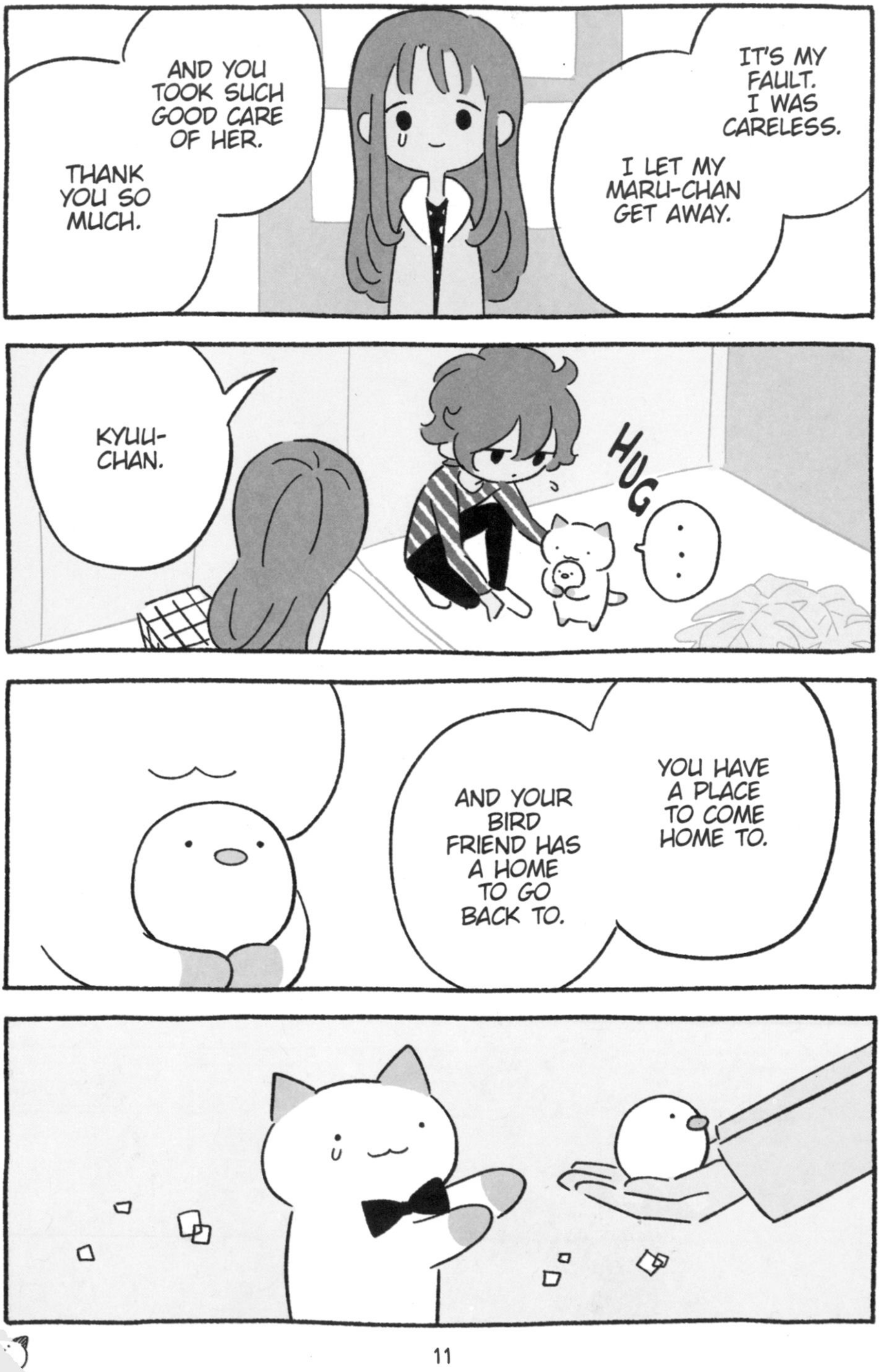
IT'S MY FAULT. I WAS CARELESS.
I LET MY MARU-CHAN GET AWAY.
AND YOU TOOK SUCH GOOD CARE OF HER.
THANK YOU SO MUCH.
HUG
...
KYUU-CHAN.
YOU HAVE A PLACE TO COME HOME TO.
AND YOUR BIRD FRIEND HAS A HOME TO GO BACK TO.

SEE YOU LATER

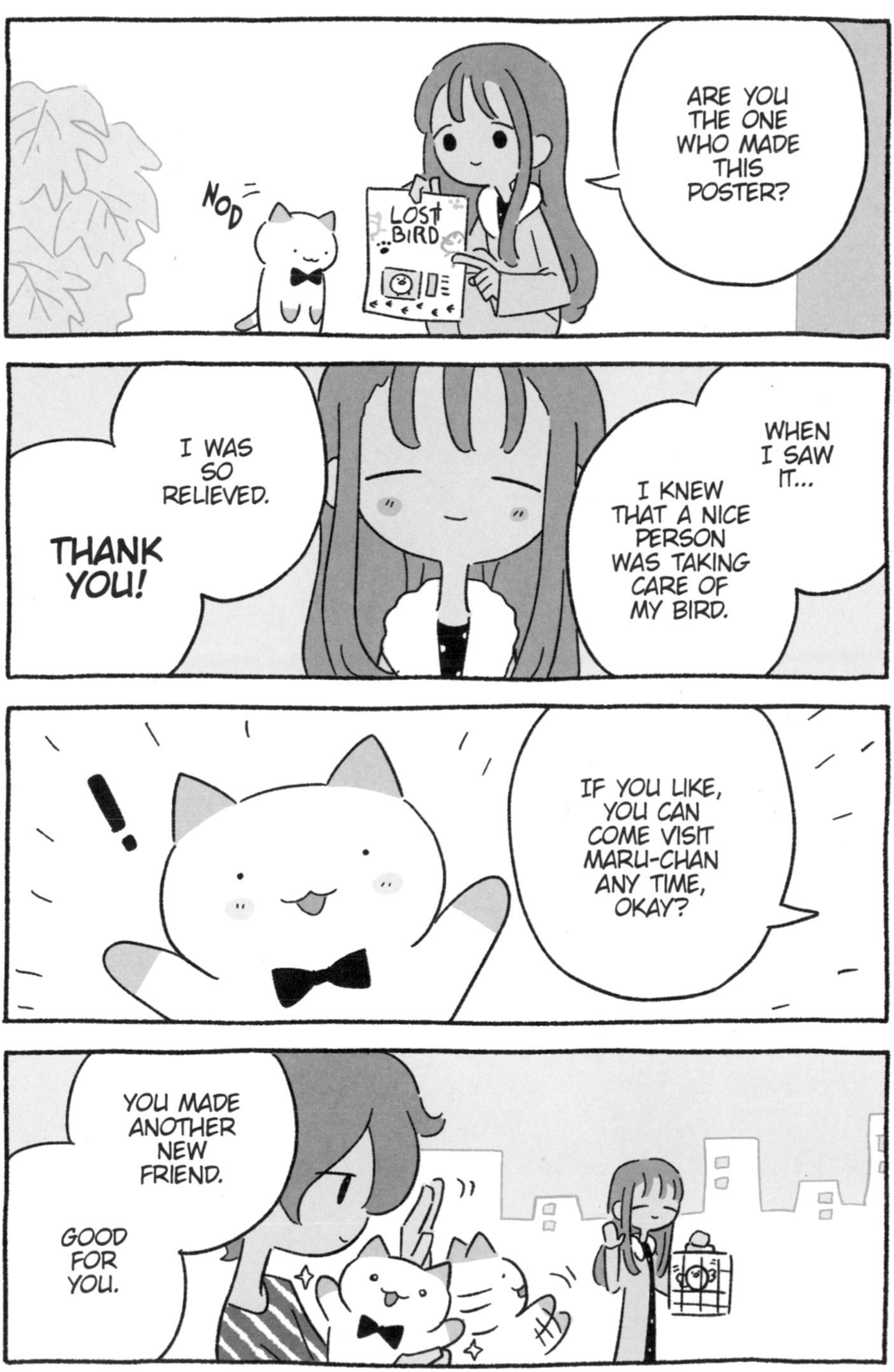

ARE YOU THE ONE WHO MADE THIS POSTER?
LOST BIRD
NOD
WHEN I SAW IT...
I KNEW THAT A NICE PERSON WAS TAKING CARE OF MY BIRD.
I WAS SO RELIEVED.
THANK YOU!
IF YOU LIKE, YOU CAN COME VISIT MARU-CHAN ANY TIME, OKAY?
!
YOU MADE ANOTHER NEW FRIEND.
GOOD FOR YOU.

LOTS OF SLEEP

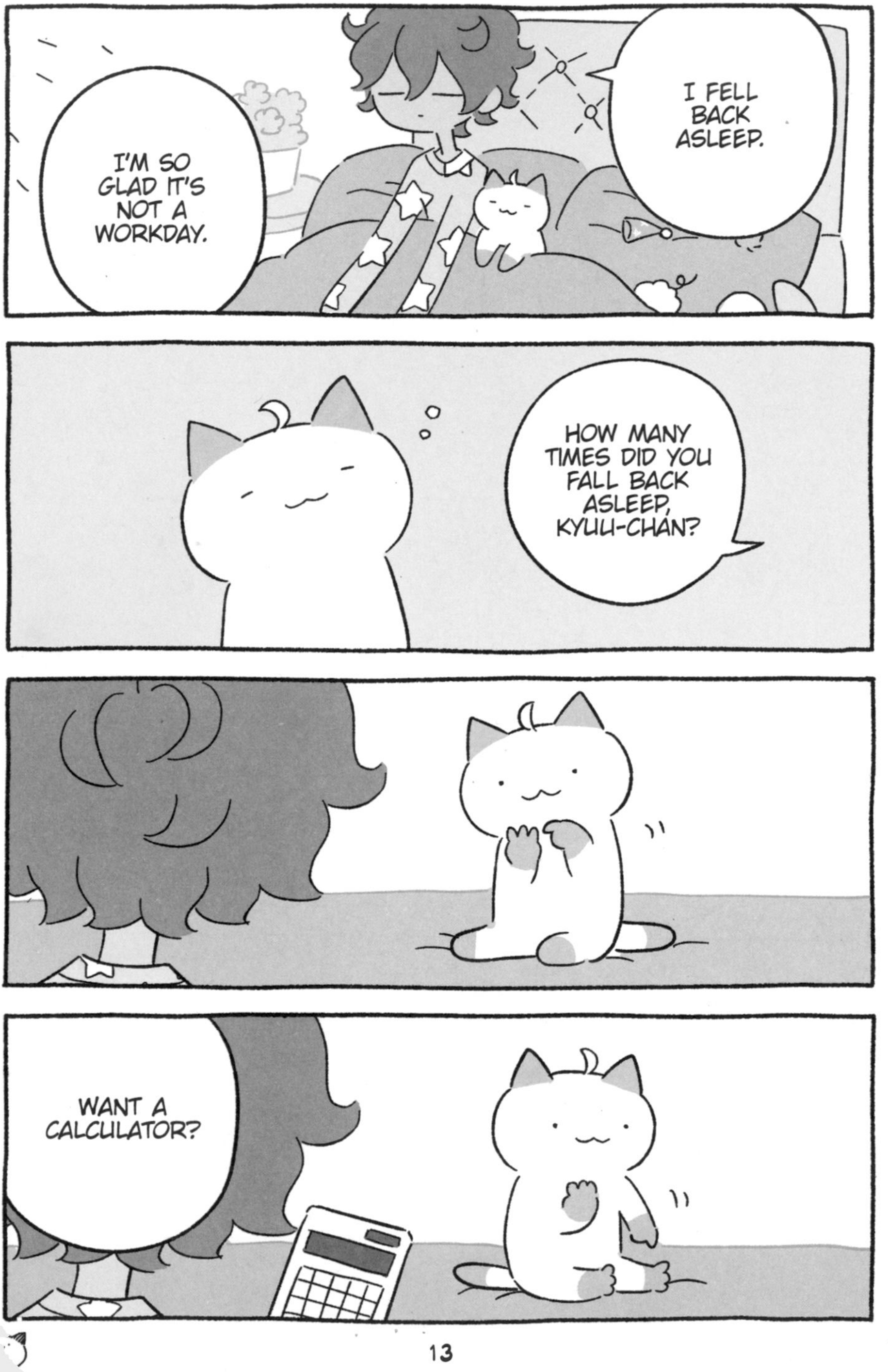
I FELL BACK ASLEEP.
I'M SO GLAD IT'S NOT A WORKDAY.
HOW MANY TIMES DID YOU FALL BACK ASLEEP, KYUU-CHAN?
WANT A CALCULATOR?

VERY IMPORTANT

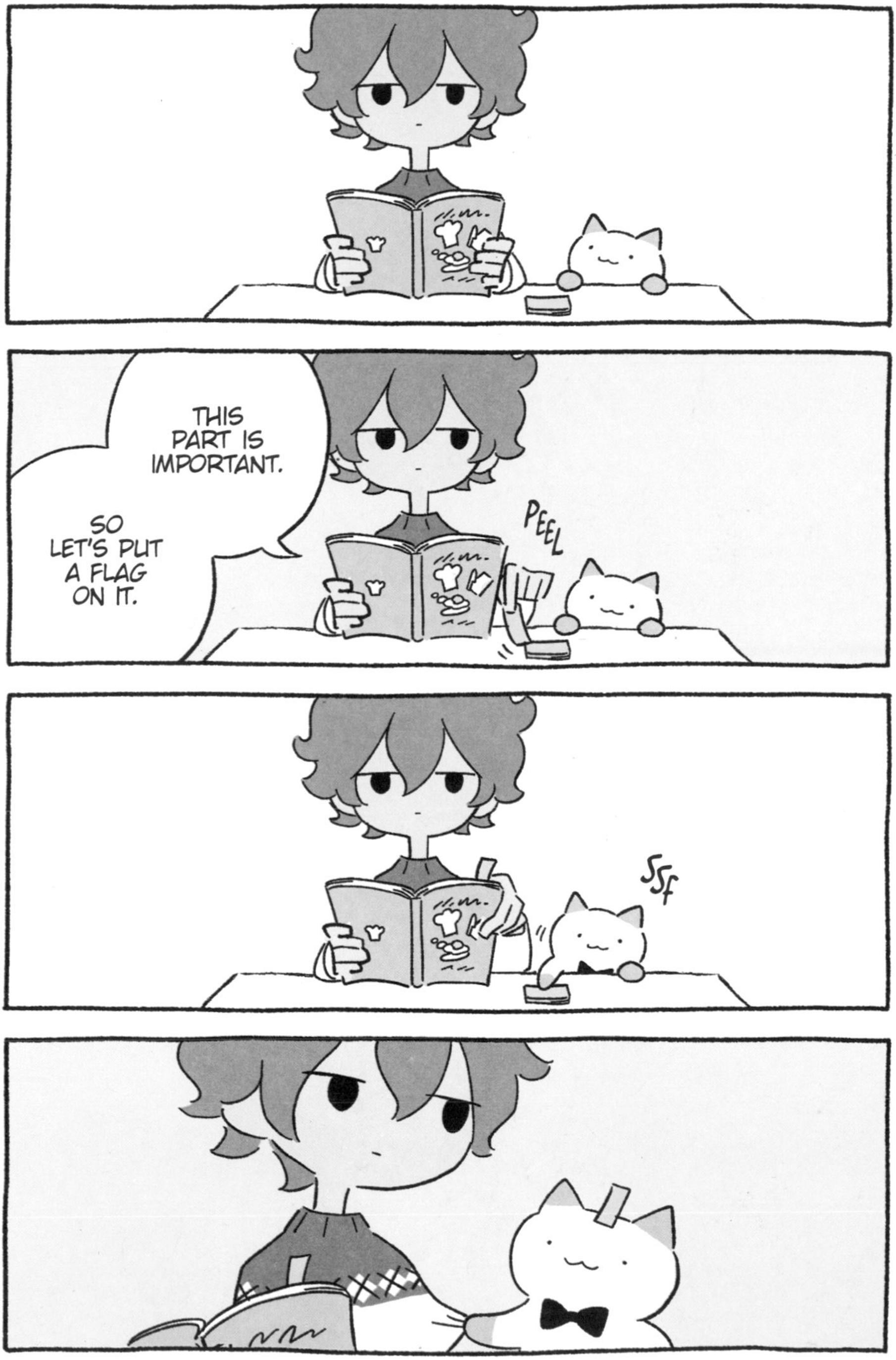
THIS PART IS IMPORTANT.
SO LET'S PUT A FLAG ON IT.
PEEL
SSF

A WONDERFUL FLUFF

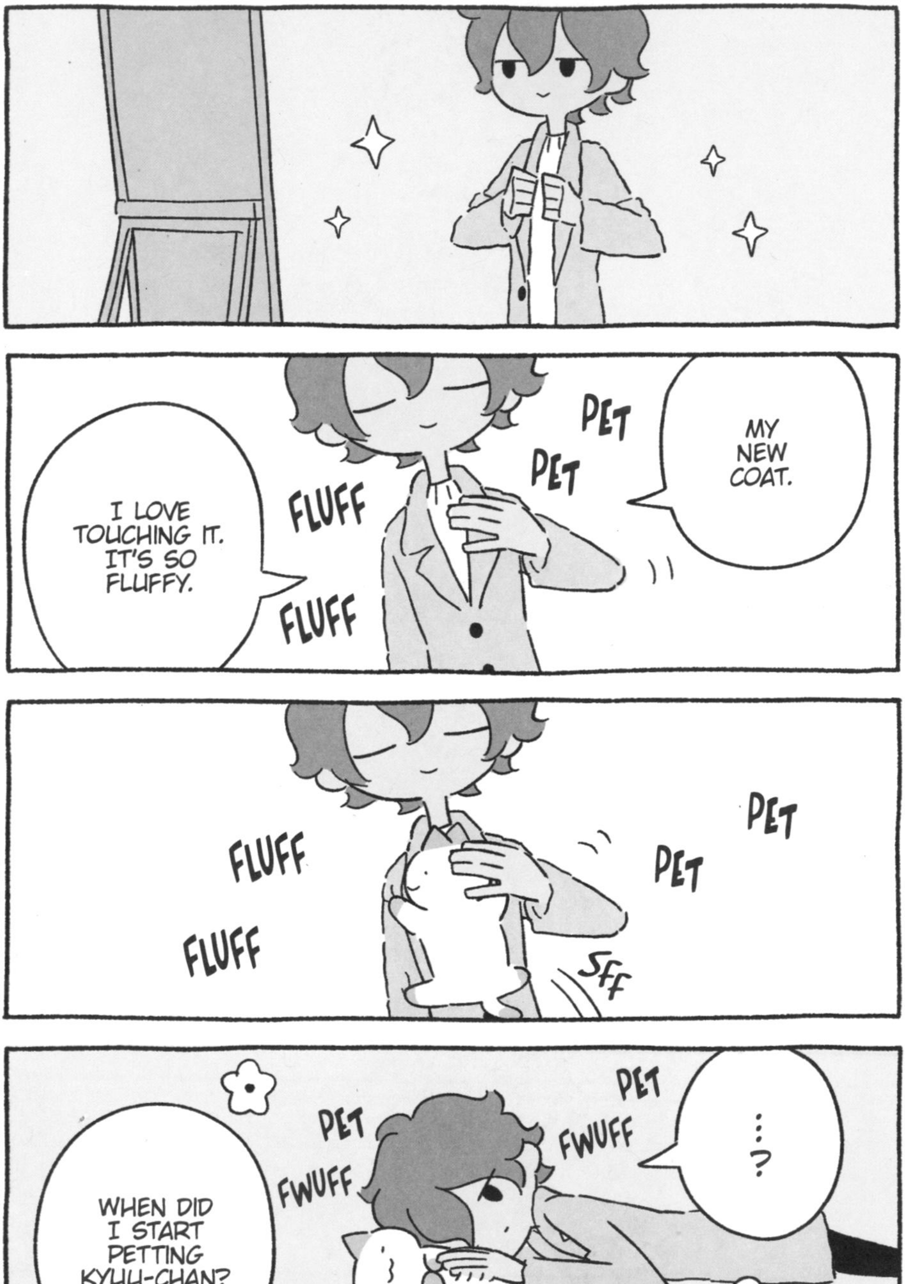
MY NEW COAT.
PET
PET
FLUFF
FLUFF
I LOVE TOUCHING IT. IT'S SO FLUFFY.
PET
PET
FLUFF
SFF
FLUFF
...?
PET
FWUFF
PET
FWUFF
WHEN DID I START PETTING KYUU-CHAN?

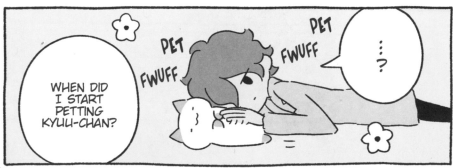

PULLING A SLED

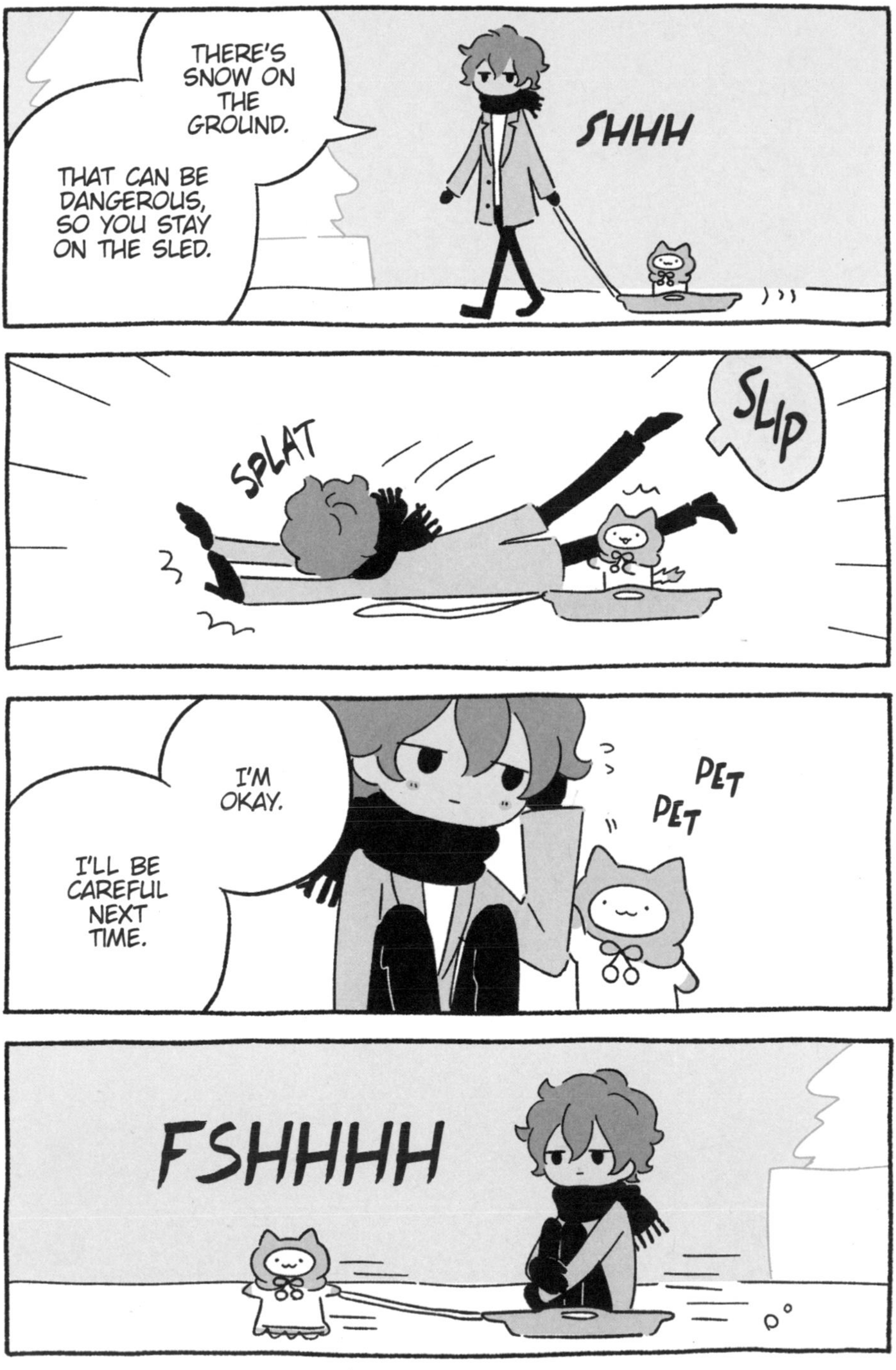
SHHH
THERE'S SNOW ON THE GROUND.
THAT CAN BE DANGEROUS, SO YOU STAY ON THE SLED.
SLIP
SPLAT
PET
PET
I'M OKAY.
I'LL BE CAREFUL NEXT TIME.
FSHHHH

SLEDDING

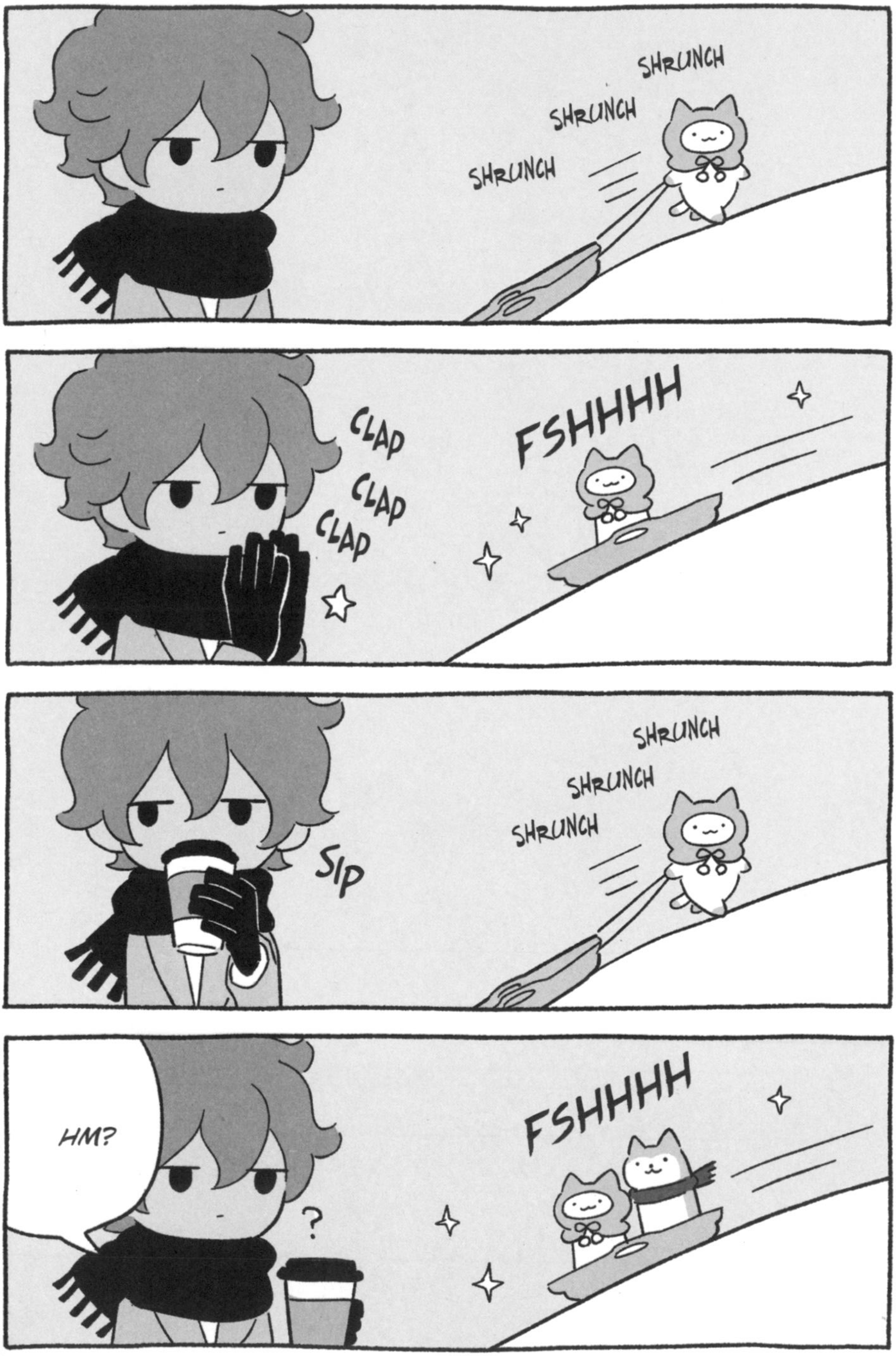
SHRUNCH
SHRUNCH
SHRUNCH
FSHHHH
CLAP
CLAP
CLAP
SHRUNCH
SHRUNCH
SHRUNCH
SIP
FSHHHH
?
HM?

INDOORS

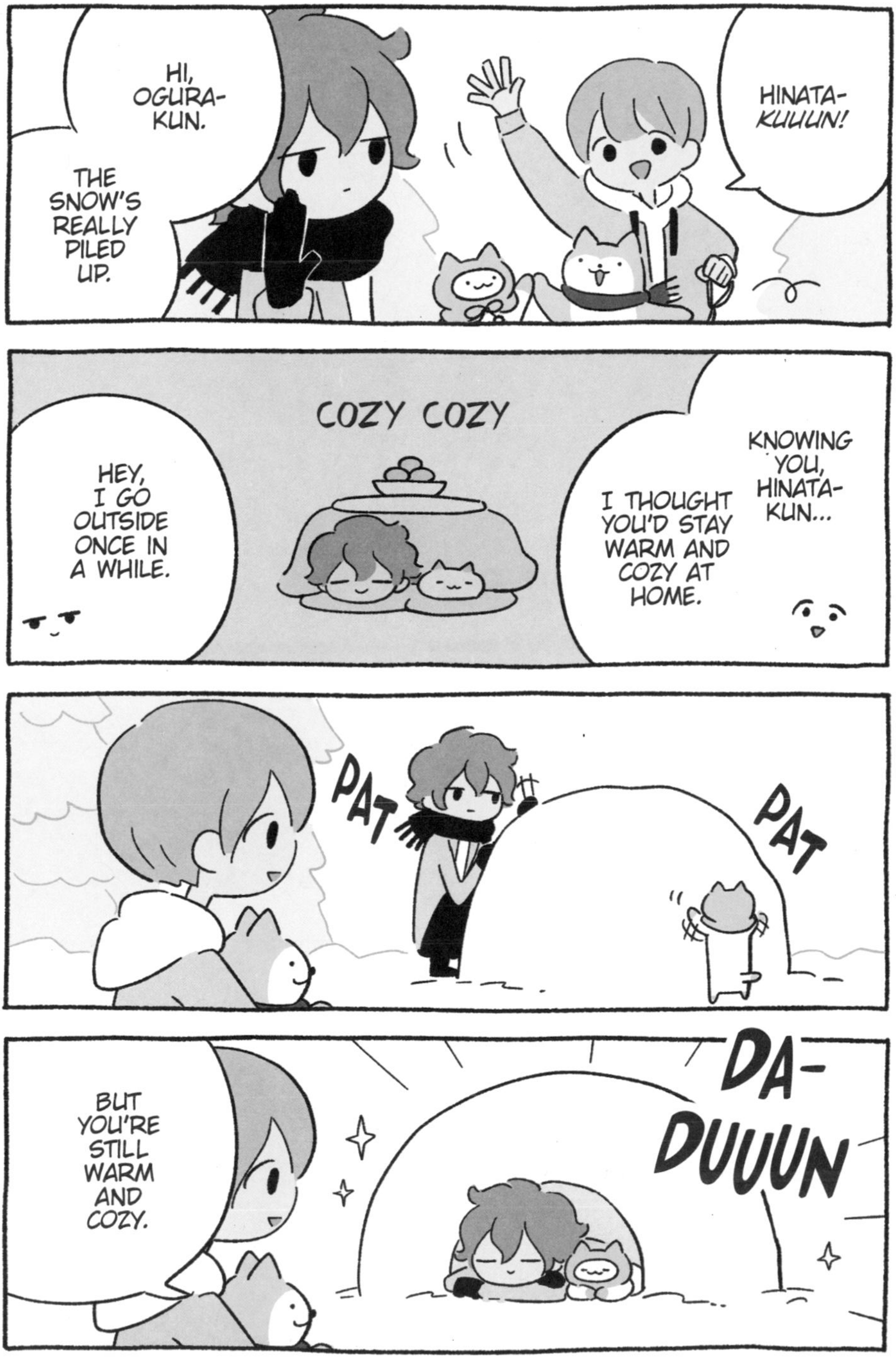
HINATA-KUUUN!
HI, OGURA-KUN.
THE SNOW'S REALLY PILED UP.
KNOWING YOU, HINATA-KUN...
I THOUGHT YOU'D STAY WARM AND COZY AT HOME.
COZY COZY
HEY, I GO OUTSIDE ONCE IN A WHILE.
PAT
PAT
DA-DUUUN
BUT YOU'RE STILL WARM AND COZY.

SNOW GAMES

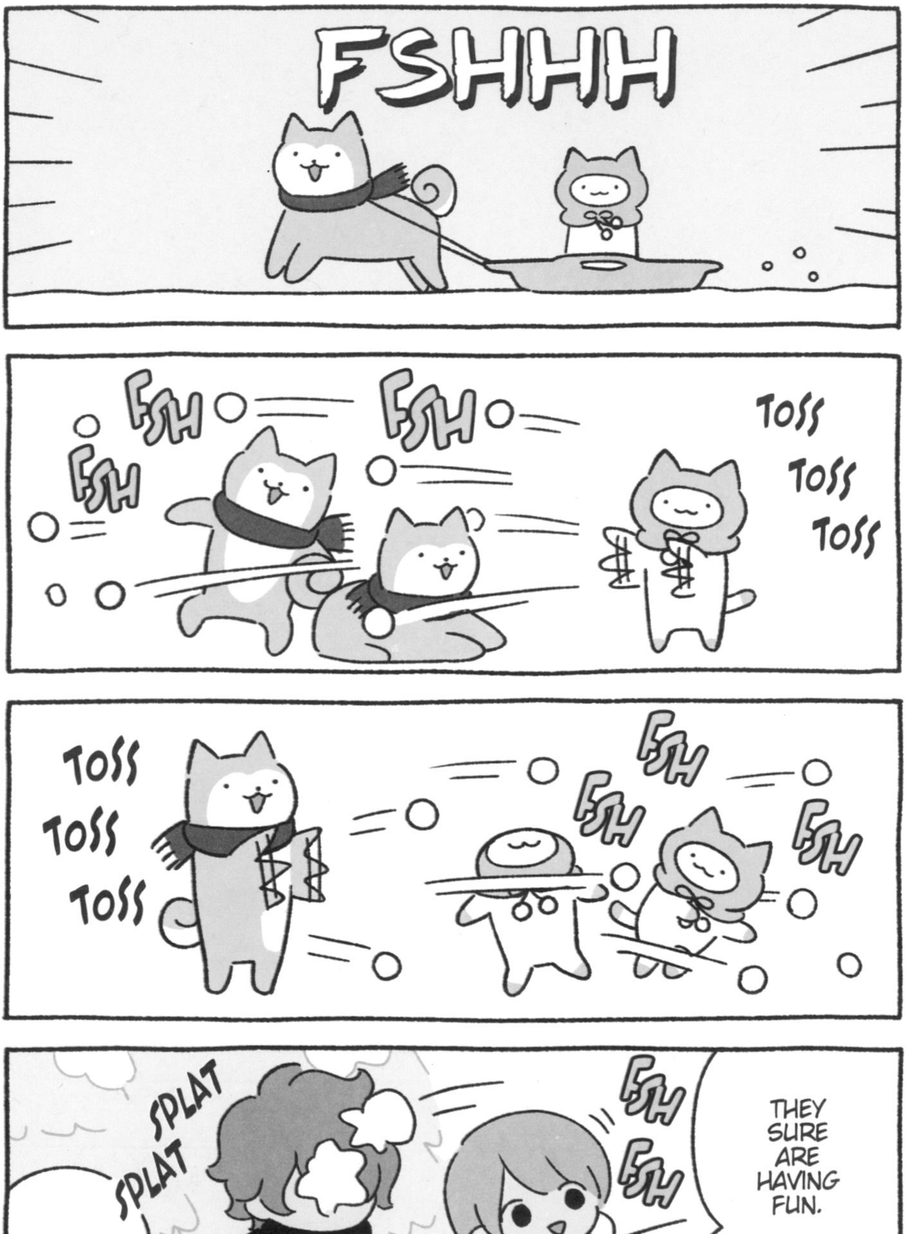
FSHHH
TOSS TOSS TOSS
FSH
FSH
FSH
FSH
FSH
FSH
TOSS TOSS TOSS
THEY SURE ARE HAVING FUN.
FSH
FSH
SPLAT
SPLAT
YEAH.

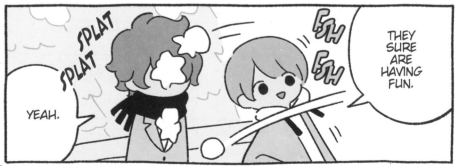

A PAIR OF GREEDY PETS

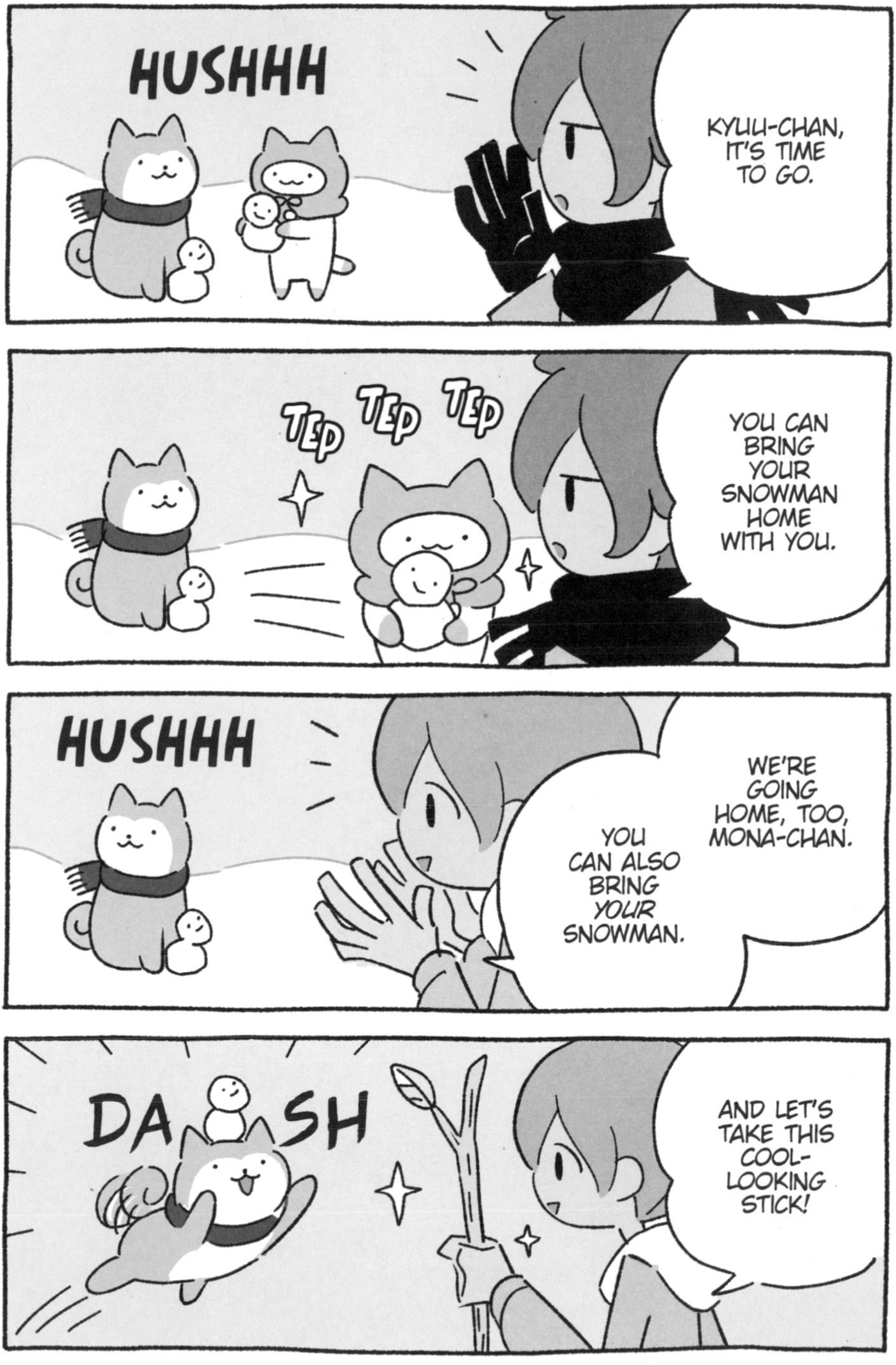
KYUU-CHAN, IT'S TIME TO GO.
HUSHHH
YOU CAN BRING YOUR SNOWMAN HOME WITH YOU.
TEP TEP TEP
WE'RE GOING HOME, TOO, MONA-CHAN.
YOU CAN ALSO BRING *YOUR* SNOWMAN.
HUSHHH
AND LET'S TAKE THIS COOL-LOOKING STICK!
DASH

STUCK

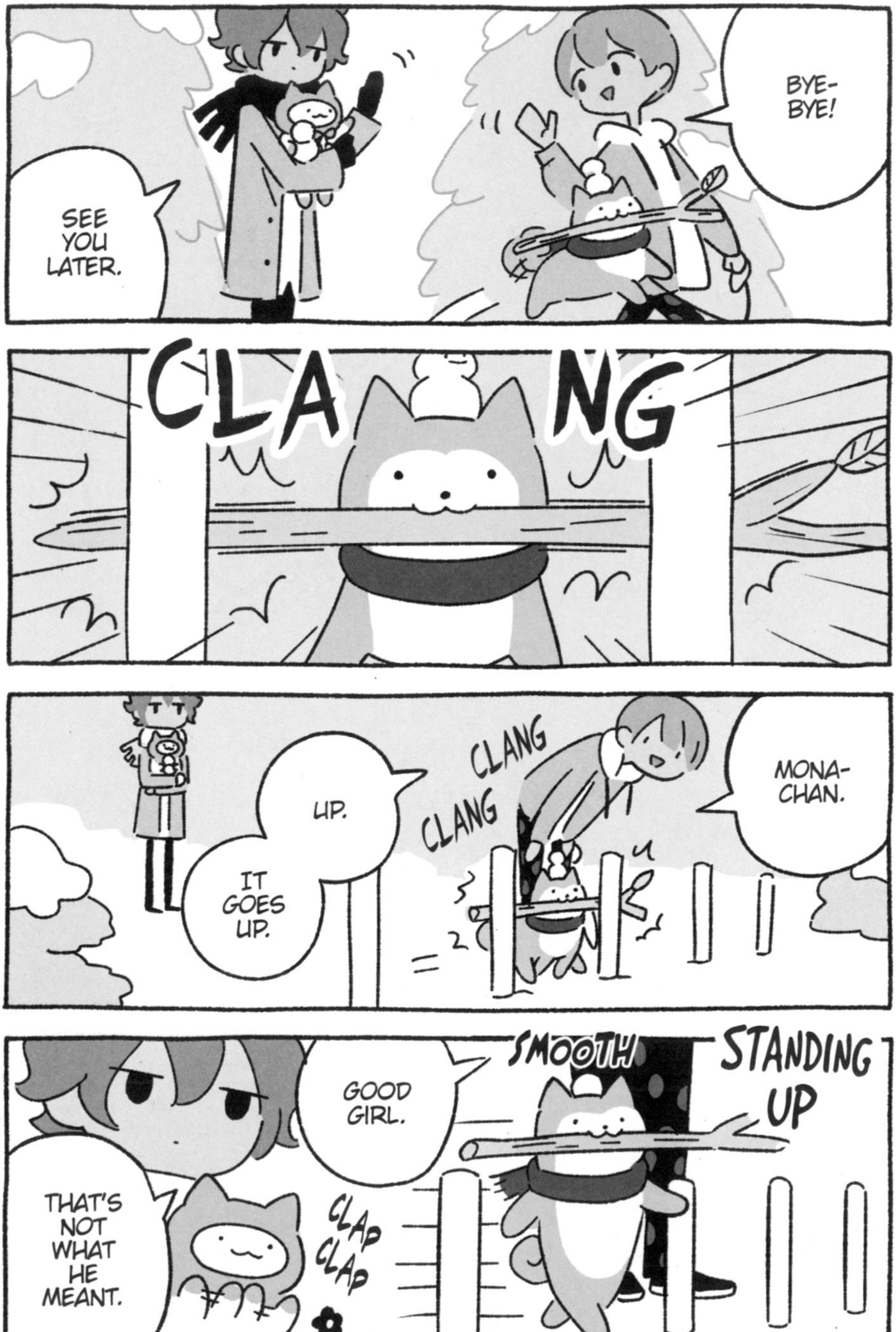
BYE-BYE!
SEE YOU LATER.
CLANG
MONA-CHAN.
CLANG CLANG
UP.
IT GOES UP.
STANDING UP
SMOOTH
GOOD GIRL.
CLAP CLAP
THAT'S NOT WHAT HE MEANT.

DISCOVERY

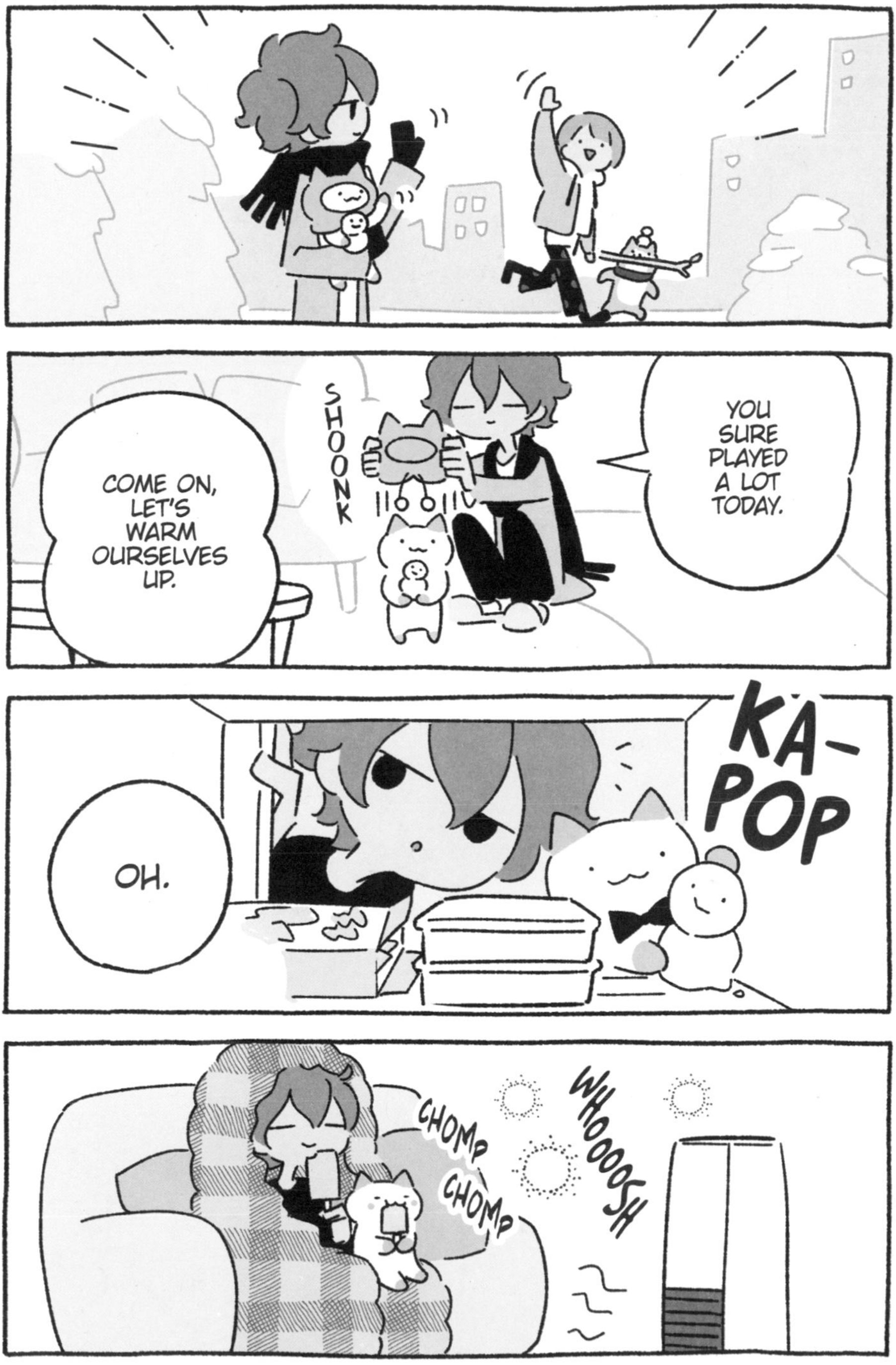
YOU SURE PLAYED A LOT TODAY.
SHOONK
COME ON, LET'S WARM OURSELVES UP.
KA-POP
OH.
WHOOOOSH
CHOMP
CHOMP

MAGIC

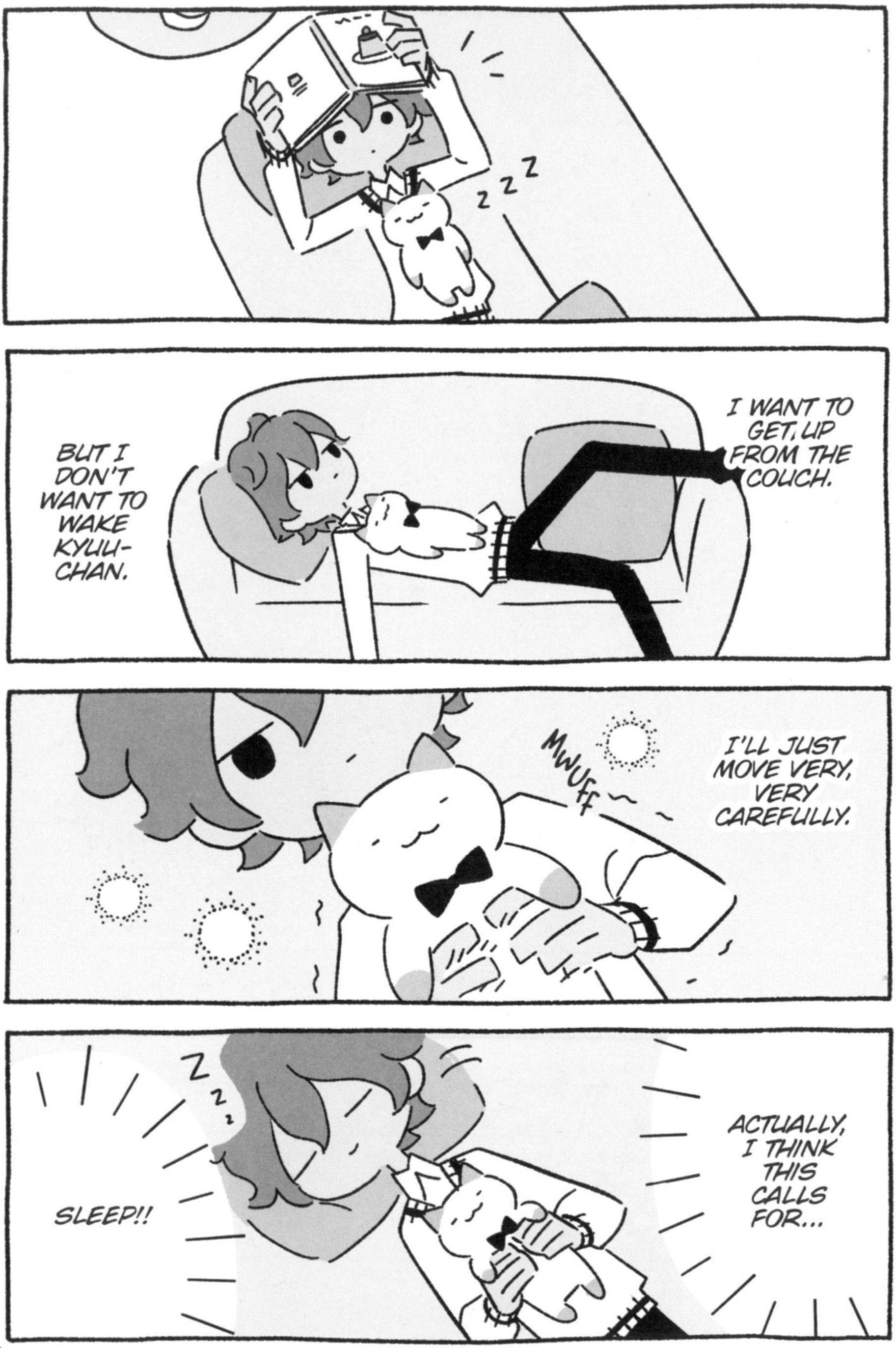

Z Z Z
I WANT TO GET UP FROM THE COUCH.
BUT I DON'T WANT TO WAKE KYUU-CHAN.
I'LL JUST MOVE VERY, VERY CAREFULLY.
MWUFF~~
Z Z Z
ACTUALLY, I THINK THIS CALLS FOR...
SLEEP!!

MULTITASKING

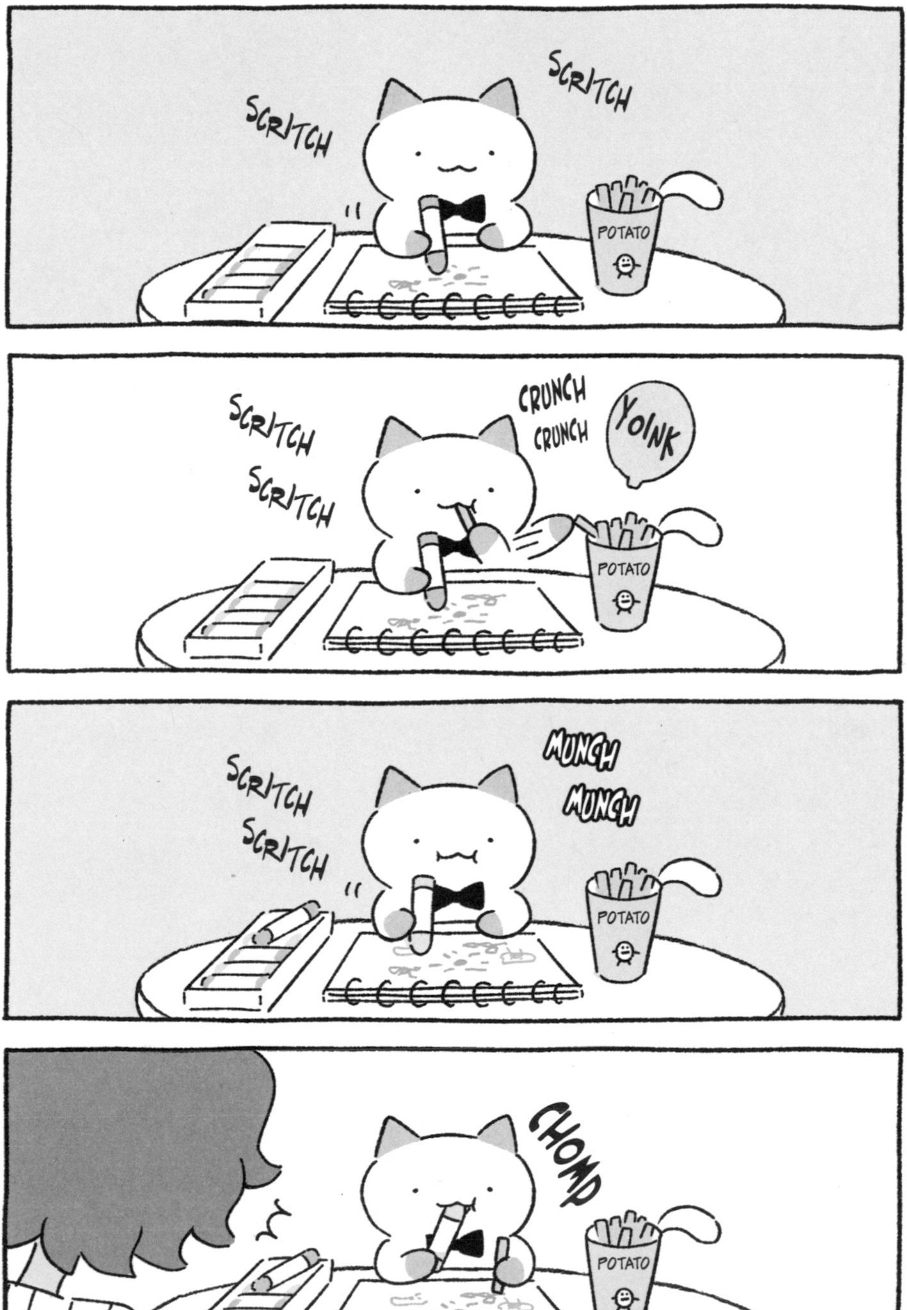
SCRITCH
SCRITCH
POTATO
YOINK
CRUNCH
CRUNCH
SCRITCH
SCRITCH
POTATO
MUNCH
MUNCH
SCRITCH
SCRITCH
POTATO
CHOMP
POTATO

BALL GAMES

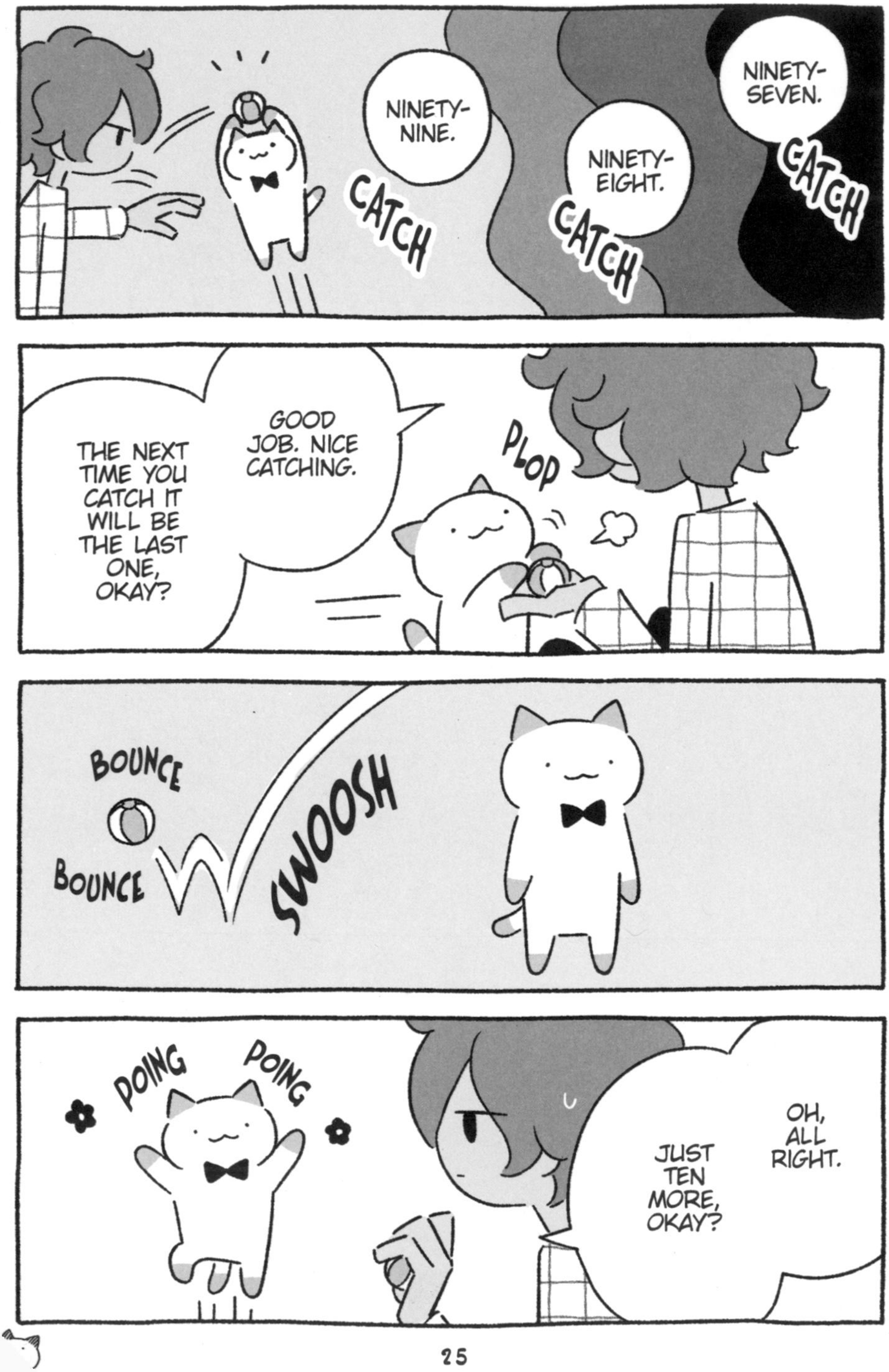
NINETY-SEVEN.
CATCH
NINETY-EIGHT.
CATCH
NINETY-NINE.
CATCH
PLOP
GOOD JOB. NICE CATCHING.
THE NEXT TIME YOU CATCH IT WILL BE THE LAST ONE, OKAY?
SWOOSH
BOUNCE
BOUNCE
OH, ALL RIGHT.
JUST TEN MORE, OKAY?
POING
POING

BUSY DAY

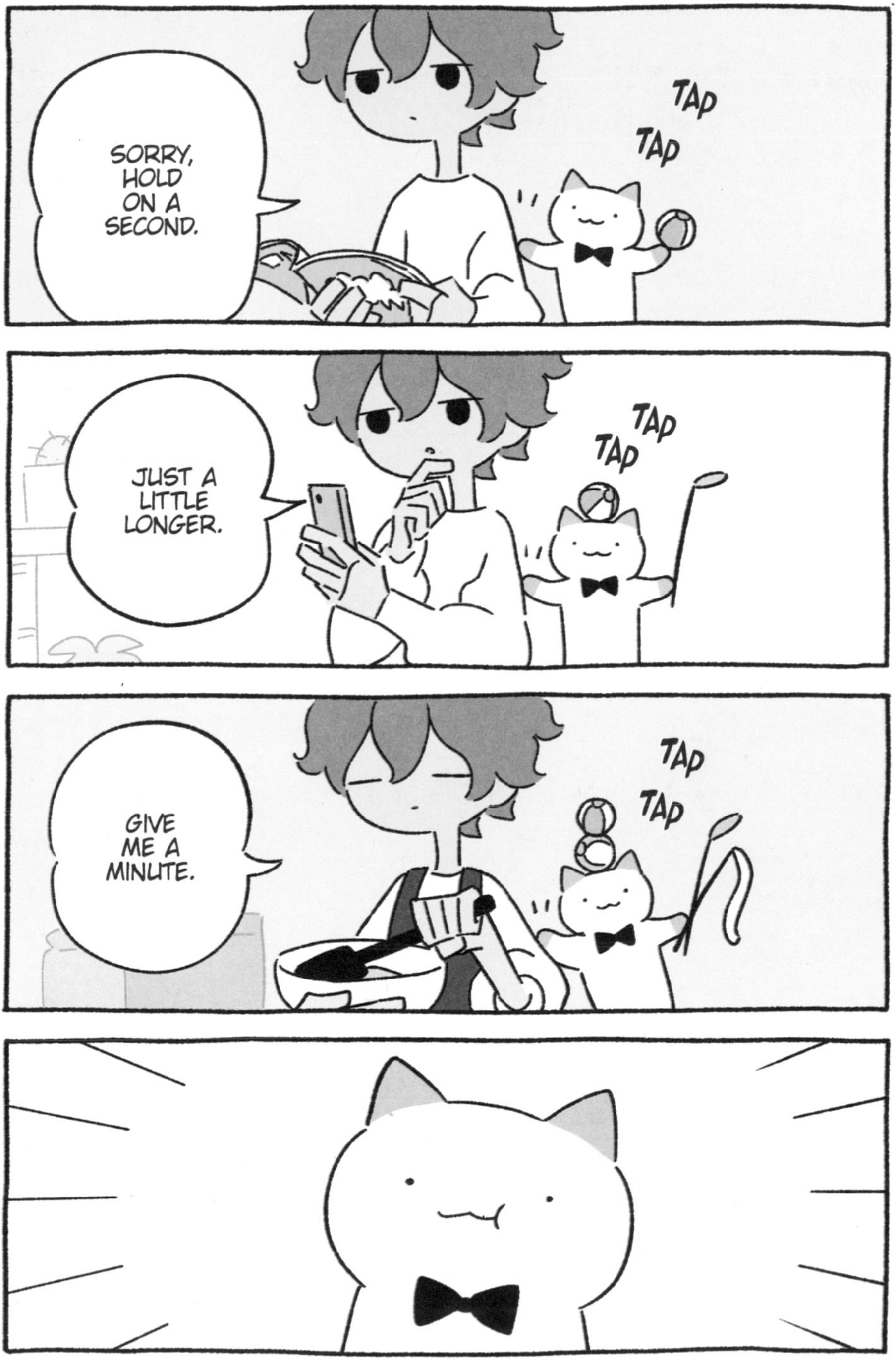
TAP
TAP
SORRY, HOLD ON A SECOND.
TAP
TAP
JUST A LITTLE LONGER.
TAP
TAP
GIVE ME A MINUTE.

DAY OF CELEBRATION

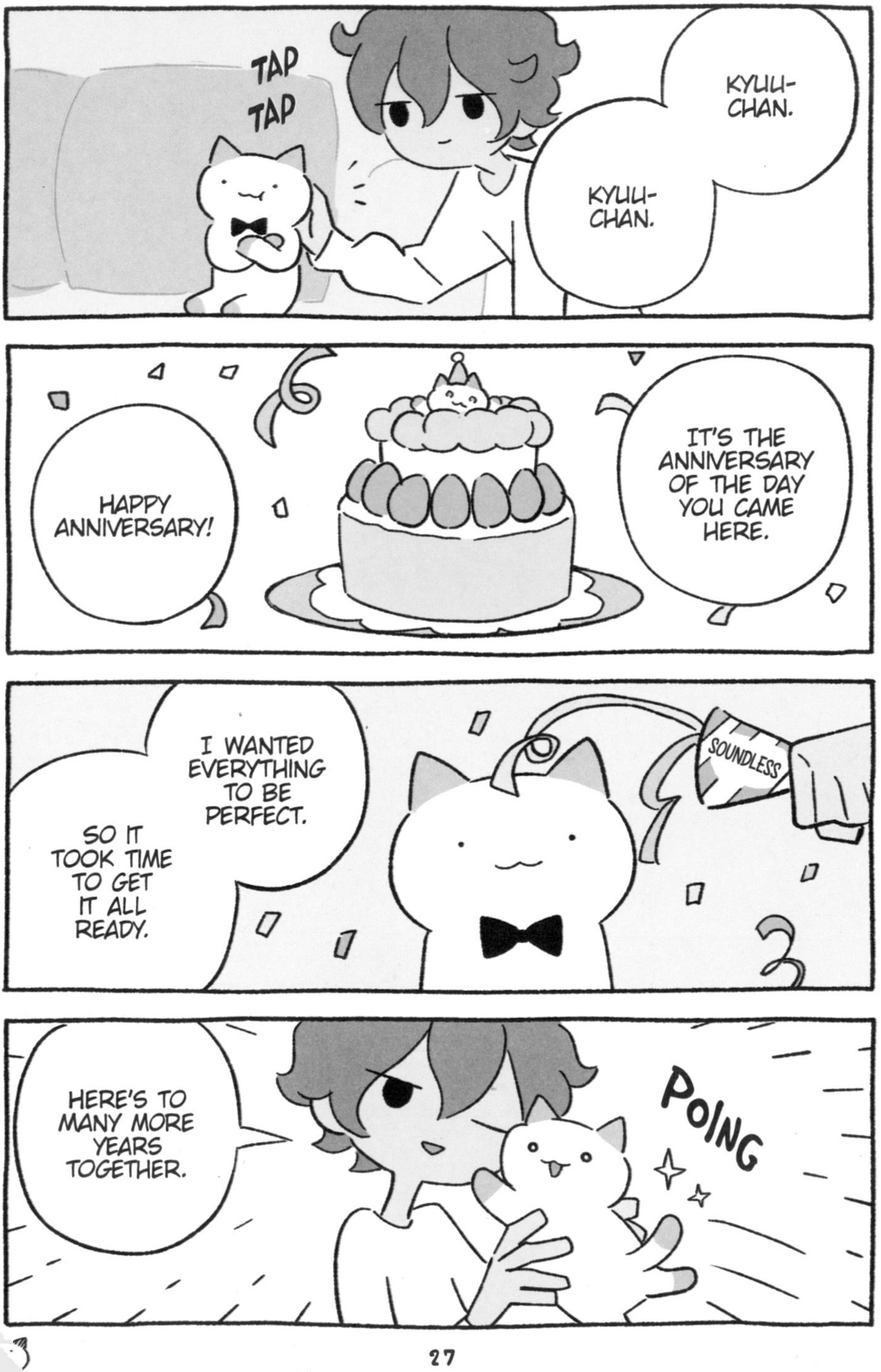
KYUU-CHAN.
KYUU-CHAN.
TAP TAP
IT'S THE ANNIVERSARY OF THE DAY YOU CAME HERE.
HAPPY ANNIVERSARY!
SOUNDLESS
I WANTED EVERYTHING TO BE PERFECT.
SO IT TOOK TIME TO GET IT ALL READY.
POING
HERE'S TO MANY MORE YEARS TOGETHER.

TRICKS

?
BALLS...
FSH
OR NOT.

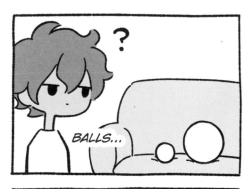

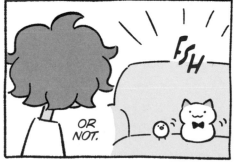

PROUD OF THEMSELVES

HELLO.
JANGLE JANGLE ♪
WELCOME!
ARE YOU ALONE TODAY?
TA-DA!
OH!
VOILA.
TEE HEE HEE!
IT'S LIKE A MAGIC TRICK.
GOOD THING WE PRACTICED, RIGHT?
TREMBLE
TREMBLE
PSST PSST

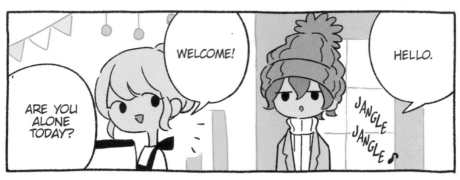

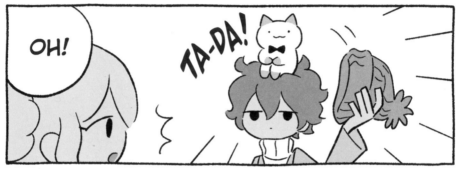

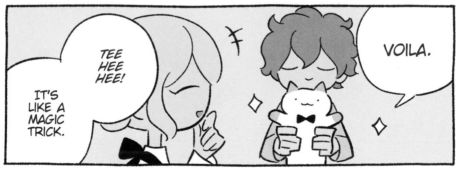

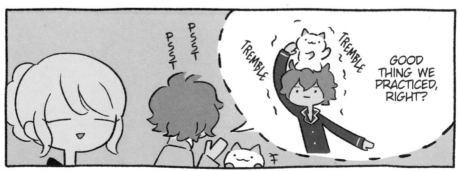

THE FRUITS OF OUR EFFORTS

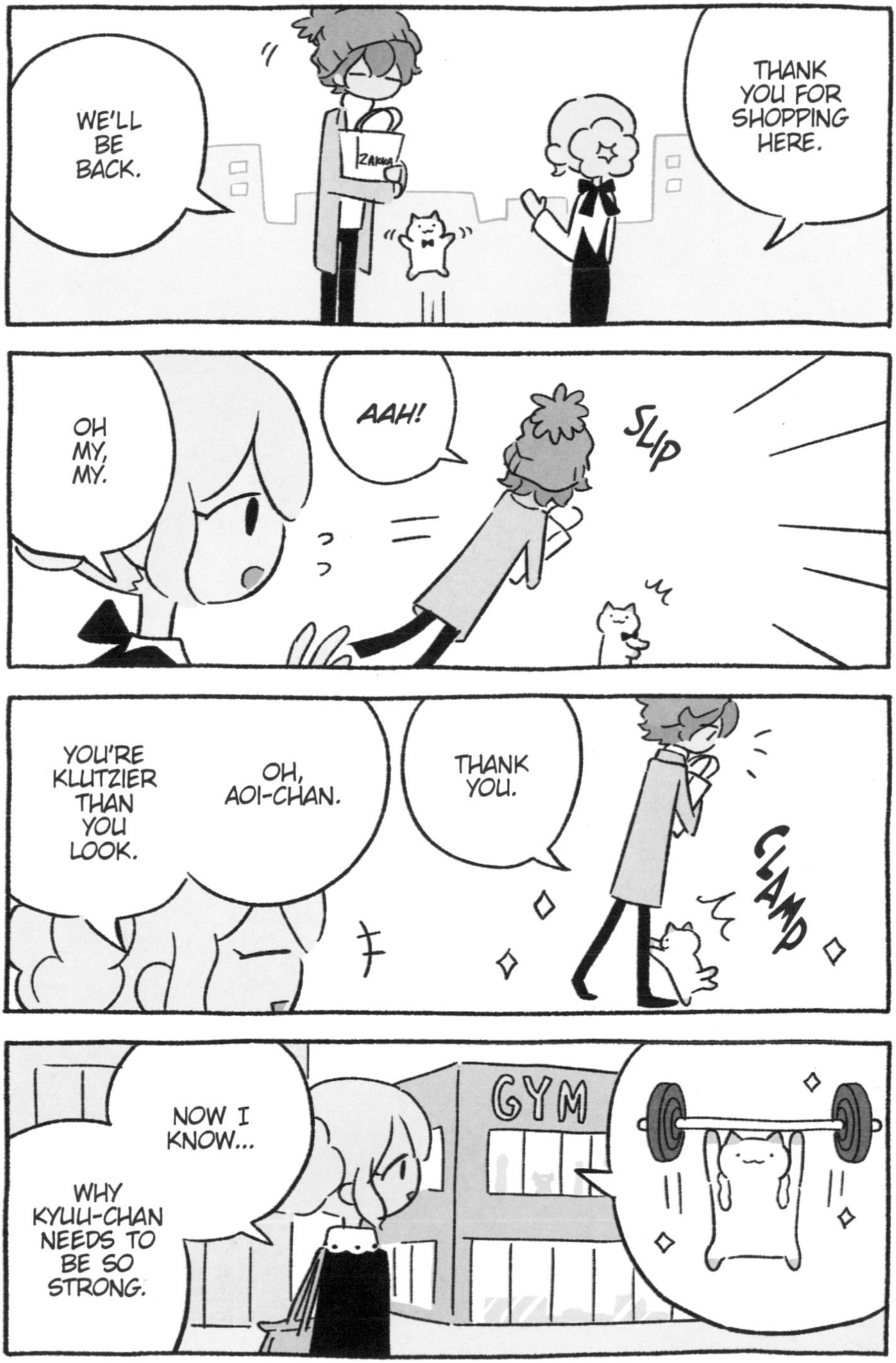
THANK YOU FOR SHOPPING HERE.
ZAKKA
WE'LL BE BACK.
SLIP
AAH!
OH MY, MY.
CLAMP
THANK YOU.
OH, AOI-CHAN.
YOU'RE KLUTZIER THAN YOU LOOK.
GYM
NOW I KNOW...
WHY KYUU-CHAN NEEDS TO BE SO STRONG.

TEAPOT

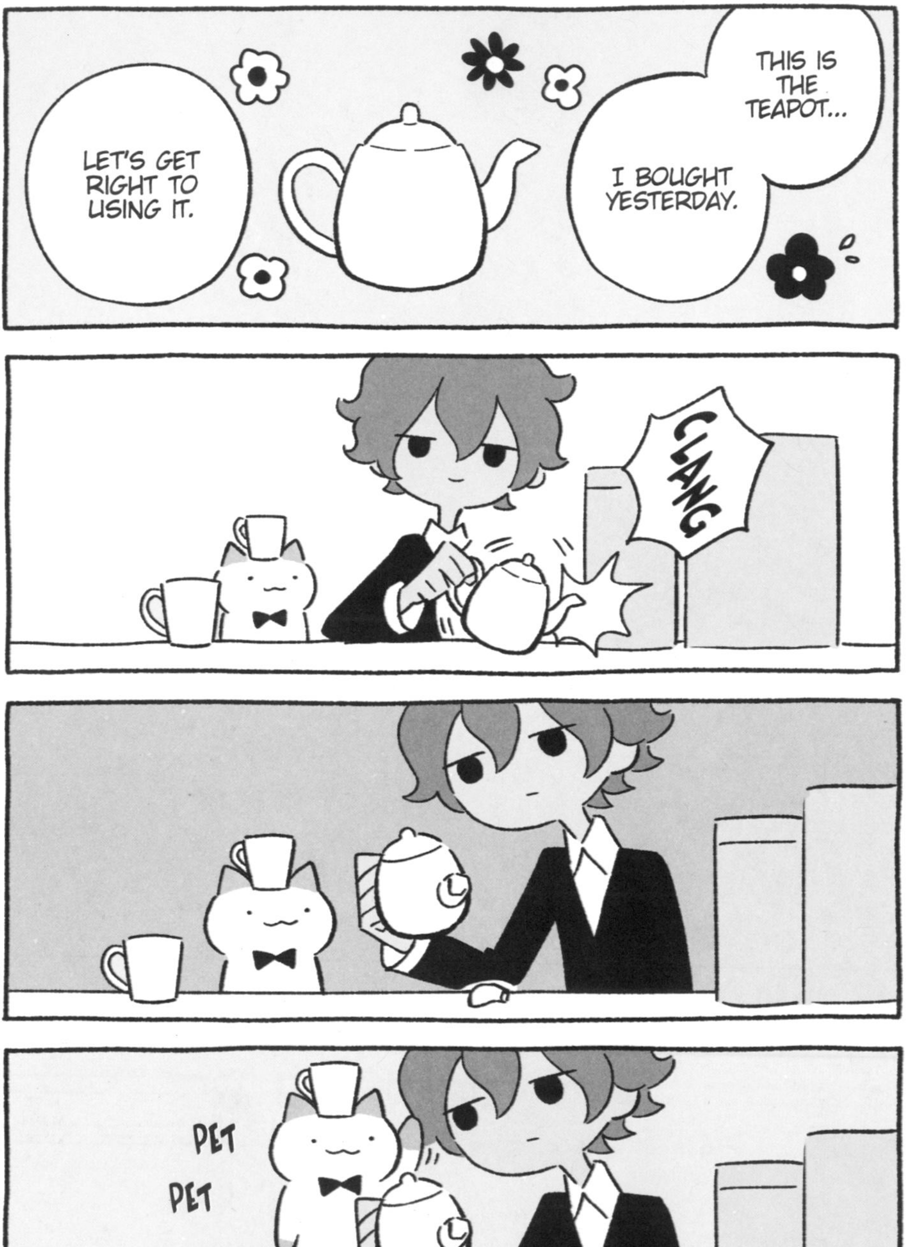
THIS IS THE TEAPOT...
I BOUGHT YESTERDAY.
LET'S GET RIGHT TO USING IT.
CLANG
PET
PET

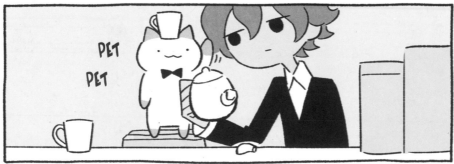

WOOLLY TRAP

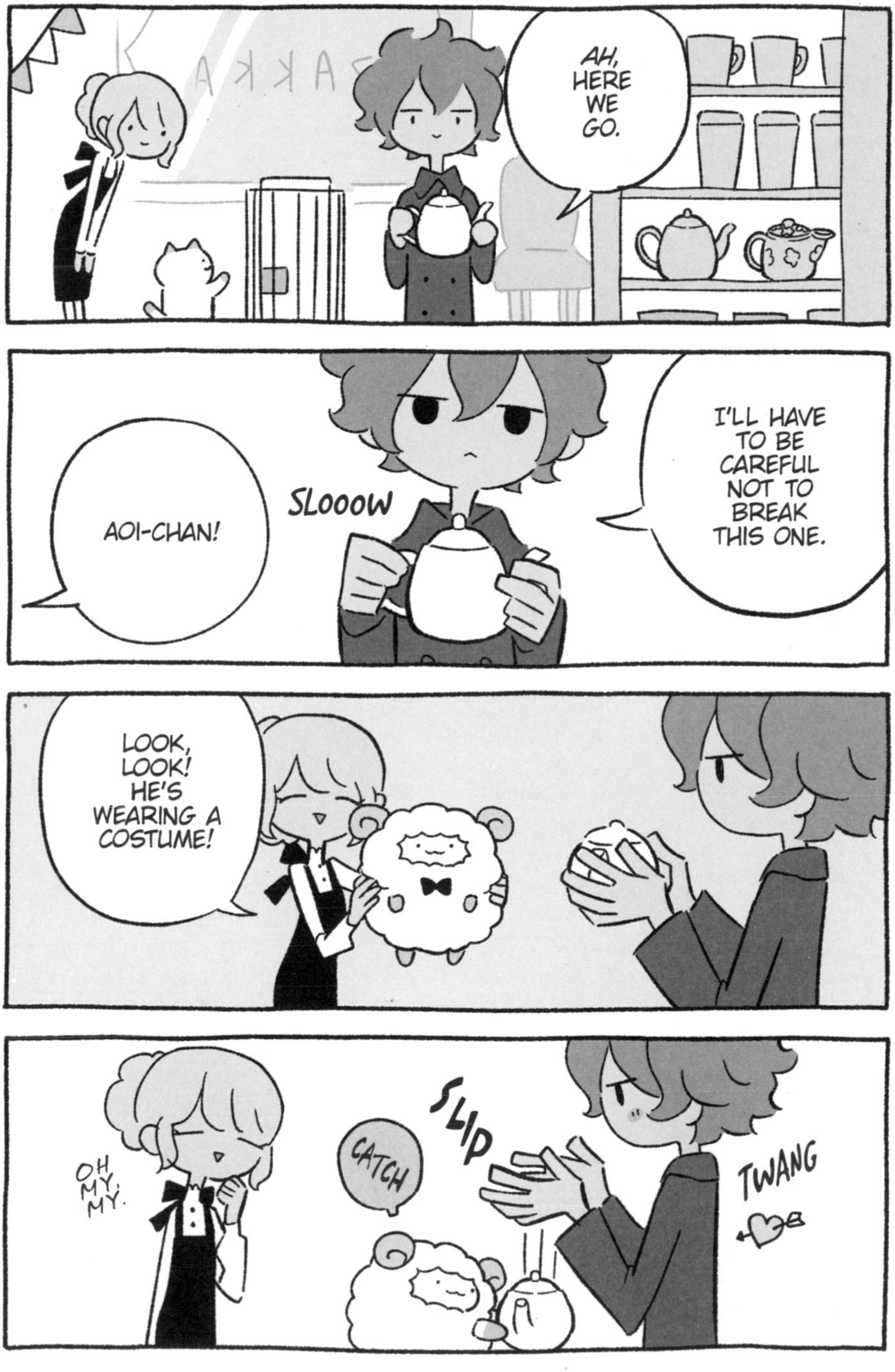

AH, HERE WE GO.
I'LL HAVE TO BE CAREFUL NOT TO BREAK THIS ONE.
SLOOOW
AOI-CHAN!
LOOK, LOOK! HE'S WEARING A COSTUME!
TWANG
SLIP
CATCH
OH MY, MY.

GOOD CHOICE

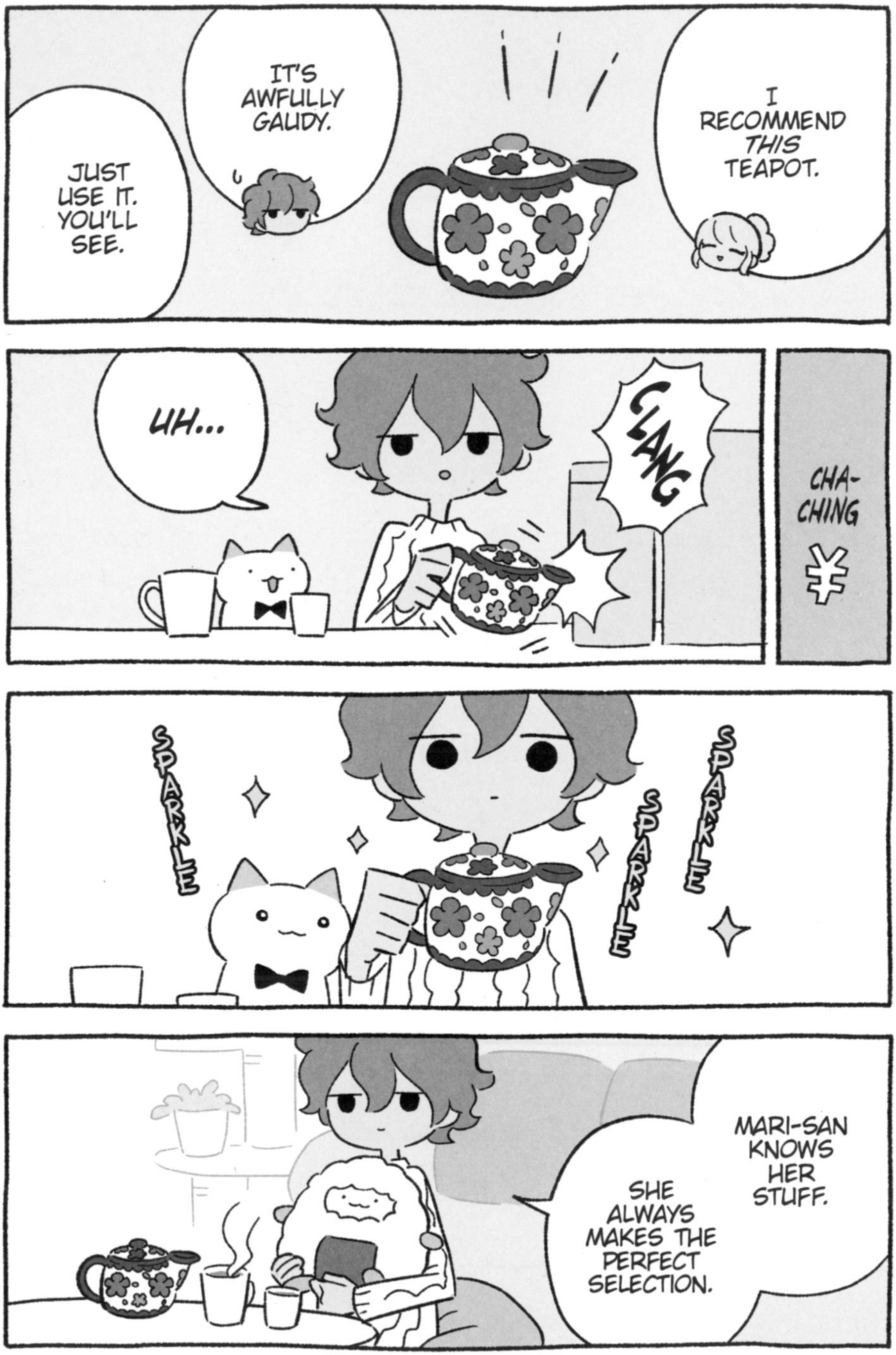
I RECOMMEND *THIS* TEAPOT.
IT'S AWFULLY GAUDY.
JUST USE IT. YOU'LL SEE.
CHA-CHING
¥
CLANG
UH...
SPARKLE
SPARKLE
SPARKLE
MARI-SAN KNOWS HER STUFF.
SHE ALWAYS MAKES THE PERFECT SELECTION.

PALATE CLEANSER

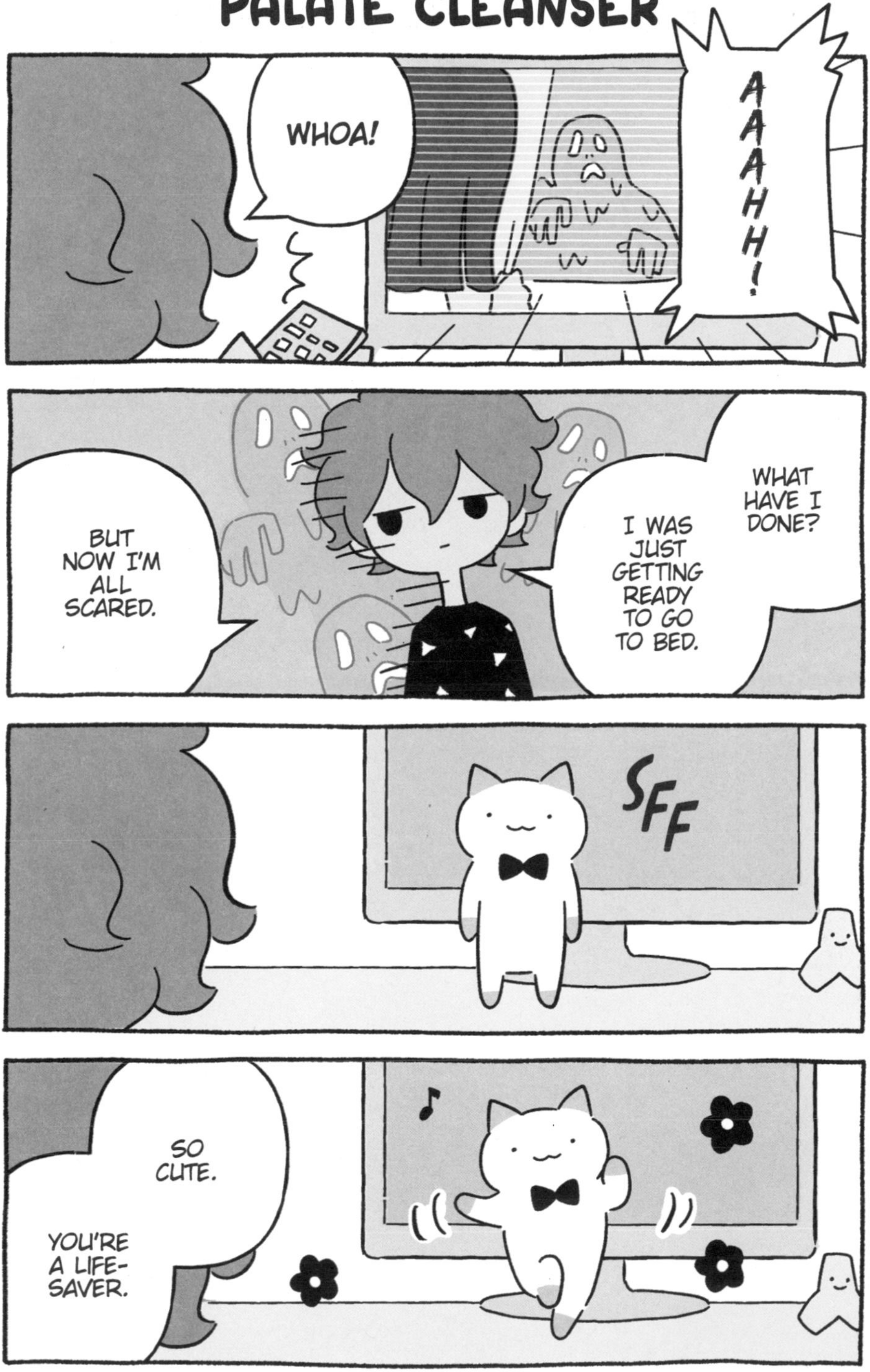
AAAAHH!
WHOA!
WHAT HAVE I DONE?
I WAS JUST GETTING READY TO GO TO BED.
BUT NOW I'M ALL SCARED.
SFF
SO CUTE.
YOU'RE A LIFE-SAVER.

BEHIND THE CURTAIN

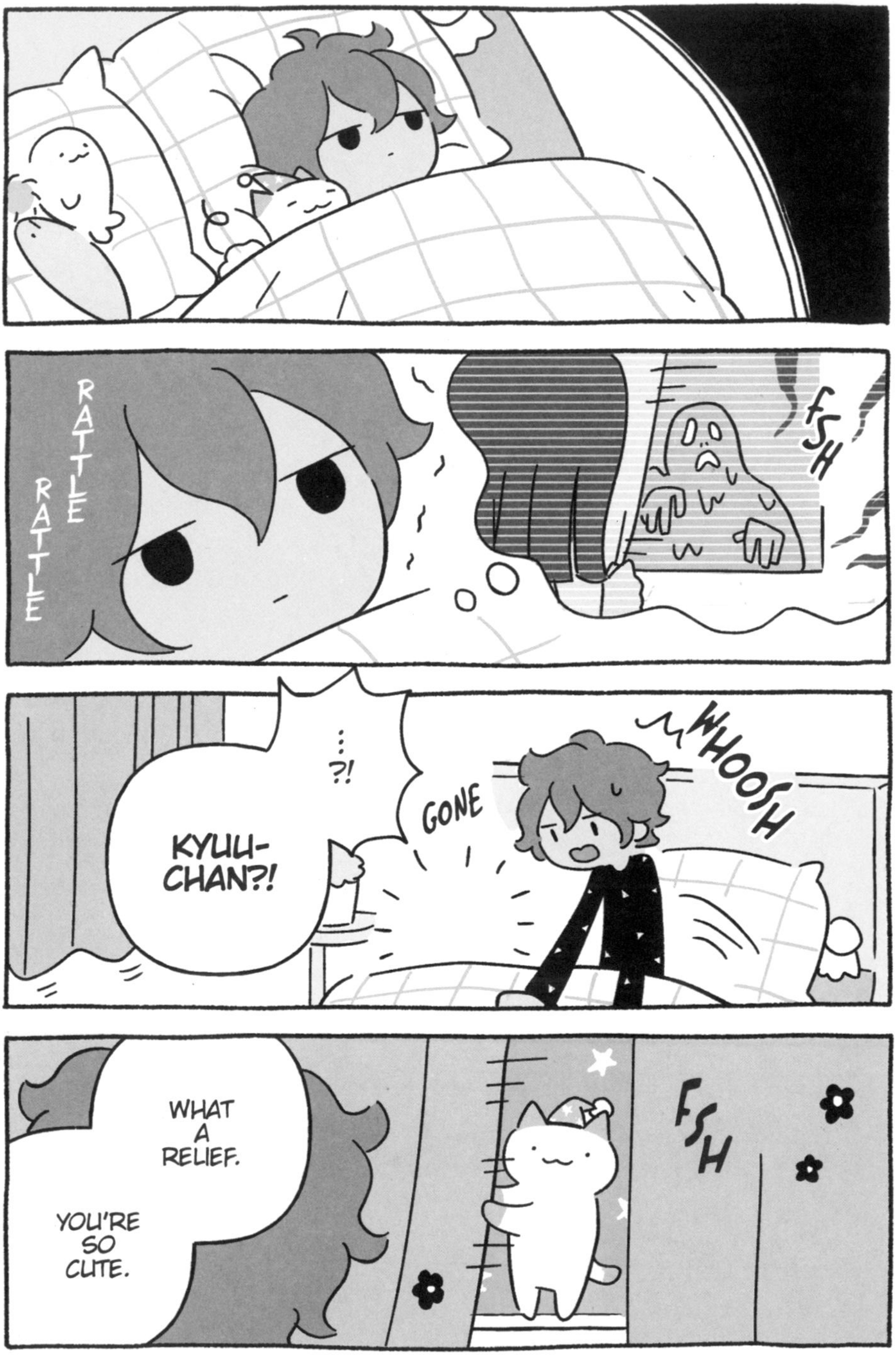
FSH
RATTLE
RATTLE
WHOOSH
GONE
...?!
KYUU-CHAN?!
FSH
WHAT A RELIEF.
YOU'RE SO CUTE.

FAVORITE SNACK BREAD

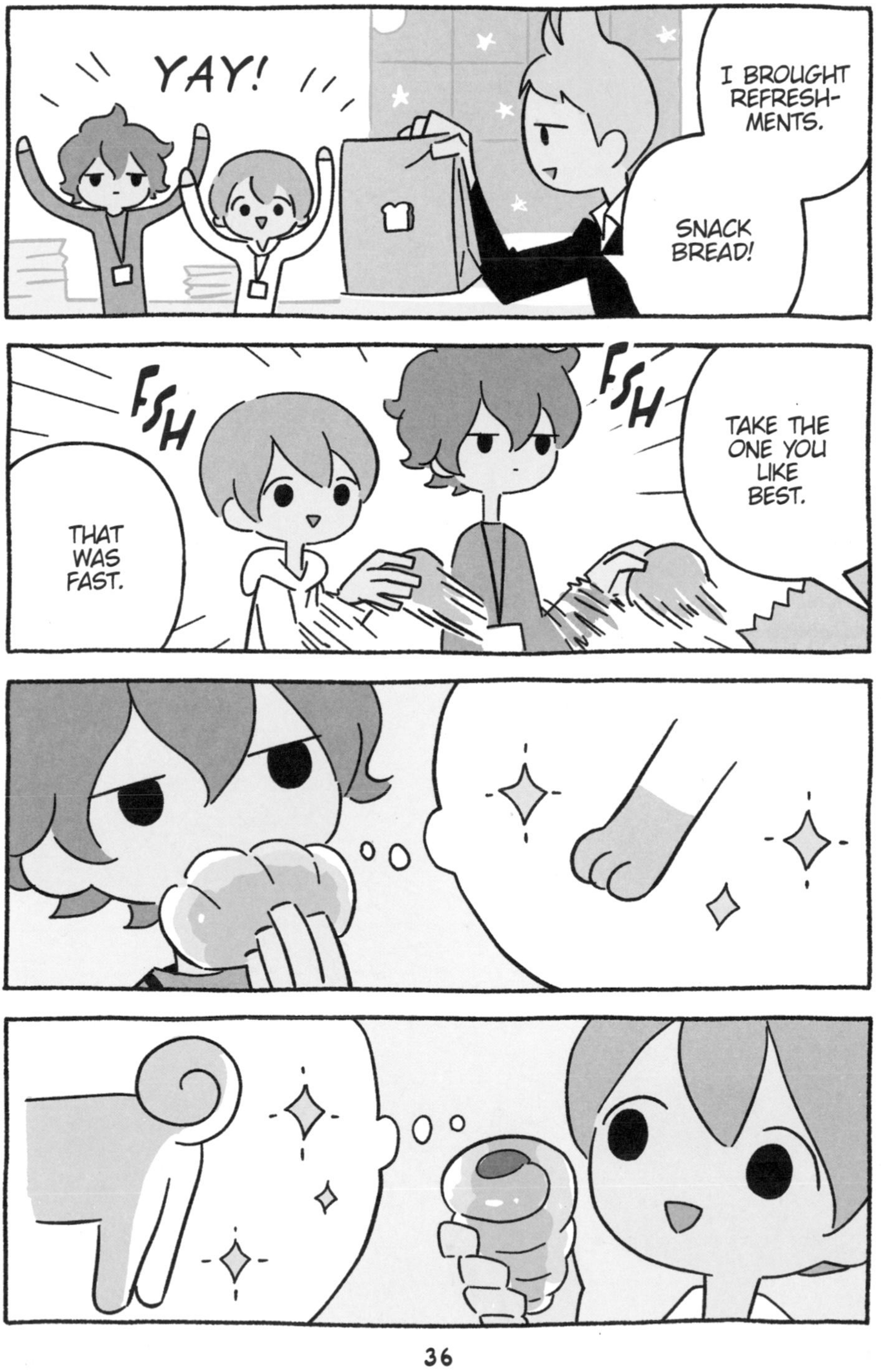
I BROUGHT REFRESH-MENTS.
SNACK BREAD!
YAY!
TAKE THE ONE YOU LIKE BEST.
FSH
FSH
THAT WAS FAST.

THE BOSS

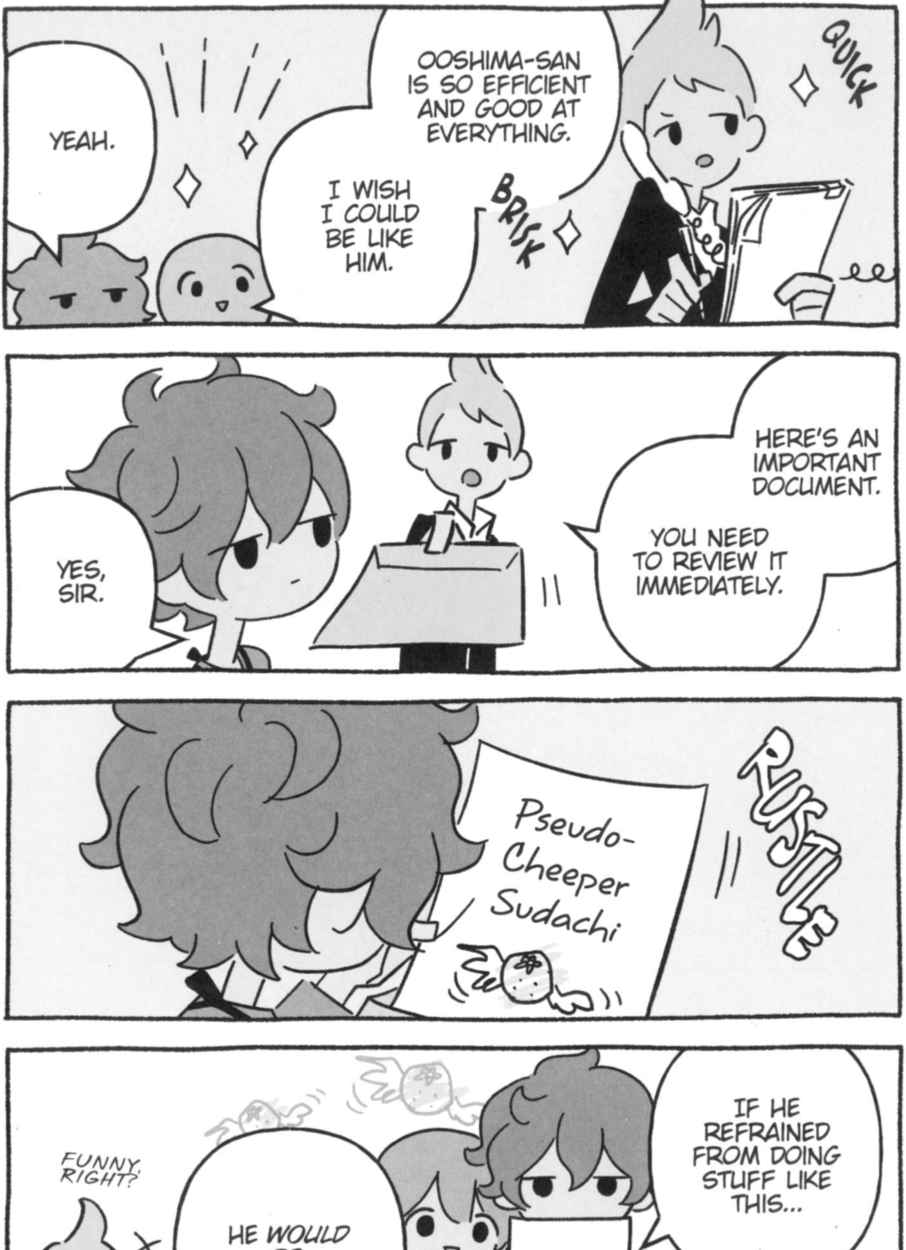
QUICK
OOSHIMA-SAN IS SO EFFICIENT AND GOOD AT EVERYTHING.
BRISK
I WISH I COULD BE LIKE HIM.
YEAH.
HERE'S AN IMPORTANT DOCUMENT.
YOU NEED TO REVIEW IT IMMEDIATELY.
YES, SIR.
RUSTLE
Pseudo-Cheeper Sudachi
IF HE REFRAINED FROM DOING STUFF LIKE THIS...
HE *WOULD* BE PERFECT.
FUNNY, RIGHT?

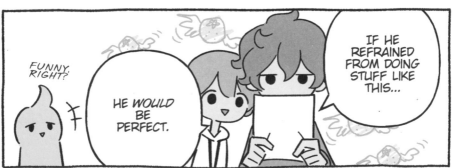

OVERLY TOUCHY-FEELY

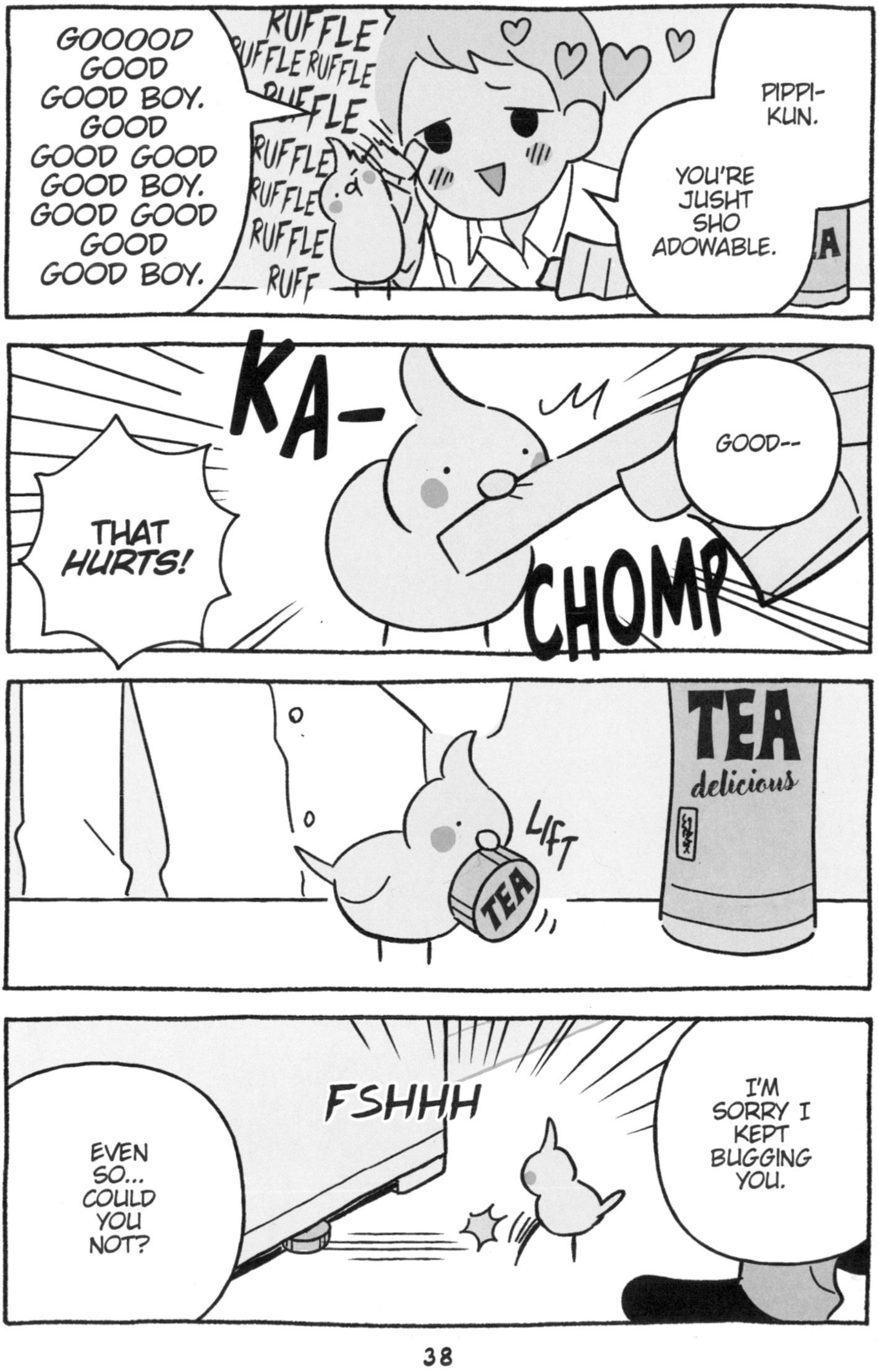
PIPPI-KUN.
YOU'RE JUSHT SHO ADOWABLE.
GOOOOD GOOD GOOD BOY. GOOD GOOD GOOD GOOD BOY. GOOD GOOD GOOD GOOD BOY.
RUFFLE RUFFLE RUFFLE RUFFLE RUFFLE RUFFLE RUFFLE RUFF
GOOD--
KA-
CHOMP
THAT HURTS!
TEA delicious
LIFT
TEA
I'M SORRY I KEPT BUGGING YOU.
FSHHH
EVEN SO... COULD YOU NOT?

PIPPI-KUN AND THE JAVA SPARROW

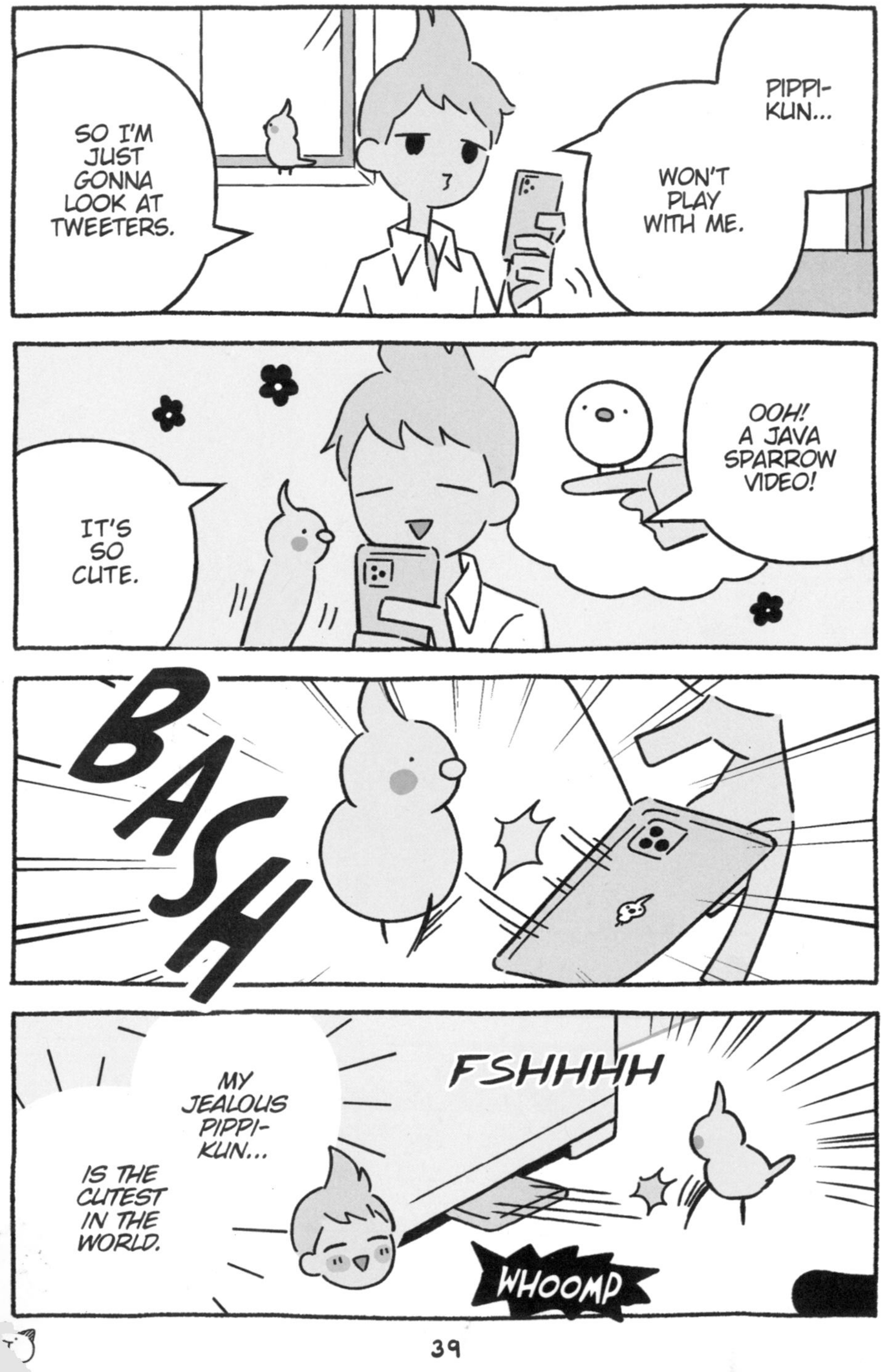

PIPPI-KUN...
WON'T PLAY WITH ME.
SO I'M JUST GONNA LOOK AT TWEETERS.
OOH! A JAVA SPARROW VIDEO!
IT'S SO CUTE.
BASH
FSHHHH
MY JEALOUS PIPPI-KUN...
IS THE CUTEST IN THE WORLD.
WHOOMP

WAITING FOR DINNER

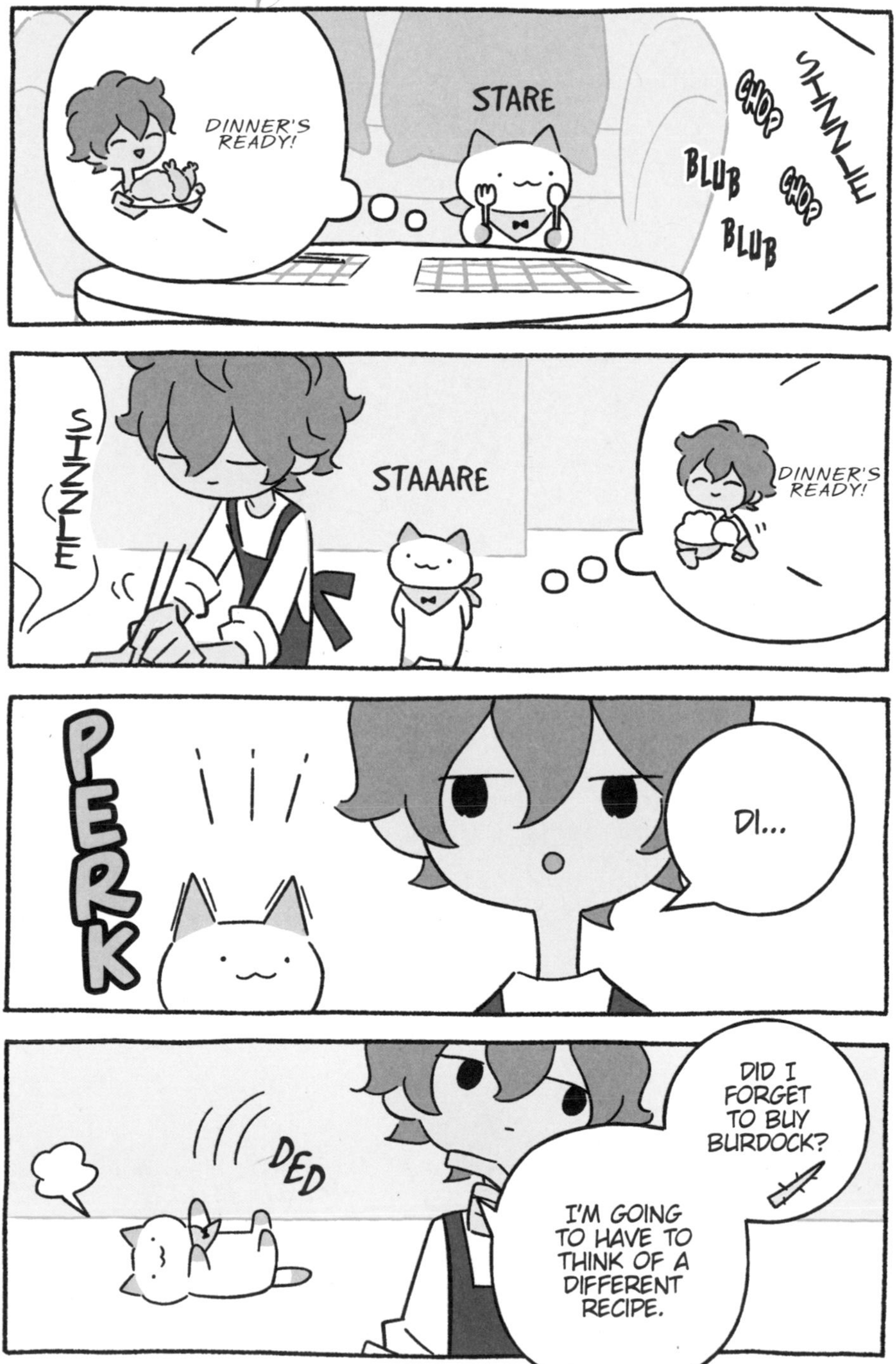

SIZZLE
CHOP
CHOP
BLUB
BLUB
STARE
DINNER'S READY!
DINNER'S READY!
STAAARE
SIZZLE
DI...
PERK
DID I FORGET TO BUY BURDOCK?
I'M GOING TO HAVE TO THINK OF A DIFFERENT RECIPE.
DED

DISTANT

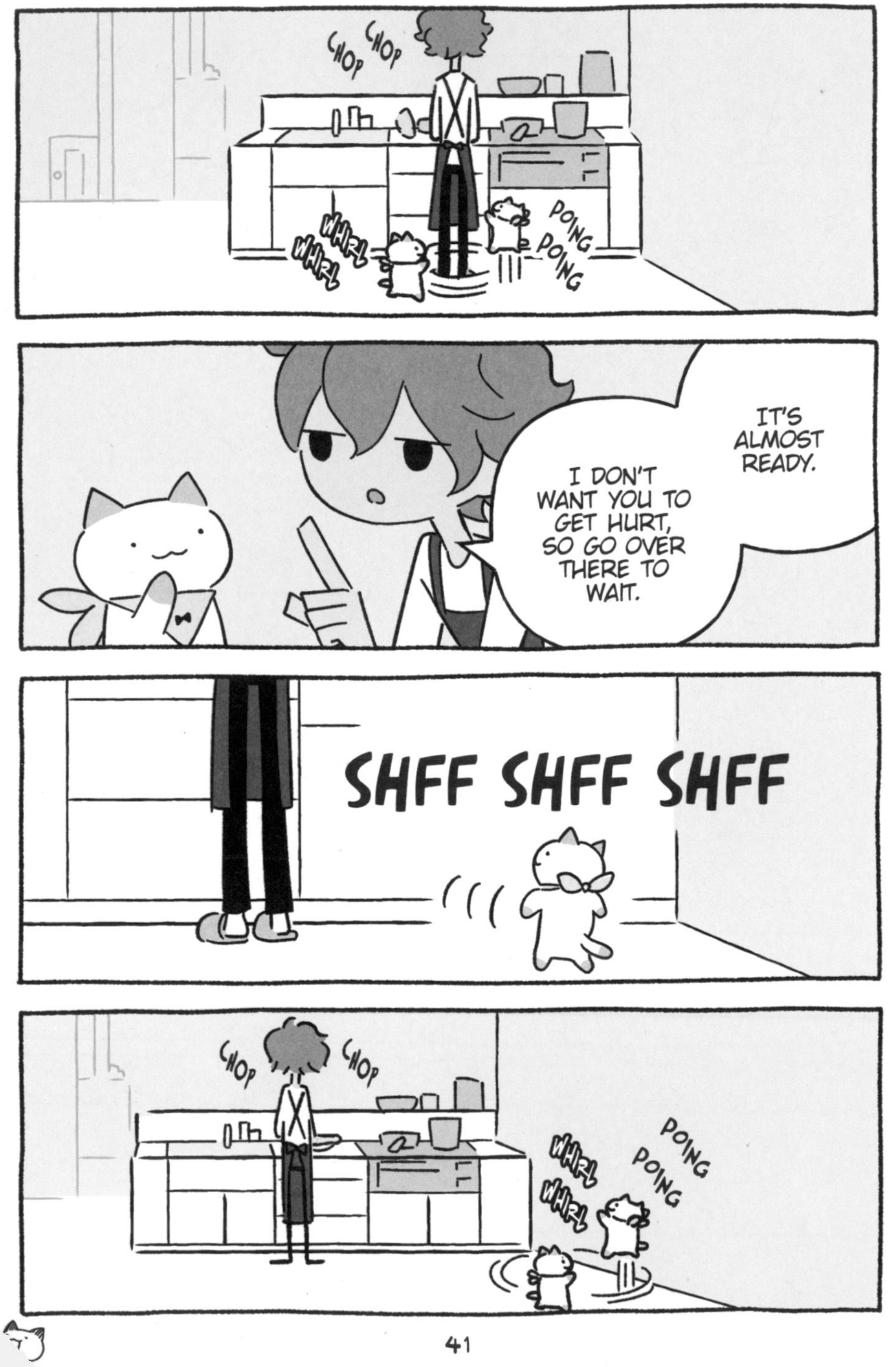
CHOP CHOP
POING POING
WHIRL WHIRL
IT'S ALMOST READY.
I DON'T WANT YOU TO GET HURT, SO GO OVER THERE TO WAIT.
SHFF SHFF SHFF
CHOP CHOP
POING POING
WHIRL WHIRL

CAP

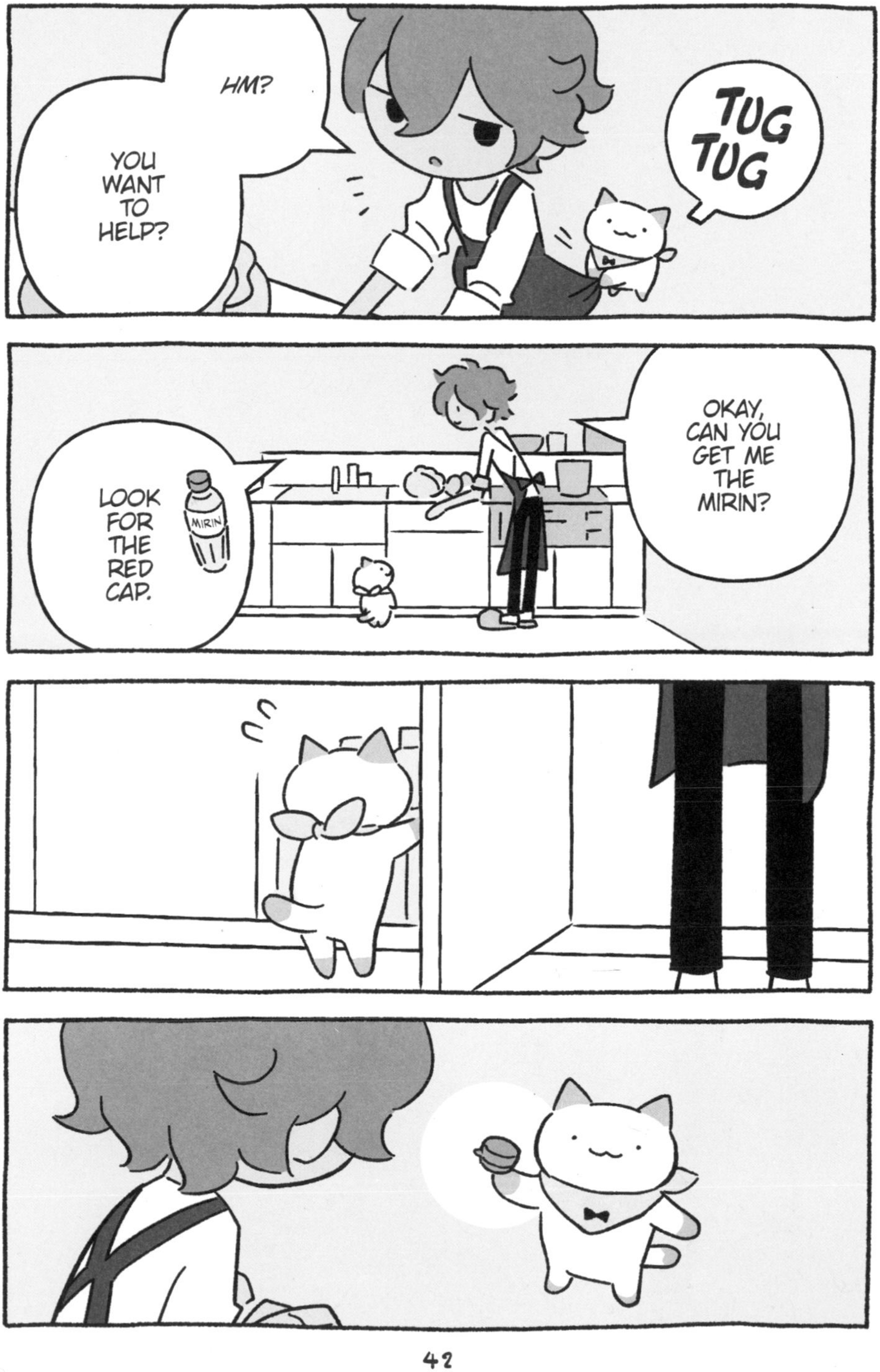
TUG TUG
HM?
YOU WANT TO HELP?
OKAY, CAN YOU GET ME THE MIRIN?
MIRIN
LOOK FOR THE RED CAP.

CAP MEMORIES

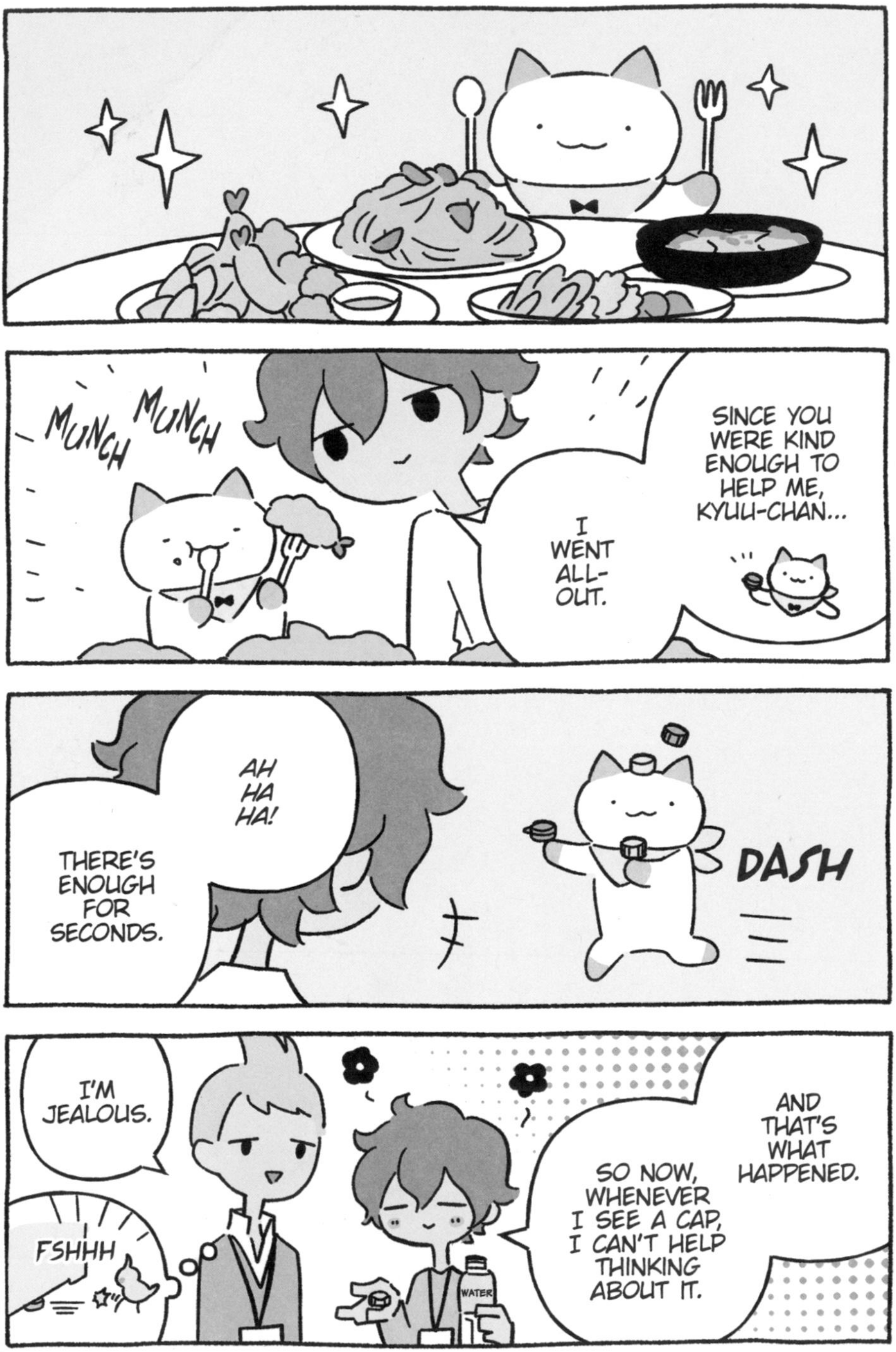
SINCE YOU WERE KIND ENOUGH TO HELP ME, KYUU-CHAN...
I WENT ALL-OUT.
MUNCH MUNCH
DASH
AH HA HA!
THERE'S ENOUGH FOR SECONDS.
AND THAT'S WHAT HAPPENED.
SO NOW, WHENEVER I SEE A CAP, I CAN'T HELP THINKING ABOUT IT.
WATER
I'M JEALOUS.
FSHHH

PURIFICATION

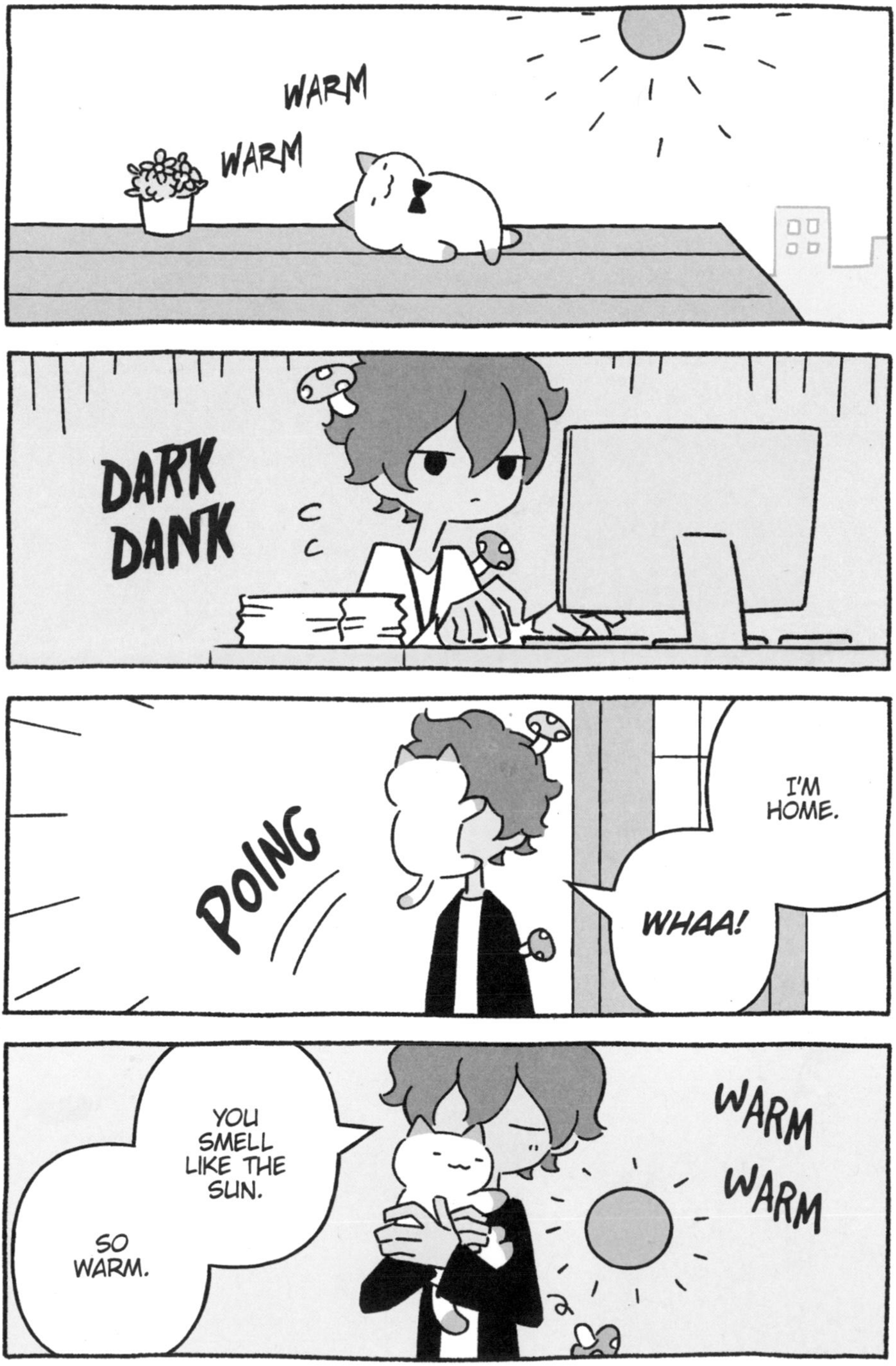
WARM
WARM
DARK
DANK
I'M HOME.
WHAA!
POING
WARM
WARM
YOU SMELL LIKE THE SUN.
SO WARM.

NEWEST MODEL

CUTE BIRD VIDEO!
WHOOMP
HEY!
YOU ALWAYS HAVE THE LATEST MODEL OF SMART-PHONE, OOSHIMA-SAN.
OOOH!
AAAH!
I'M JEALOUS.
Y...
YEAH, WELL.

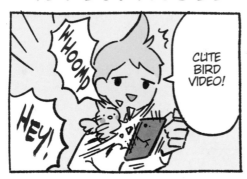

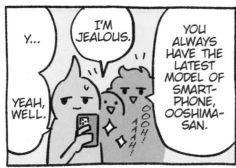

WHACK-A-MOLE

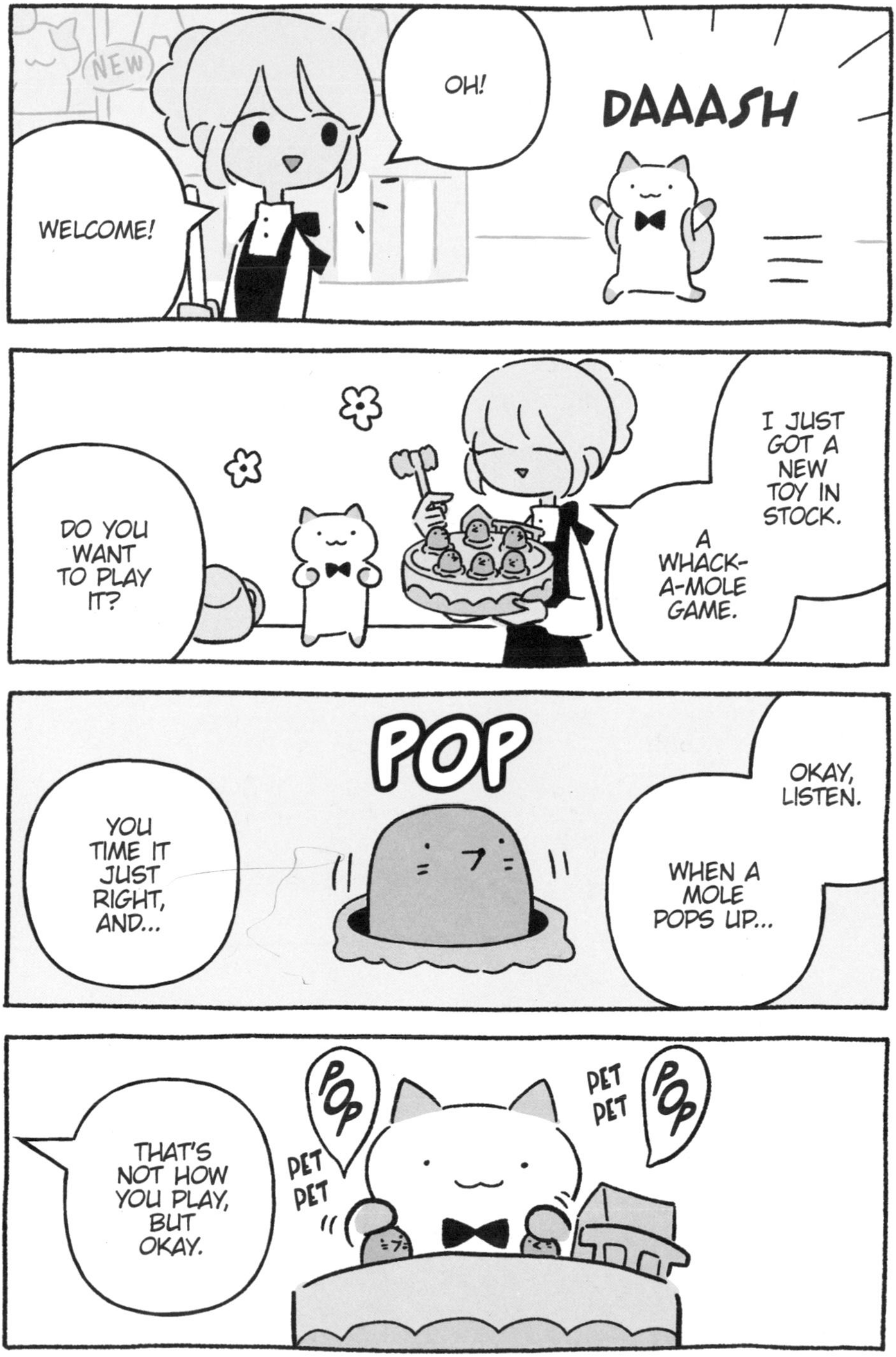
DAAASH
OH!
WELCOME!
I JUST GOT A NEW TOY IN STOCK.
A WHACK-A-MOLE GAME.
DO YOU WANT TO PLAY IT?
POP
OKAY, LISTEN.
WHEN A MOLE POPS UP...
YOU TIME IT JUST RIGHT, AND...
POP
PET PET
POP
PET PET
THAT'S NOT HOW YOU PLAY, BUT OKAY.

THIS AND THAT

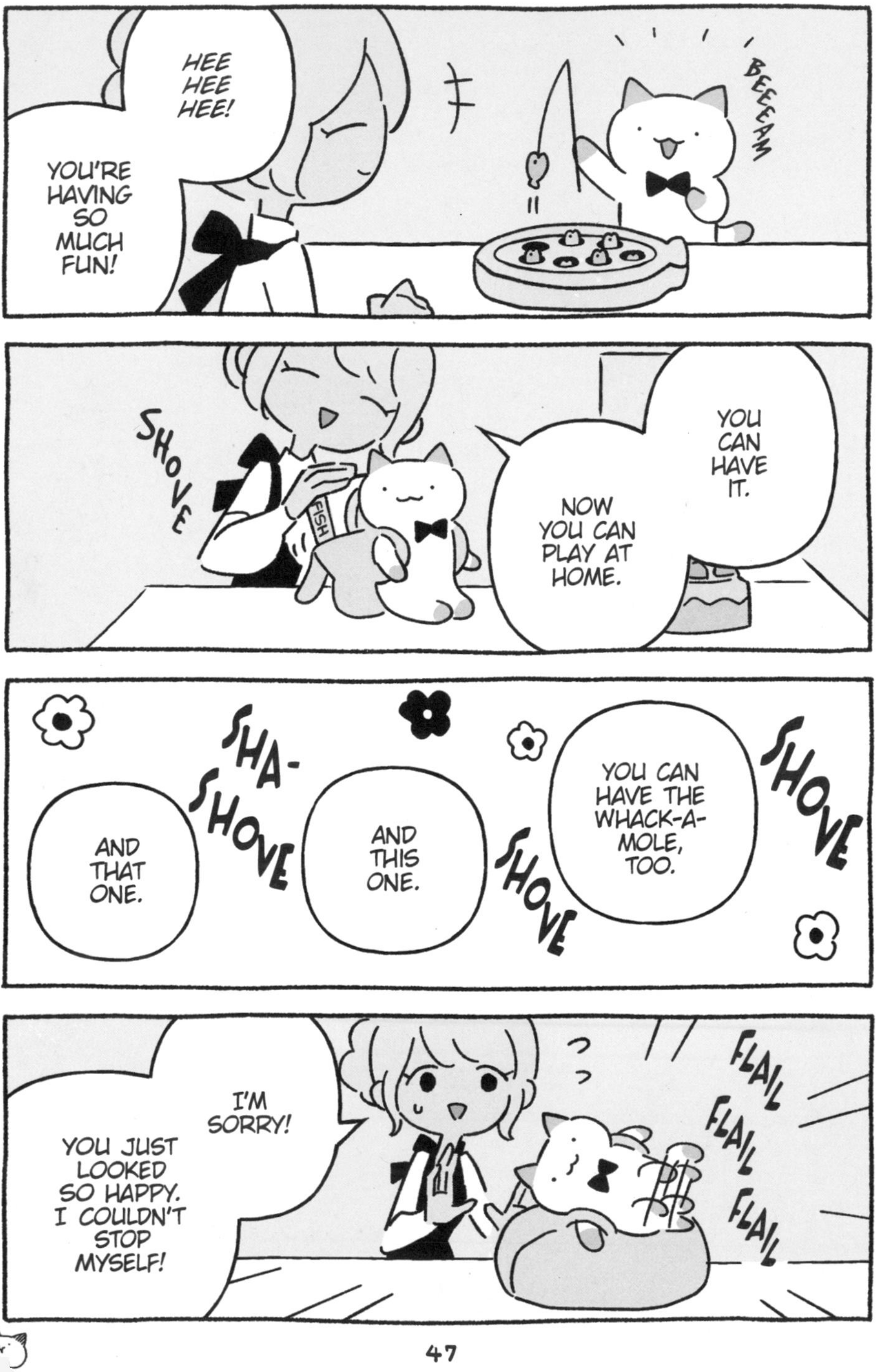
BEEEAM
HEE HEE HEE!
YOU'RE HAVING SO MUCH FUN!
YOU CAN HAVE IT.
NOW YOU CAN PLAY AT HOME.
FISH
SHOVE
SHOVE
YOU CAN HAVE THE WHACK-A-MOLE, TOO.
SHOVE
SHA-SHOVE
AND THIS ONE.
AND THAT ONE.
FLAIL
FLAIL
FLAIL
I'M SORRY!
YOU JUST LOOKED SO HAPPY. I COULDN'T STOP MYSELF!

BOX GAMES

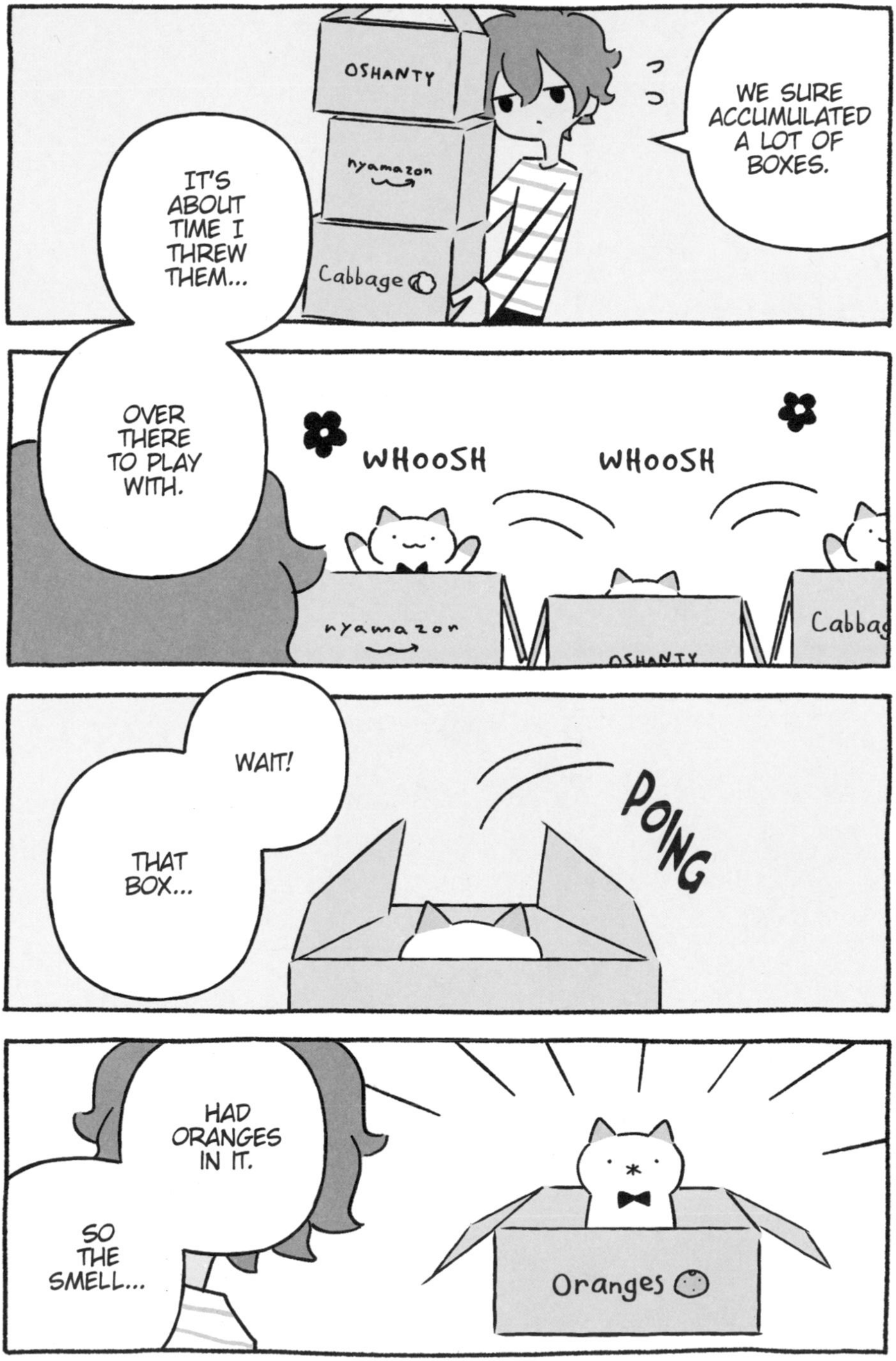
WE SURE ACCUMULATED A LOT OF BOXES.
OSHANTY
nyamazon
Cabbage
IT'S ABOUT TIME I THREW THEM...
OVER THERE TO PLAY WITH.
WHOOSH
WHOOSH
nyamazon
OSHANTY
WAIT!
POING
THAT BOX...
HAD ORANGES IN IT.
SO THE SMELL...
Oranges

PET-A-CAT

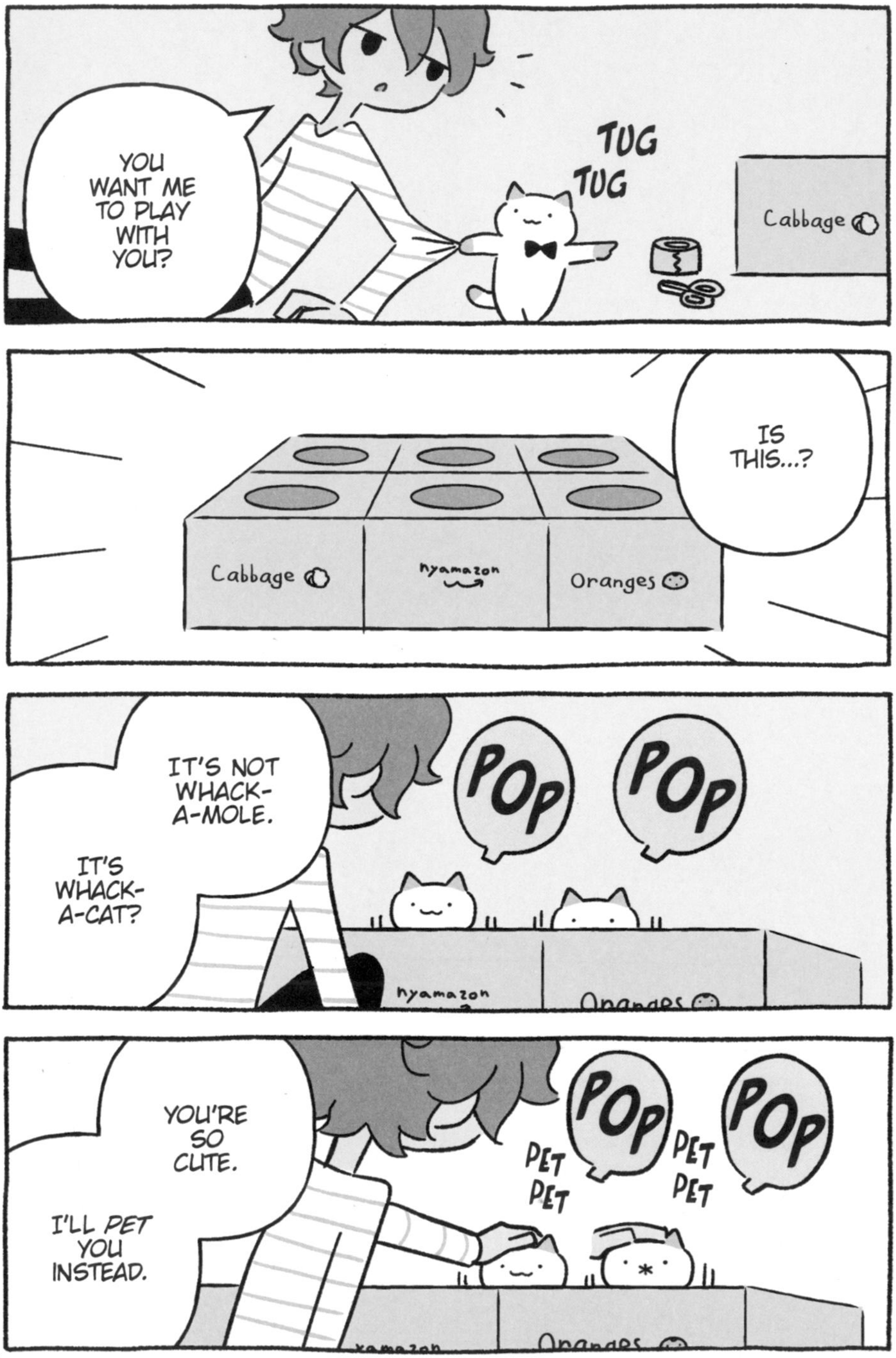
TUG
TUG
Cabbage
YOU WANT ME TO PLAY WITH YOU?
IS THIS...?
Oranges
nyamazon
Cabbage
POP
POP
IT'S NOT WHACK-A-MOLE.
IT'S WHACK-A-CAT?
nyamazon
POP
POP
PET
PET
PET
PET
YOU'RE SO CUTE.
I'LL *PET* YOU INSTEAD.

DANCING NIGHT

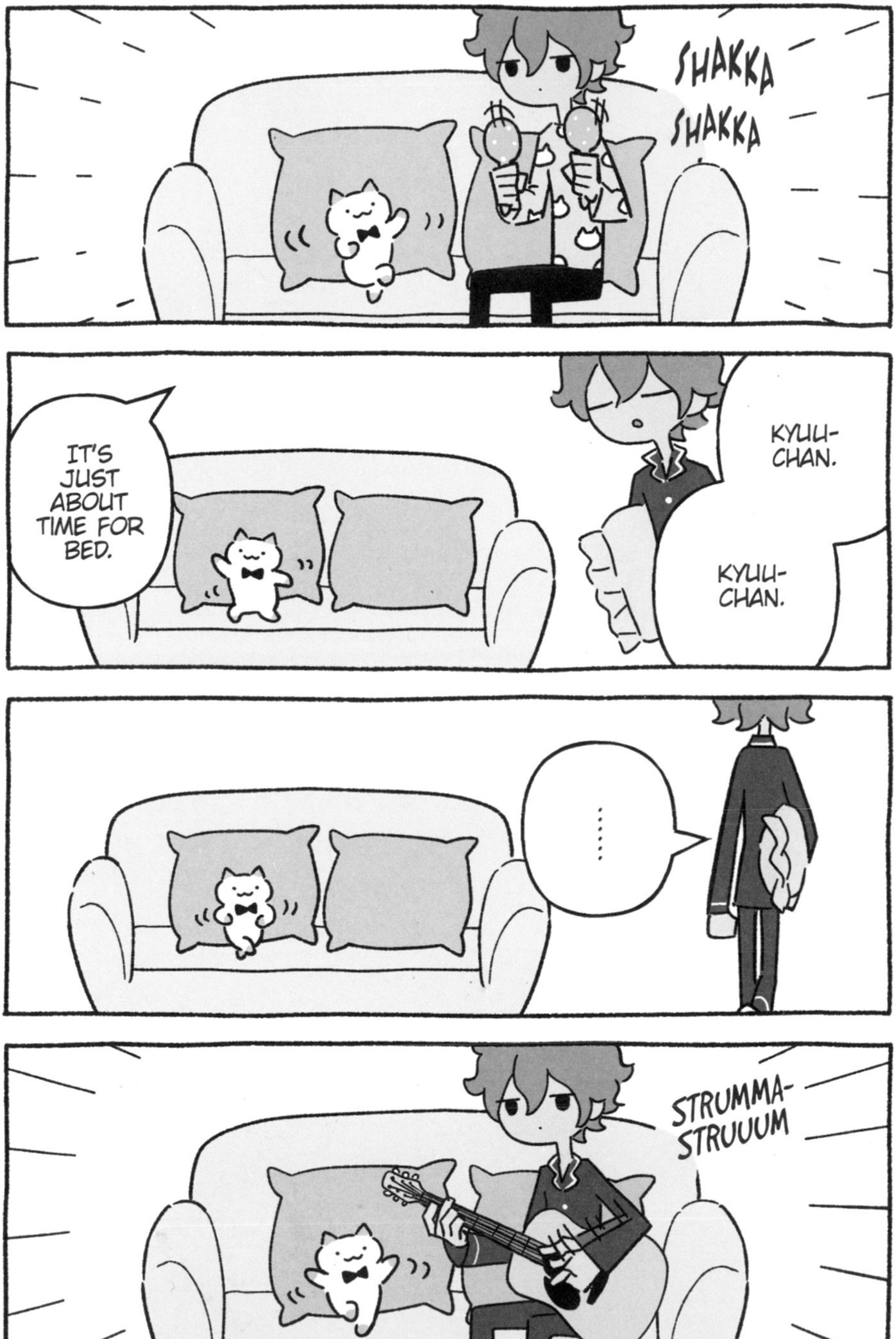
SHAKKA SHAKKA
KYUU-CHAN.
KYUU-CHAN.
IT'S JUST ABOUT TIME FOR BED.
......
STRUMMA-STRUUUM

WARM WELCOME

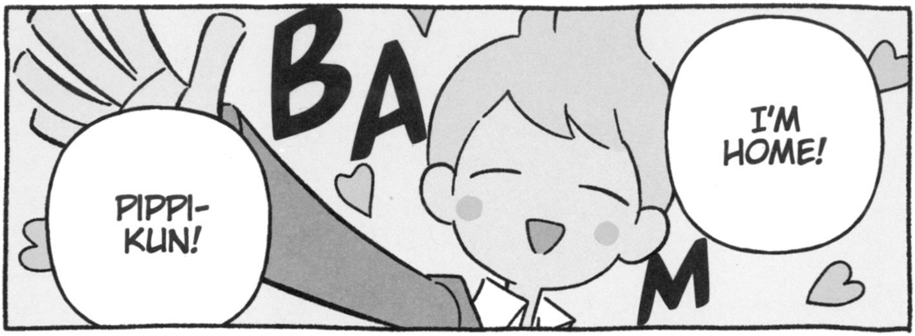
I'M HOME!
BAM
PIPPI-KUN!

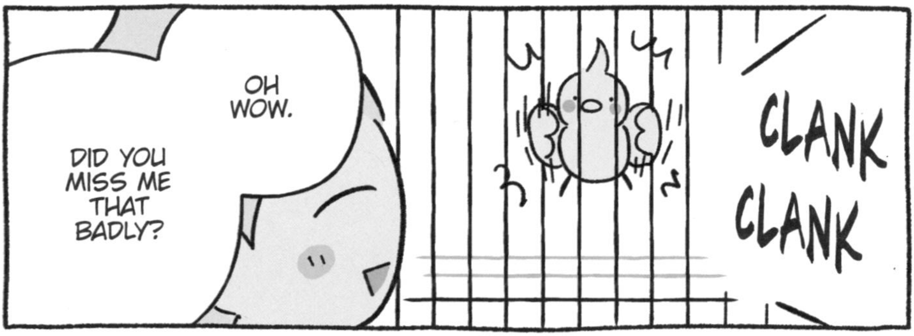
CLANK CLANK
OH WOW.
DID YOU MISS ME THAT BADLY?

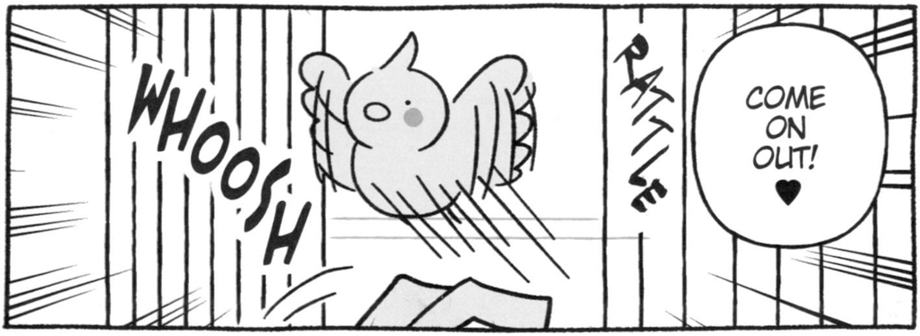
COME ON OUT! ♥
RATTLE
WHOOSH

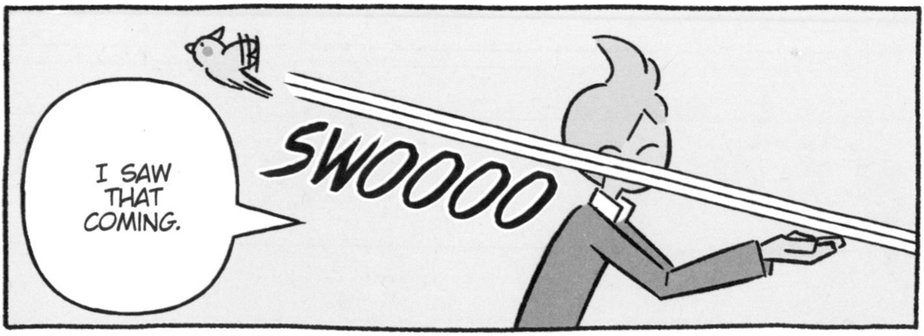
SWOOOO
I SAW THAT COMING.

FLUFFY DISPENSER

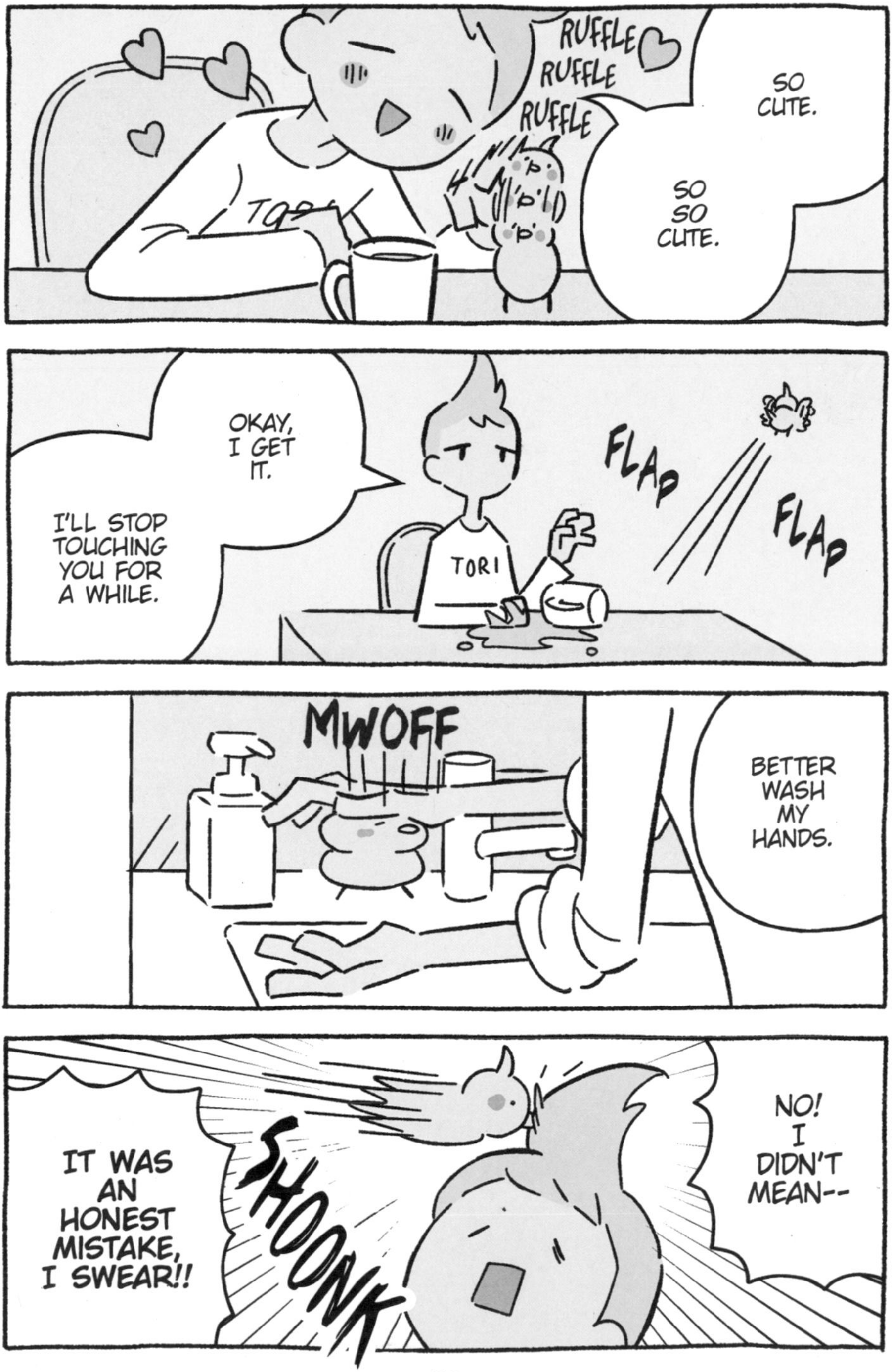
SO CUTE.
SO SO CUTE.
RUFFLE RUFFLE RUFFLE
FLAP FLAP
OKAY, I GET IT.
TORI
I'LL STOP TOUCHING YOU FOR A WHILE.
BETTER WASH MY HANDS.
MWOFF
NO! I DIDN'T MEAN--
SHOONK
IT WAS AN HONEST MISTAKE, I SWEAR!!

HE NEVER LEARNS

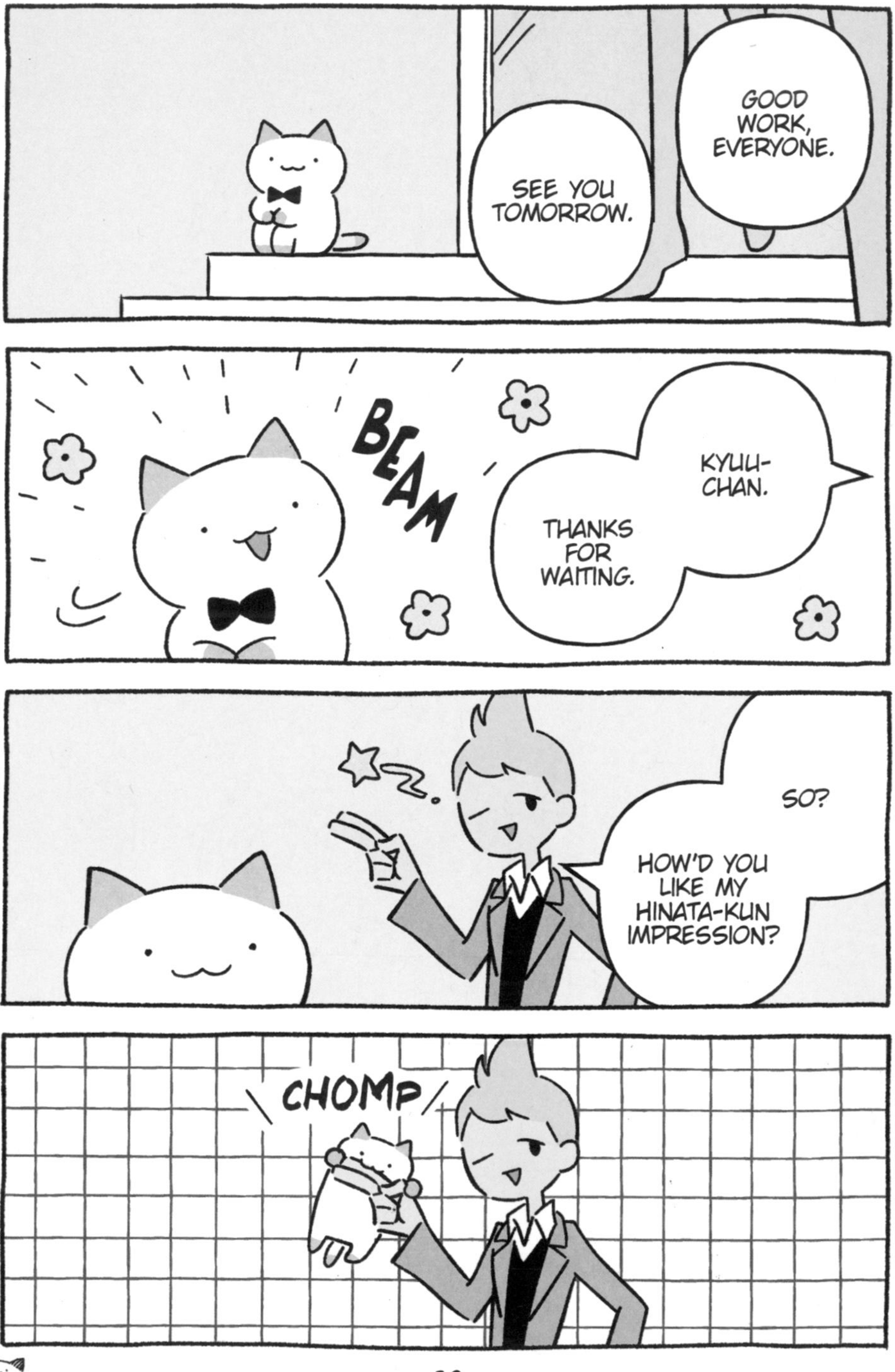
GOOD WORK, EVERYONE.
SEE YOU TOMORROW.
KYUU-CHAN.
THANKS FOR WAITING.
BEAM
SO?
HOW'D YOU LIKE MY HINATA-KUN IMPRESSION?
CHOMP

OPERATION: LET'S BE FRIENDS

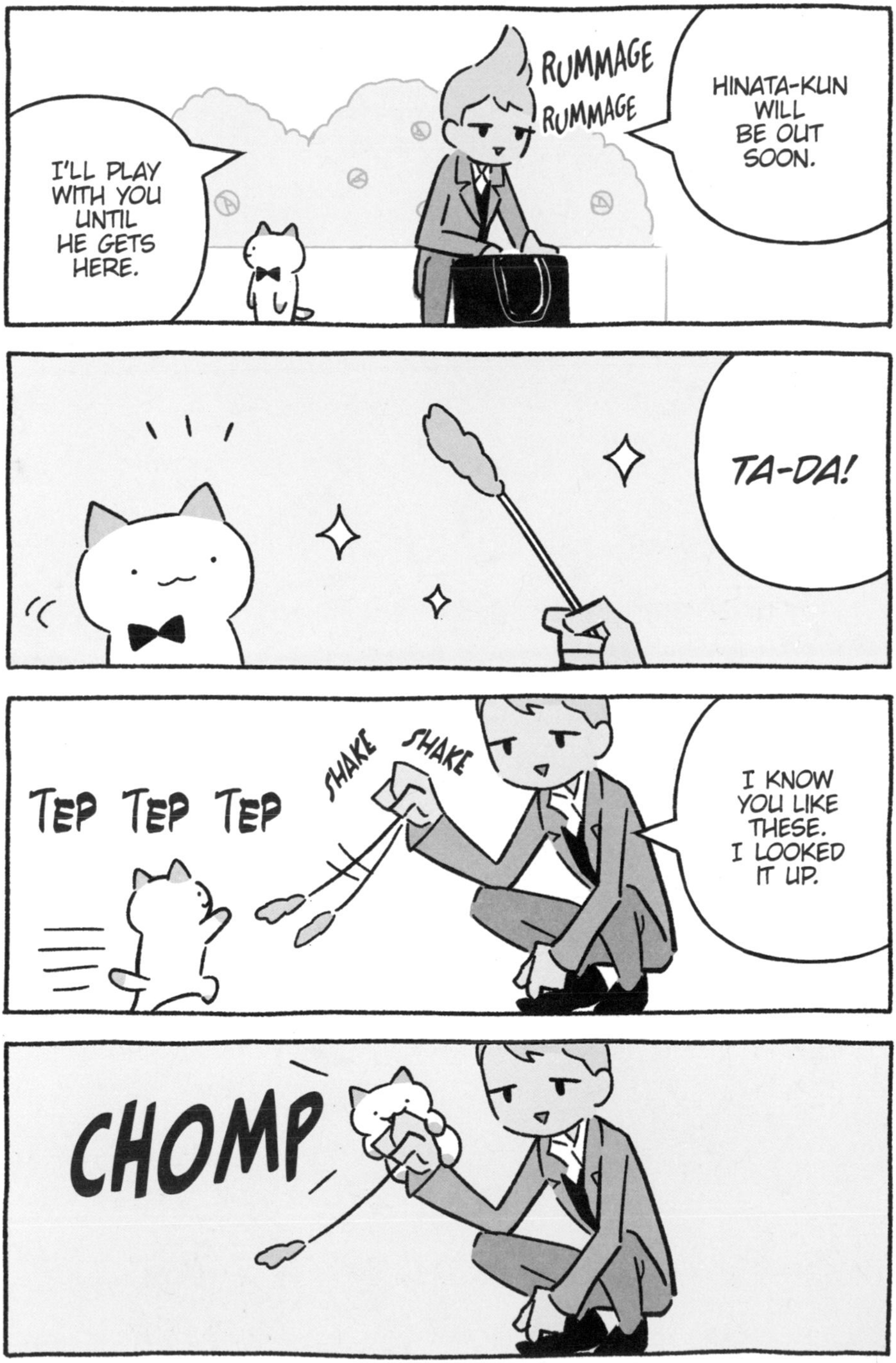
HINATA-KUN WILL BE OUT SOON.
RUMMAGE
RUMMAGE
I'LL PLAY WITH YOU UNTIL HE GETS HERE.
TA-DA!
I KNOW YOU LIKE THESE. I LOOKED IT UP.
SHAKE SHAKE
TEP TEP TEP
CHOMP

A LITTLE BIRD TOLD ME

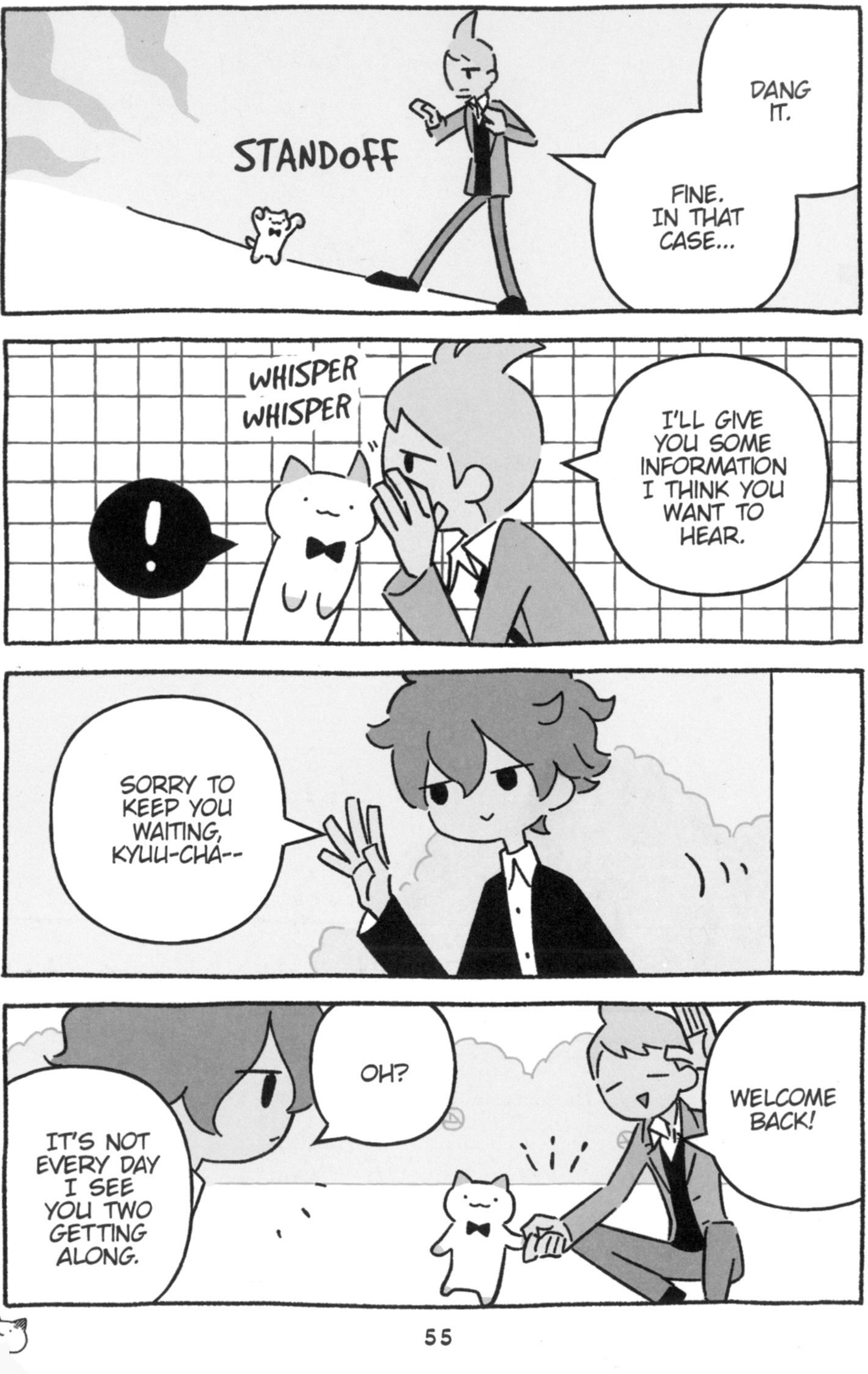
DANG IT.
FINE. IN THAT CASE...
STANDOFF
I'LL GIVE YOU SOME INFORMATION I THINK YOU WANT TO HEAR.
WHISPER WHISPER
!
SORRY TO KEEP YOU WAITING, KYUU-CHA--
WELCOME BACK!
OH?
IT'S NOT EVERY DAY I SEE YOU TWO GETTING ALONG.

CAKE SHOP

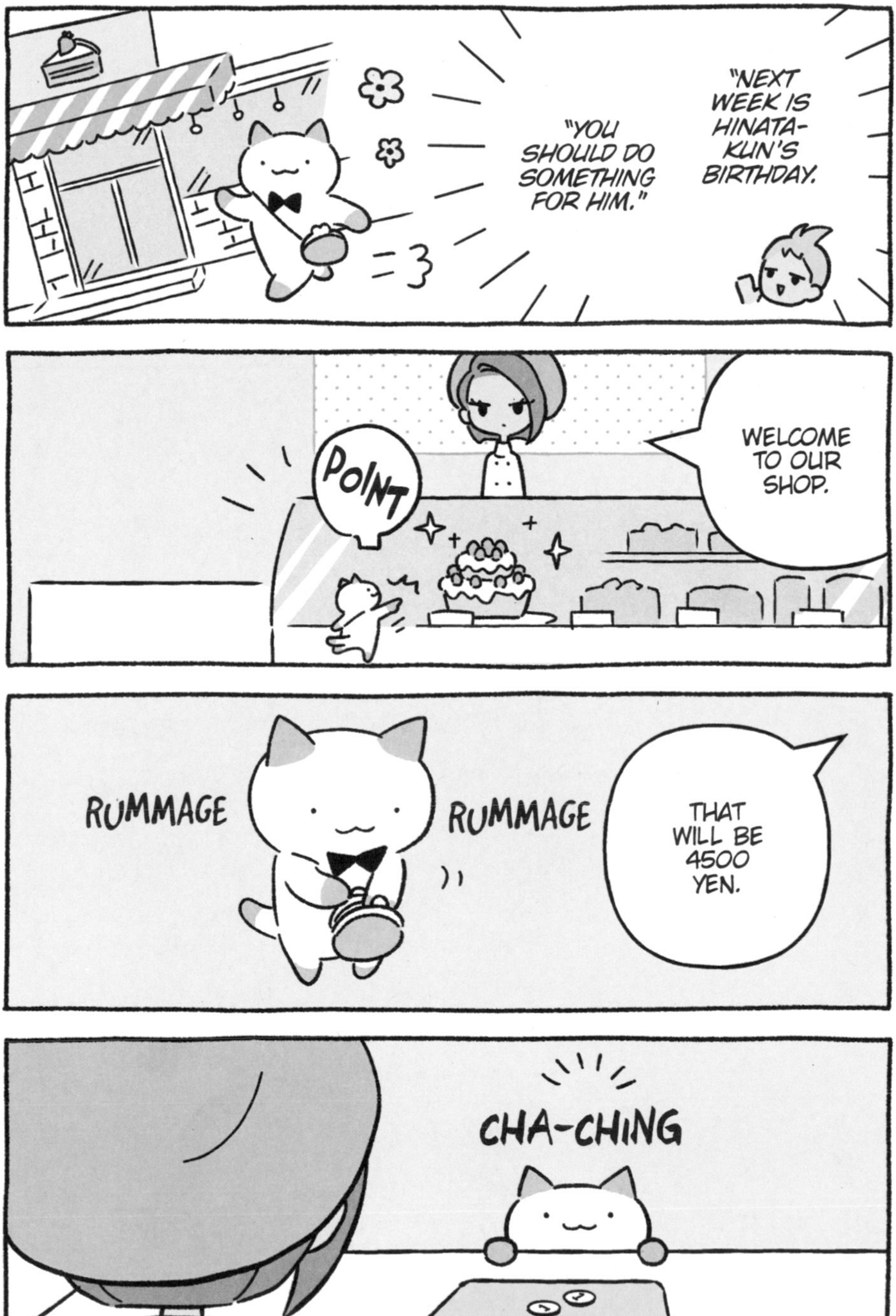
"NEXT WEEK IS HINATA-KUN'S BIRTHDAY.
"YOU SHOULD DO SOMETHING FOR HIM."
WELCOME TO OUR SHOP.
POINT
THAT WILL BE 4500 YEN.
RUMMAGE
RUMMAGE
CHA-CHING

TAKE HIM AWAY

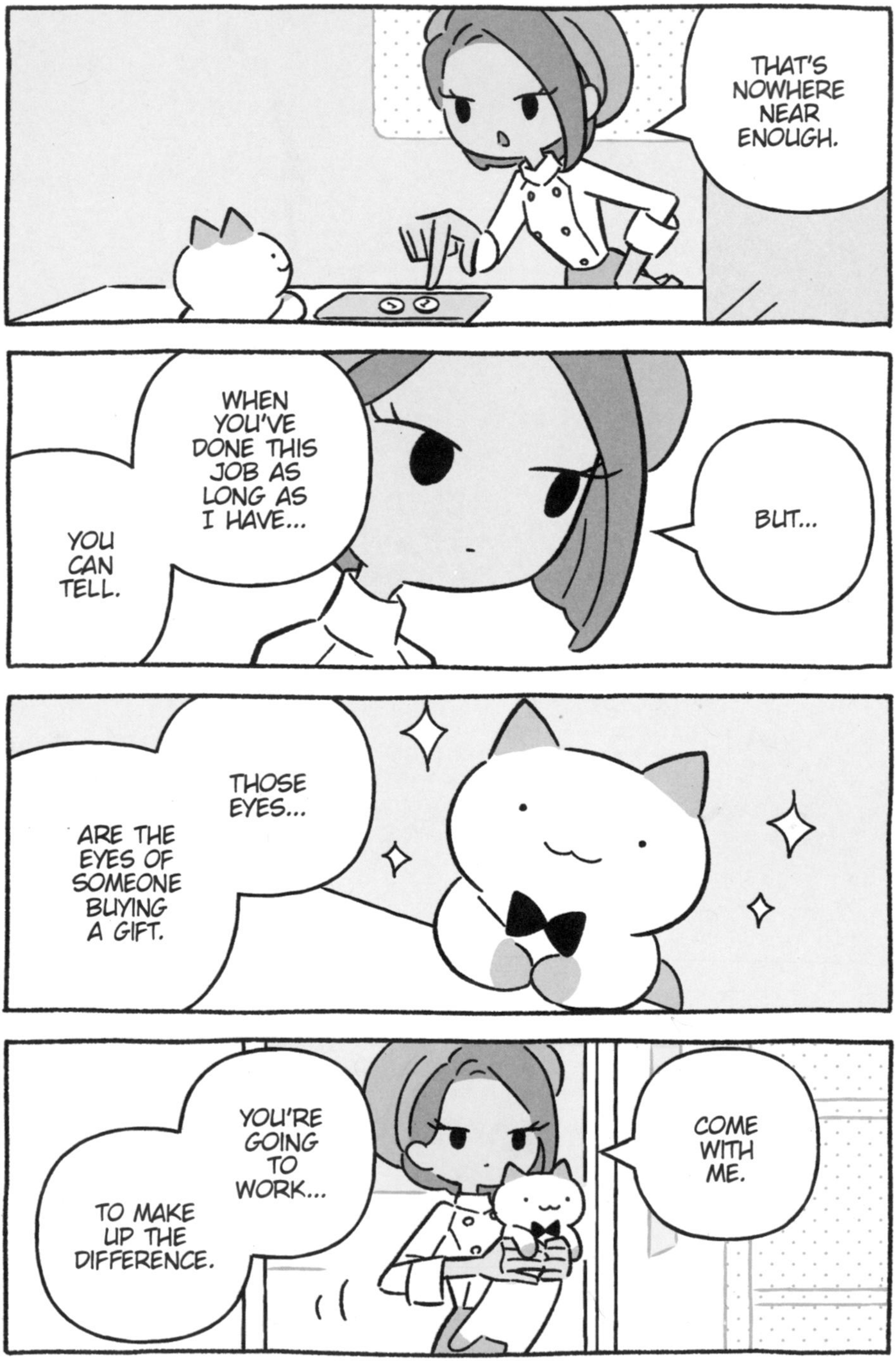
THAT'S NOWHERE NEAR ENOUGH.
BUT...
WHEN YOU'VE DONE THIS JOB AS LONG AS I HAVE...
YOU CAN TELL.
THOSE EYES...
ARE THE EYES OF SOMEONE BUYING A GIFT.
COME WITH ME.
YOU'RE GOING TO WORK...
TO MAKE UP THE DIFFERENCE.

MAKING CAKE

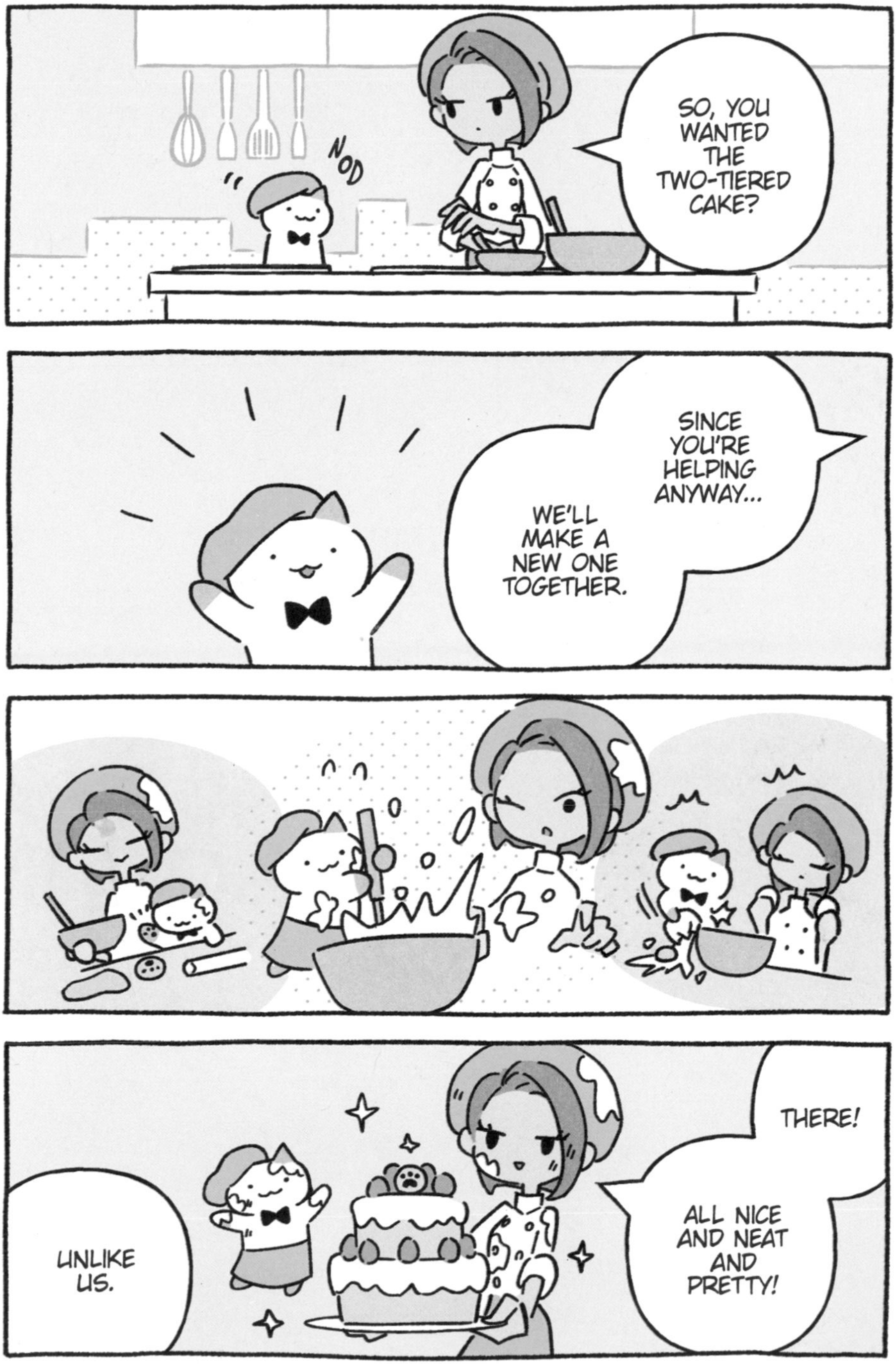
SO, YOU WANTED THE TWO-TIERED CAKE?
NOD
SINCE YOU'RE HELPING ANYWAY...
WE'LL MAKE A NEW ONE TOGETHER.
THERE!
ALL NICE AND NEAT AND PRETTY!
UNLIKE US.

NEW EMPLOYEE

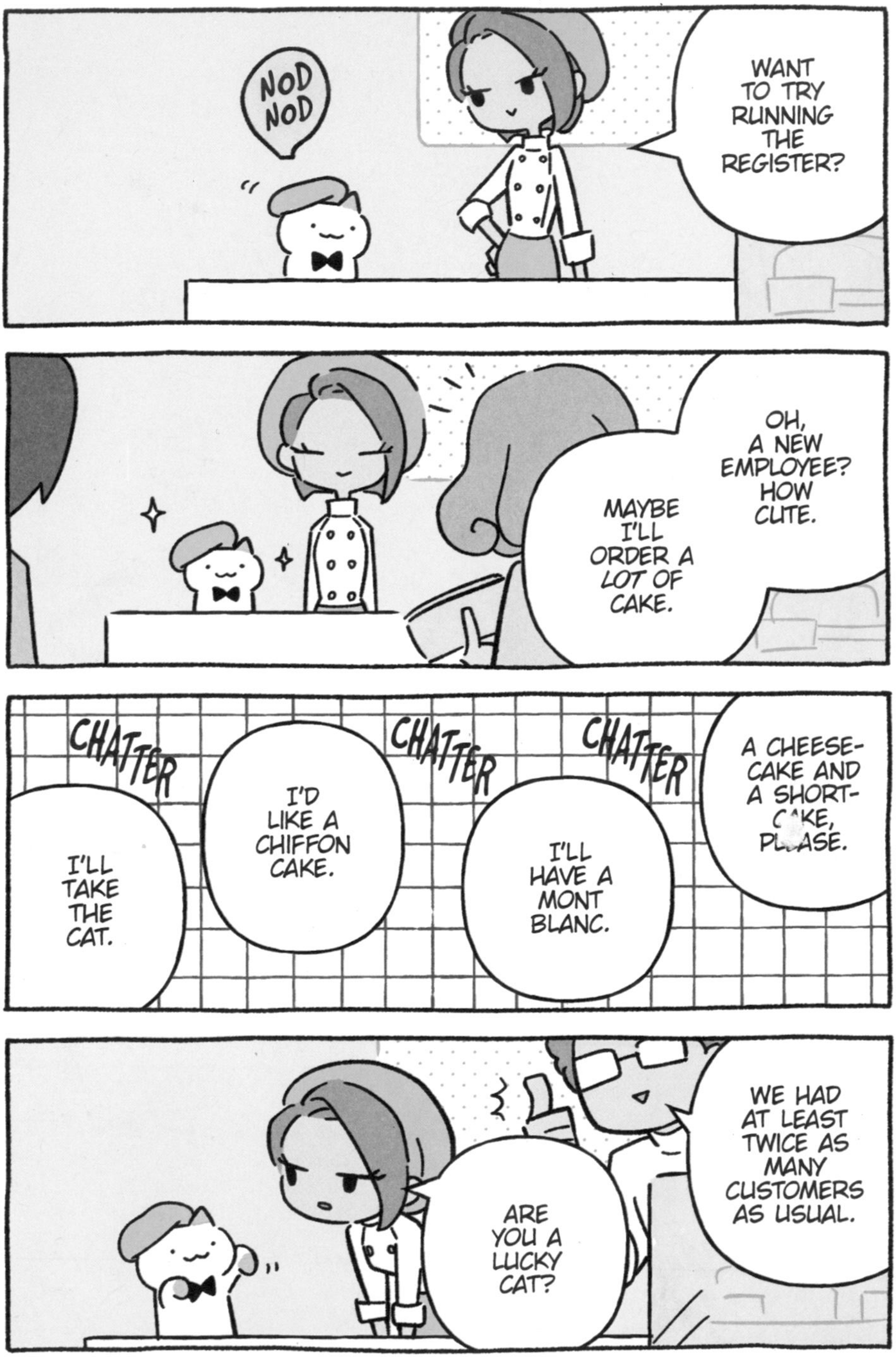
WANT TO TRY RUNNING THE REGISTER?
NOD NOD
OH, A NEW EMPLOYEE? HOW CUTE.
MAYBE I'LL ORDER A LOT OF CAKE.
A CHEESE-CAKE AND A SHORT-CAKE, PLEASE.
CHATTER
I'LL HAVE A MONT BLANC.
CHATTER
I'D LIKE A CHIFFON CAKE.
CHATTER
I'LL TAKE THE CAT.
WE HAD AT LEAST TWICE AS MANY CUSTOMERS AS USUAL.
ARE YOU A LUCKY CAT?

9

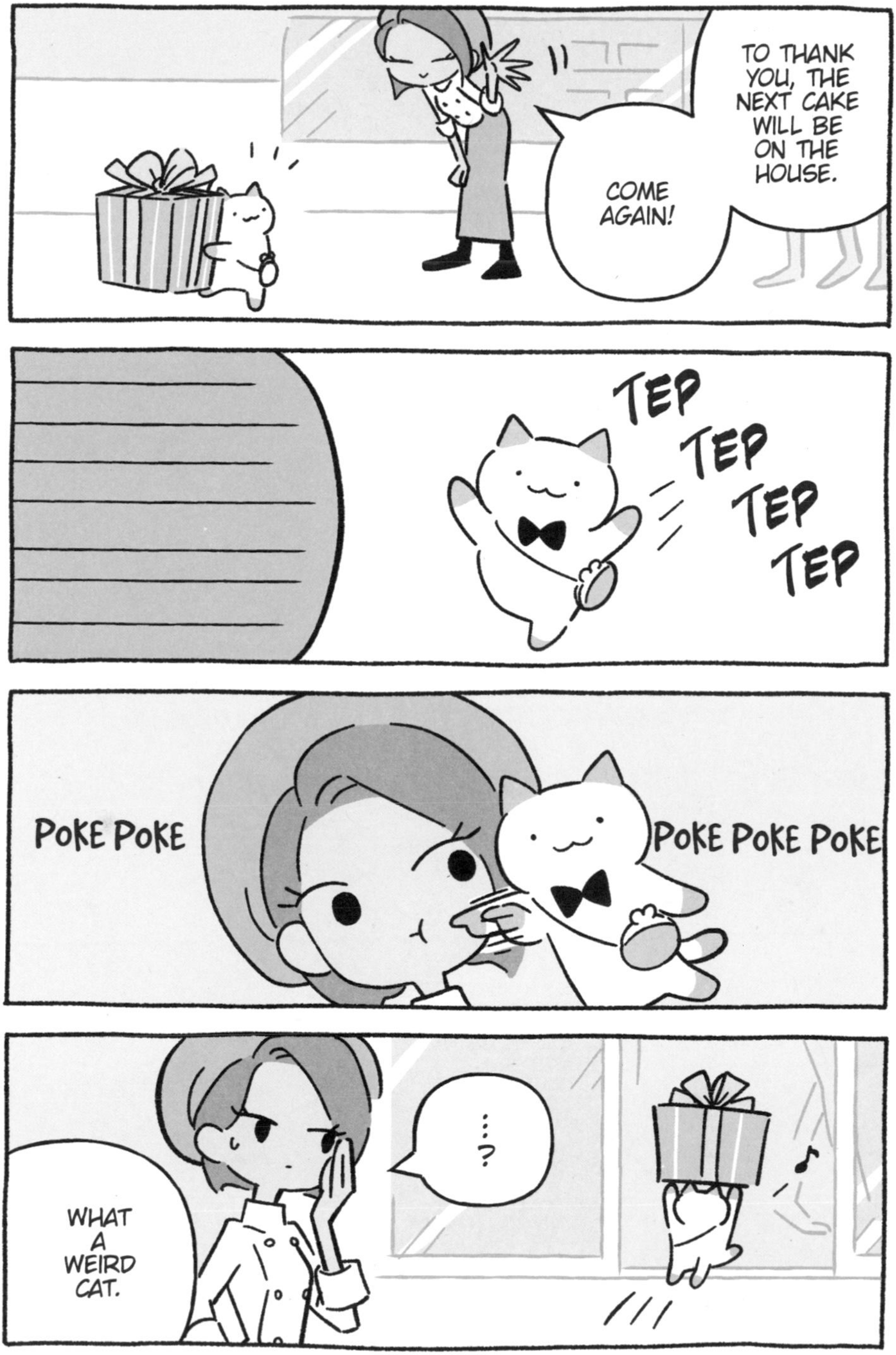
TO THANK YOU, THE NEXT CAKE WILL BE ON THE HOUSE.
COME AGAIN!
TEP TEP TEP TEP
POKE POKE POKE
POKE POKE
...?
WHAT A WEIRD CAT.

COMMENCE PREPARATIONS

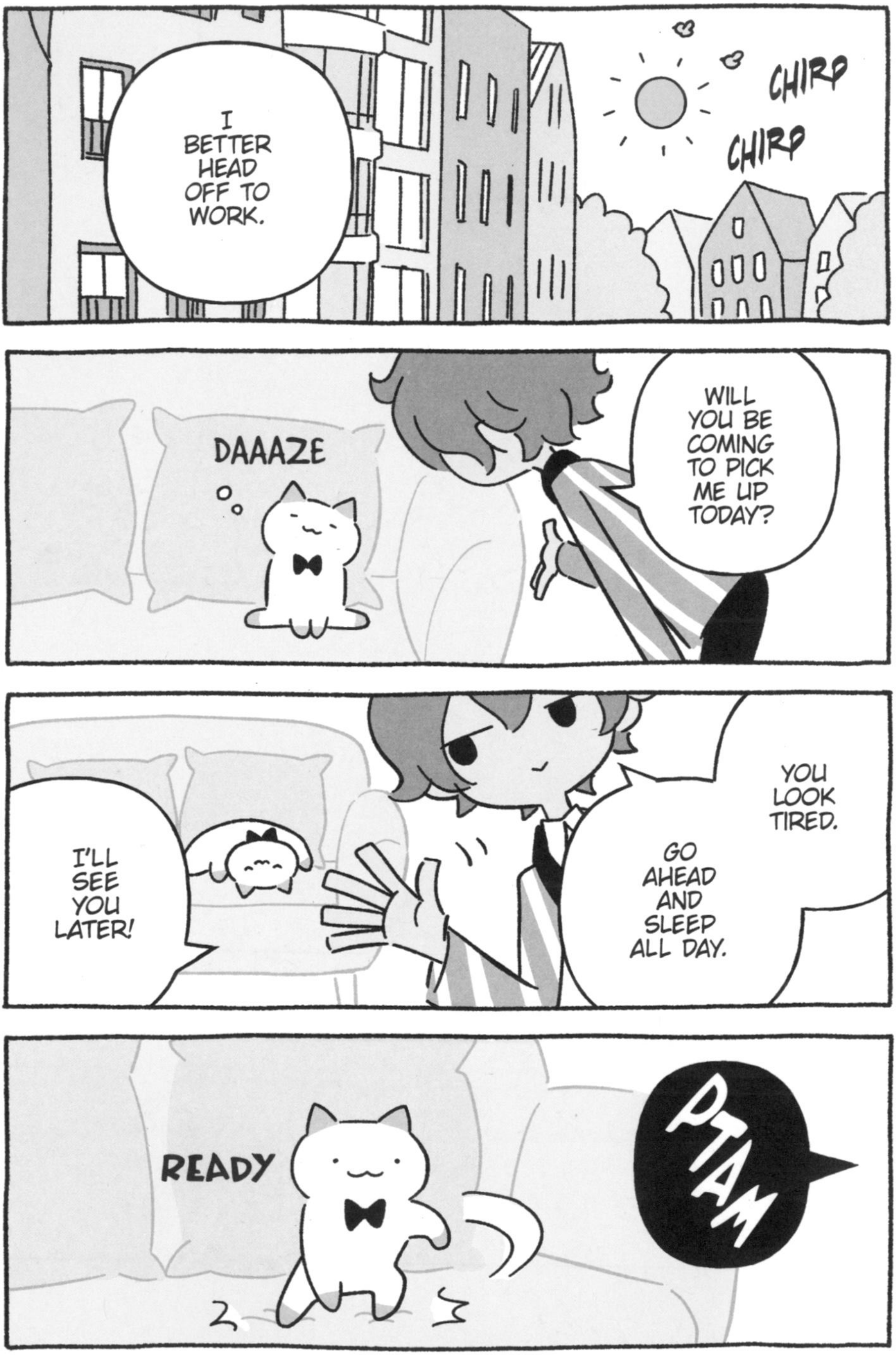
CHIRP
CHIRP
I BETTER HEAD OFF TO WORK.
WILL YOU BE COMING TO PICK ME UP TODAY?
DAAAZE
YOU LOOK TIRED.
GO AHEAD AND SLEEP ALL DAY.
I'LL SEE YOU LATER!
PTAM
READY

ULTIMATE CRISIS

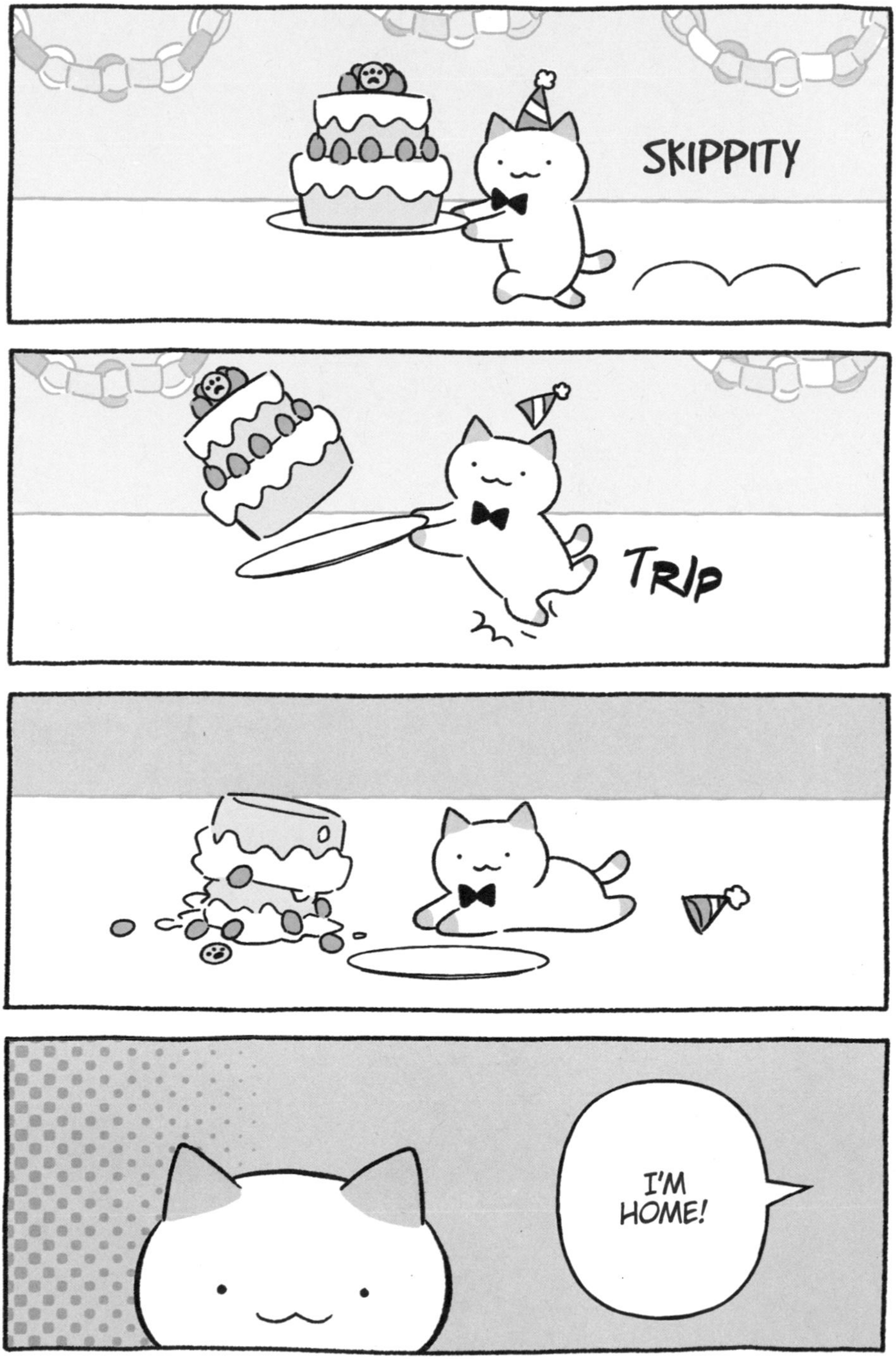
SKIPPITY
TRIP
I'M HOME!

ANGUISH

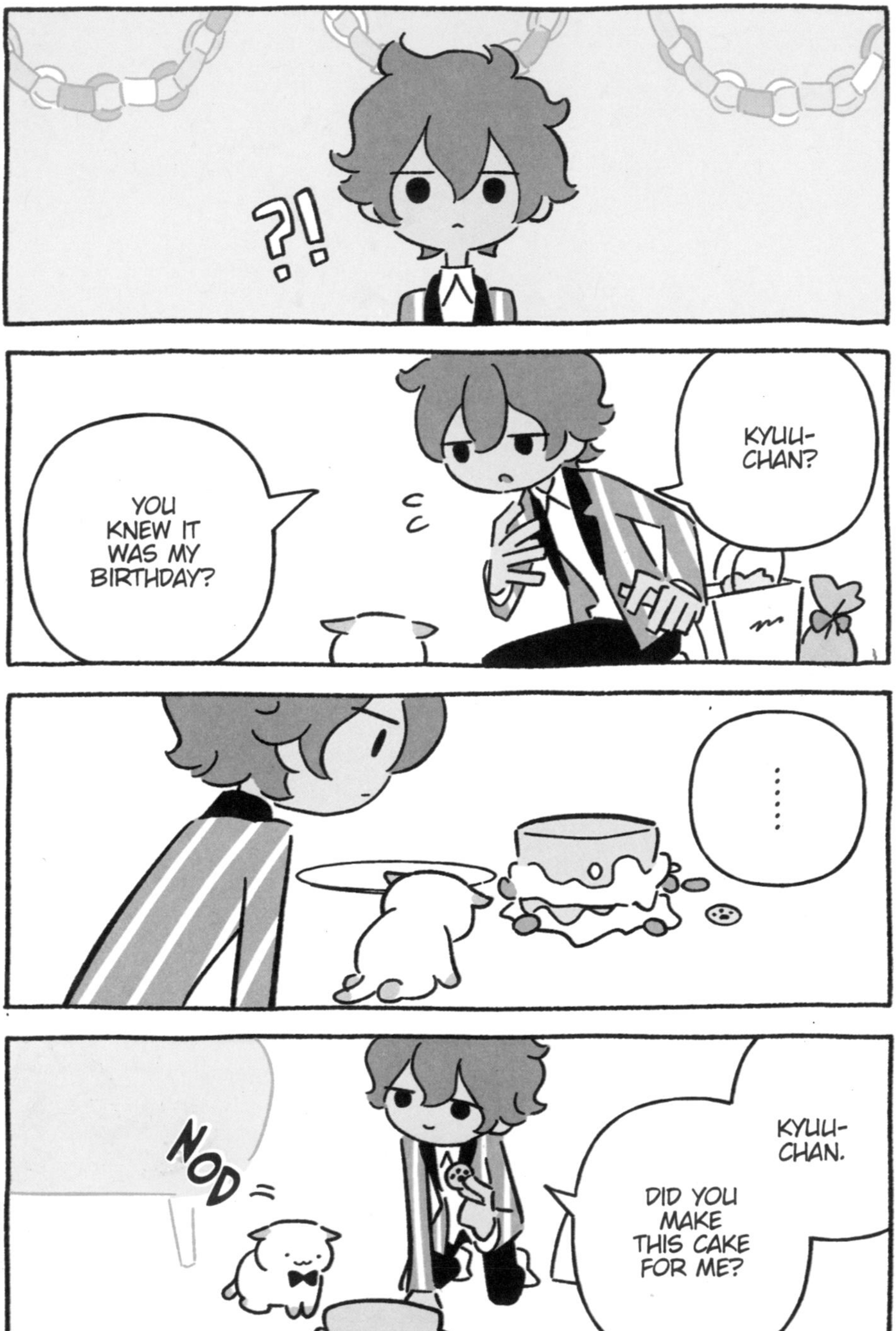
?!
KYUU-CHAN?
YOU KNEW IT WAS MY BIRTHDAY?
......
KYUU-CHAN.
DID YOU MAKE THIS CAKE FOR ME?
NOD

JOY

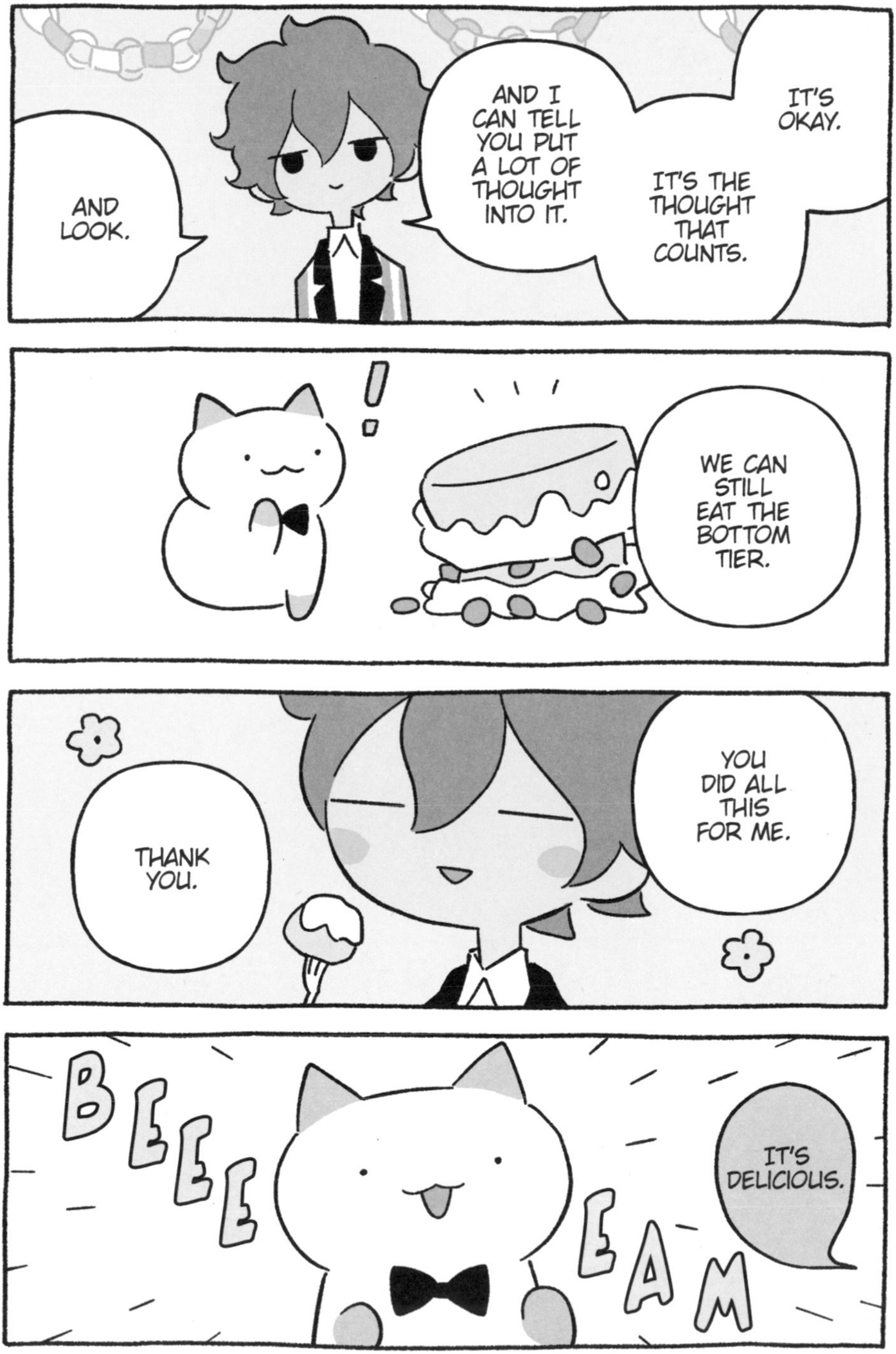
IT'S OKAY.
IT'S THE THOUGHT THAT COUNTS.
AND I CAN TELL YOU PUT A LOT OF THOUGHT INTO IT.
AND LOOK.
!
WE CAN STILL EAT THE BOTTOM TIER.
YOU DID ALL THIS FOR ME.
THANK YOU.
IT'S DELICIOUS.
BEEEEAM

EXPRESSIONS OF LOVE

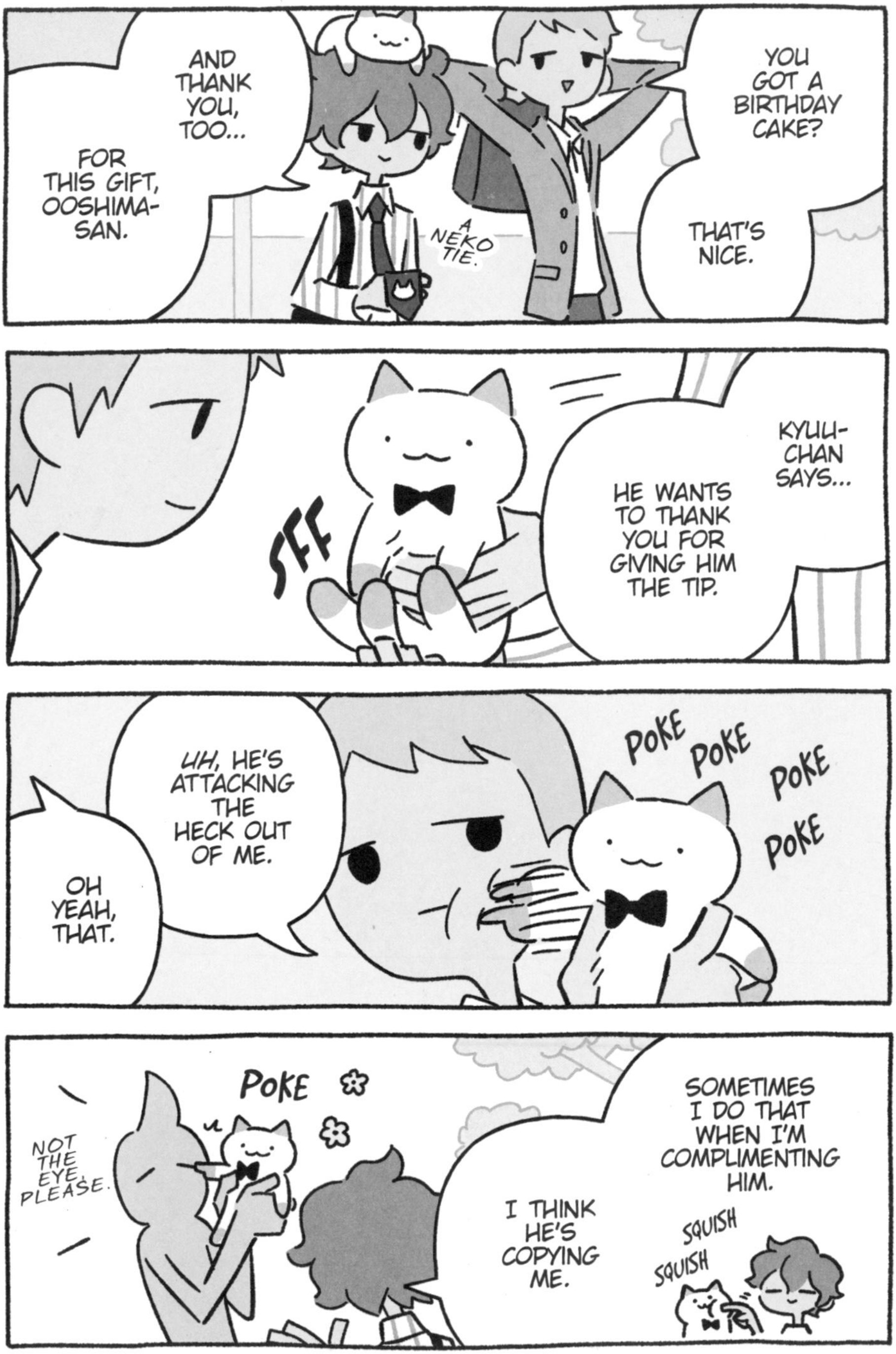
YOU GOT A BIRTHDAY CAKE?
THAT'S NICE.
AND THANK YOU, TOO...
FOR THIS GIFT, OOSHIMA-SAN.
A NEKO TIE.
KYUU-CHAN SAYS...
HE WANTS TO THANK YOU FOR GIVING HIM THE TIP.
SFF
POKE POKE POKE POKE
UH, HE'S ATTACKING THE HECK OUT OF ME.
OH YEAH, THAT.
SOMETIMES I DO THAT WHEN I'M COMPLIMENTING HIM.
I THINK HE'S COPYING ME.
SQUISH SQUISH
POKE
NOT THE EYE, PLEASE.

MATCHING

YOU SURE ARE CLOSE.
MY IDENTITY.
IT'S CUTE, LIKE A CAT.

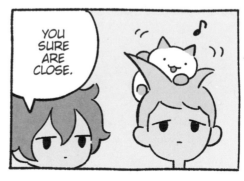

MASKS

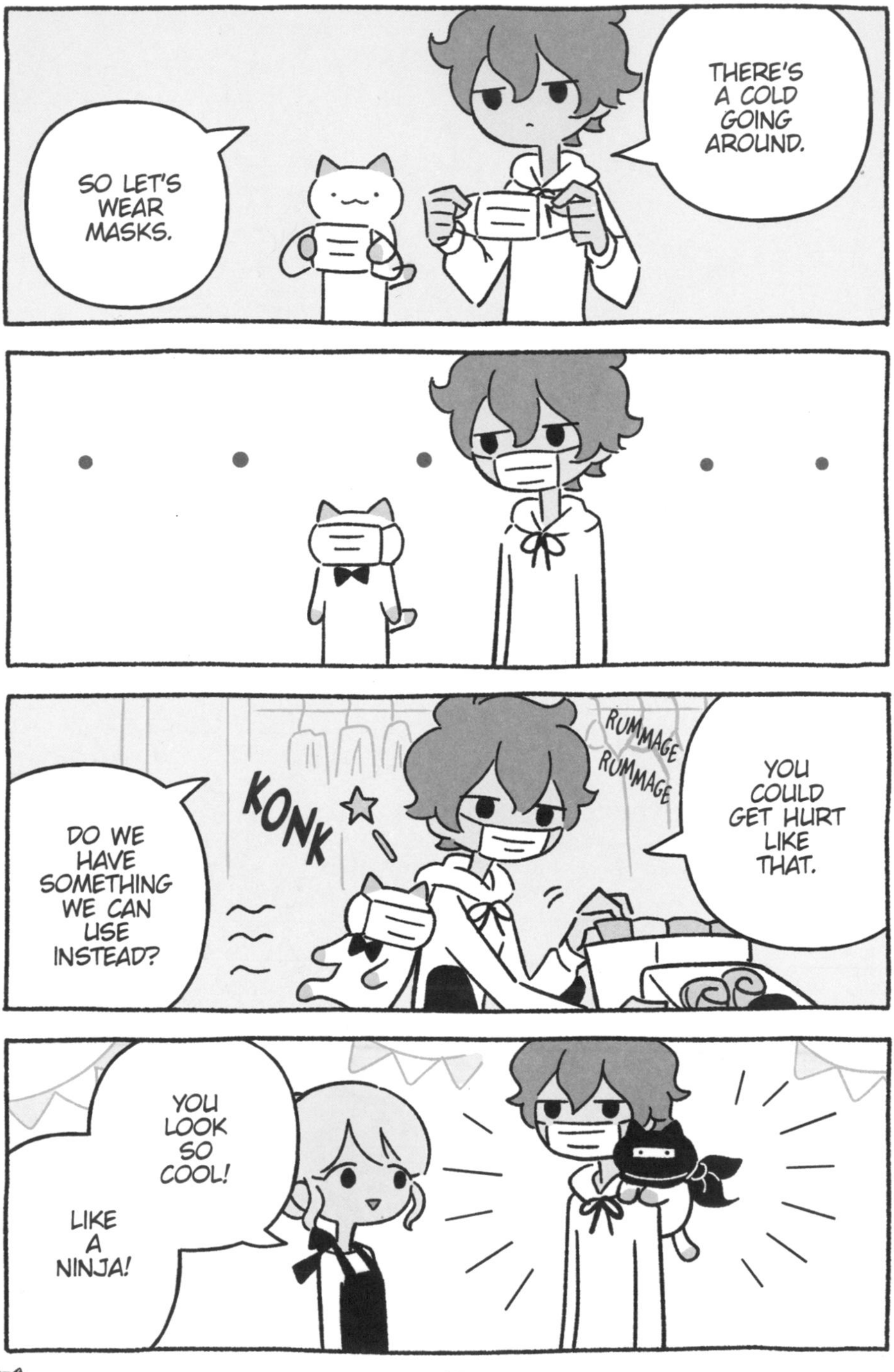

THERE'S A COLD GOING AROUND.
SO LET'S WEAR MASKS.
RUMMAGE RUMMAGE
YOU COULD GET HURT LIKE THAT.
KONK
DO WE HAVE SOMETHING WE CAN USE INSTEAD?
YOU LOOK SO COOL!
LIKE A NINJA!

SUPER HIGH SPEED

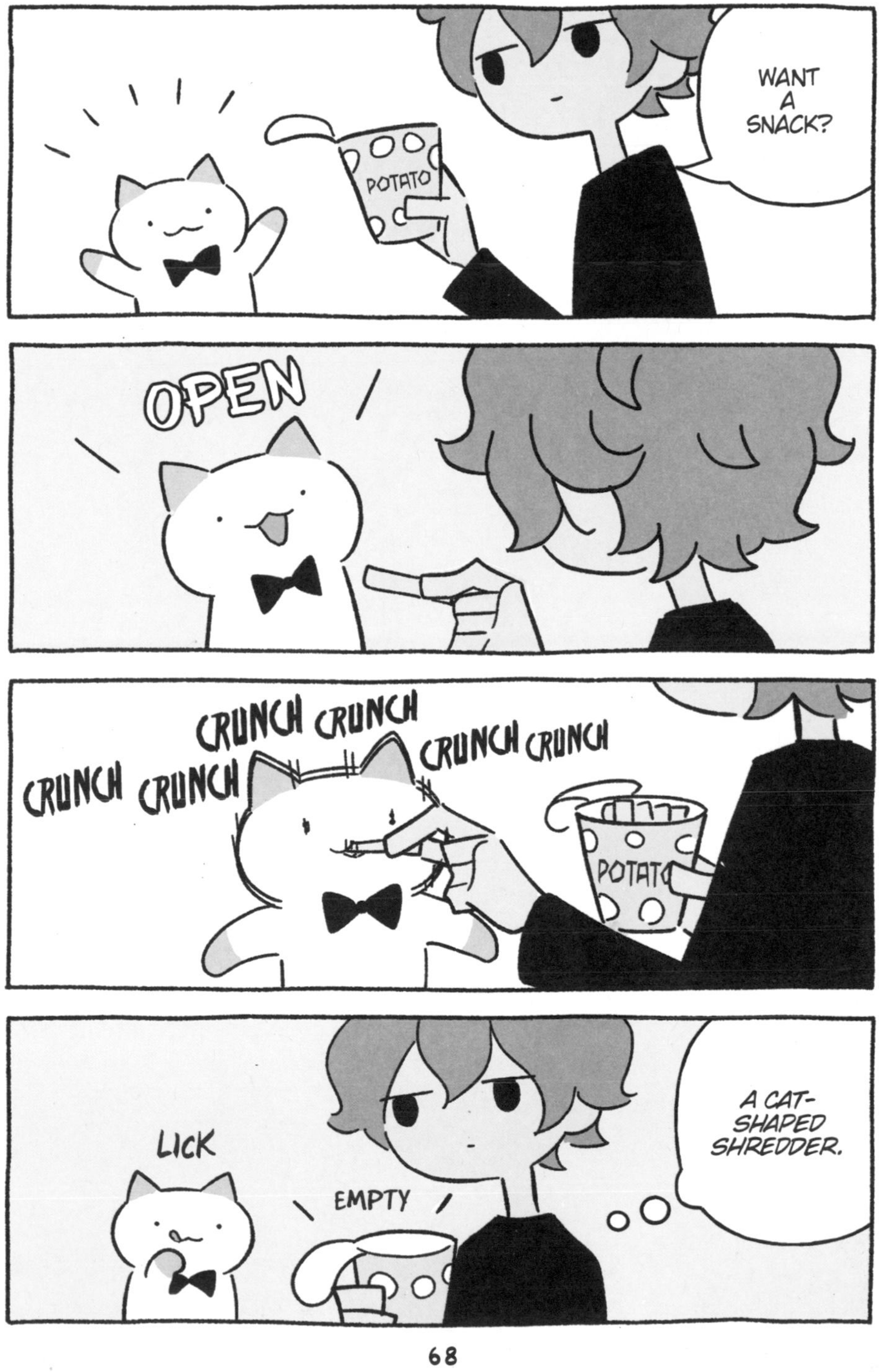

WANT A SNACK?
POTATO
OPEN
CRUNCH CRUNCH
CRUNCH CRUNCH
CRUNCH CRUNCH
A CAT-SHAPED SHREDDER.
EMPTY
LICK

GO AHEAD

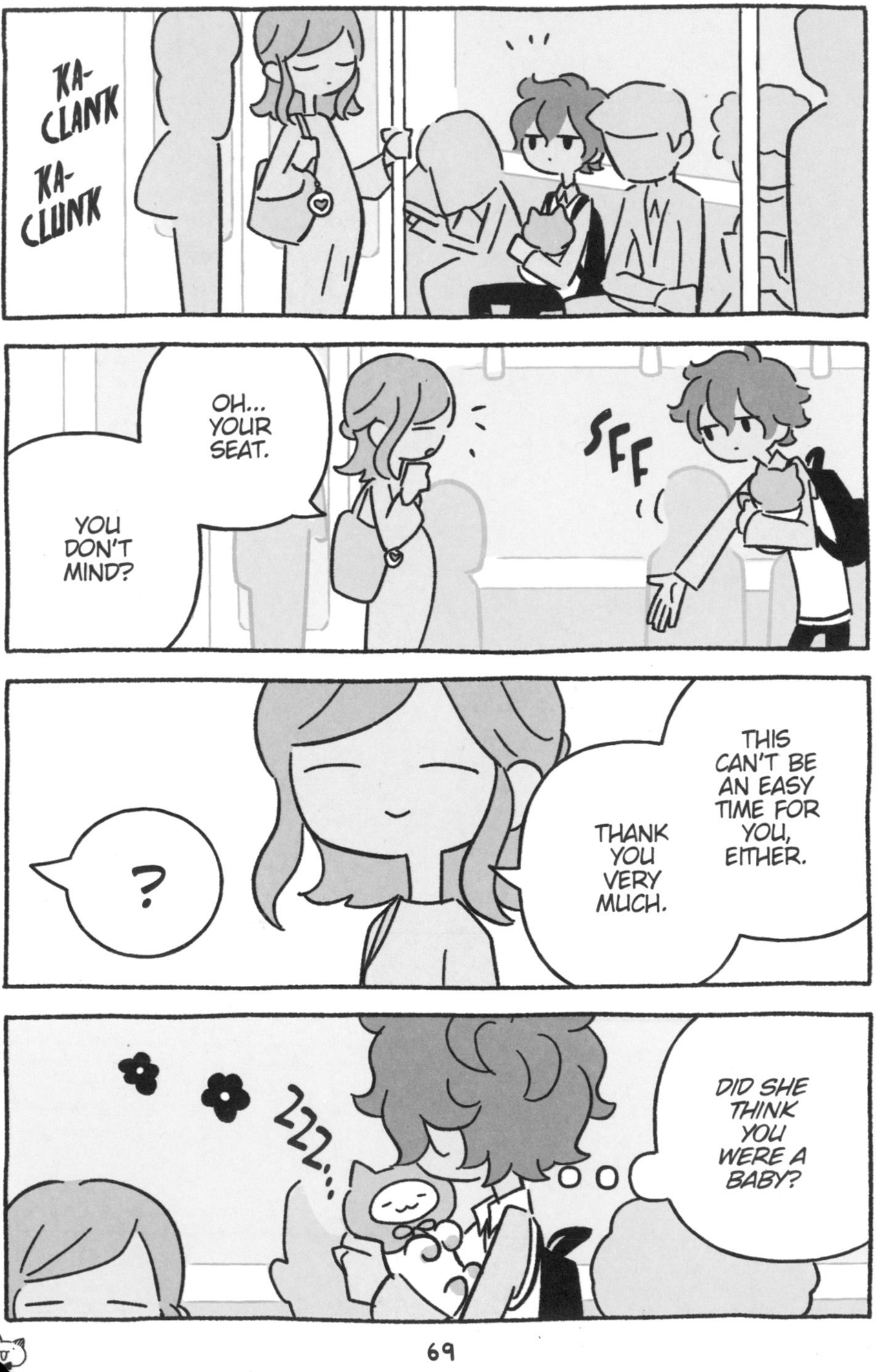
KA-CLANK
KA-CLUNK
SFF
OH... YOUR SEAT.
YOU DON'T MIND?
THIS CAN'T BE AN EASY TIME FOR YOU, EITHER.
THANK YOU VERY MUCH.
?
DID SHE THINK YOU WERE A BABY?
ZZZ...

MASCOT

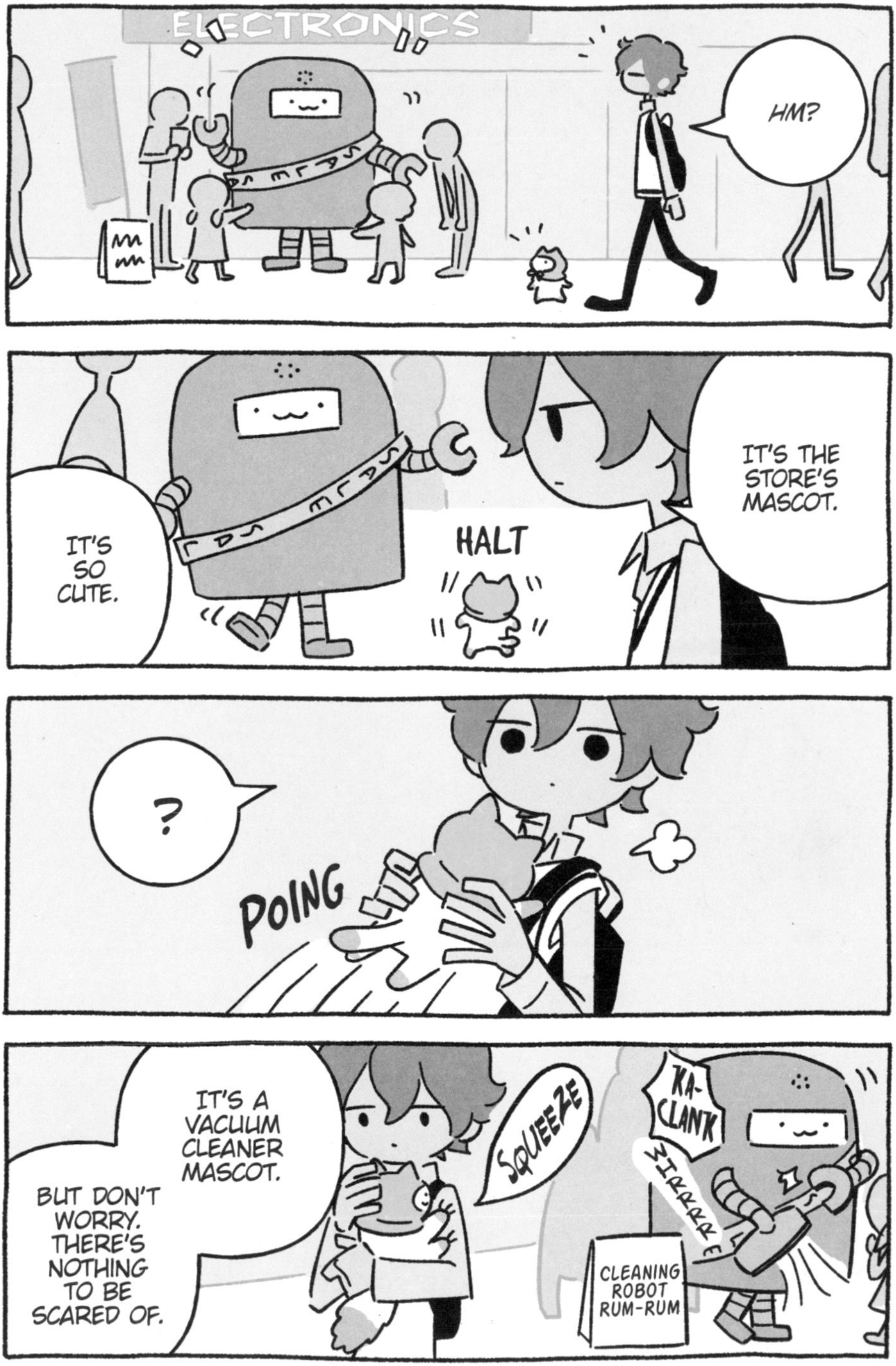
HM?
ELECTRONICS
IT'S THE STORE'S MASCOT.
HALT
IT'S SO CUTE.
?
POING
KA-CLANK
WHIRRRR
CLEANING ROBOT RUM-RUM
SQUEEZE
IT'S A VACUUM CLEANER MASCOT.
BUT DON'T WORRY. THERE'S NOTHING TO BE SCARED OF.

BUY IT

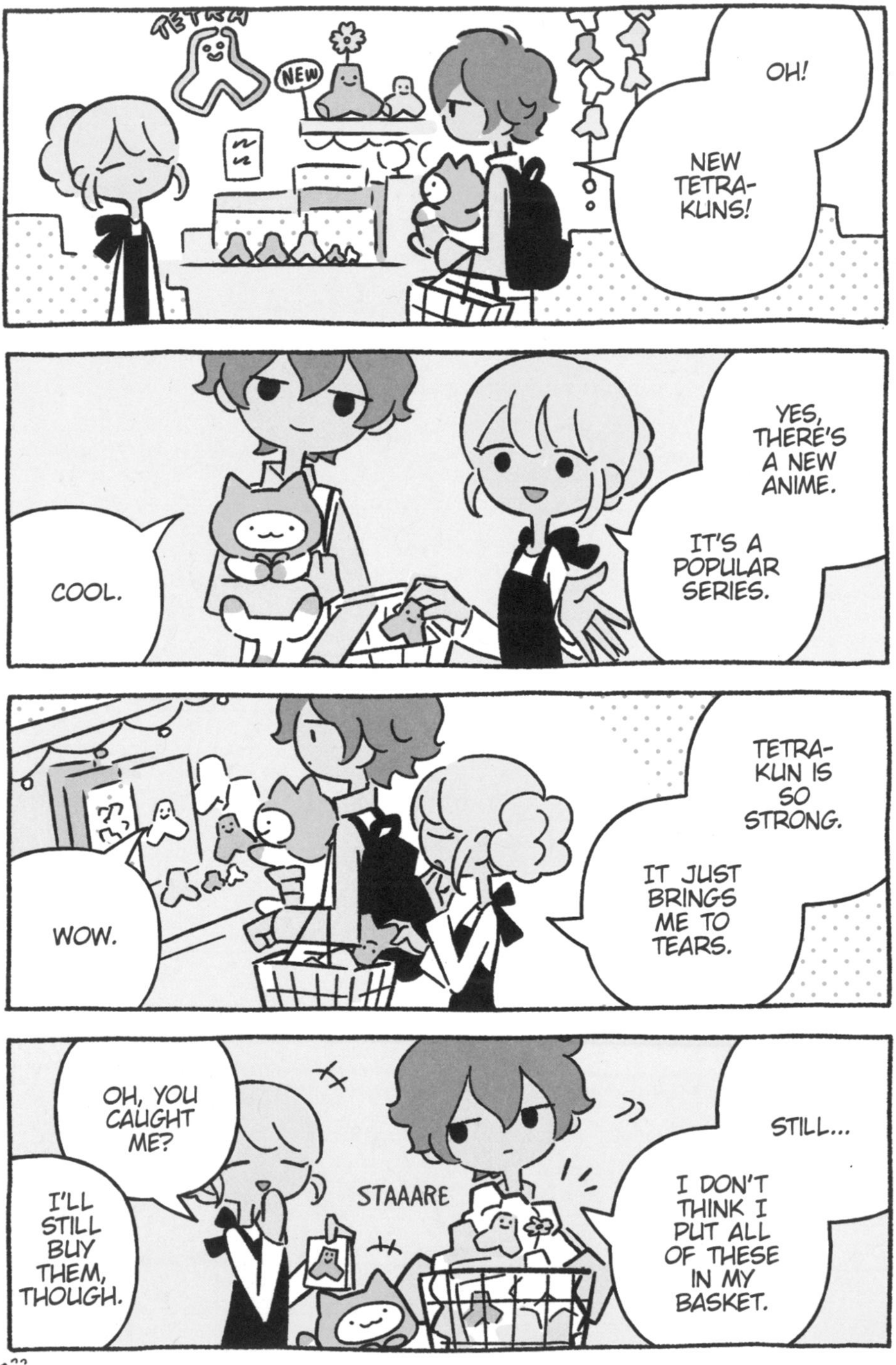
OH! NEW TETRA-KUNS!
NEW
YES, THERE'S A NEW ANIME.
IT'S A POPULAR SERIES.
COOL.
TETRA-KUN IS SO STRONG.
IT JUST BRINGS ME TO TEARS.
WOW.
STILL...
I DON'T THINK I PUT ALL OF THESE IN MY BASKET.
STAAARE
OH, YOU CAUGHT ME?
I'LL STILL BUY THEM, THOUGH.

FIGHT! TETRA-KUN

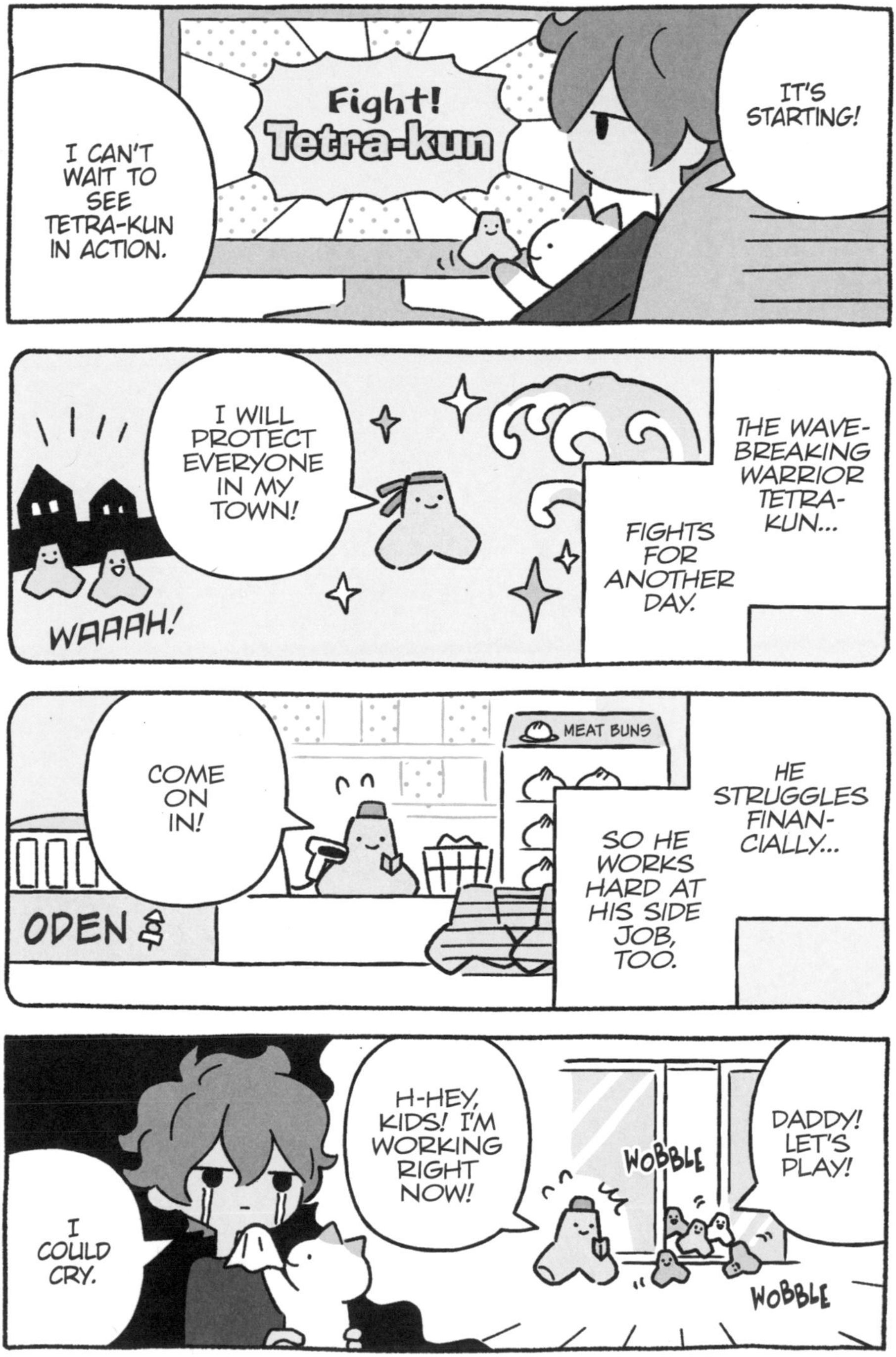
IT'S STARTING!
Fight! Tetra-kun
I CAN'T WAIT TO SEE TETRA-KUN IN ACTION.
THE WAVE-BREAKING WARRIOR TETRA-KUN...
FIGHTS FOR ANOTHER DAY.
I WILL PROTECT EVERYONE IN MY TOWN!
WAAAH!
HE STRUGGLES FINANCIALLY...
SO HE WORKS HARD AT HIS SIDE JOB, TOO.
MEAT BUNS
COME ON IN!
ODEN
DADDY! LET'S PLAY!
WOBBLE
H-HEY, KIDS! I'M WORKING RIGHT NOW!
WOBBLE
I COULD CRY.

DISPOSABLE CHOPSTICKS

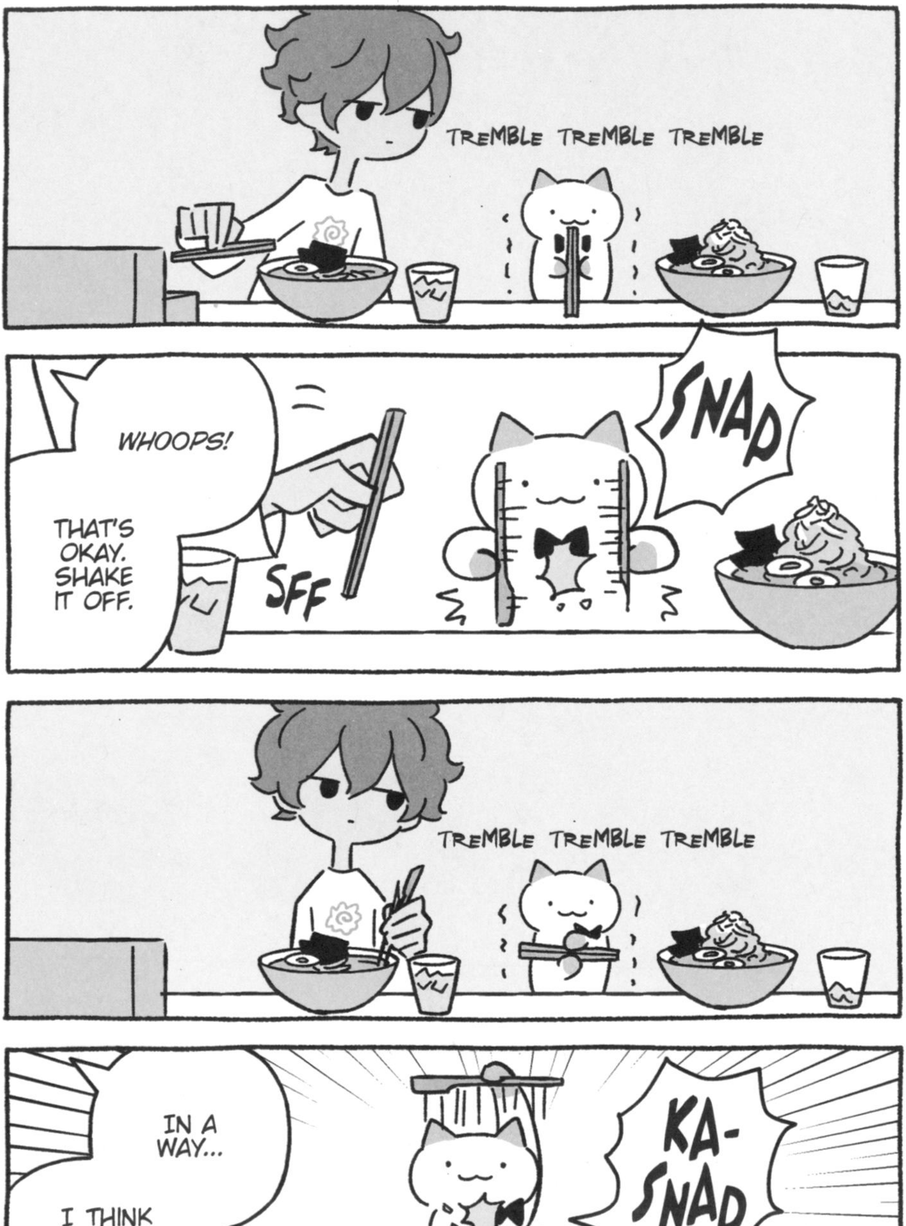
TREMBLE TREMBLE TREMBLE
SNAP
WHOOPS!
SFF
THAT'S OKAY. SHAKE IT OFF.
TREMBLE TREMBLE TREMBLE
KA-SNAP
IN A WAY...
I THINK THAT TAKES ITS OWN KIND OF LUCK.

KITTY

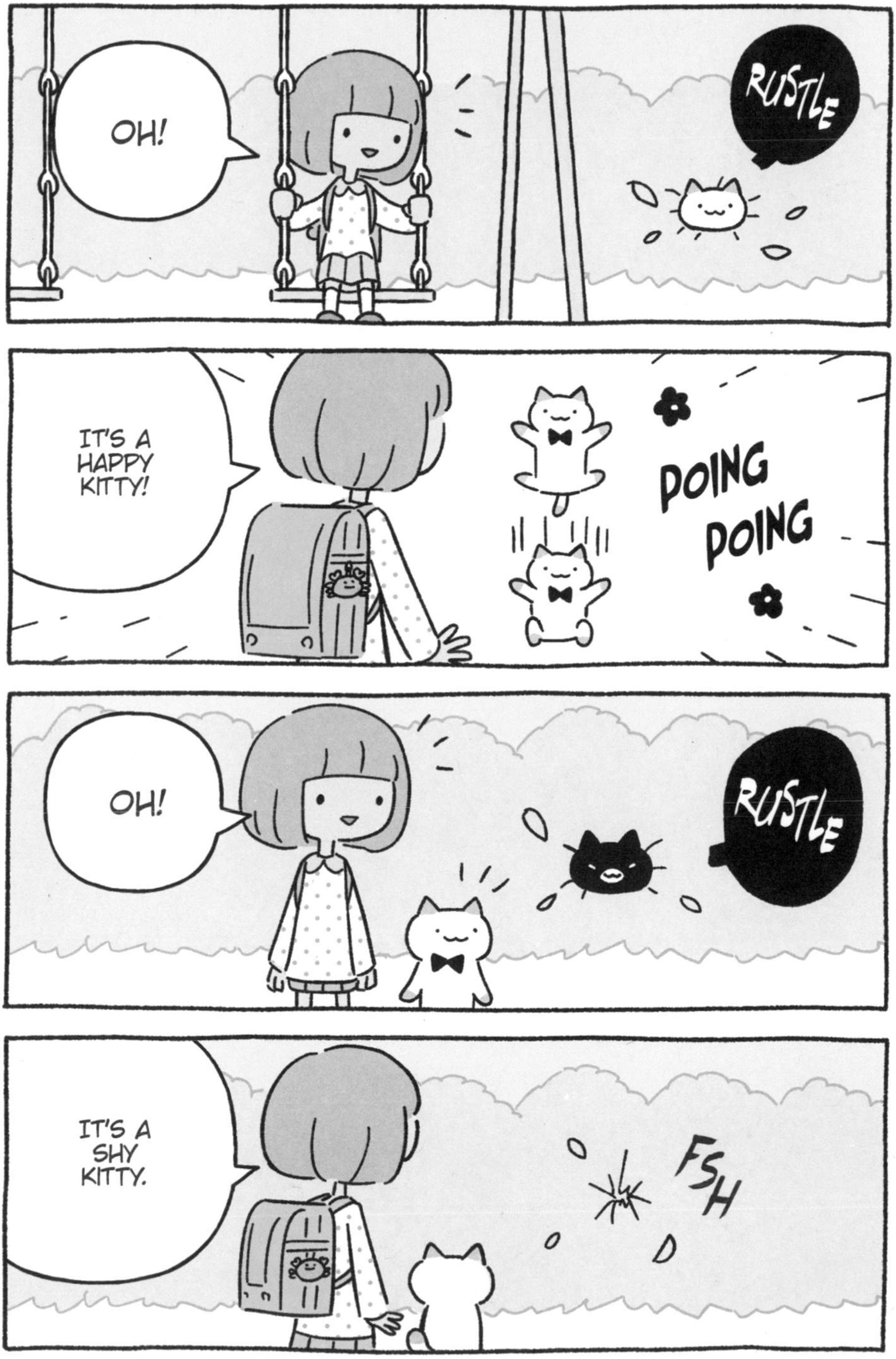
RUSTLE
OH!
POING POING
IT'S A HAPPY KITTY!
RUSTLE
OH!
FSH
IT'S A SHY KITTY.

LURKING

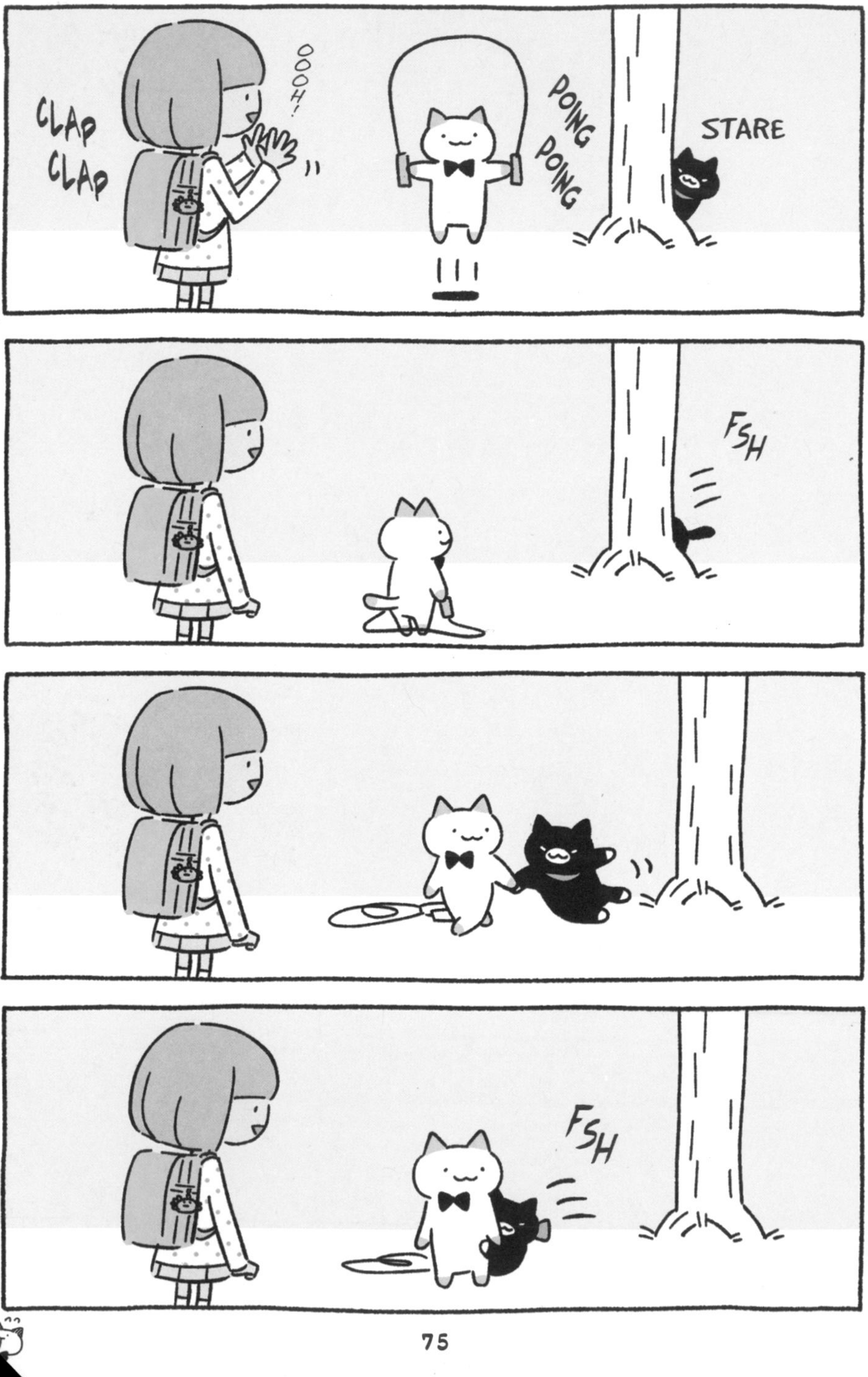
STARE
POING POING
OOOOH!
CLAP CLAP
FSH
FSH

FRIENDS

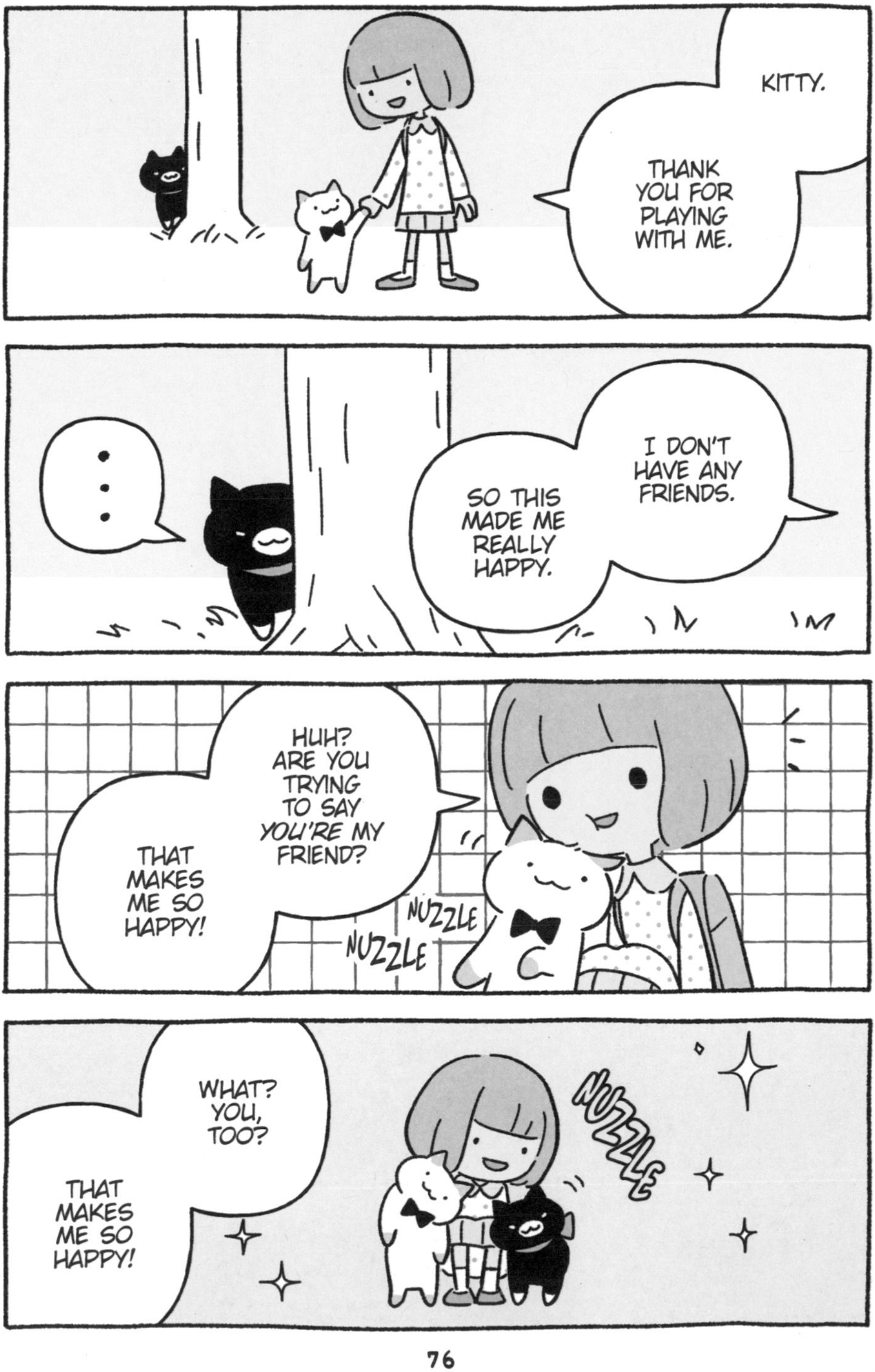

KITTY.
THANK YOU FOR PLAYING WITH ME.
I DON'T HAVE ANY FRIENDS.
SO THIS MADE ME REALLY HAPPY.
...
HUH? ARE YOU TRYING TO SAY *YOU'RE* MY FRIEND?
THAT MAKES ME SO HAPPY!
NUZZLE
NUZZLE
NUZZLE
WHAT? YOU, TOO?
THAT MAKES ME SO HAPPY!

HIDE-AND-SEEK

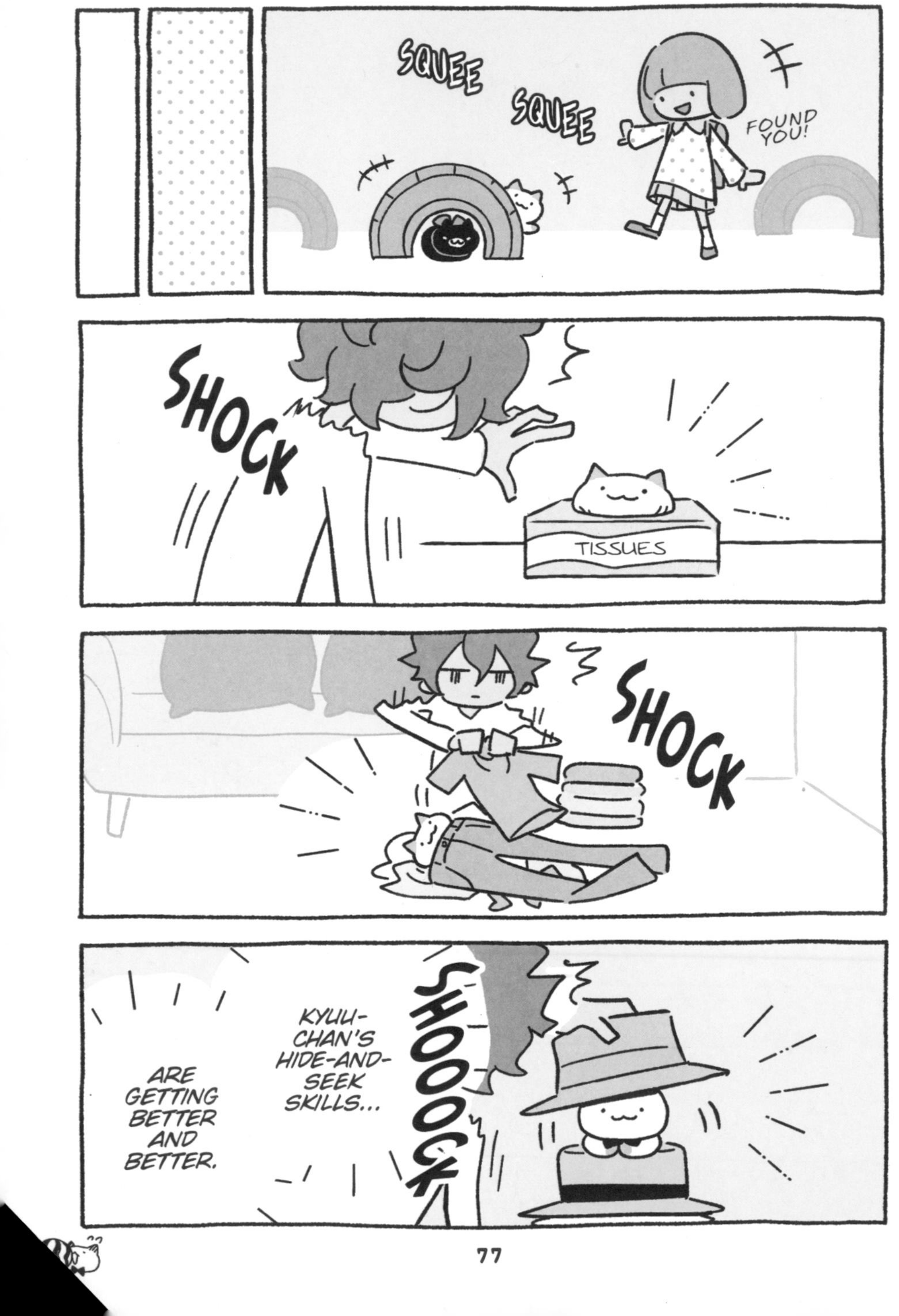
FOUND YOU!
SQUEE
SQUEE
SHOCK
TISSUES
SHOCK
SHOOOCK
KYUU-CHAN'S HIDE-AND-SEEK SKILLS...
ARE GETTING BETTER AND BETTER.

SURPRISE

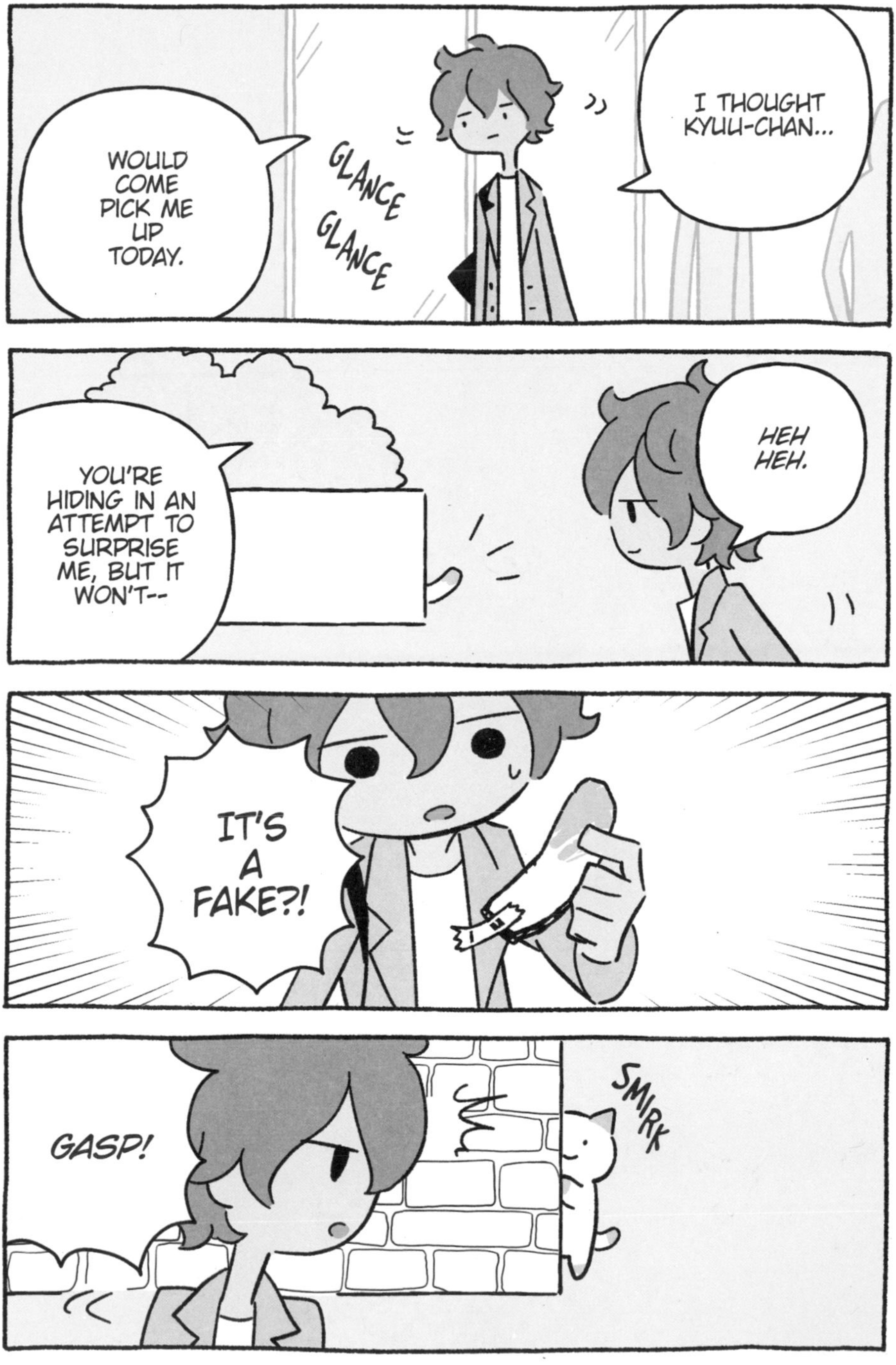
I THOUGHT KYUU-CHAN...
GLANCE GLANCE
WOULD COME PICK ME UP TODAY.
HEH HEH.
YOU'RE HIDING IN AN ATTEMPT TO SURPRISE ME, BUT IT WON'T--
IT'S A FAKE?!
SMIRK
GASP!

NO MATTER WHAT HE DOES

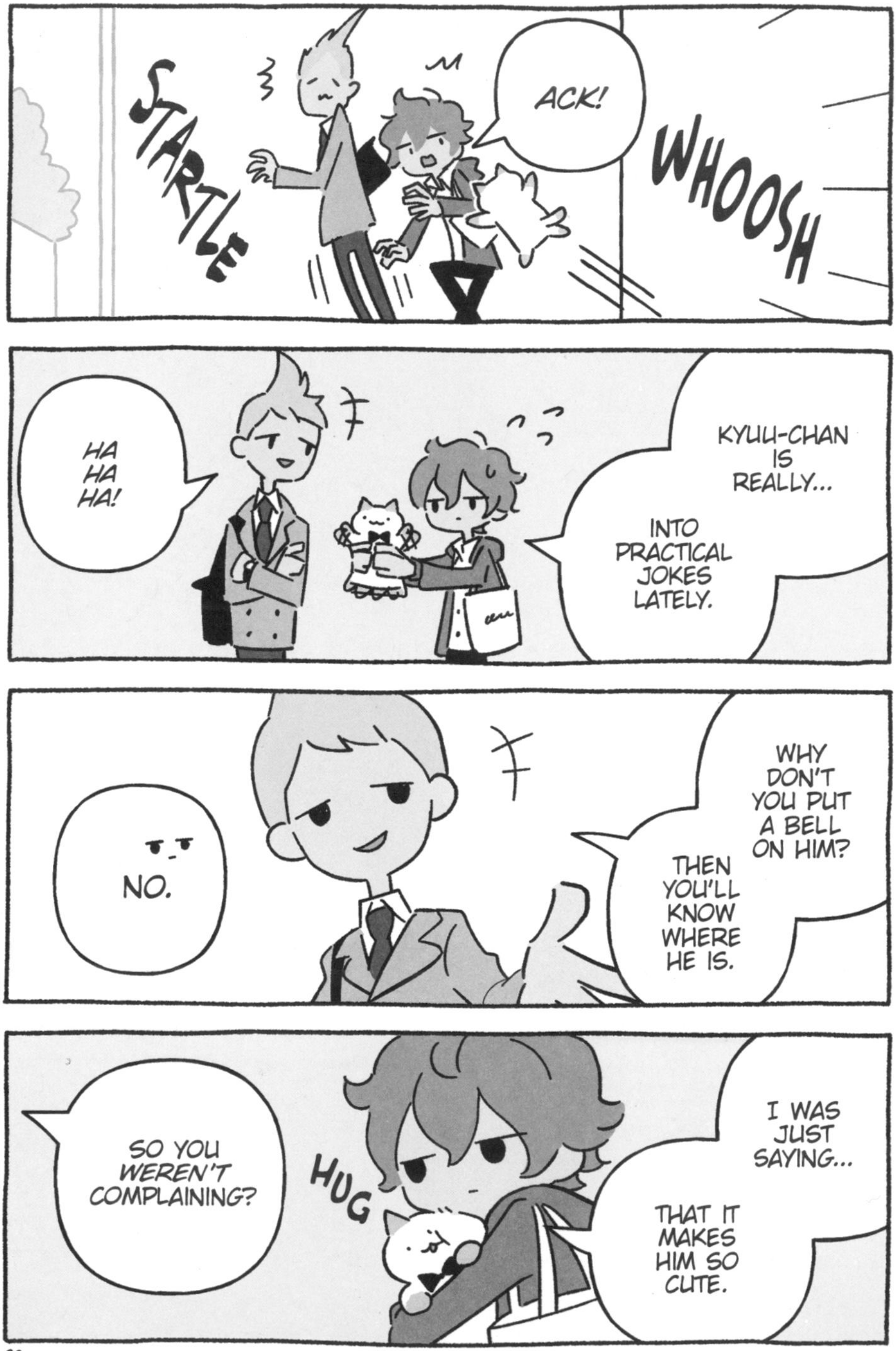

WHOOSH
ACK!
STARTLE
KYUU-CHAN IS REALLY...
INTO PRACTICAL JOKES LATELY.
HA HA HA!
WHY DON'T YOU PUT A BELL ON HIM?
THEN YOU'LL KNOW WHERE HE IS.
NO.
I WAS JUST SAYING...
THAT IT MAKES HIM SO CUTE.
HUG
SO YOU WEREN'T COMPLAINING?

SNEEZE FACE

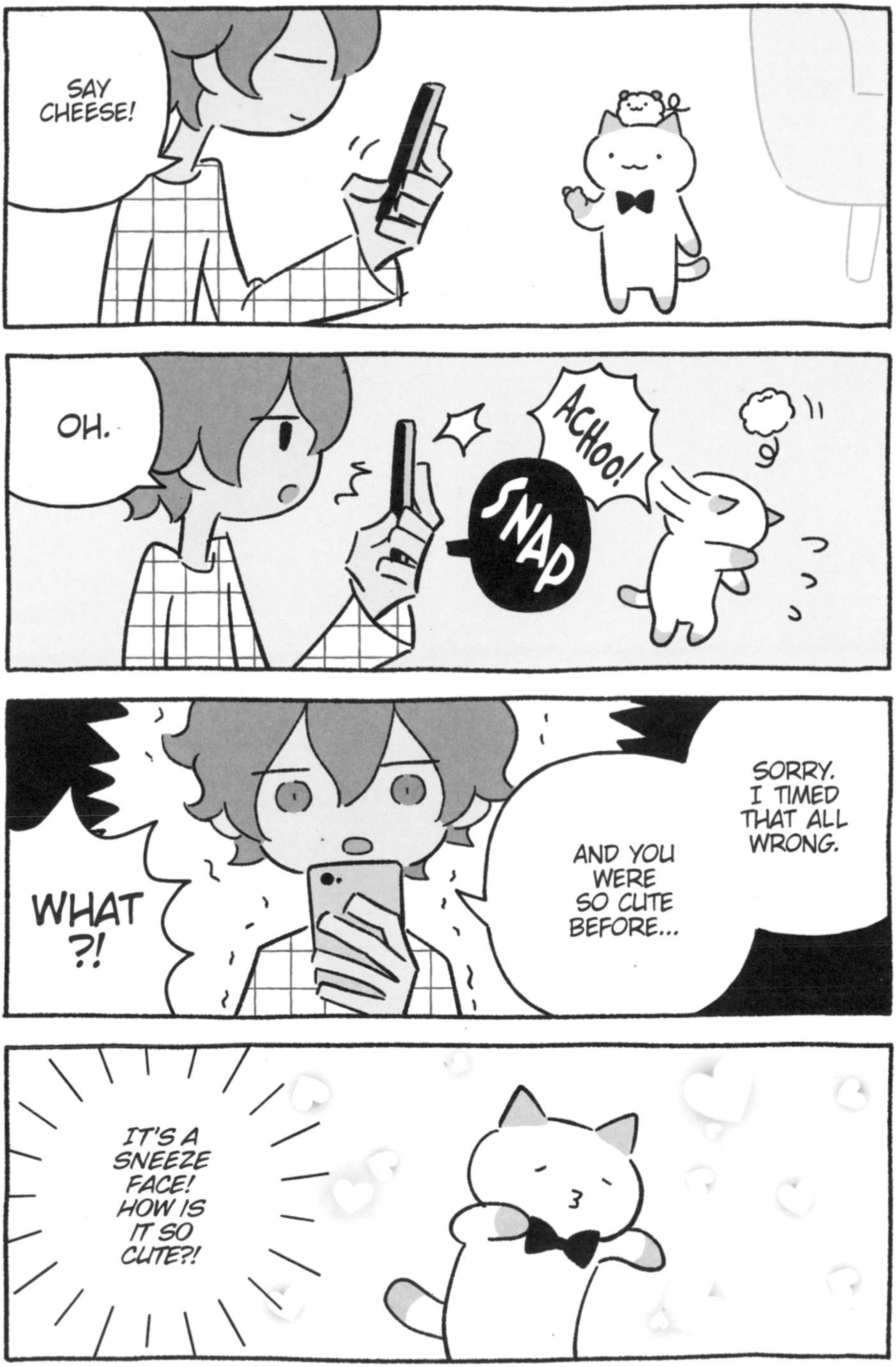
SAY CHEESE!
ACHOO!
SNAP
OH.
SORRY. I TIMED THAT ALL WRONG.
AND YOU WERE SO CUTE BEFORE...
WHAT?!
IT'S A SNEEZE FACE! HOW IS IT SO CUTE?!

SAND FACE

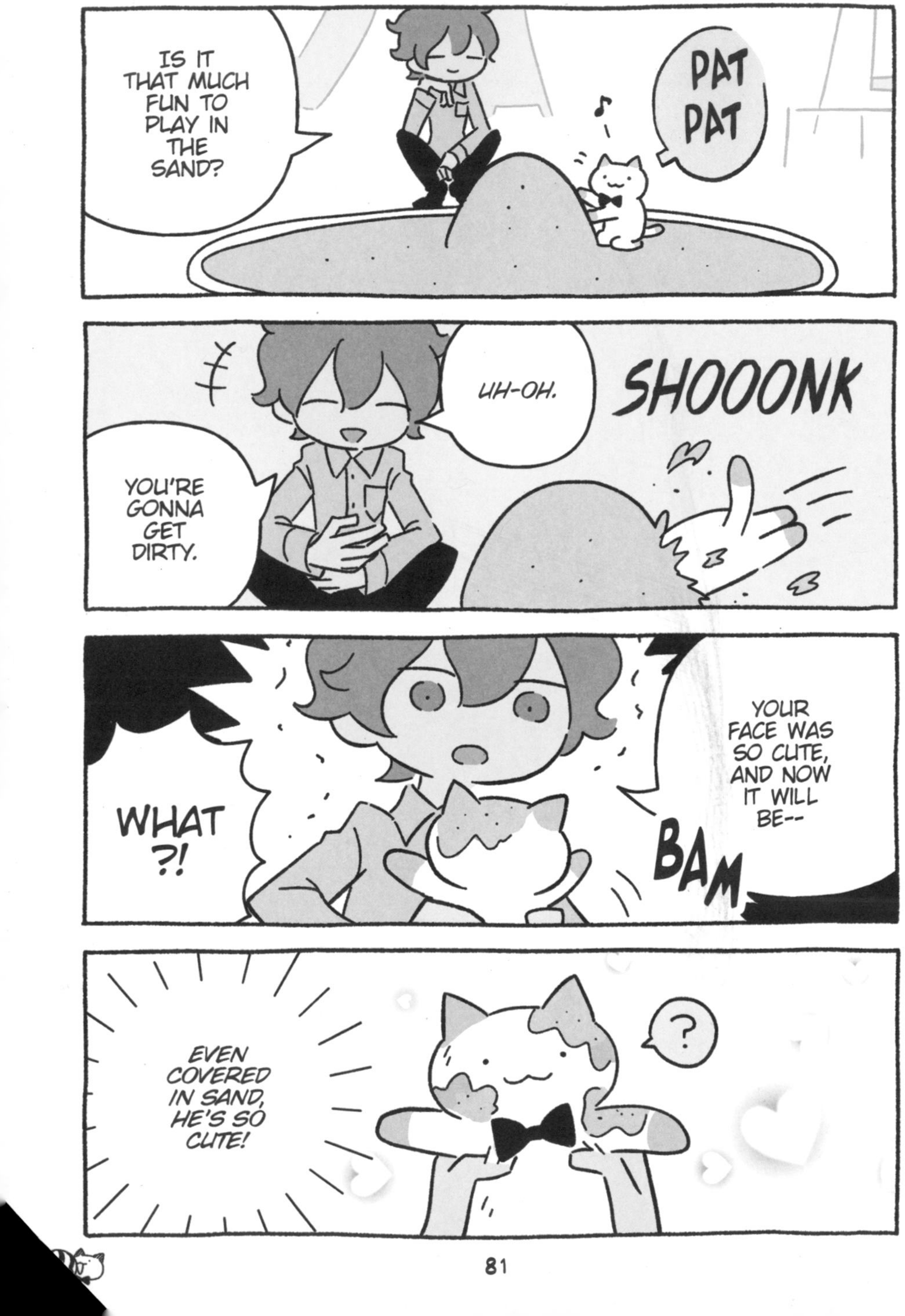
PAT PAT
IS IT THAT MUCH FUN TO PLAY IN THE SAND?
SHOOONK
UH-OH.
YOU'RE GONNA GET DIRTY.
YOUR FACE WAS SO CUTE, AND NOW IT WILL BE--
BAM
WHAT ?!
?
EVEN COVERED IN SAND, HE'S SO CUTE!

FOOD SENSOR

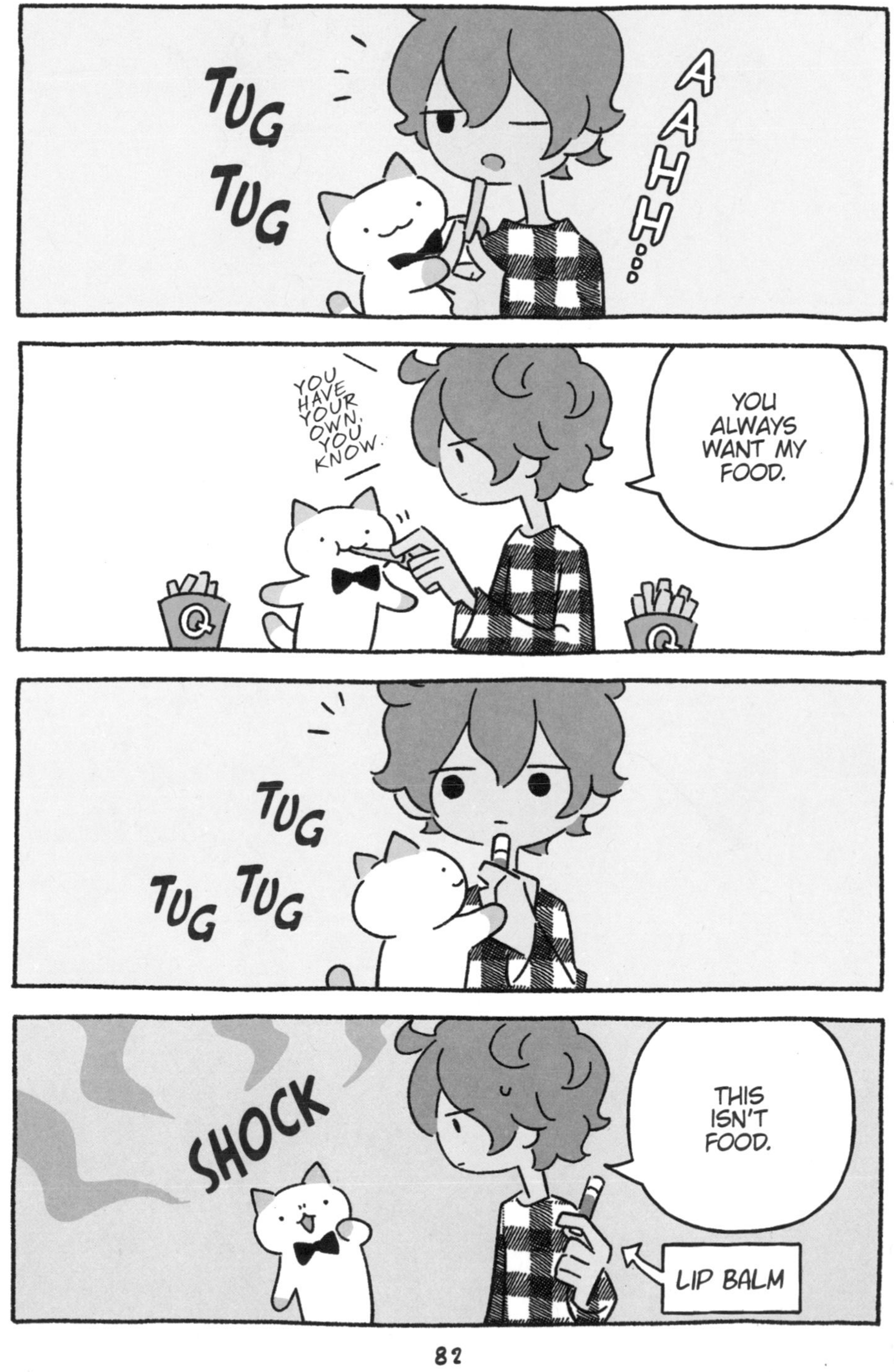
AAHH...
TUG TUG
YOU ALWAYS WANT MY FOOD.
YOU HAVE YOUR OWN, YOU KNOW.
TUG
TUG
TUG
THIS ISN'T FOOD.
LIP BALM
SHOCK

SUPER-SIZED RICE OMELET

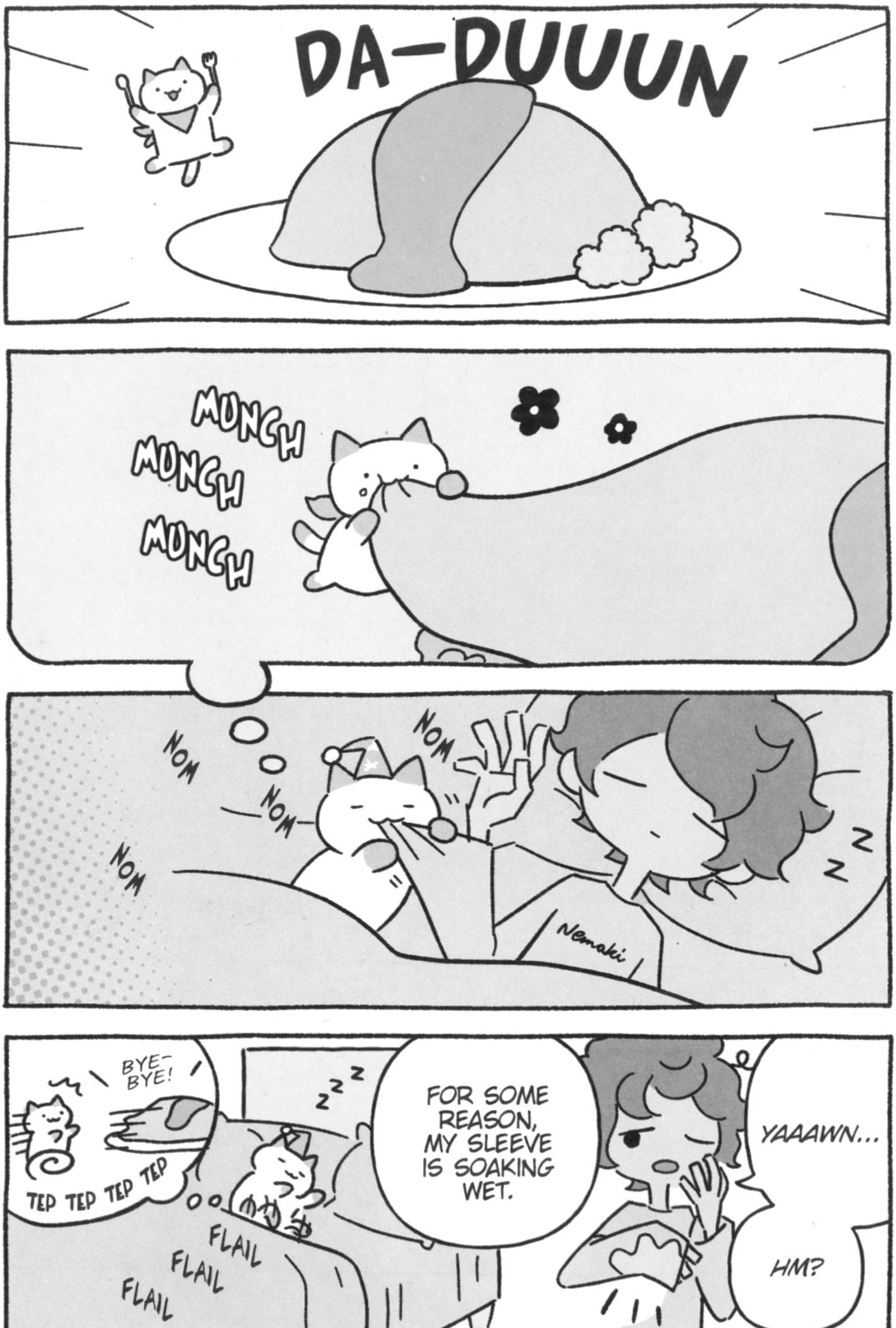
DA-DUUUN
MUNCH
MUNCH
MUNCH
NOM
NOM
NOM
NOM
Z Z
Nemaki
YAAAWN...
HM?
FOR SOME REASON, MY SLEEVE IS SOAKING WET.
Z Z Z
BYE-BYE!
TEP TEP TEP TEP
FLAIL
FLAIL
FLAIL

I LIKE IT OUTSIDE

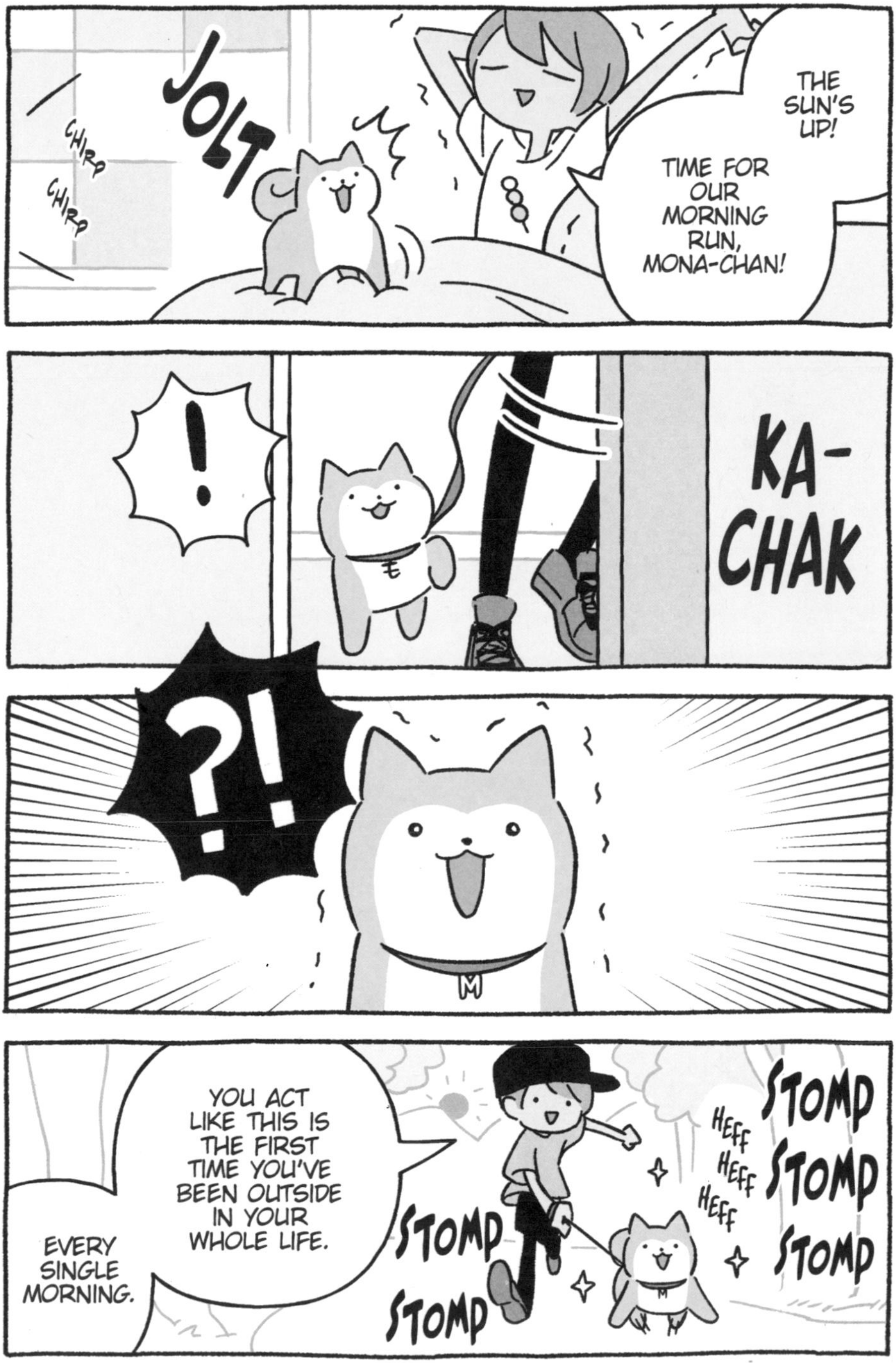
THE SUN'S UP!
TIME FOR OUR MORNING RUN, MONA-CHAN!
JOLT
CHIRP
CHIRP
KA-CHAK
!
?!
STOMP STOMP STOMP
HEFF HEFF HEFF
STOMP STOMP
YOU ACT LIKE THIS IS THE FIRST TIME YOU'VE BEEN OUTSIDE IN YOUR WHOLE LIFE.
EVERY SINGLE MORNING.

SURPRISE ATTACK

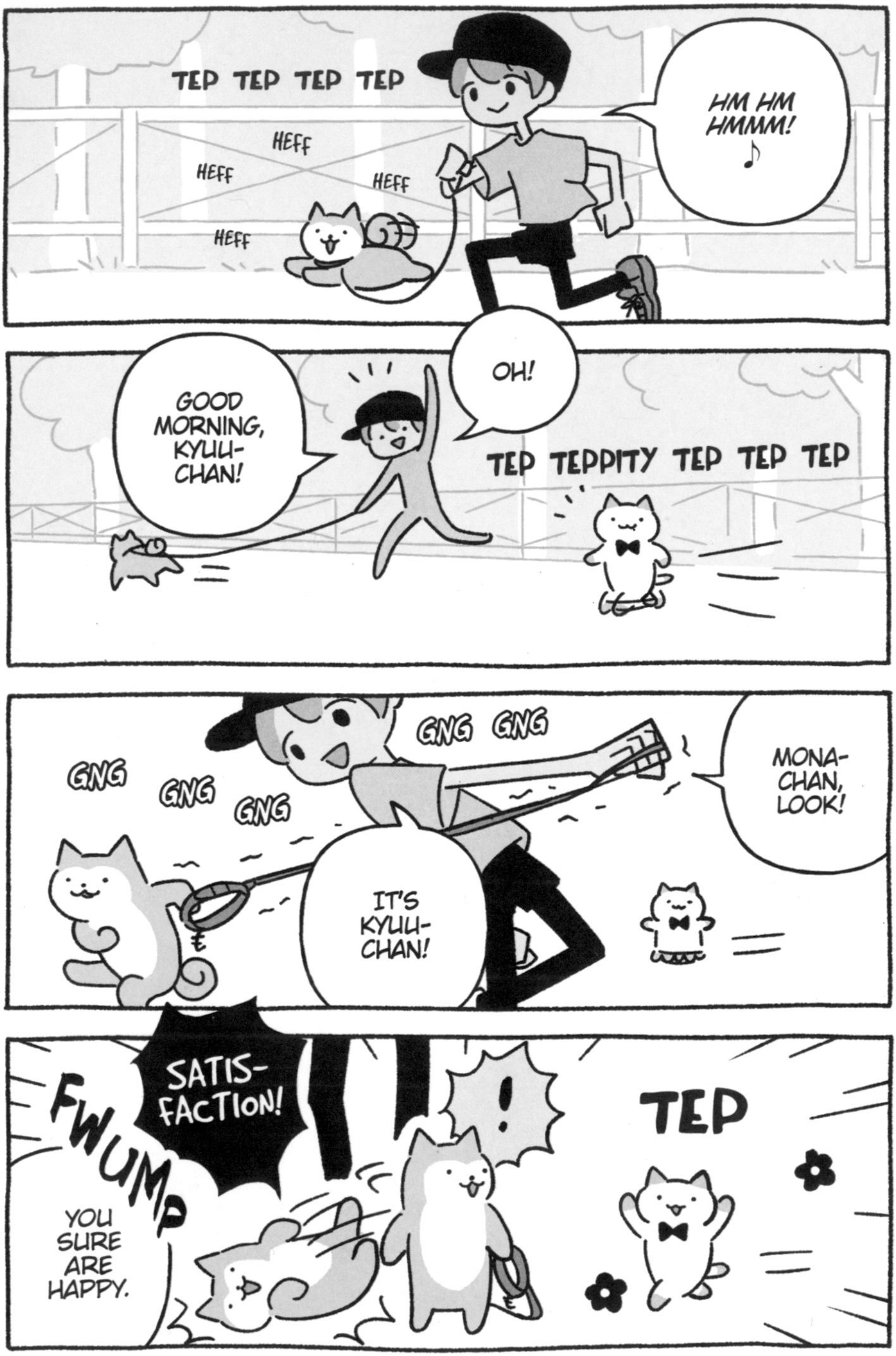
HM HM HMMM! ♪
TEP TEP TEP TEP
HEFF
HEFF
HEFF
HEFF
OH!
GOOD MORNING, KYUU-CHAN!
TEP TEPPITY TEP TEP TEP
MONA-CHAN, LOOK!
GNG GNG
GNG
GNG
GNG
IT'S KYUU-CHAN!
TEP
!
SATIS-FACTION!
FWUMP
YOU SURE ARE HAPPY.

DOING WELL

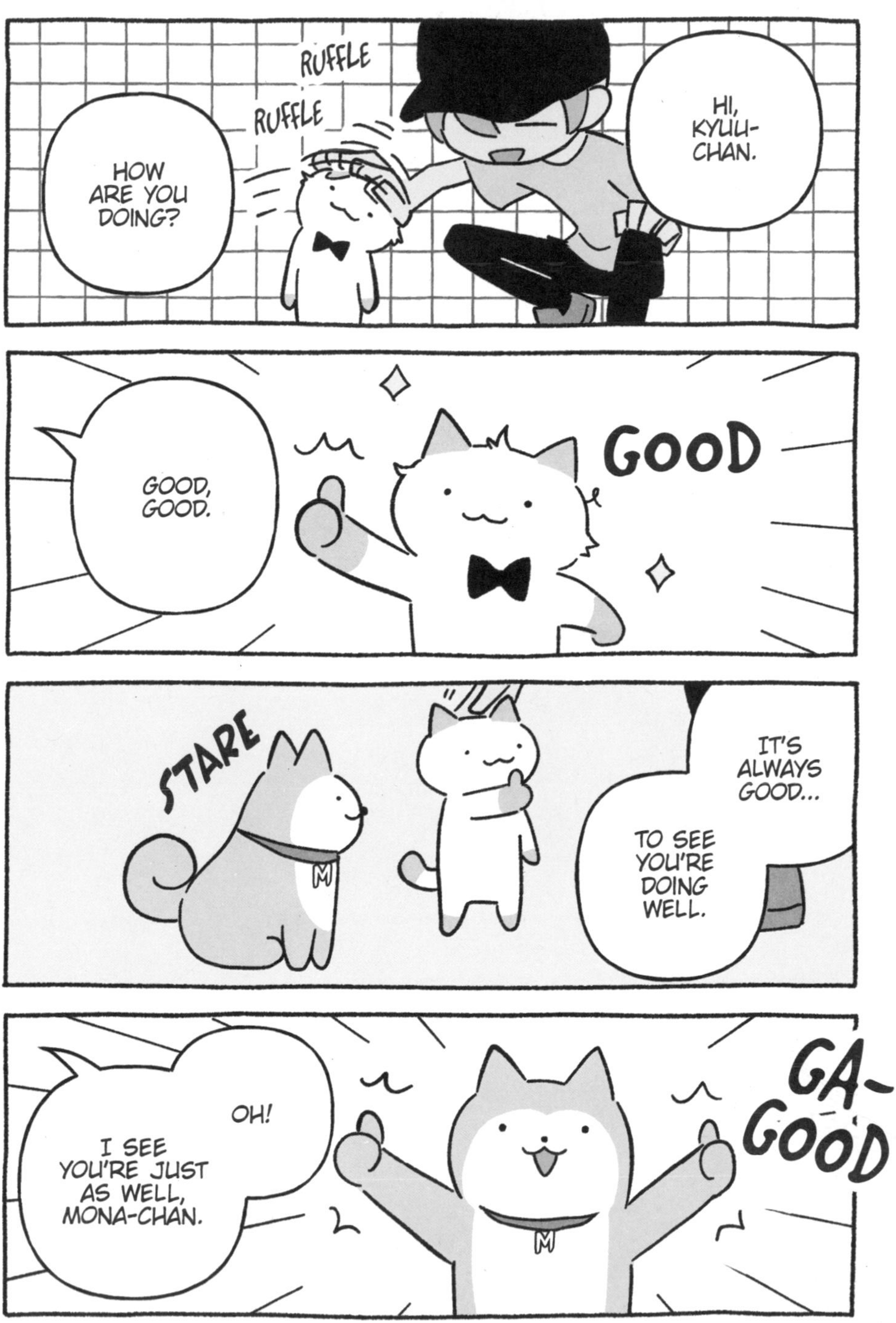
HI, KYUU-CHAN.
RUFFLE
RUFFLE
HOW ARE YOU DOING?
GOOD
GOOD, GOOD.
IT'S ALWAYS GOOD...
TO SEE YOU'RE DOING WELL.
STARE
GA-GOOD
OH!
I SEE YOU'RE JUST AS WELL, MONA-CHAN.

DETOURS

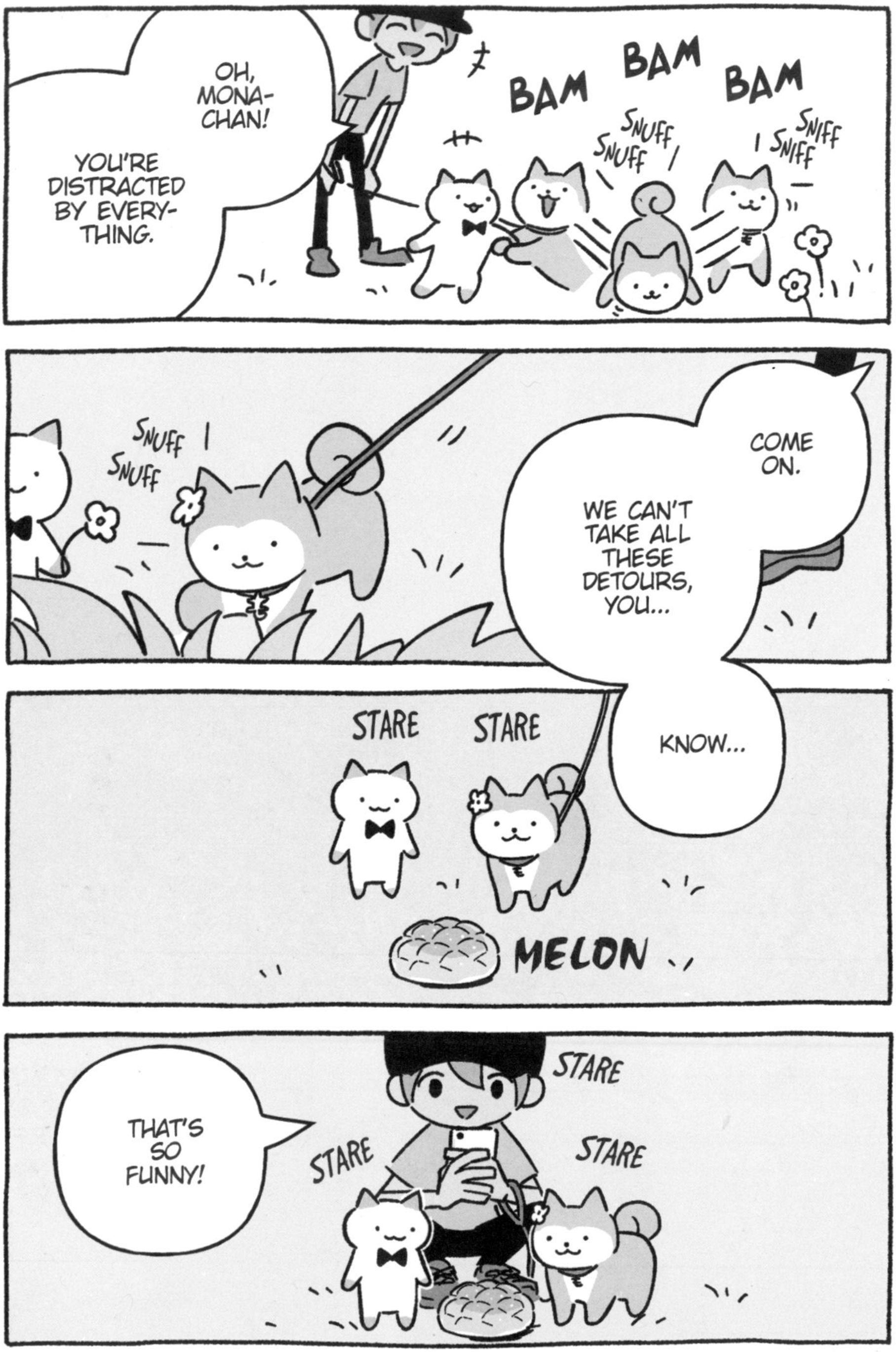

BAM BAM BAM
SNIFF SNIFF
SNUFF SNUFF
OH, MONA-CHAN! YOU'RE DISTRACTED BY EVERY-THING.
COME ON. WE CAN'T TAKE ALL THESE DETOURS, YOU... KNOW...
SNUFF SNUFF
STARE STARE
MELON
STARE
STARE
STARE
THAT'S SO FUNNY!

WIZARD

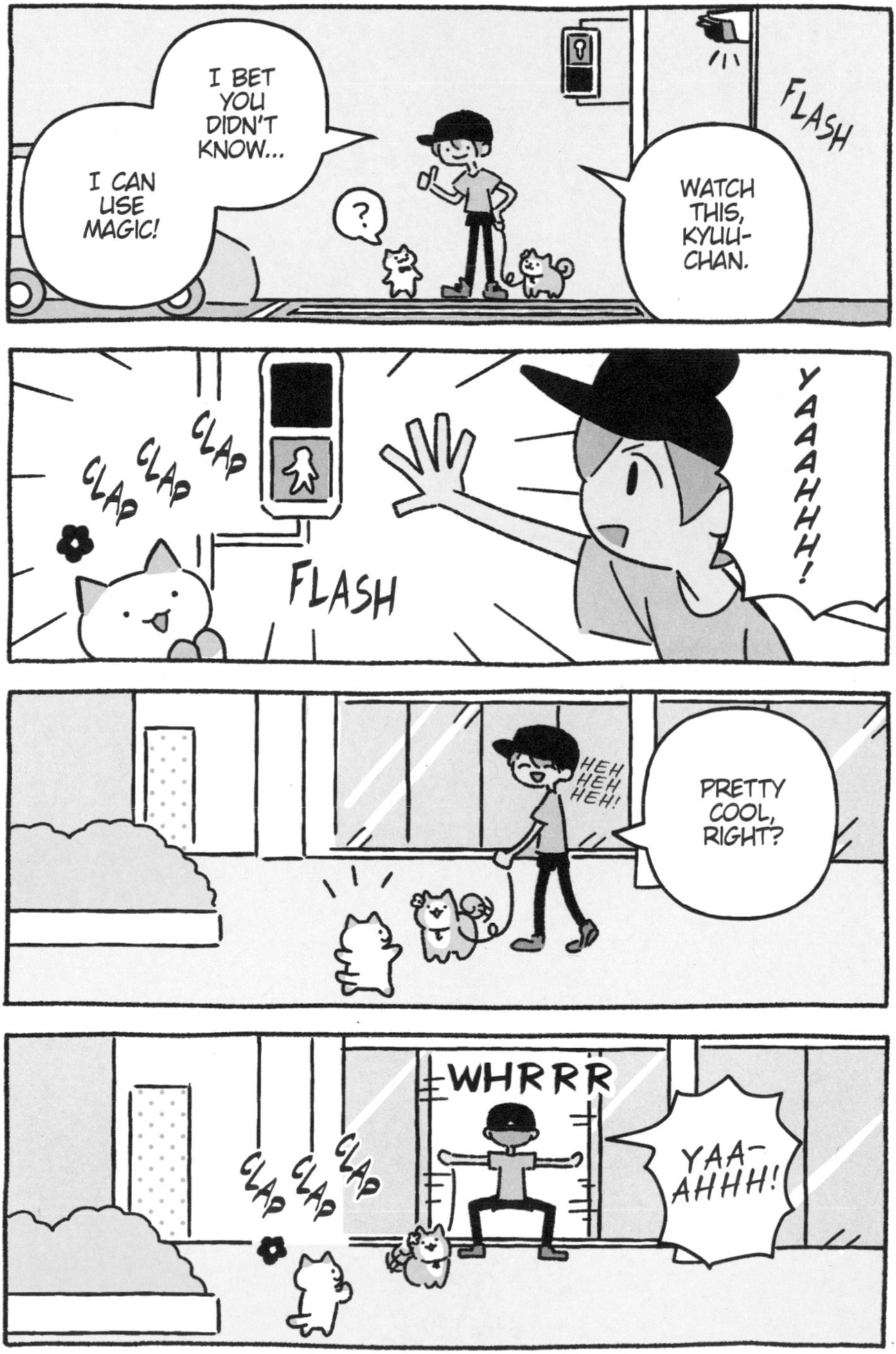
FLASH
WATCH THIS, KYUU-CHAN.
I BET YOU DIDN'T KNOW...
I CAN USE MAGIC!
?
YAAAAHHHH!
FLASH
CLAP
CLAP
CLAP
PRETTY COOL, RIGHT?
HEH HEH HEH!
YAA-AHHH!
WHRRR
CLAP
CLAP
CLAP

OVERPROTECTIVE

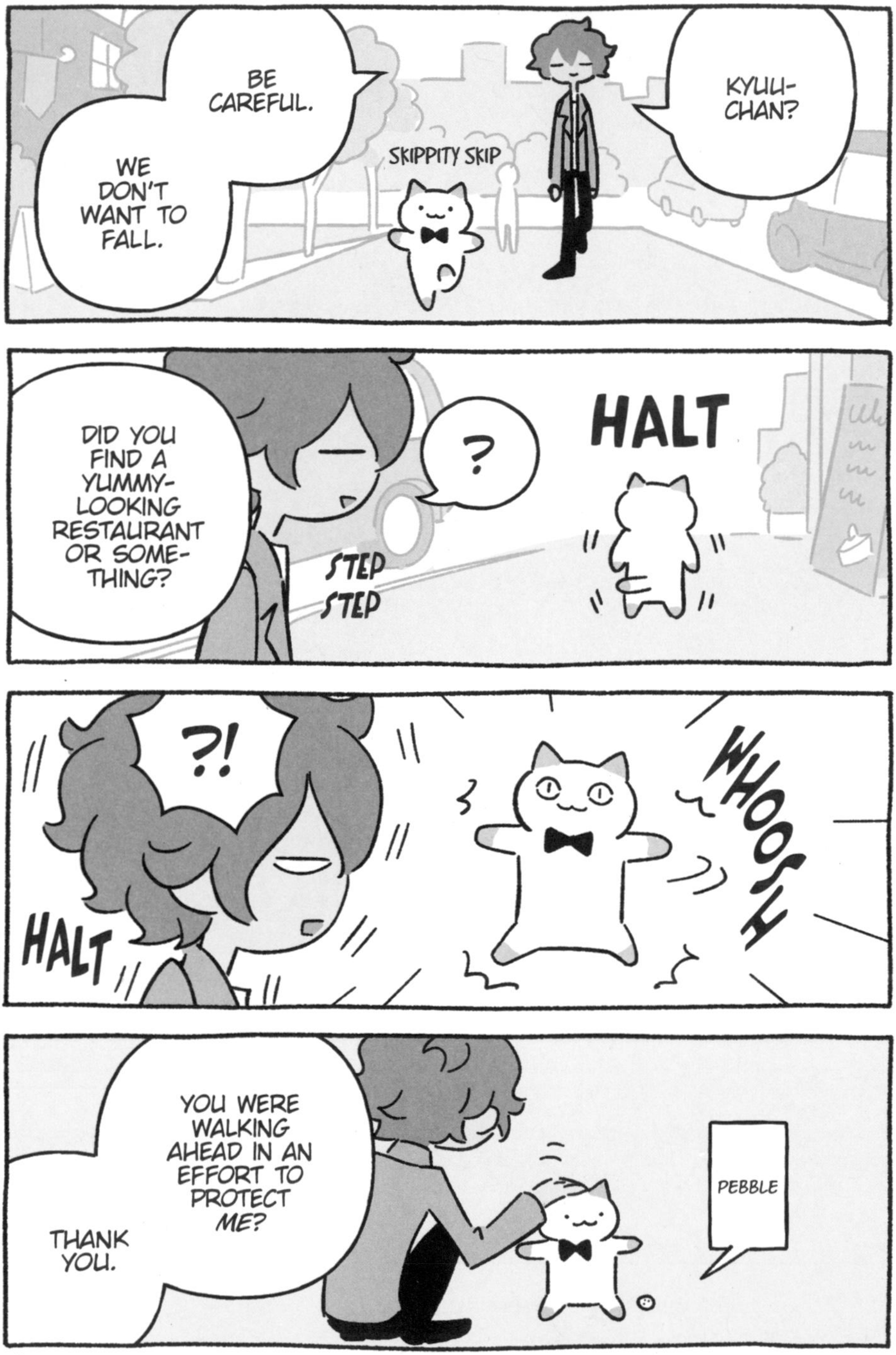

KYUU-CHAN?
SKIPPITY SKIP
BE CAREFUL.
WE DON'T WANT TO FALL.
HALT
?
STEP STEP
DID YOU FIND A YUMMY-LOOKING RESTAURANT OR SOME-THING?
WHOOSH
?!
HALT
PEBBLE
YOU WERE WALKING AHEAD IN AN EFFORT TO PROTECT ME?
THANK YOU.

RESCUE VEHICLE

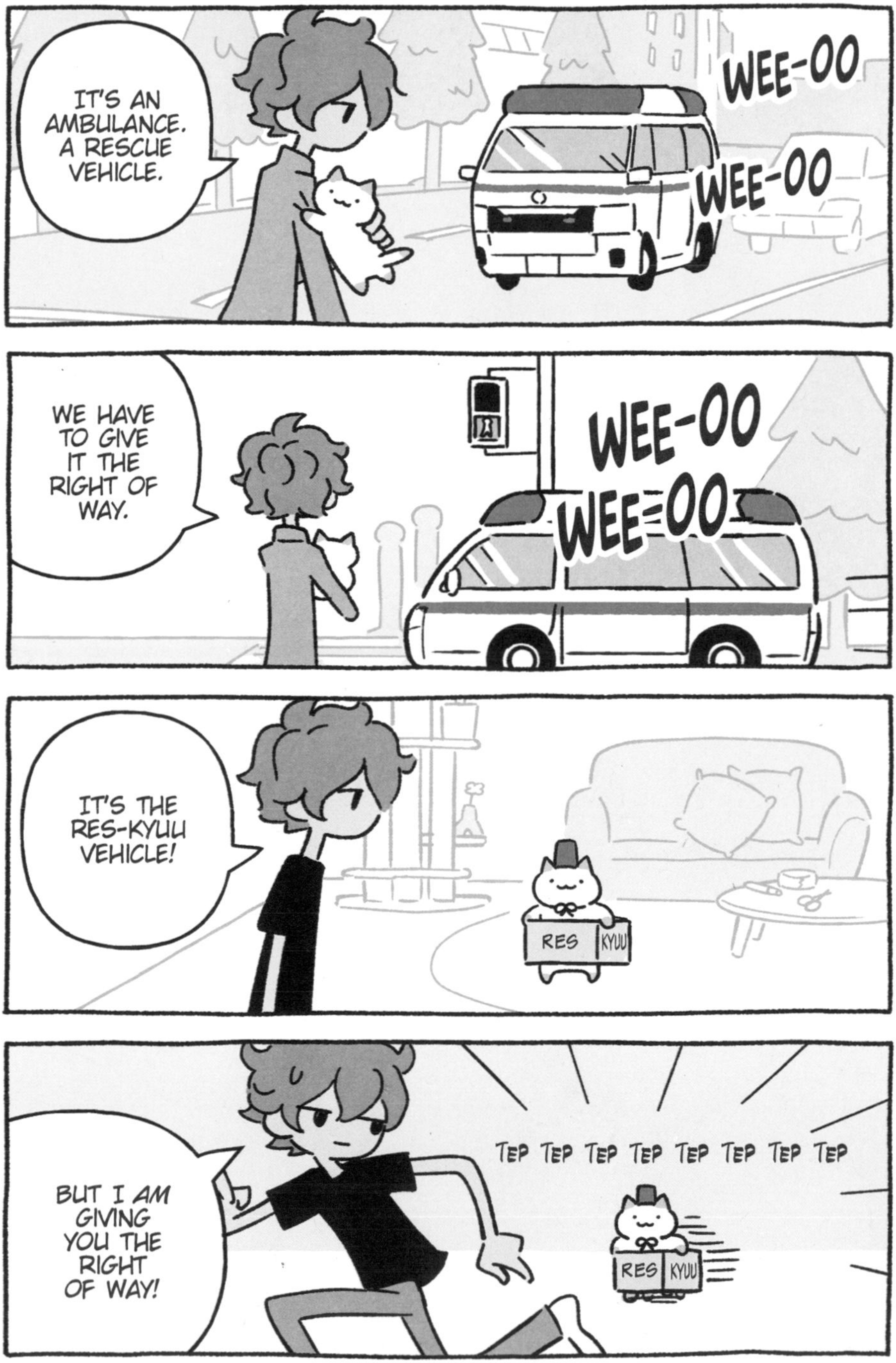
WEE-OO
WEE-OO
IT'S AN AMBULANCE. A RESCUE VEHICLE.
WEE-OO
WEE-OO
WE HAVE TO GIVE IT THE RIGHT OF WAY.
IT'S THE RES-KYUU VEHICLE!
RES
KYUU
TEP TEP TEP TEP TEP TEP TEP TEP
RES
KYUU
BUT I *AM* GIVING YOU THE RIGHT OF WAY!

RES-KYUU SQUAD ①

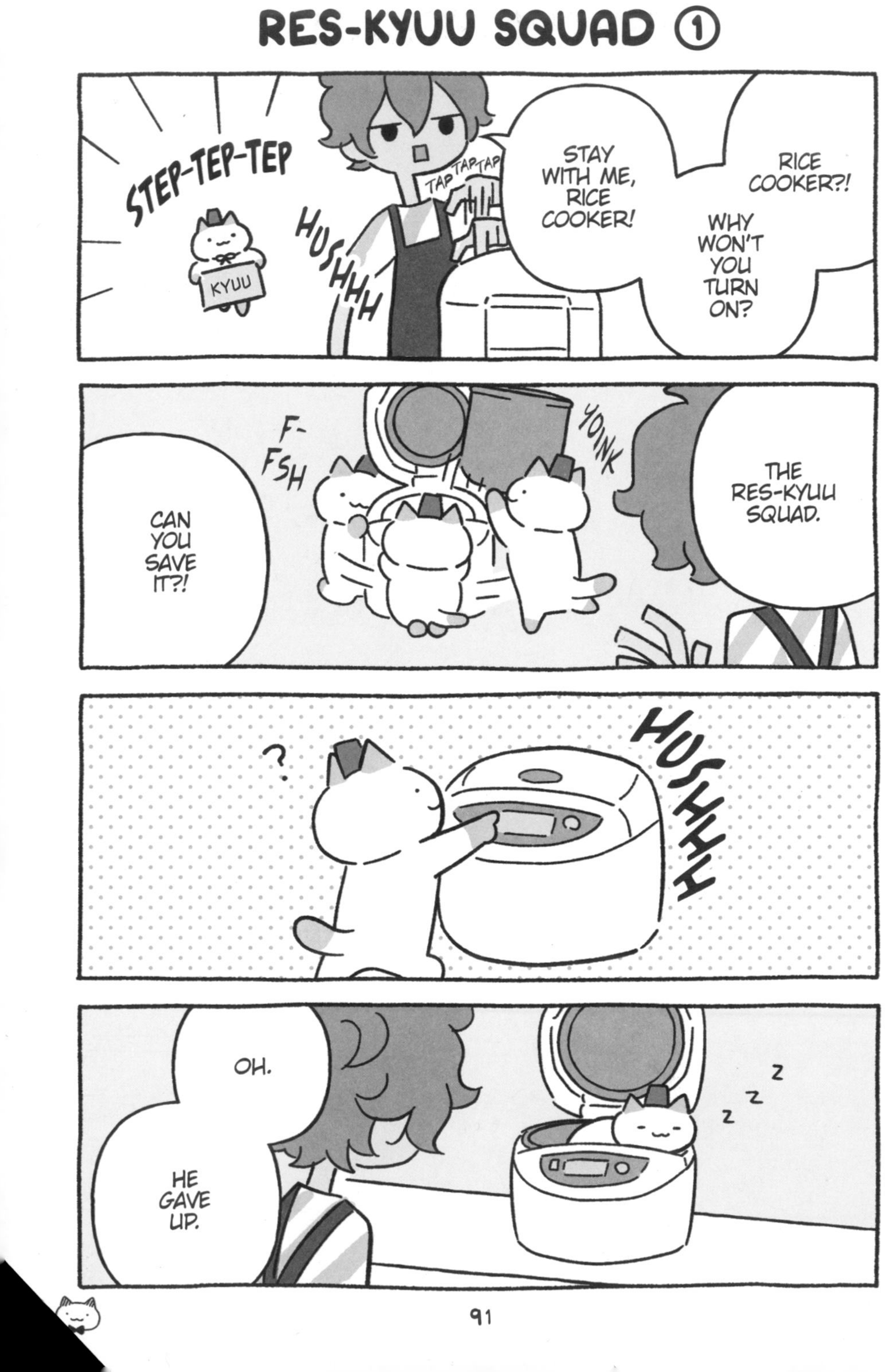
RICE COOKER?!
WHY WON'T YOU TURN ON?
STAY WITH ME, RICE COOKER!
TAP TAP TAP
HUSHHH
STEP-TEP-TEP
KYUU
THE RES-KYUU SQUAD.
YOINK
F-FSH
CAN YOU SAVE IT?!
HUSHHH
?
Z Z Z
OH.
HE GAVE UP.

RES-KYUU SQUAD ②

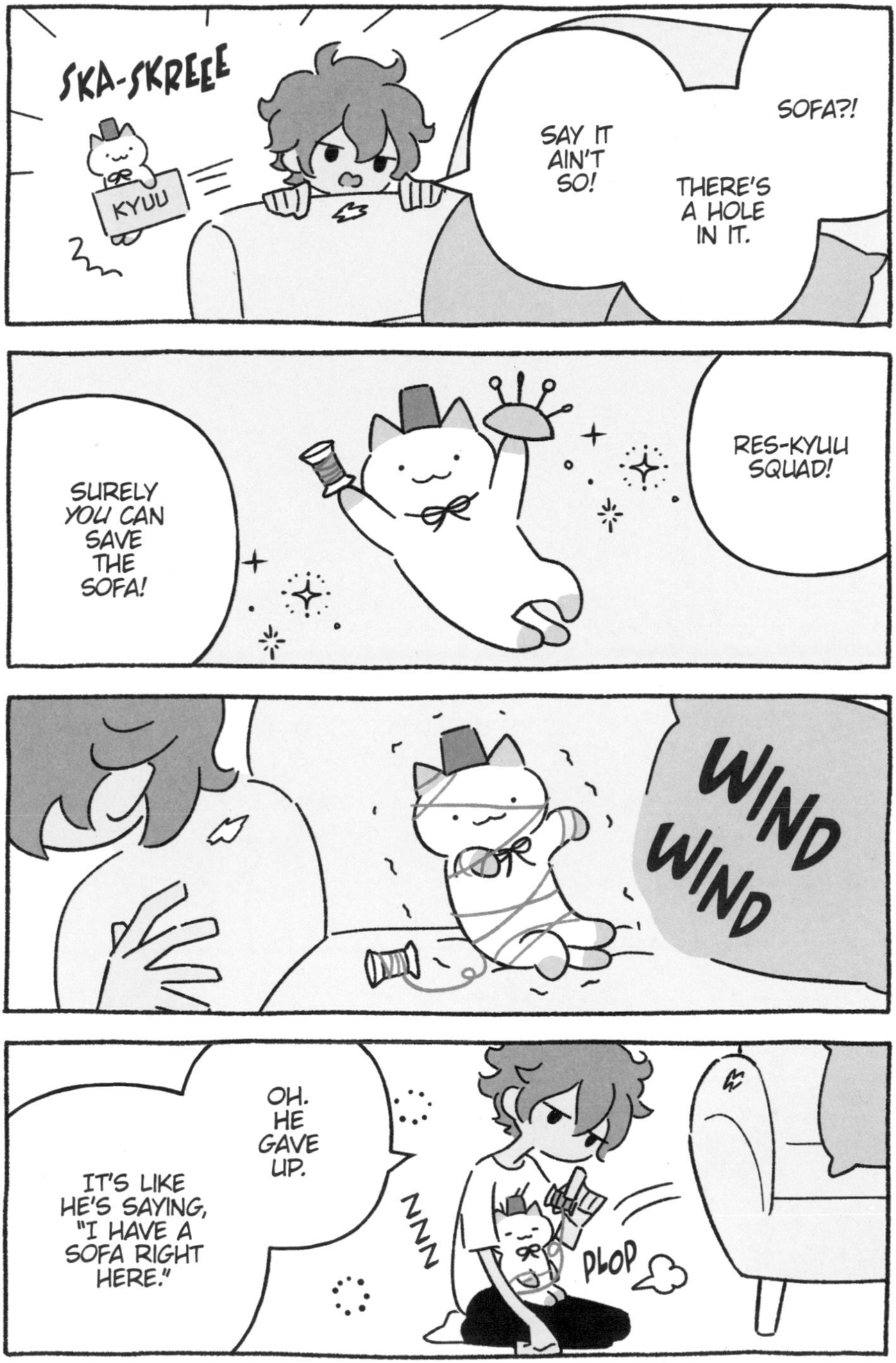

SOFA?!
THERE'S A HOLE IN IT.
SAY IT AIN'T SO!
SKA-SKREEE
KYUU
RES-KYUU SQUAD!
SURELY *YOU* CAN SAVE THE SOFA!
WIND WIND
PLOP
OH. HE GAVE UP.
IT'S LIKE HE'S SAYING, "I HAVE A SOFA RIGHT HERE."

CHAOS

YOU'VE GOT UNIQUE PHOTO-GRAPHIC SENSIBILI-TIES.
YOU THINK SO?
KYUU-CHAN?!

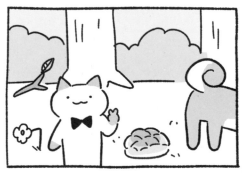

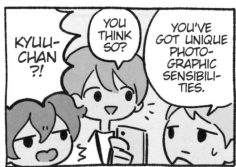

THE USUAL CAFÉ

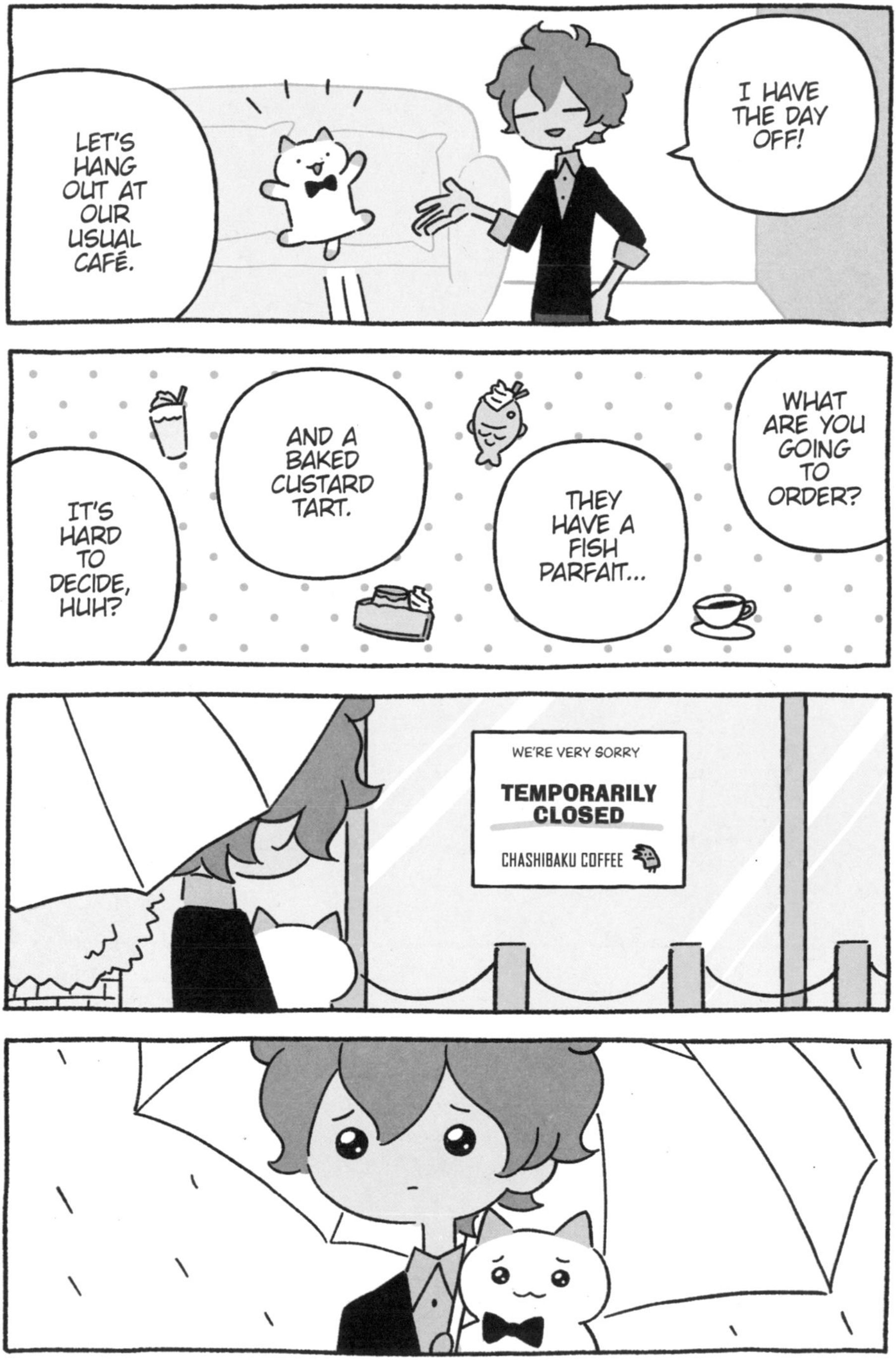
I HAVE THE DAY OFF!
LET'S HANG OUT AT OUR USUAL CAFÉ.
WHAT ARE YOU GOING TO ORDER?
THEY HAVE A FISH PARFAIT...
AND A BAKED CUSTARD TART.
IT'S HARD TO DECIDE, HUH?
WE'RE VERY SORRY
TEMPORARILY CLOSED
CHASHIBAKU COFFEE

DOG PARK

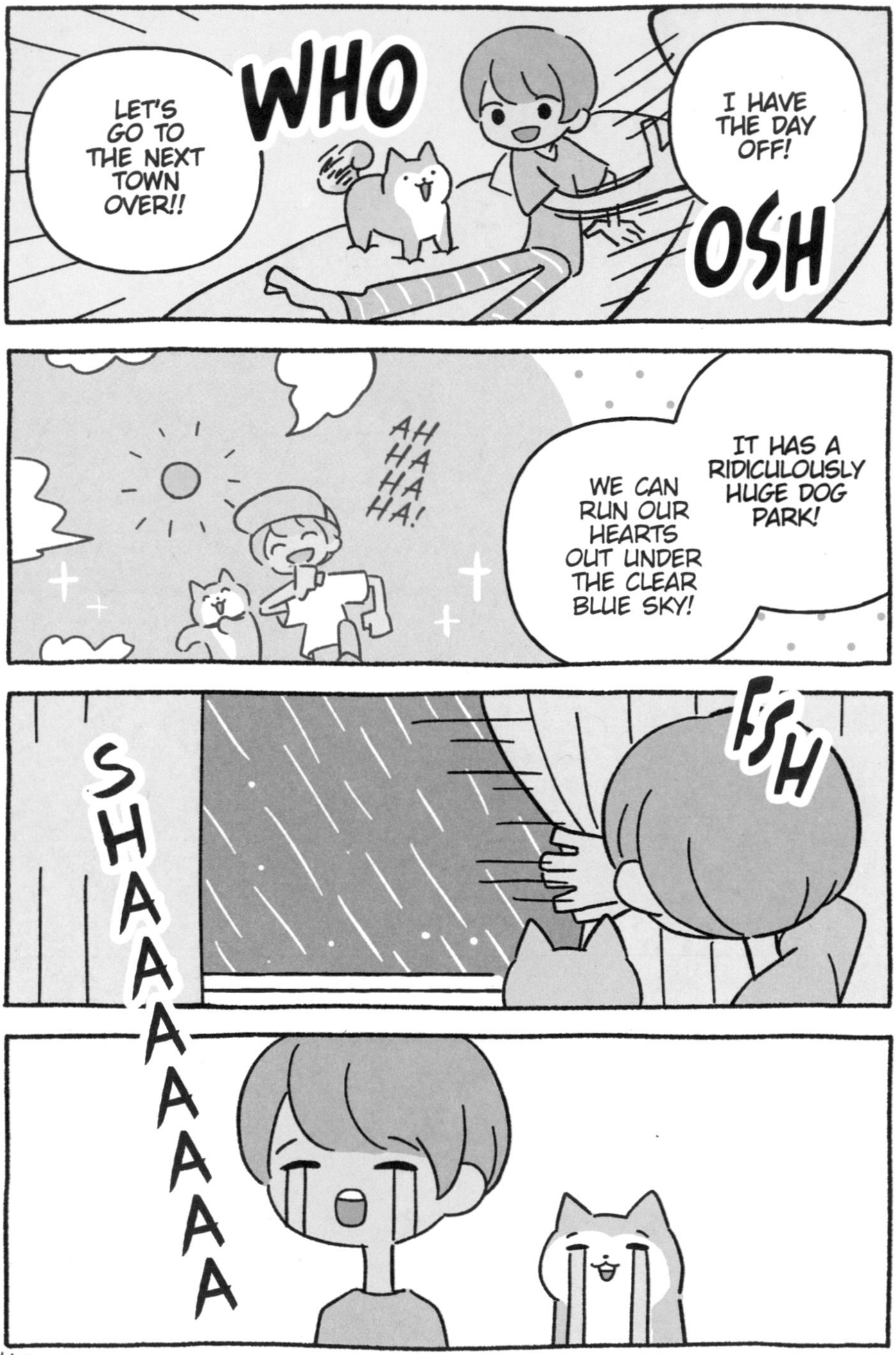

I HAVE THE DAY OFF!
WHO
OSH
LET'S GO TO THE NEXT TOWN OVER!!
IT HAS A RIDICULOUSLY HUGE DOG PARK!
WE CAN RUN OUR HEARTS OUT UNDER THE CLEAR BLUE SKY!
AH HA HA HA!
FSH
SHAAAAAAA

RAIN AND SWEETS

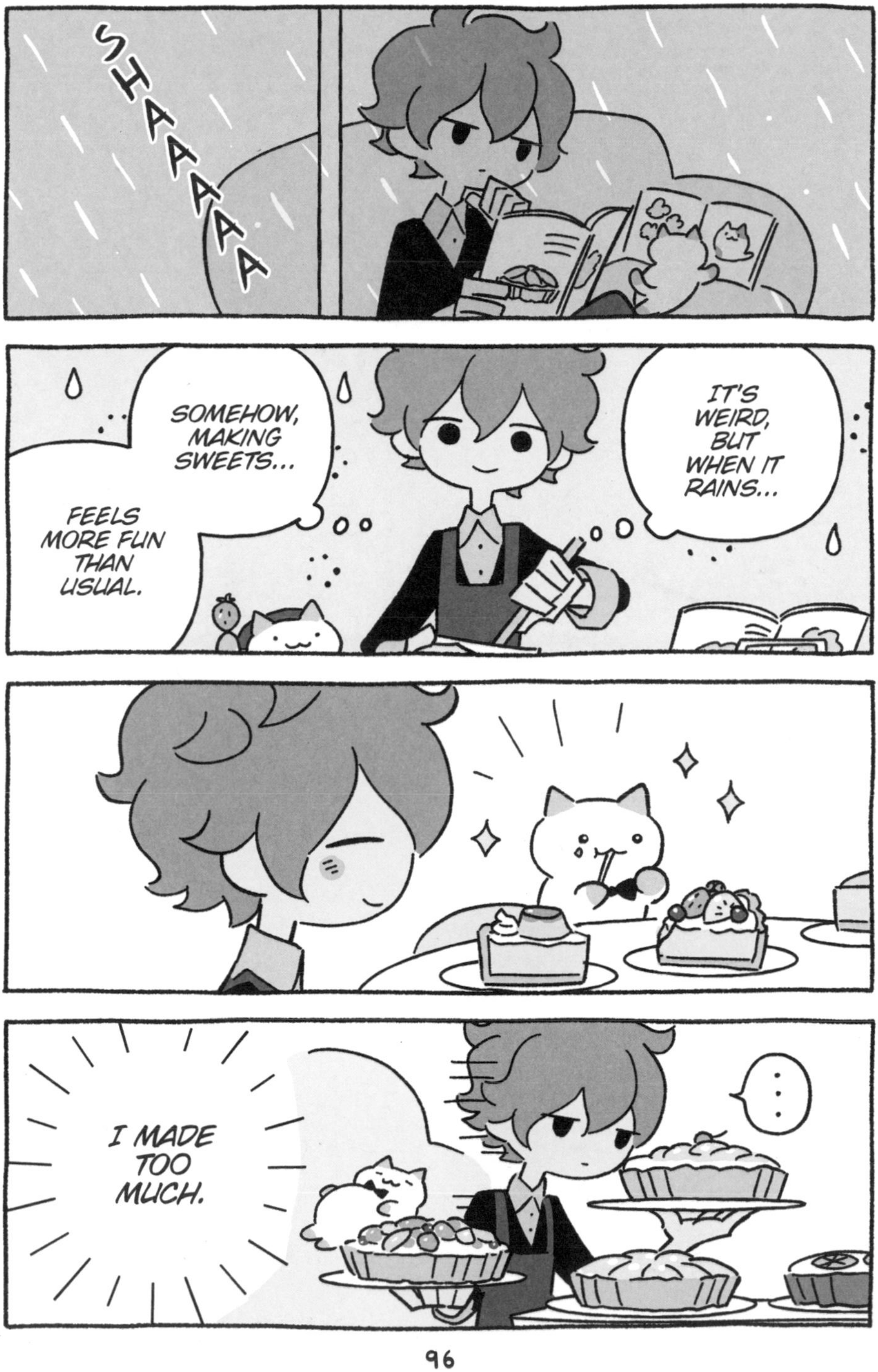
SHAAAAAA
IT'S WEIRD, BUT WHEN IT RAINS...
SOMEHOW, MAKING SWEETS...
FEELS MORE FUN THAN USUAL.
...
I MADE TOO MUCH.

COME ON IN

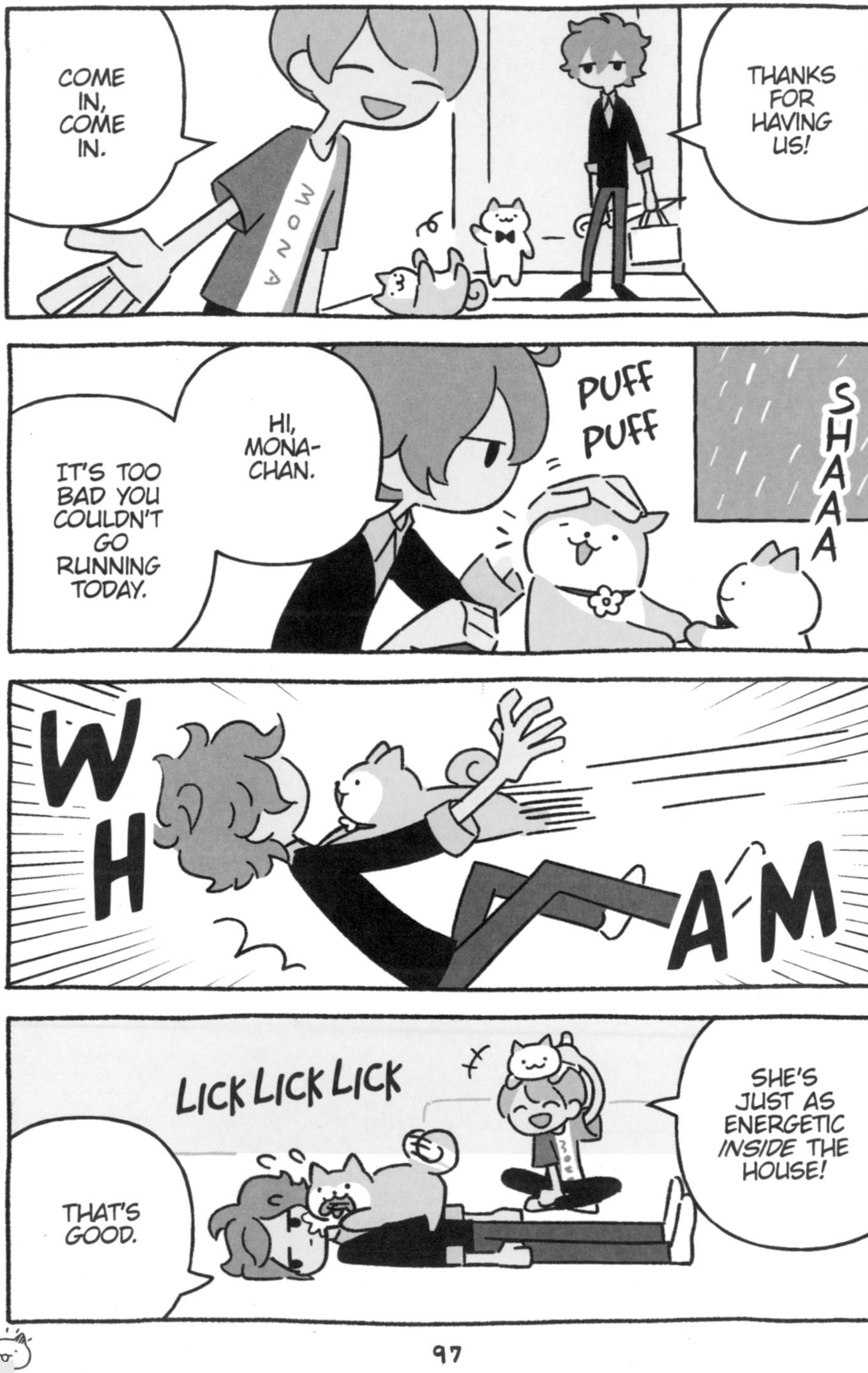

THANKS FOR HAVING US!
COME IN, COME IN.
SHAAAA
PUFF PUFF
HI, MONA-CHAN.
IT'S TOO BAD YOU COULDN'T GO RUNNING TODAY.
WHAM
SHE'S JUST AS ENERGETIC *INSIDE* THE HOUSE!
LICK LICK LICK
THAT'S GOOD.

TAKING POSITION

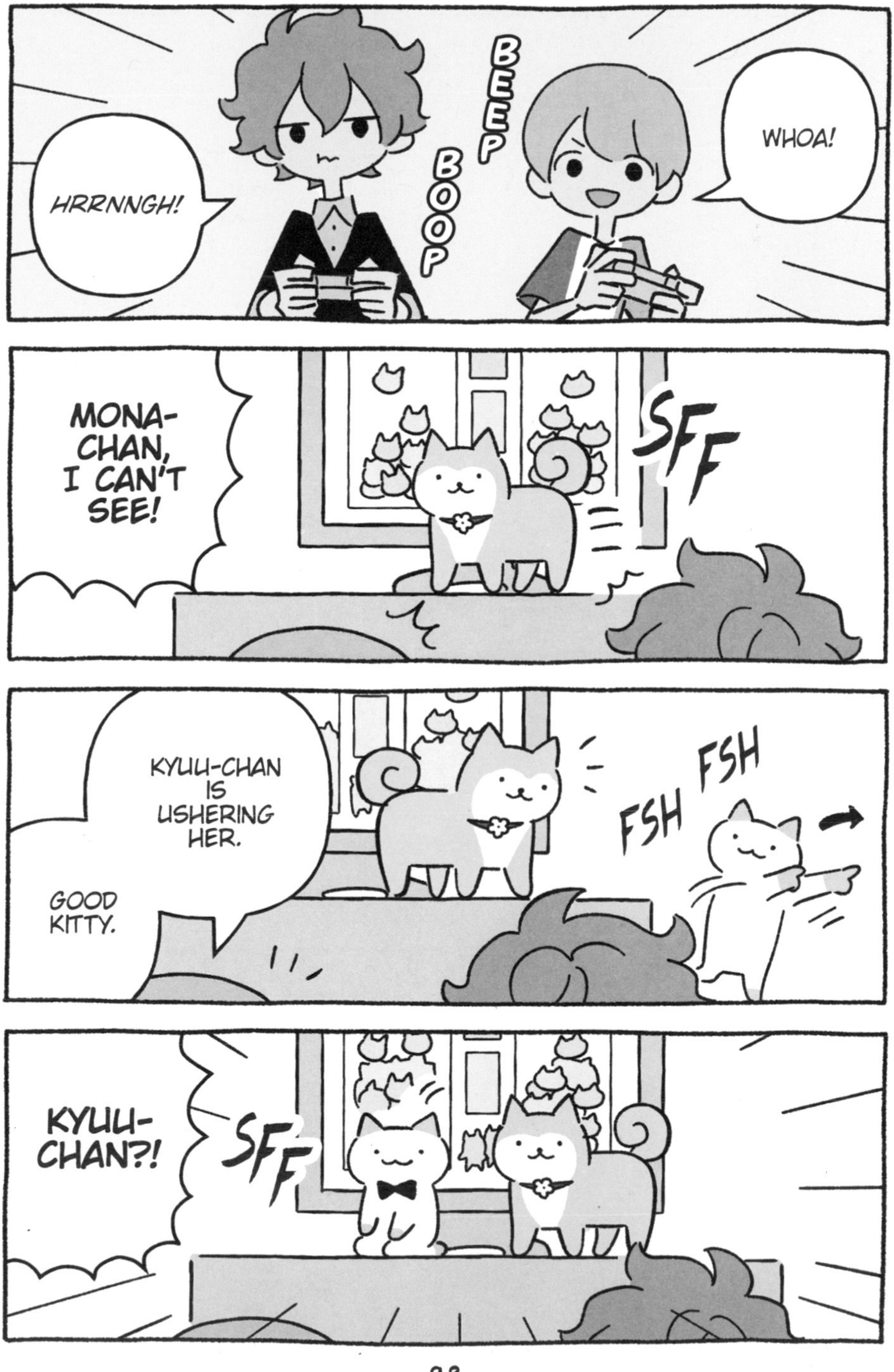
WHOA!
BEEP
BOOP
HRRNNGH!
SFF
MONA-CHAN, I CAN'T SEE!
FSH FSH
KYUU-CHAN IS USHERING HER.
GOOD KITTY.
SFF
KYUU-CHAN?!

FLUFFY PEOPLE

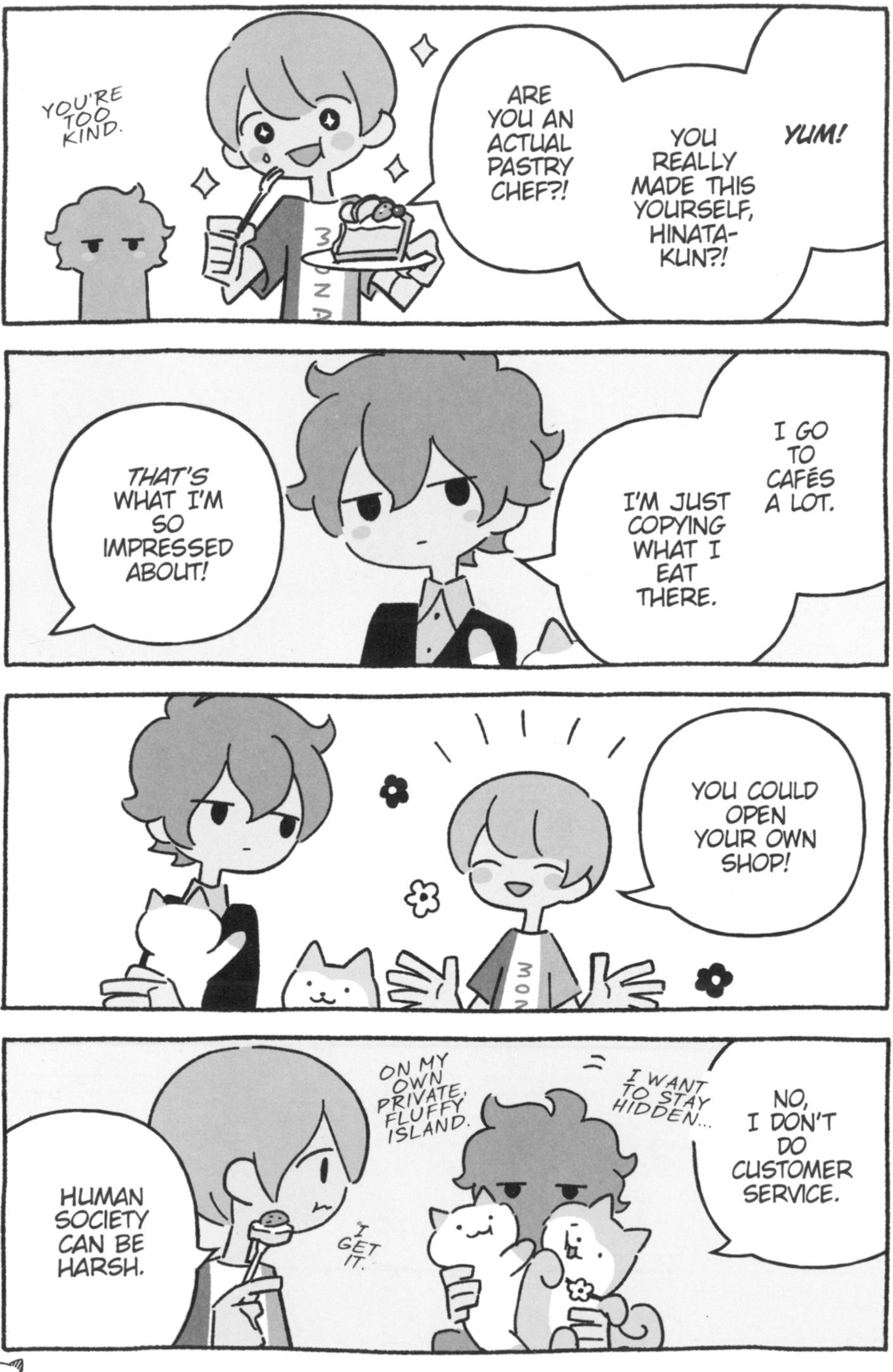

YUM!
YOU REALLY MADE THIS YOURSELF, HINATA-KUN?!
ARE YOU AN ACTUAL PASTRY CHEF?!
YOU'RE TOO KIND.
I GO TO CAFÉS A LOT.
I'M JUST COPYING WHAT I EAT THERE.
THAT'S WHAT I'M SO IMPRESSED ABOUT!
YOU COULD OPEN YOUR OWN SHOP!
NO, I DON'T DO CUSTOMER SERVICE.
I WANT TO STAY HIDDEN...
ON MY OWN PRIVATE, FLUFFY ISLAND.
I GET IT.
HUMAN SOCIETY CAN BE HARSH.

OGURA CROSSING

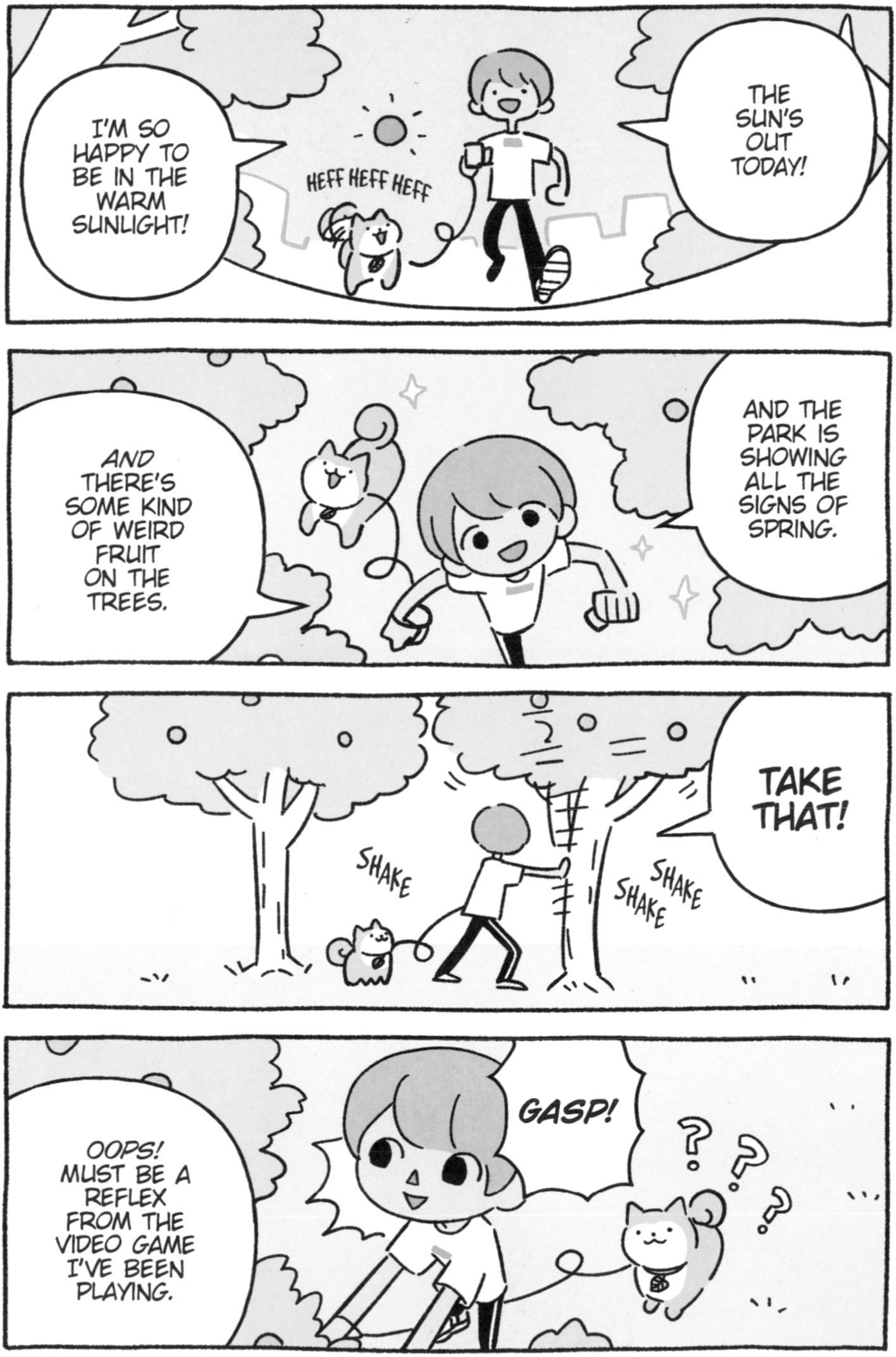
THE SUN'S OUT TODAY!
HEFF HEFF HEFF
I'M SO HAPPY TO BE IN THE WARM SUNLIGHT!
AND THE PARK IS SHOWING ALL THE SIGNS OF SPRING.
AND THERE'S SOME KIND OF WEIRD FRUIT ON THE TREES.
TAKE THAT!
SHAKE SHAKE
SHAKE
GASP!
OOPS! MUST BE A REFLEX FROM THE VIDEO GAME I'VE BEEN PLAYING.

YOU DROPPED SOMETHING

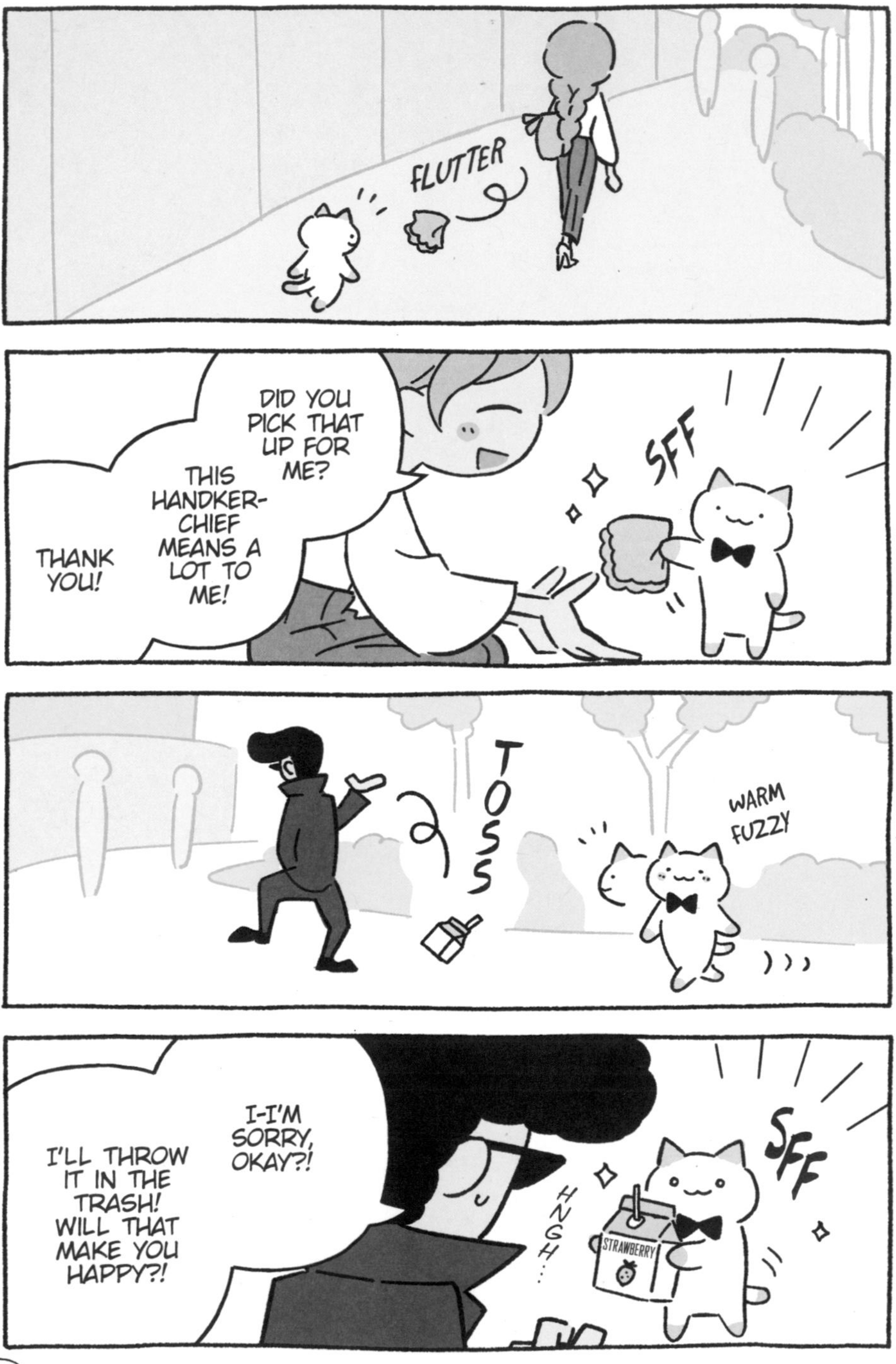
FLUTTER
SFF
DID YOU PICK THAT UP FOR ME?
THIS HANDKERCHIEF MEANS A LOT TO ME!
THANK YOU!
WARM FUZZY
TOSS
SFF
STRAWBERRY
HNGH...
I-I'M SORRY, OKAY?!
I'LL THROW IT IN THE TRASH! WILL THAT MAKE YOU HAPPY?!

CAT-LOVING CHERRY BLOSSOMS

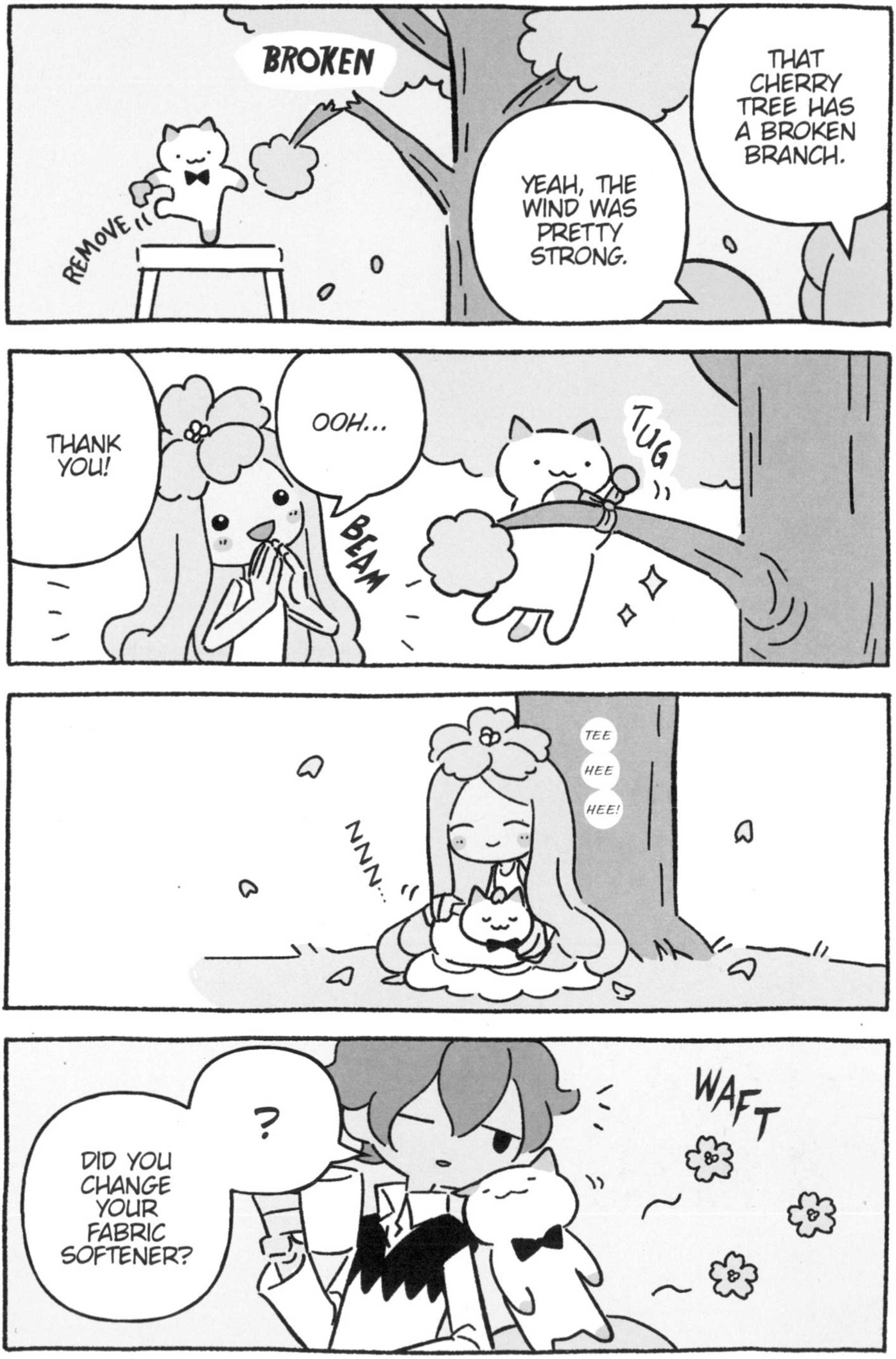
THAT CHERRY TREE HAS A BROKEN BRANCH.
YEAH, THE WIND WAS PRETTY STRONG.
BROKEN
REMOVE
TUG
OOH...
BEAM
THANK YOU!
TEE
HEE
HEE!
NNN...
WAFT
?
DID YOU CHANGE YOUR FABRIC SOFTENER?

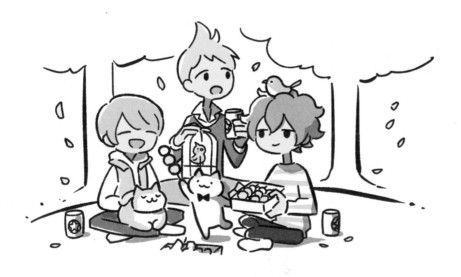

COLOR CONSULTING

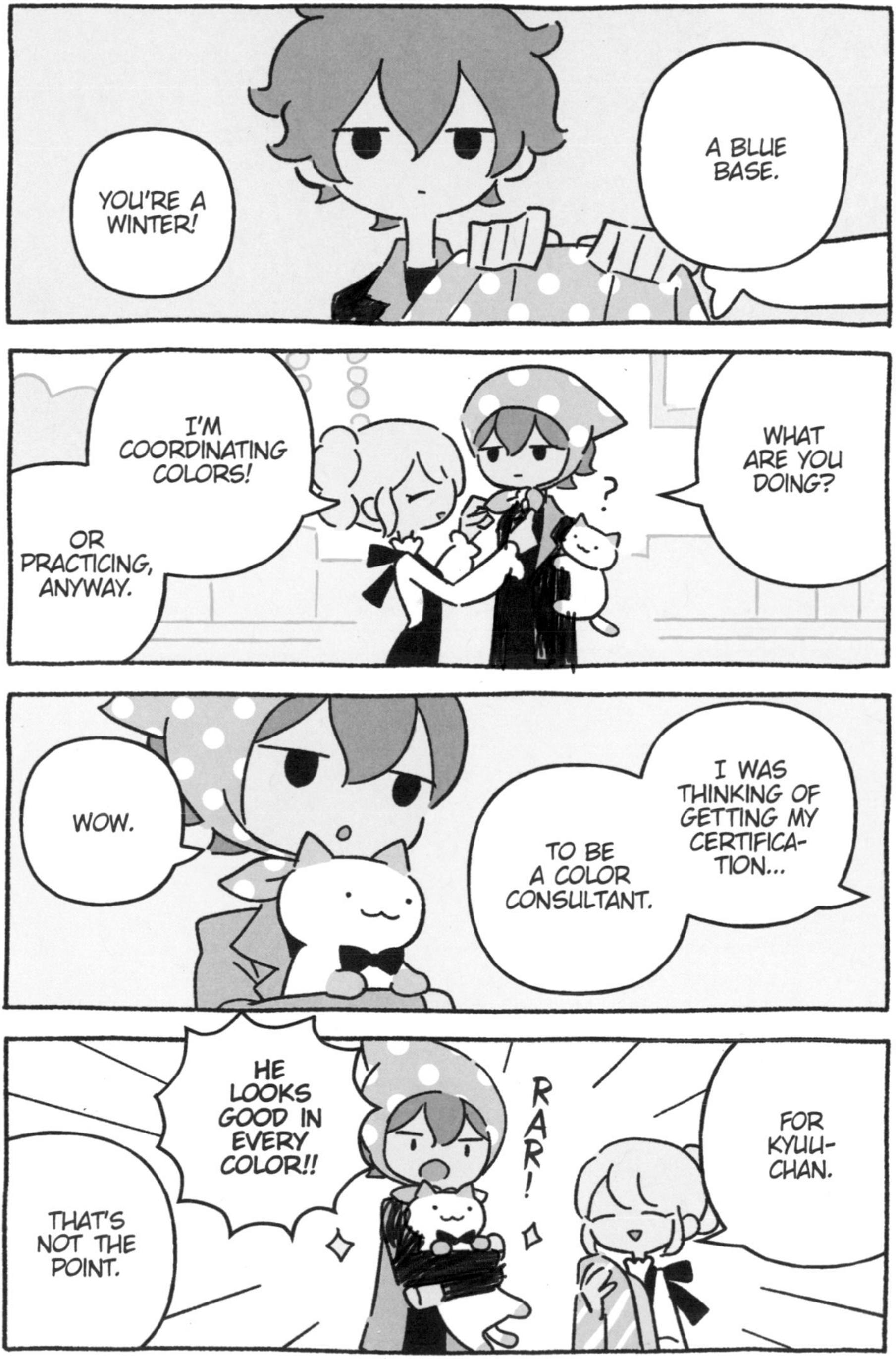
A BLUE BASE.
YOU'RE A WINTER!
WHAT ARE YOU DOING?
I'M COORDINATING COLORS!
OR PRACTICING, ANYWAY.
I WAS THINKING OF GETTING MY CERTIFICA-TION...
TO BE A COLOR CONSULTANT.
WOW.
FOR KYUU-CHAN.
RAR!
HE LOOKS GOOD IN EVERY COLOR!!
THAT'S NOT THE POINT.

CERTIFICATION

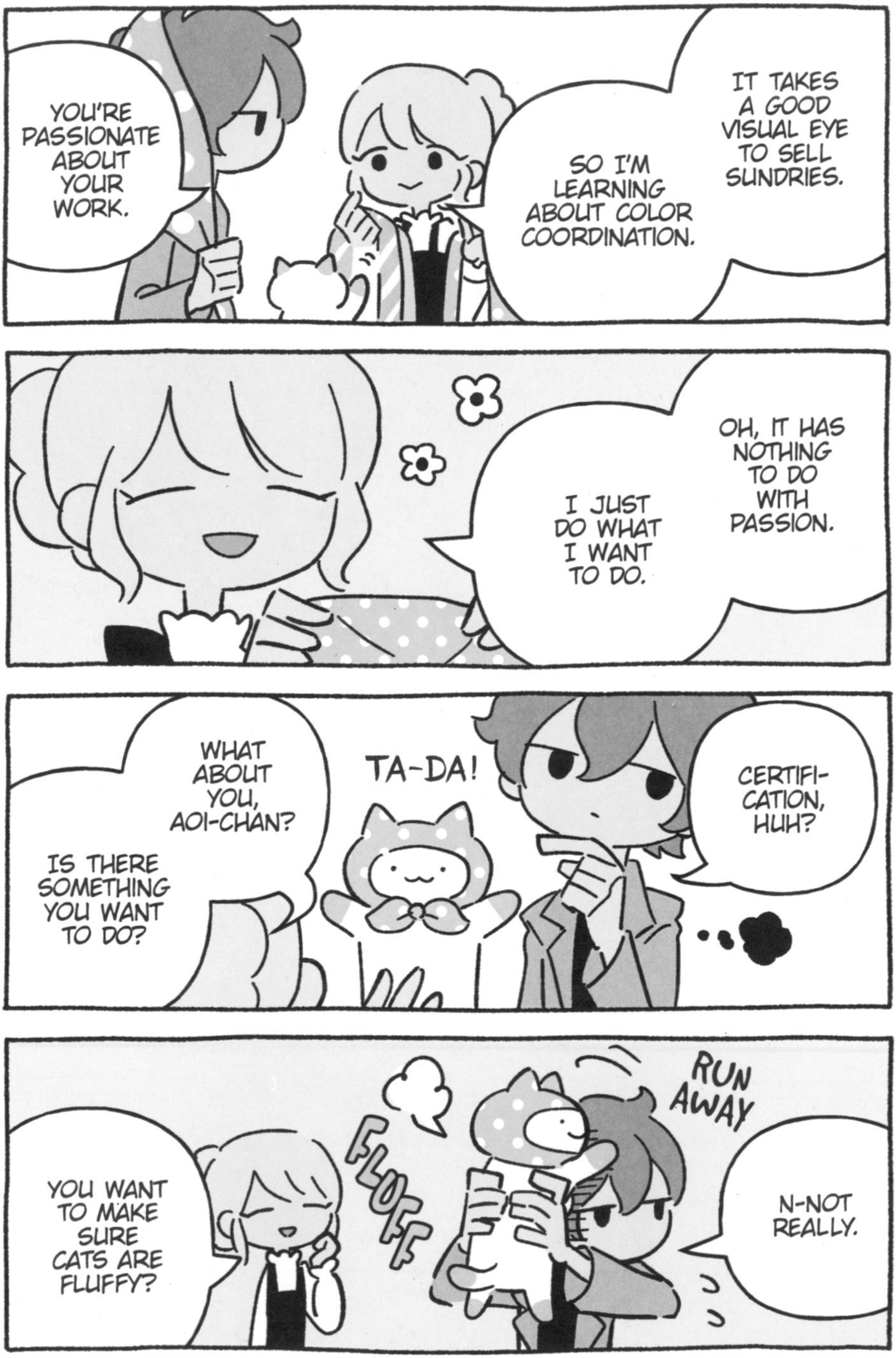
IT TAKES A GOOD VISUAL EYE TO SELL SUNDRIES.
SO I'M LEARNING ABOUT COLOR COORDINATION.
YOU'RE PASSIONATE ABOUT YOUR WORK.
OH, IT HAS NOTHING TO DO WITH PASSION.
I JUST DO WHAT I WANT TO DO.
CERTIFI-CATION, HUH?
TA-DA!
WHAT ABOUT YOU, AOI-CHAN?
IS THERE SOMETHING YOU WANT TO DO?
RUN AWAY
N-NOT REALLY.
FLUFF
YOU WANT TO MAKE SURE CATS ARE FLUFFY?

OBSESSED WITH SUNDRIES

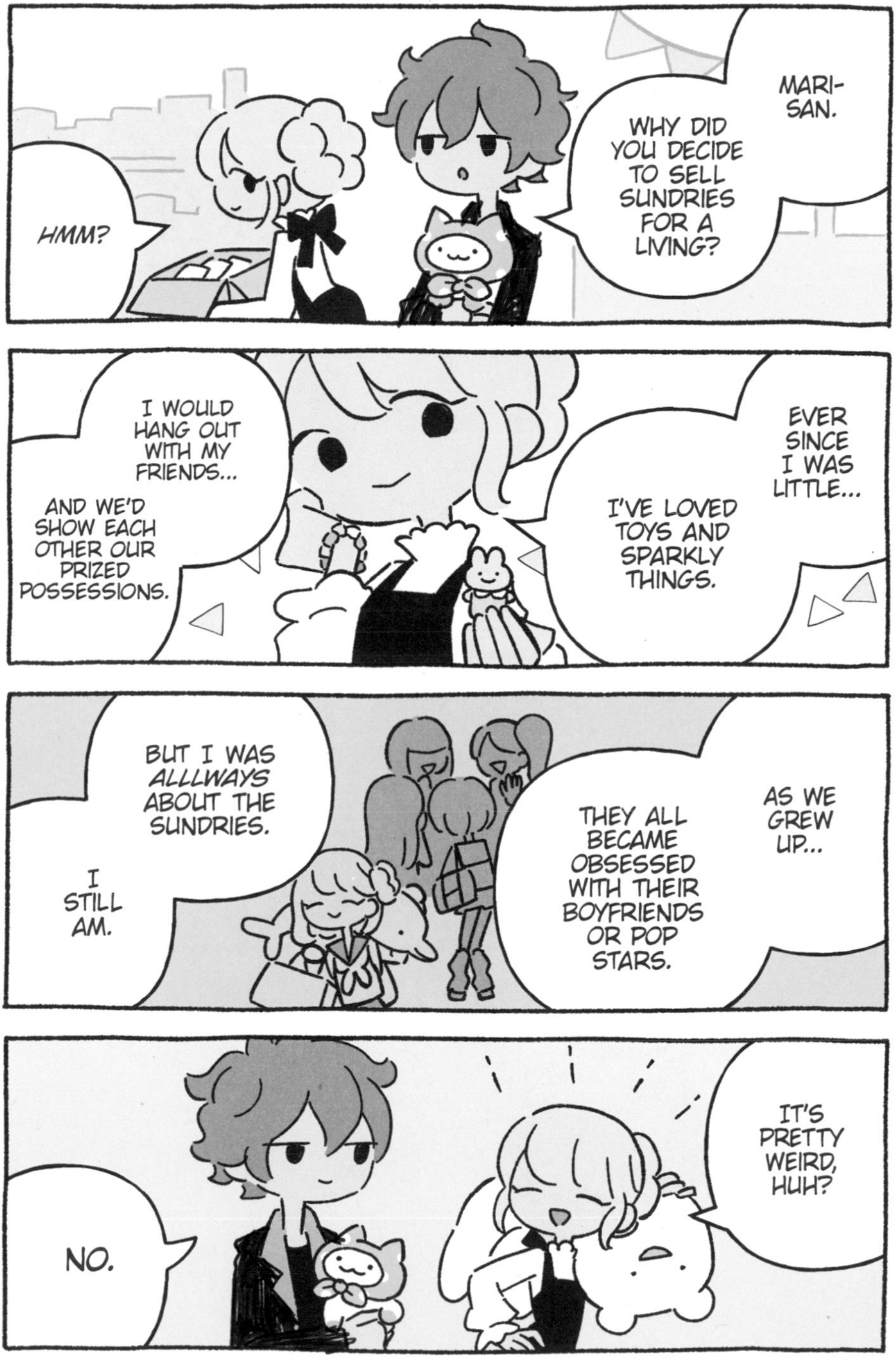
MARI-SAN.
WHY DID YOU DECIDE TO SELL SUNDRIES FOR A LIVING?
HMM?
EVER SINCE I WAS LITTLE...
I'VE LOVED TOYS AND SPARKLY THINGS.
I WOULD HANG OUT WITH MY FRIENDS...
AND WE'D SHOW EACH OTHER OUR PRIZED POSSESSIONS.
AS WE GREW UP...
THEY ALL BECAME OBSESSED WITH THEIR BOYFRIENDS OR POP STARS.
BUT I WAS *ALLLWAYS* ABOUT THE SUNDRIES.
I STILL AM.
IT'S PRETTY WEIRD, HUH?
NO.

IDENTICAL SURPRISES

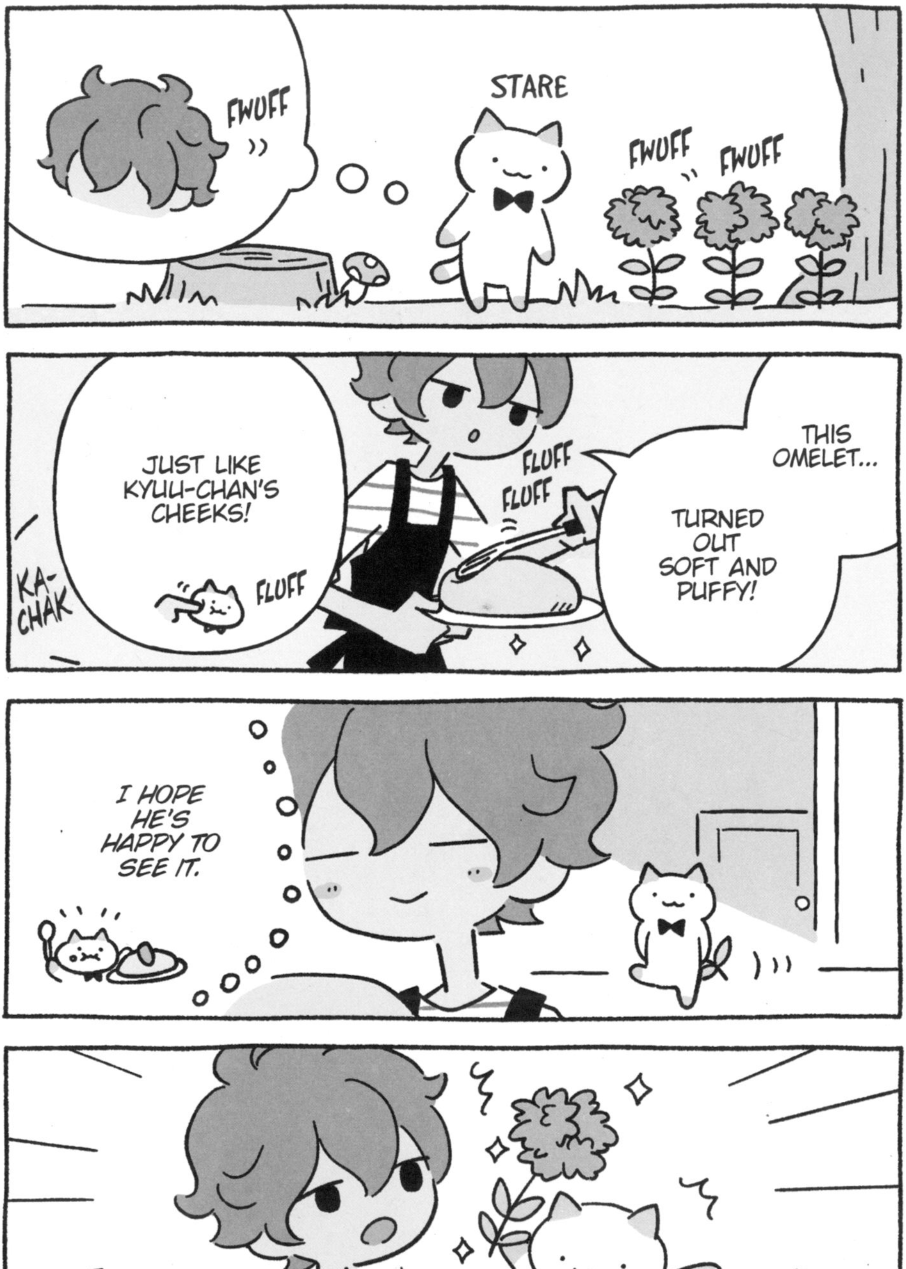
FWUFF
FWUFF
STARE
FWUFF
THIS OMELET...
TURNED OUT SOFT AND PUFFY!
FLUFF
FLUFF
JUST LIKE KYUU-CHAN'S CHEEKS!
FLUFF
KA-CHAK
I HOPE HE'S HAPPY TO SEE IT.

INFORMATION SOCIETY

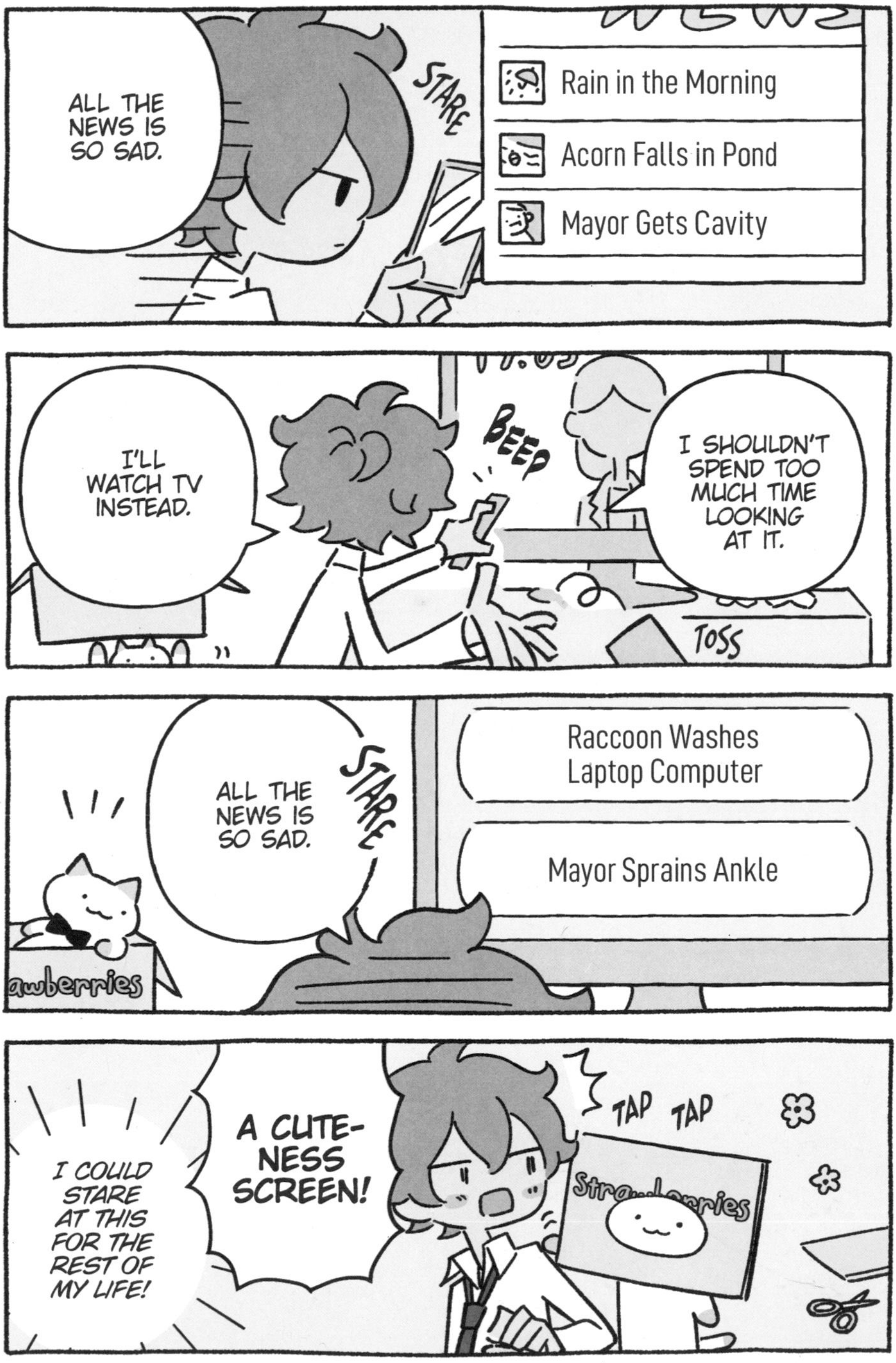
Rain in the Morning
Acorn Falls in Pond
Mayor Gets Cavity
STARE
ALL THE NEWS IS SO SAD.
I SHOULDN'T SPEND TOO MUCH TIME LOOKING AT IT.
BEEP
TOSS
I'LL WATCH TV INSTEAD.
Raccoon Washes Laptop Computer
Mayor Sprains Ankle
STARE
ALL THE NEWS IS SO SAD.
awberries
TAP TAP
A CUTE-NESS SCREEN!
I COULD STARE AT THIS FOR THE REST OF MY LIFE!

ASAP

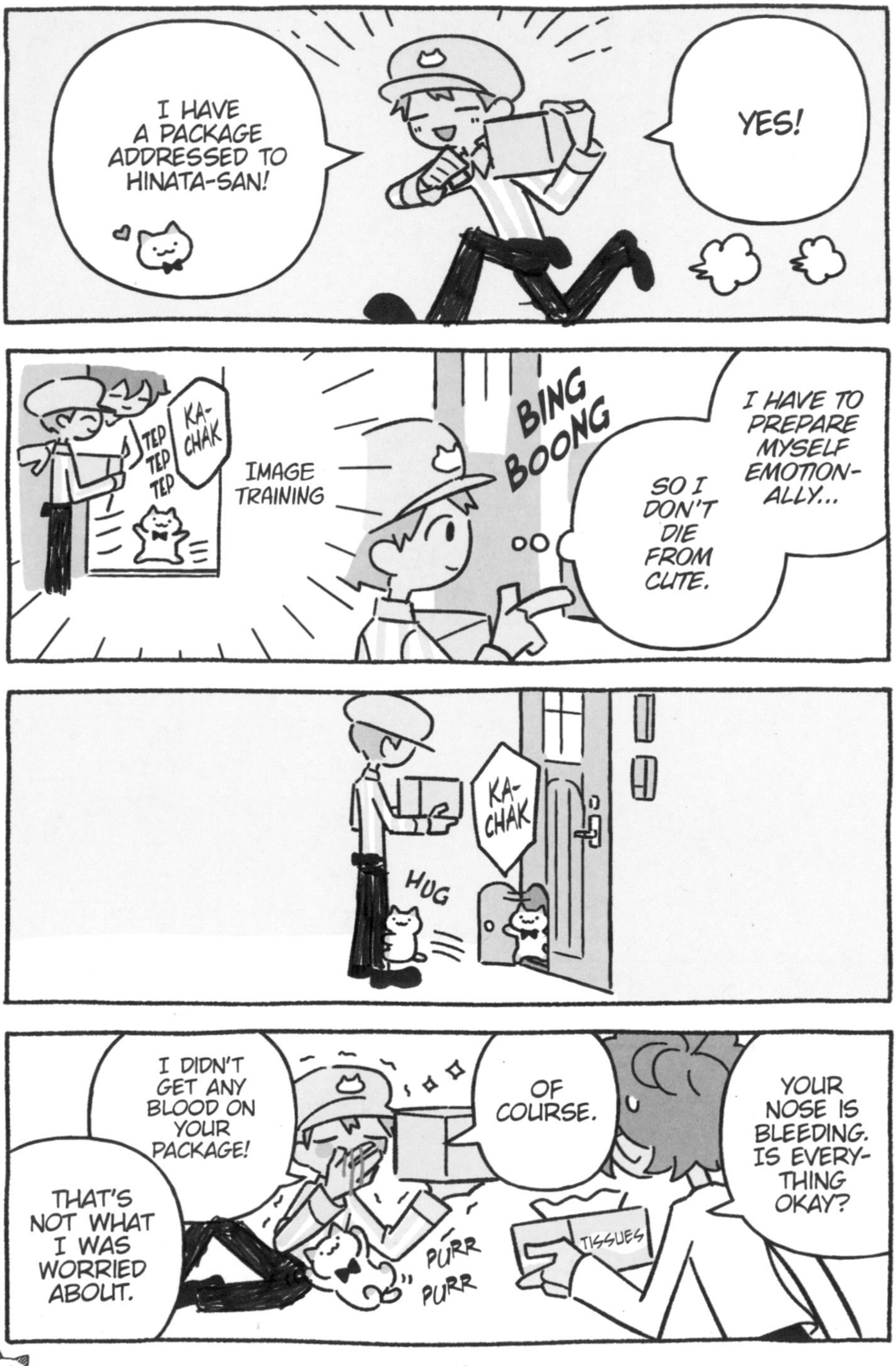
YES!
I HAVE A PACKAGE ADDRESSED TO HINATA-SAN!
BING BOONG
I HAVE TO PREPARE MYSELF EMOTION-ALLY...
SO I DON'T DIE FROM CUTE.
IMAGE TRAINING
KA-CHAK
TEP TEP TEP
KA-CHAK
HUG
YOUR NOSE IS BLEEDING. IS EVERY-THING OKAY?
OF COURSE.
I DIDN'T GET ANY BLOOD ON YOUR PACKAGE!
TISSUES
THAT'S NOT WHAT I WAS WORRIED ABOUT.
PURR PURR

CALMING DOWN

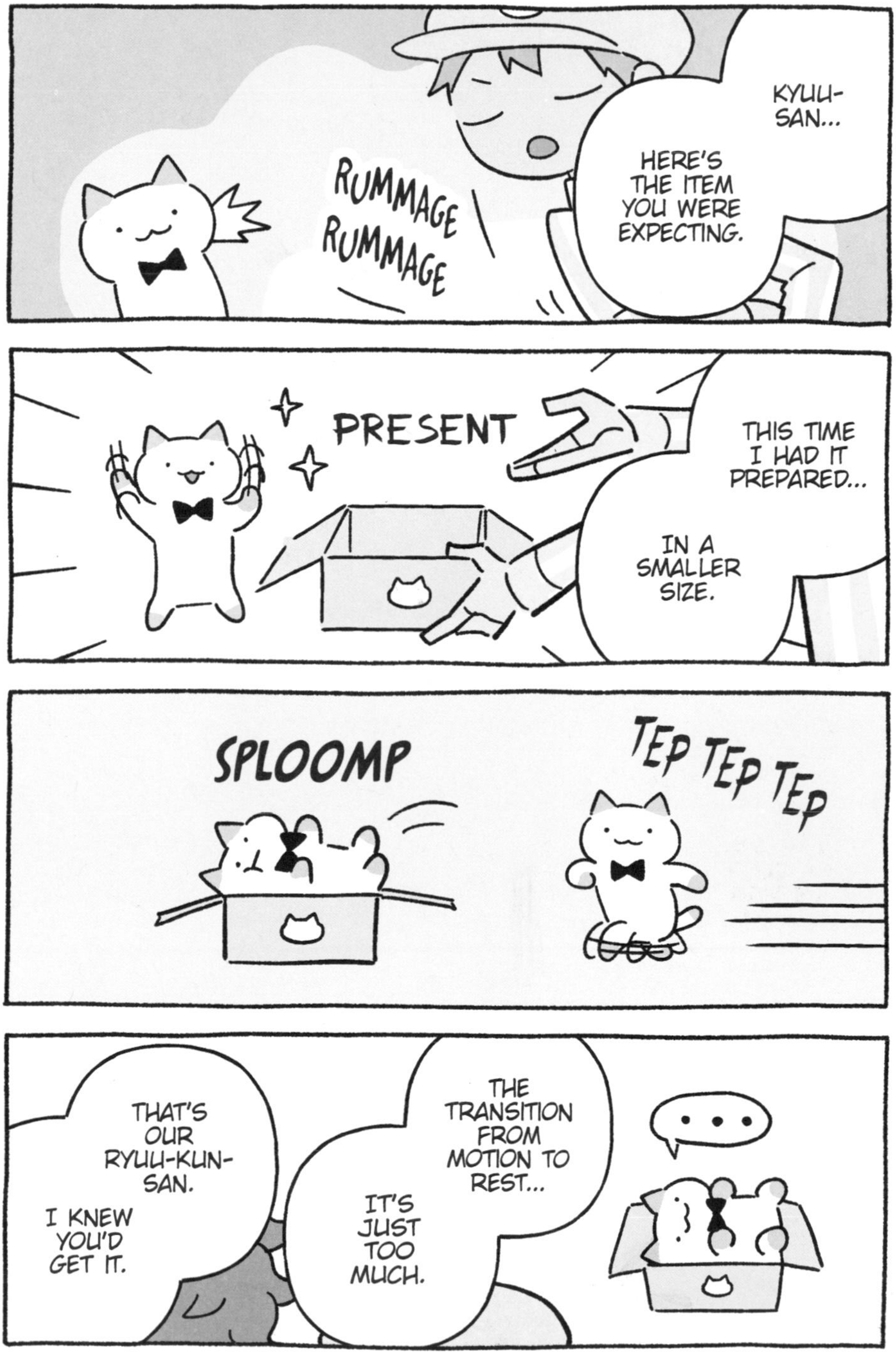
KYUU-SAN...
HERE'S THE ITEM YOU WERE EXPECTING.
RUMMAGE RUMMAGE
THIS TIME I HAD IT PREPARED...
IN A SMALLER SIZE.
PRESENT
TEP TEP TEP
SPLOOMP
...
THE TRANSITION FROM MOTION TO REST...
IT'S JUST TOO MUCH.
THAT'S OUR RYUU-KUN-SAN.
I KNEW YOU'D GET IT.

LOST SOUL

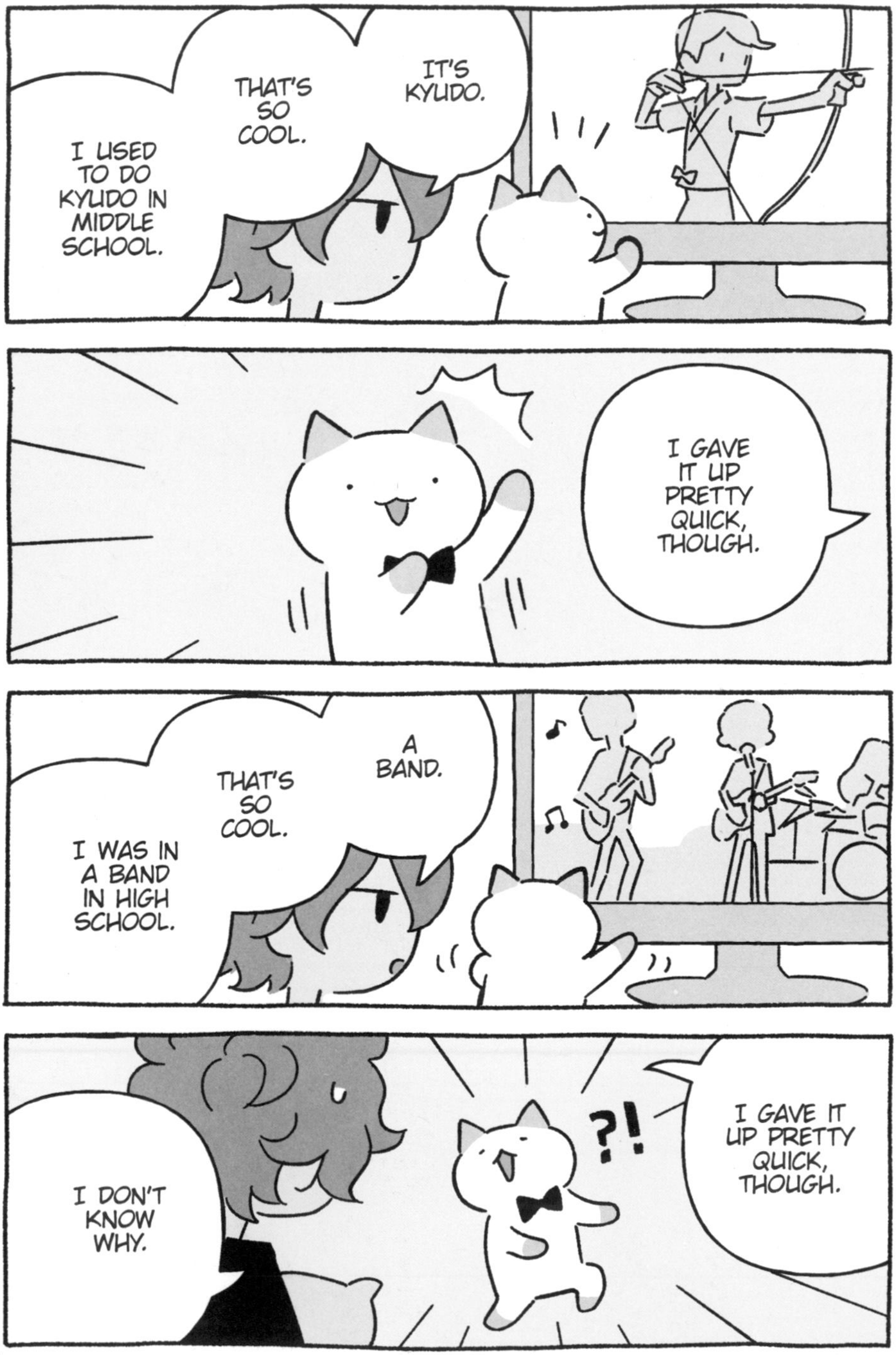
IT'S KYUDO.
THAT'S SO COOL.
I USED TO DO KYUDO IN MIDDLE SCHOOL.
I GAVE IT UP PRETTY QUICK, THOUGH.
A BAND.
THAT'S SO COOL.
I WAS IN A BAND IN HIGH SCHOOL.
I GAVE IT UP PRETTY QUICK, THOUGH.
?!
I DON'T KNOW WHY.

GUIDANCE COUNSELOR

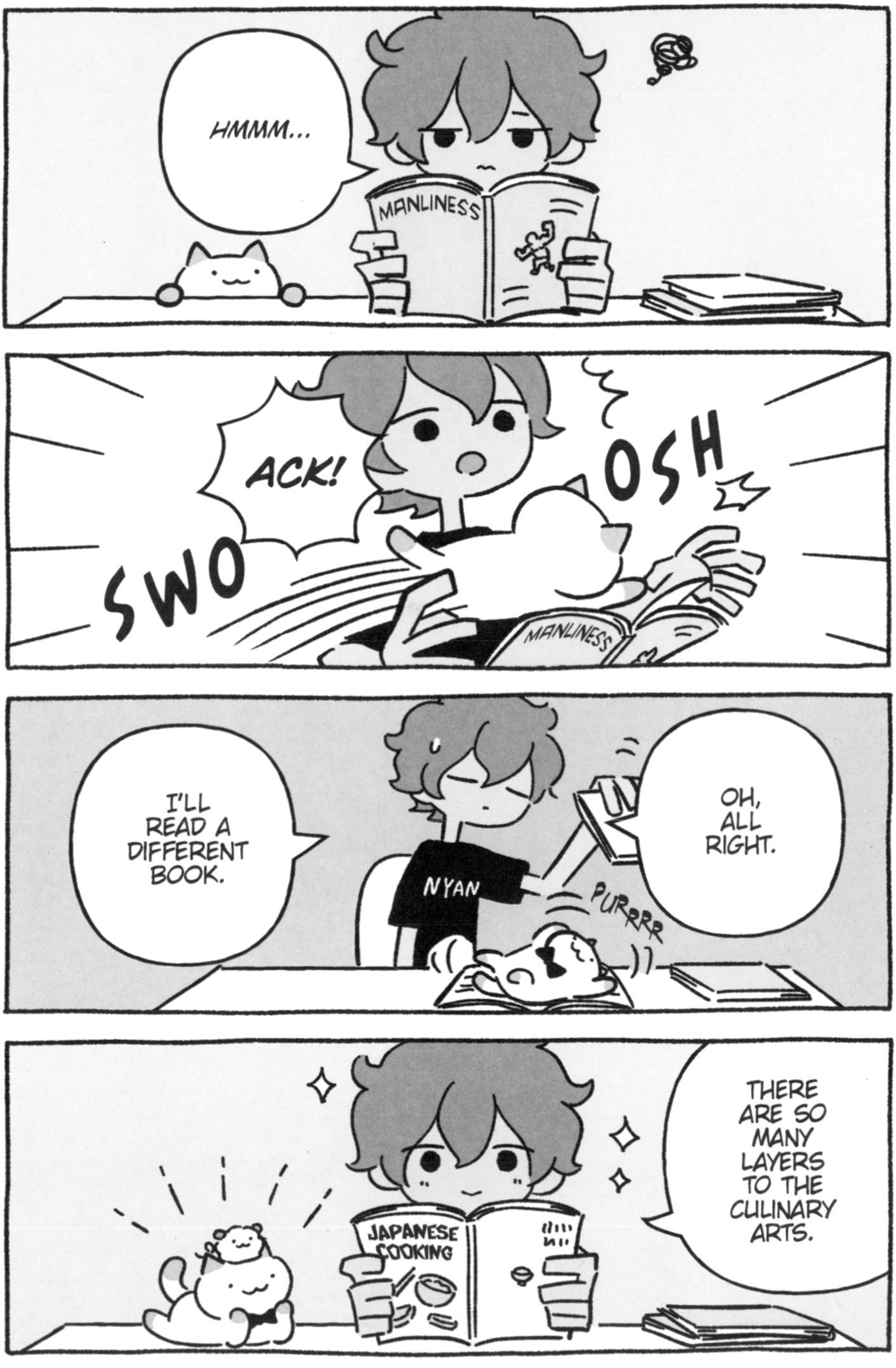
HMMM...
MANLINESS
OSH
ACK!
SWO
MANLINESS
OH, ALL RIGHT.
PURRRR
NYAN
I'LL READ A DIFFERENT BOOK.
THERE ARE SO MANY LAYERS TO THE CULINARY ARTS.
JAPANESE COOKING

BLANKET MONITOR

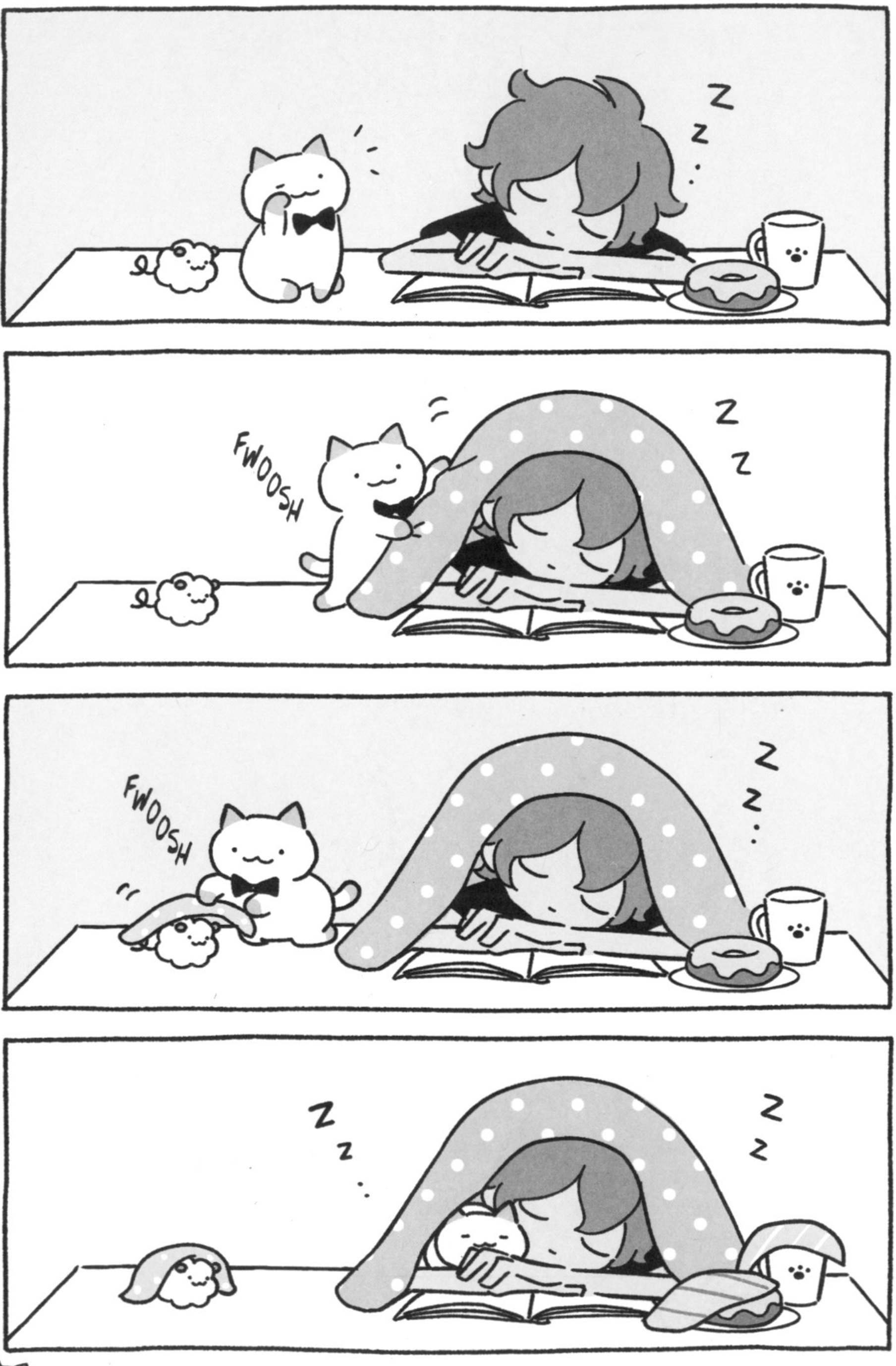
Z
Z
FWOOSH
Z
Z
FWOOSH
Z
Z
Z
Z
Z
Z

TOE BEANS AND TV

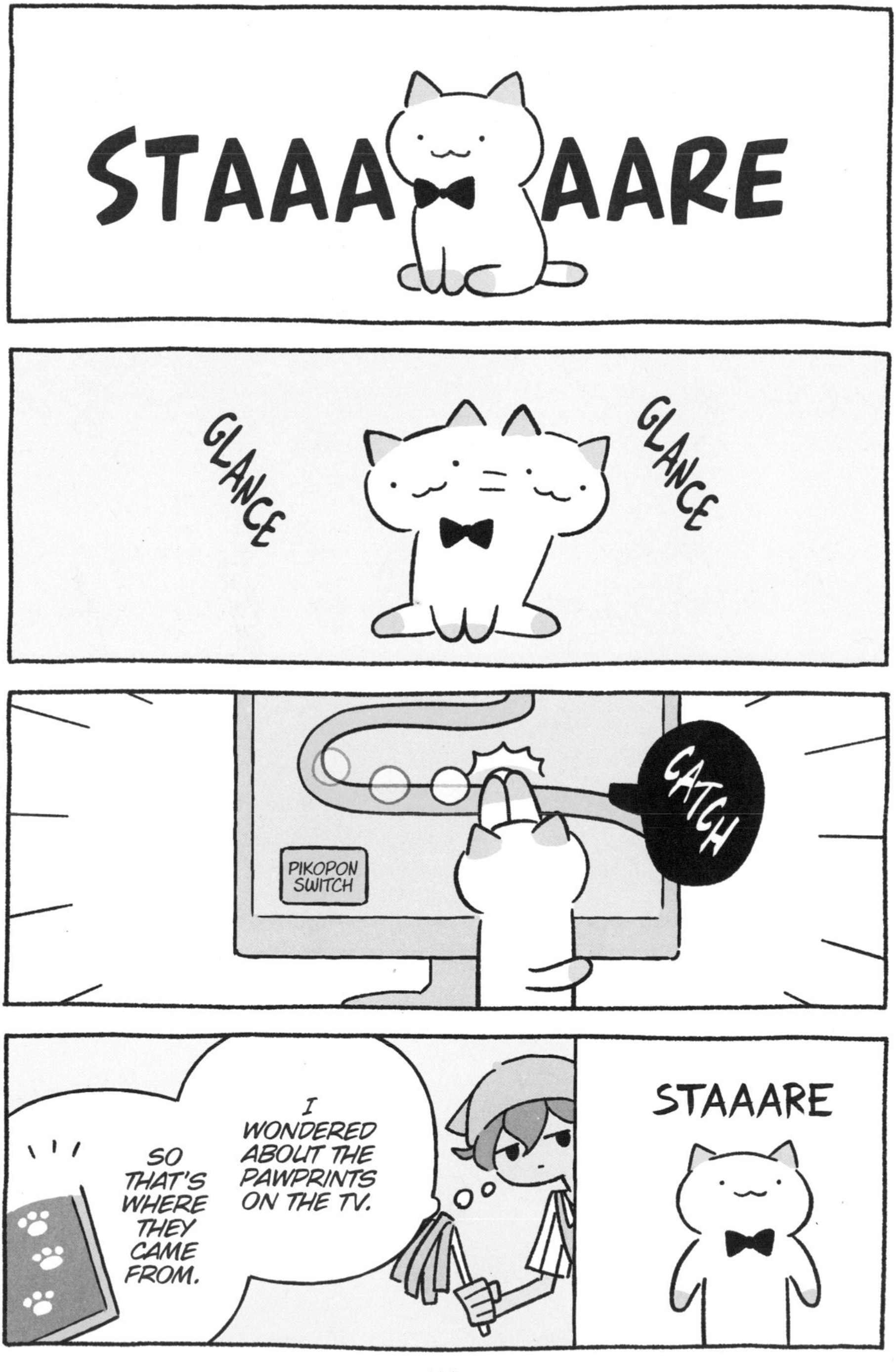
STAAA AARE
GLANCE
GLANCE
CATCH
PIKOPON SWITCH
STAAARE
I WONDERED ABOUT THE PAWPRINTS ON THE TV.
SO THAT'S WHERE THEY CAME FROM.

WHEN DID...?

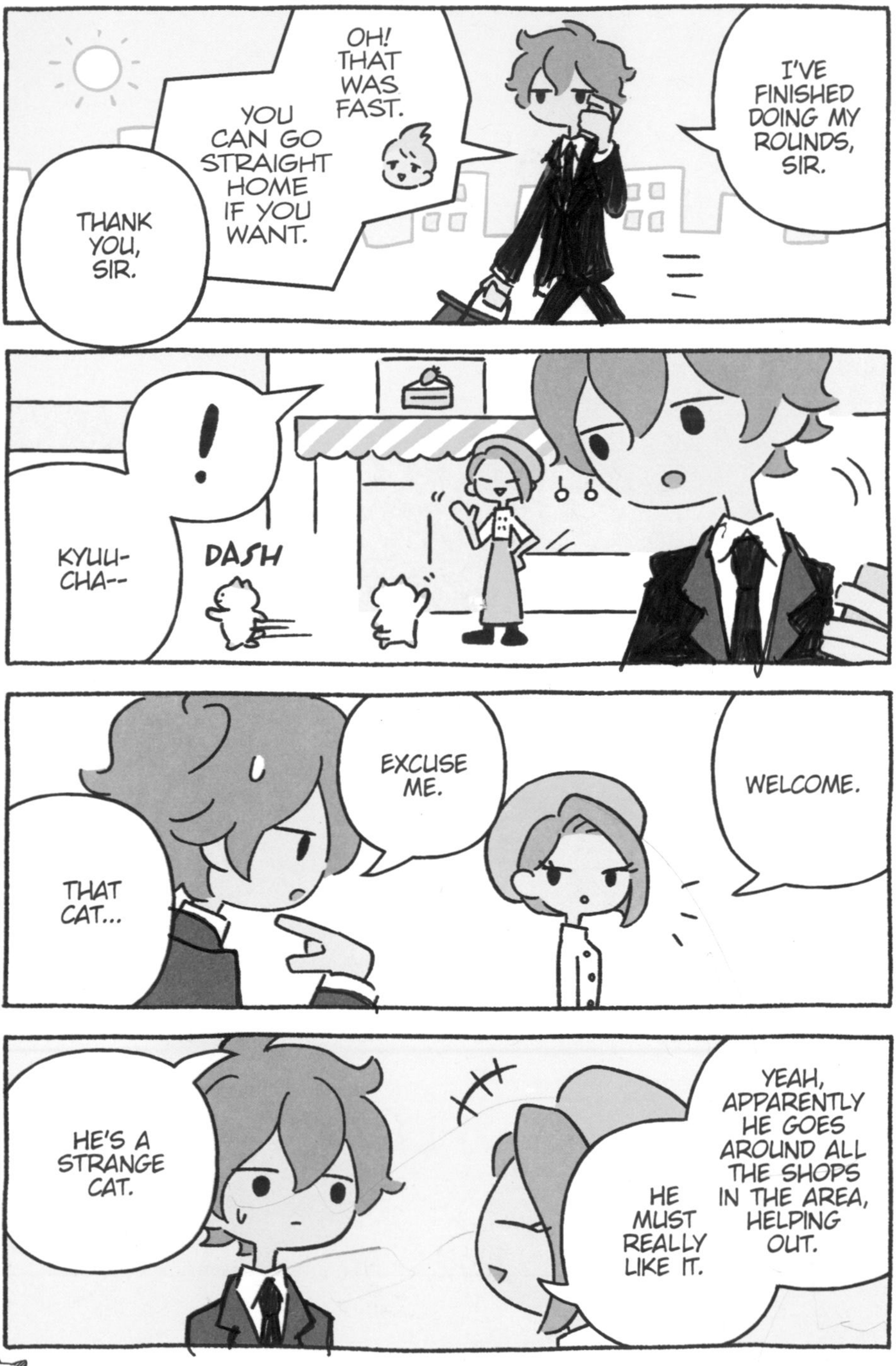
I'VE FINISHED DOING MY ROUNDS, SIR.
OH! THAT WAS FAST.
YOU CAN GO STRAIGHT HOME IF YOU WANT.
THANK YOU, SIR.
!
DASH
KYUU-CHA--
WELCOME.
EXCUSE ME.
THAT CAT...
YEAH, APPARENTLY HE GOES AROUND ALL THE SHOPS IN THE AREA, HELPING OUT.
HE MUST REALLY LIKE IT.
HE'S A STRANGE CAT.

CAT STATIONERY

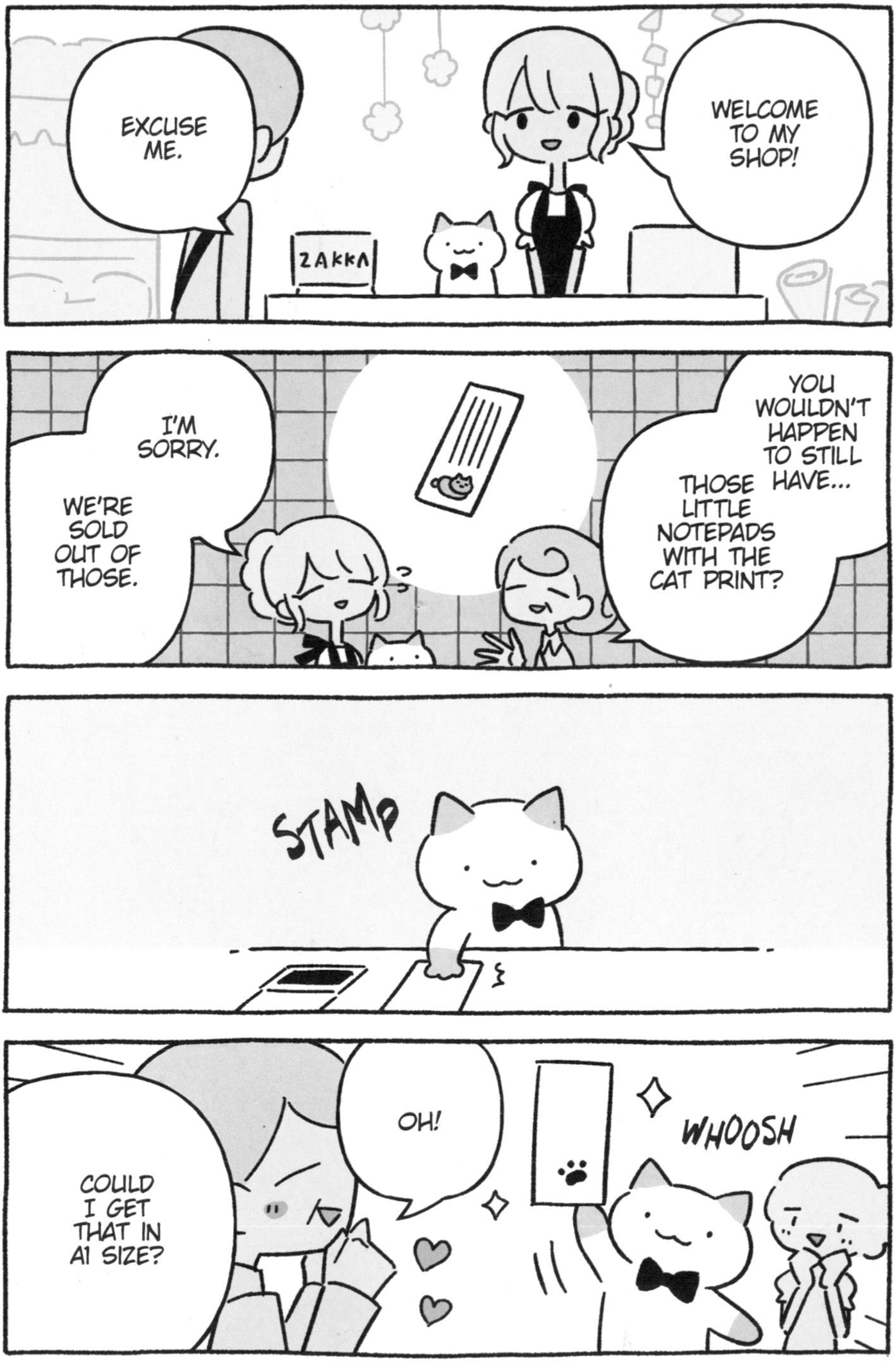
WELCOME TO MY SHOP!
ZAKKA
EXCUSE ME.
YOU WOULDN'T HAPPEN TO STILL HAVE...
THOSE LITTLE NOTEPADS WITH THE CAT PRINT?
I'M SORRY.
WE'RE SOLD OUT OF THOSE.
STAMP
WHOOSH
OH!
COULD I GET THAT IN A1 SIZE?

WHAT STARTED IT ALL

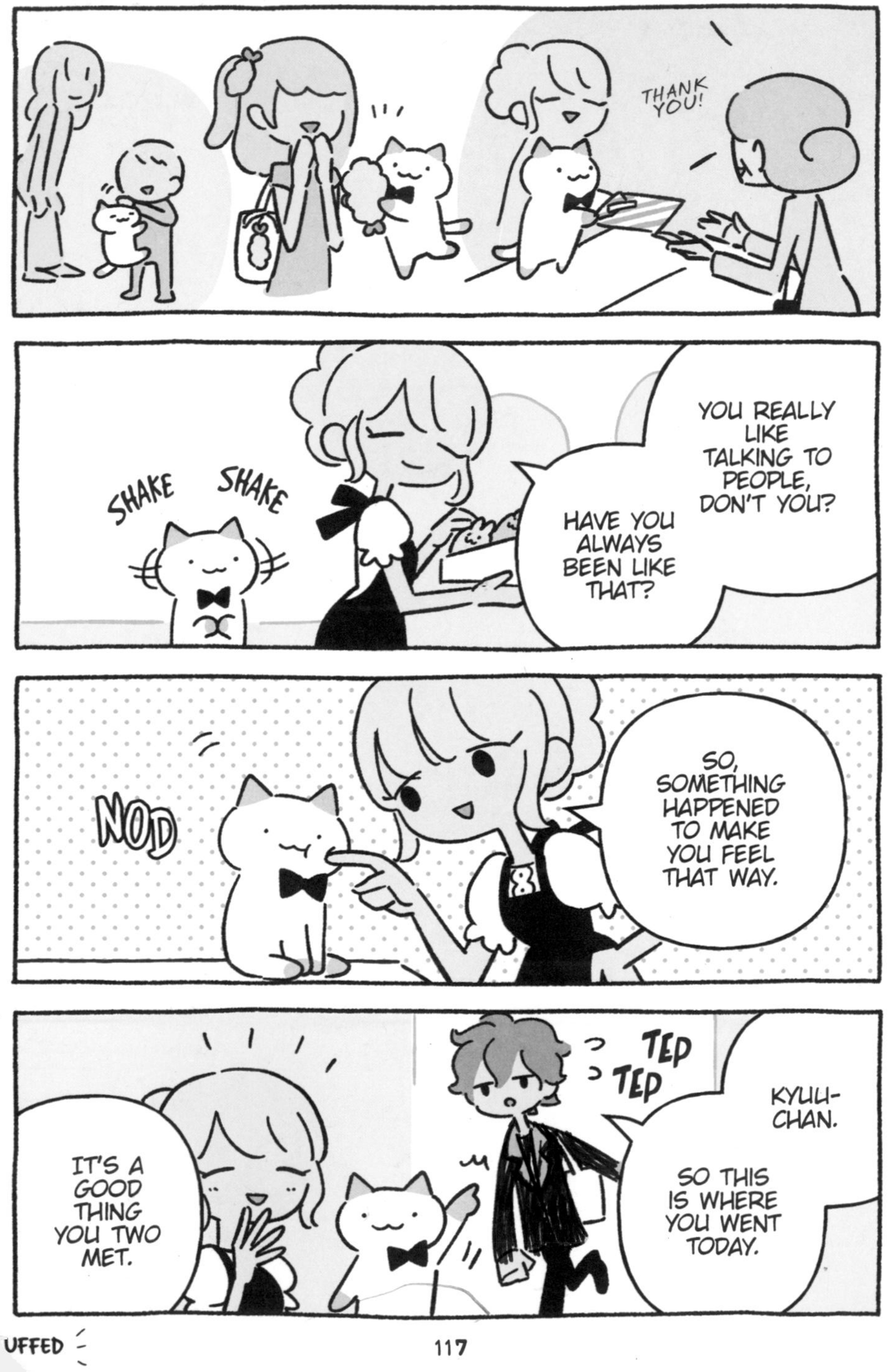
THANK YOU!
YOU REALLY LIKE TALKING TO PEOPLE, DON'T YOU?
HAVE YOU ALWAYS BEEN LIKE THAT?
SHAKE SHAKE
SO, SOMETHING HAPPENED TO MAKE YOU FEEL THAT WAY.
NOD
TEP TEP
KYUU-CHAN.
SO THIS IS WHERE YOU WENT TODAY.
IT'S A GOOD THING YOU TWO MET.

UFFED

DREAM

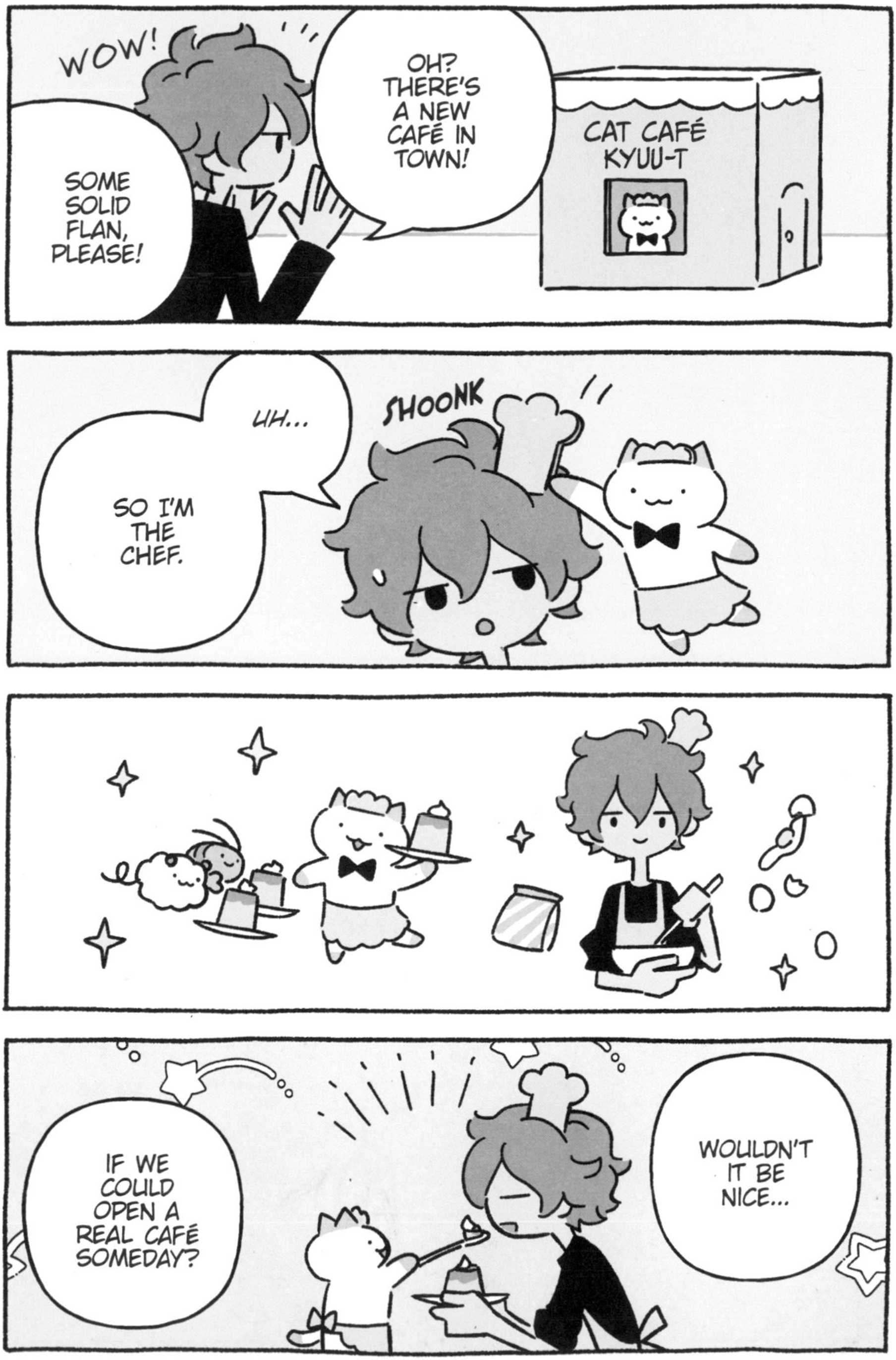
OH? THERE'S A NEW CAFÉ IN TOWN!
CAT CAFÉ KYUU-T
WOW!
SOME SOLID FLAN, PLEASE!
SHOONK
UH...
SO I'M THE CHEF.
WOULDN'T IT BE NICE...
IF WE COULD OPEN A REAL CAFÉ SOMEDAY?

THE LAMP OF DAYS GONE BY

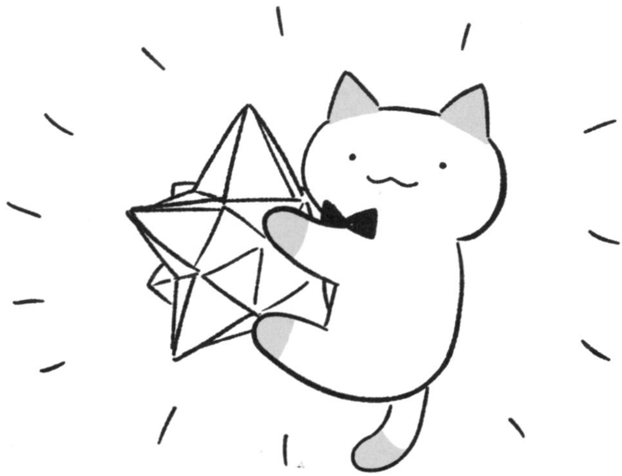

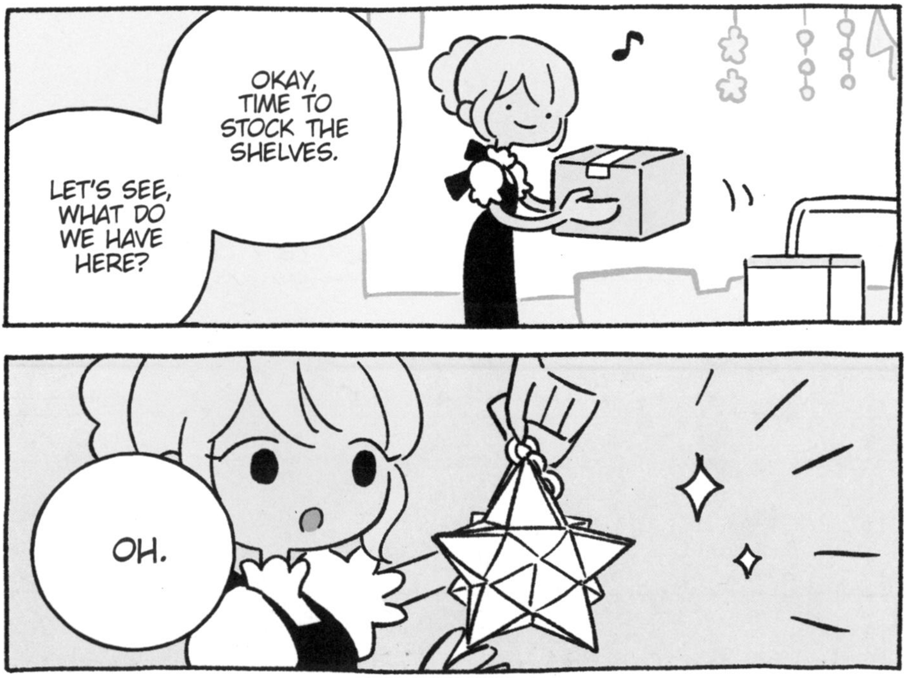
OKAY, TIME TO STOCK THE SHELVES.
LET'S SEE, WHAT DO WE HAVE HERE?
OH.

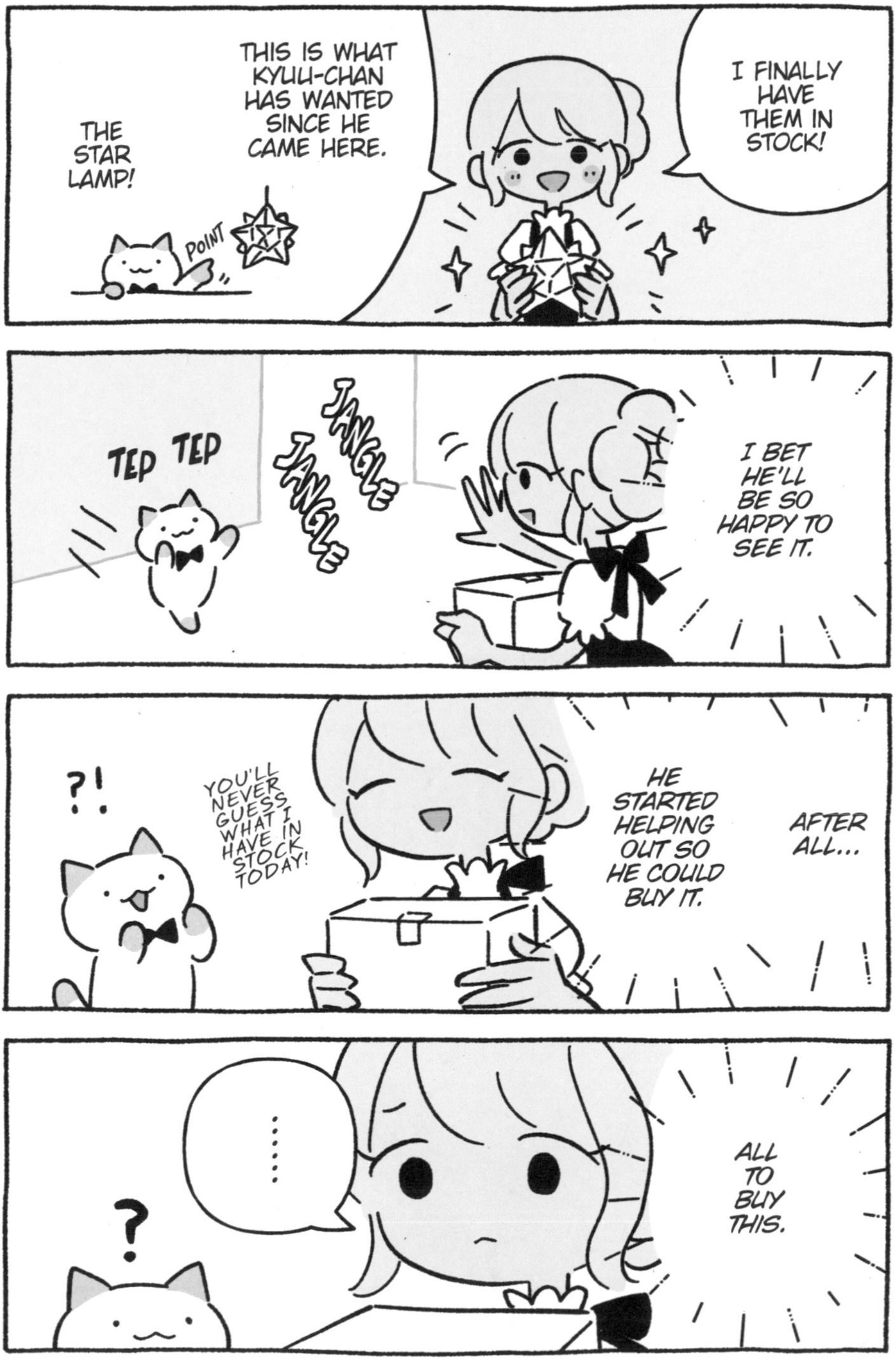
I FINALLY HAVE THEM IN STOCK!
THIS IS WHAT KYUU-CHAN HAS WANTED SINCE HE CAME HERE.
THE STAR LAMP!
POINT
I BET HE'LL BE SO HAPPY TO SEE IT.
JANGLE
JANGLE
TEP TEP
AFTER ALL...
HE STARTED HELPING OUT SO HE COULD BUY IT.
YOU'LL NEVER GUESS WHAT I HAVE IN STOCK TODAY!
?!
ALL TO BUY THIS.
......
?

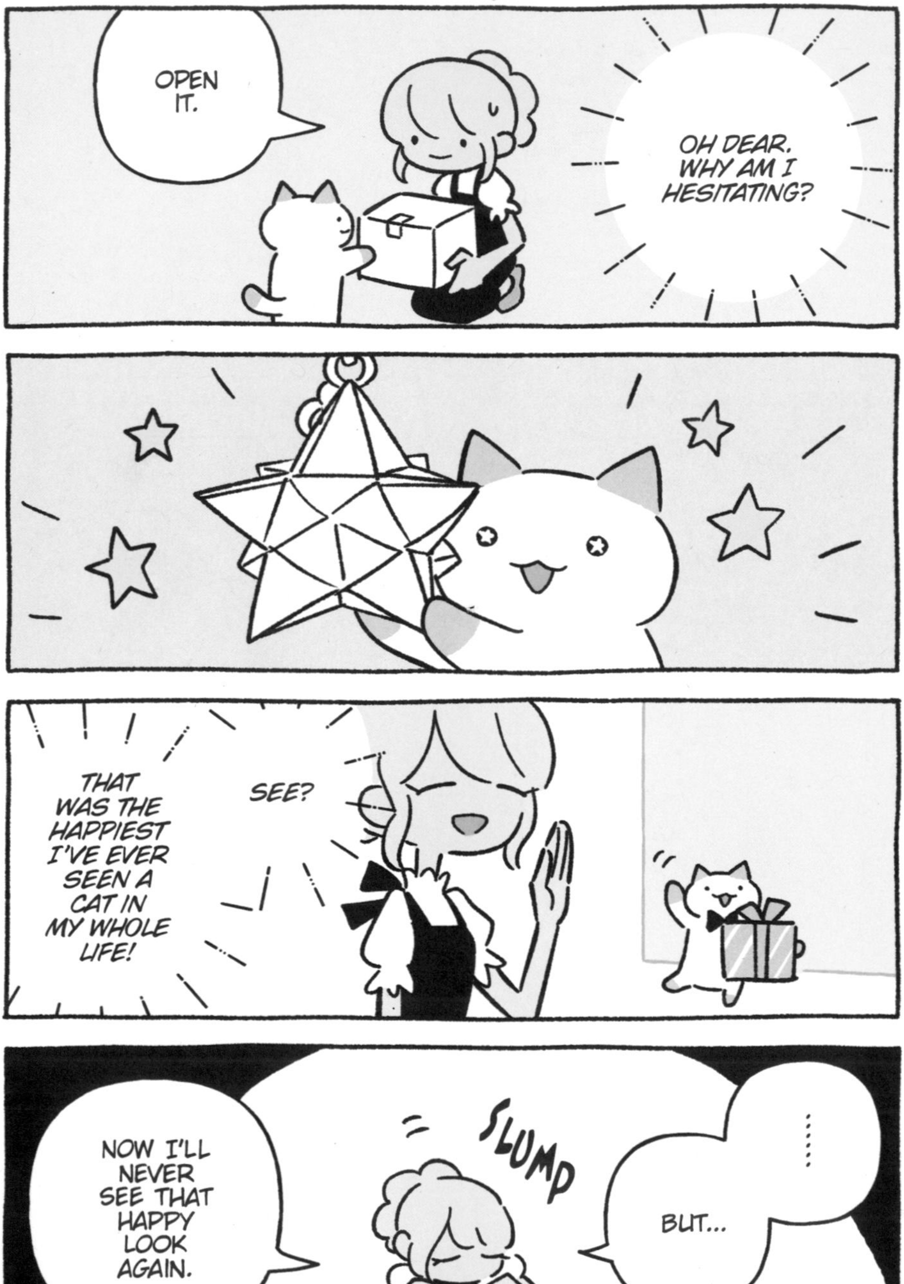
OH DEAR. WHY AM I HESITATING?
OPEN IT.
SEE?
THAT WAS THE HAPPIEST I'VE EVER SEEN A CAT IN MY WHOLE LIFE!
......
BUT...
SLUMP
NOW I'LL NEVER SEE THAT HAPPY LOOK AGAIN.

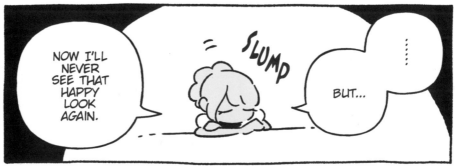

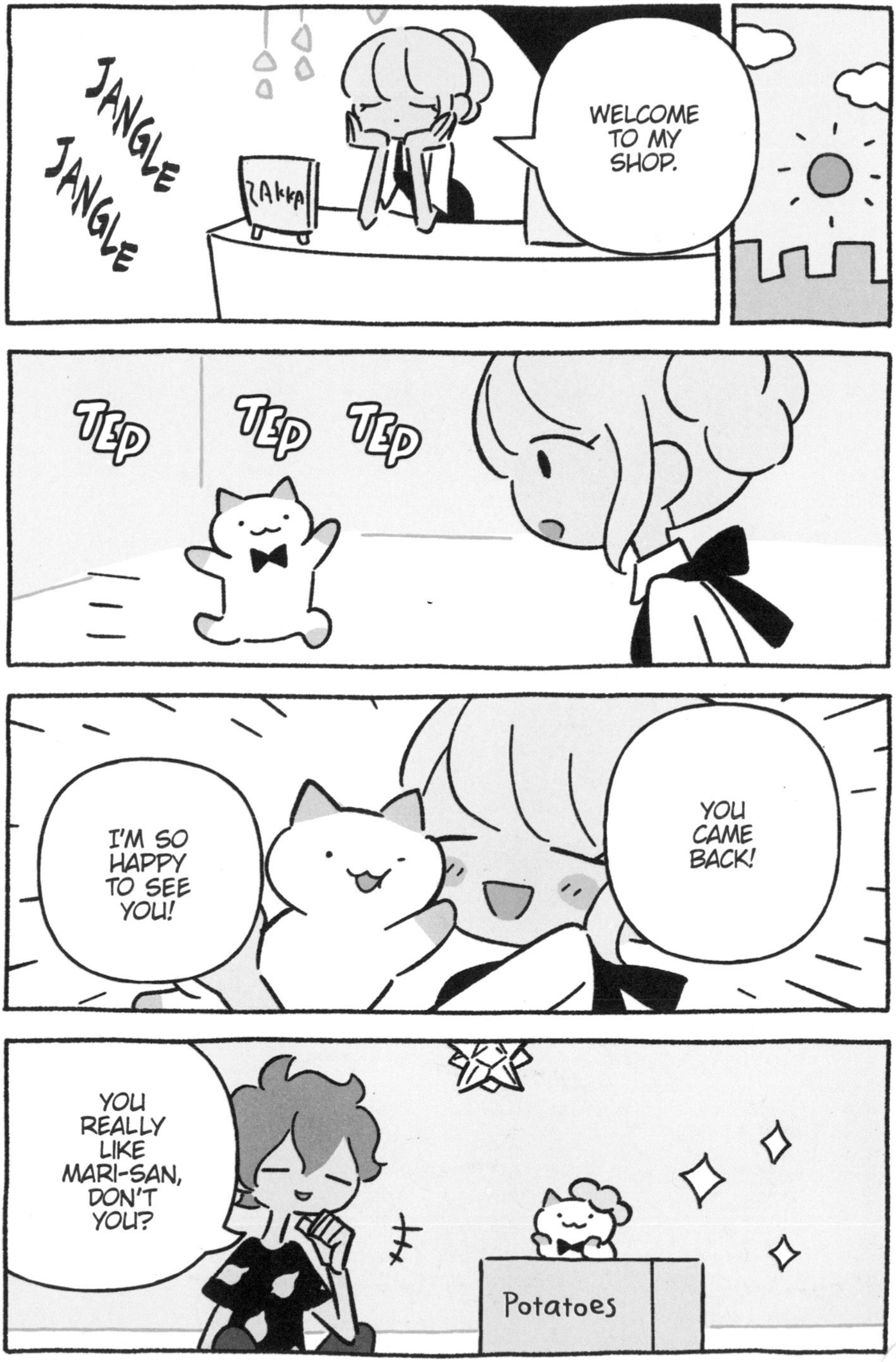
WELCOME TO MY SHOP.
ZAkka
JANGLE JANGLE
TEP TEP TEP
YOU CAME BACK!
I'M SO HAPPY TO SEE YOU!
YOU REALLY LIKE MARI-SAN, DON'T YOU?
Potatoes

FLUFFY CROSSING

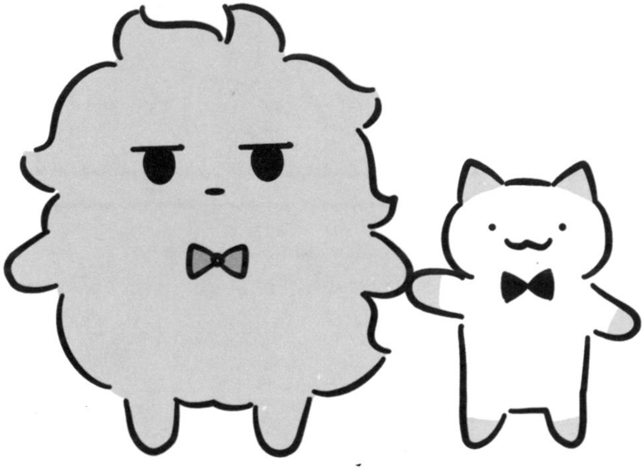

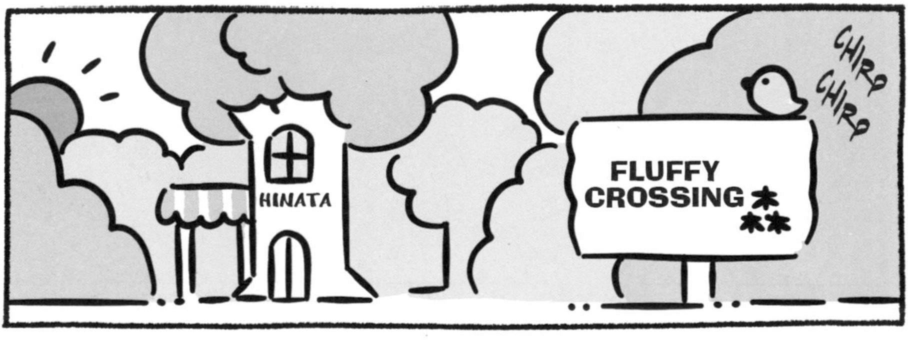
CHIRP
CHIRP
FLUFFY
CROSSING
HINATA

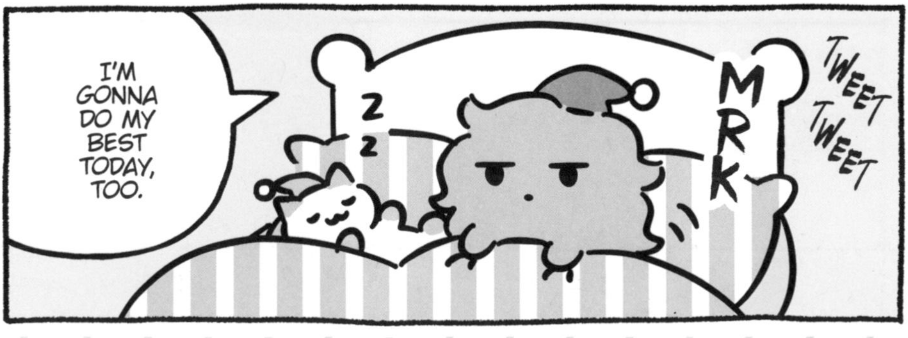
TWEET
TWEET
MRK
Z
Z
I'M GONNA DO MY BEST TODAY, TOO.

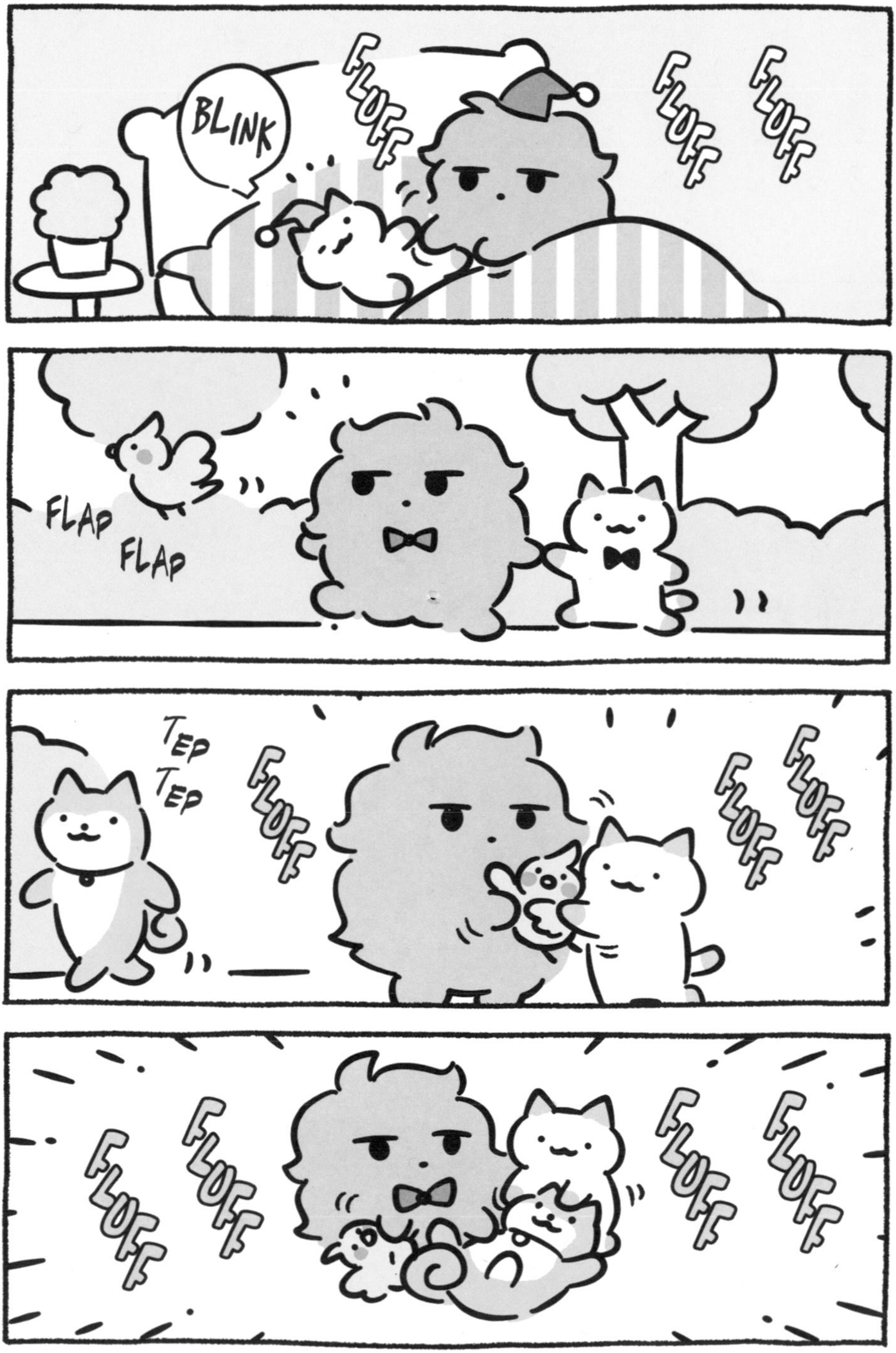
FLUFF
FLUFF
FLUFF
BLINK
FLAP
FLAP
FLUFF
FLUFF
FLUFF
TEP
TEP
FLUFF
FLUFF
FLUFF
FLUFF

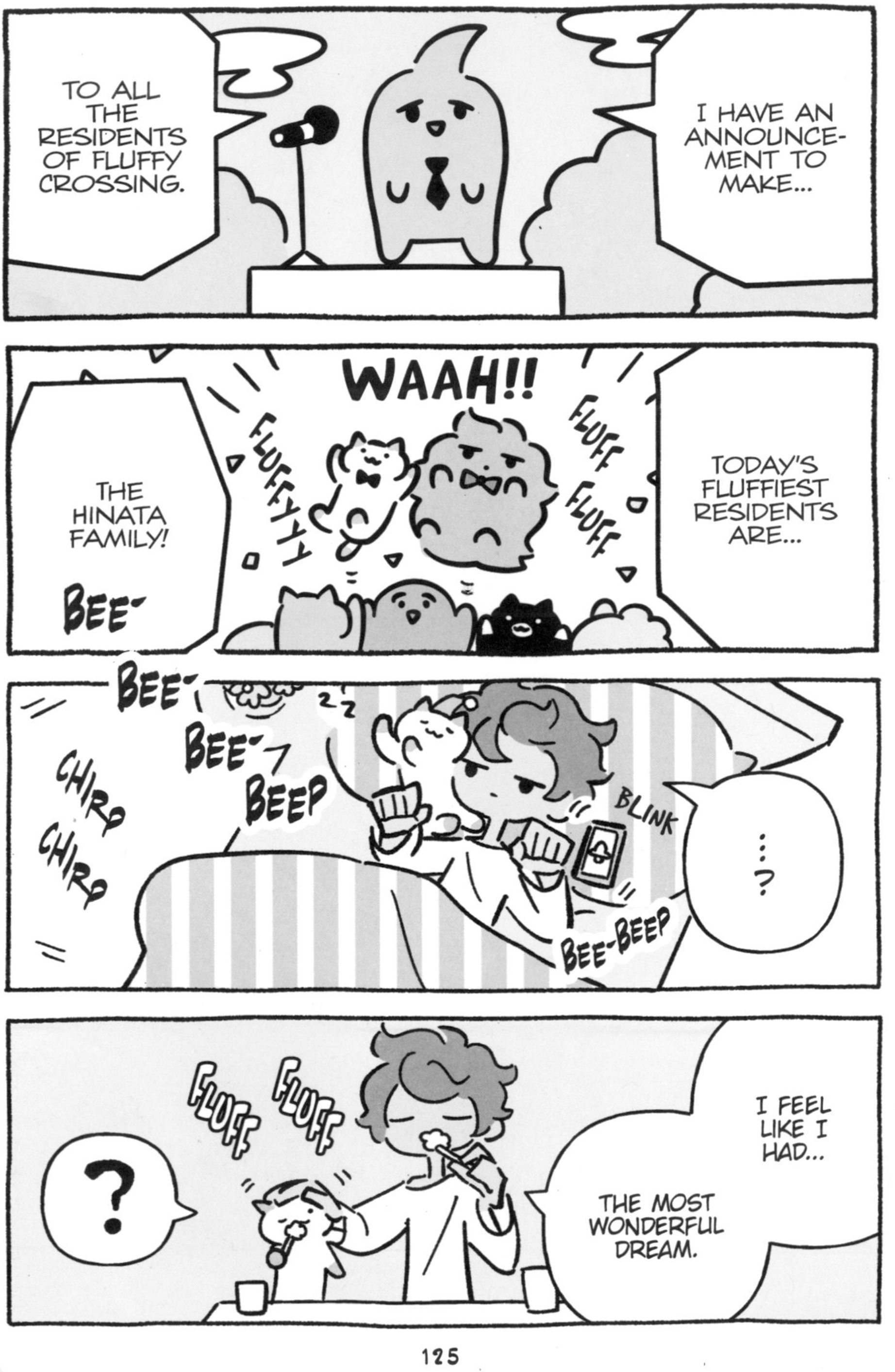
I HAVE AN ANNOUNCEMENT TO MAKE...
TO ALL THE RESIDENTS OF FLUFFY CROSSING.
TODAY'S FLUFFIEST RESIDENTS ARE...
WAAH!!
FLUFF
FLUFF
FLUFFYYY
THE HINATA FAMILY!
BEE-
...?
BLINK
BEE-BEEP
BEEP
BEE-
BEE-
CHIRP
CHIRP
I FEEL LIKE I HAD...
THE MOST WONDERFUL DREAM.
FLUFF
FLUFF
?

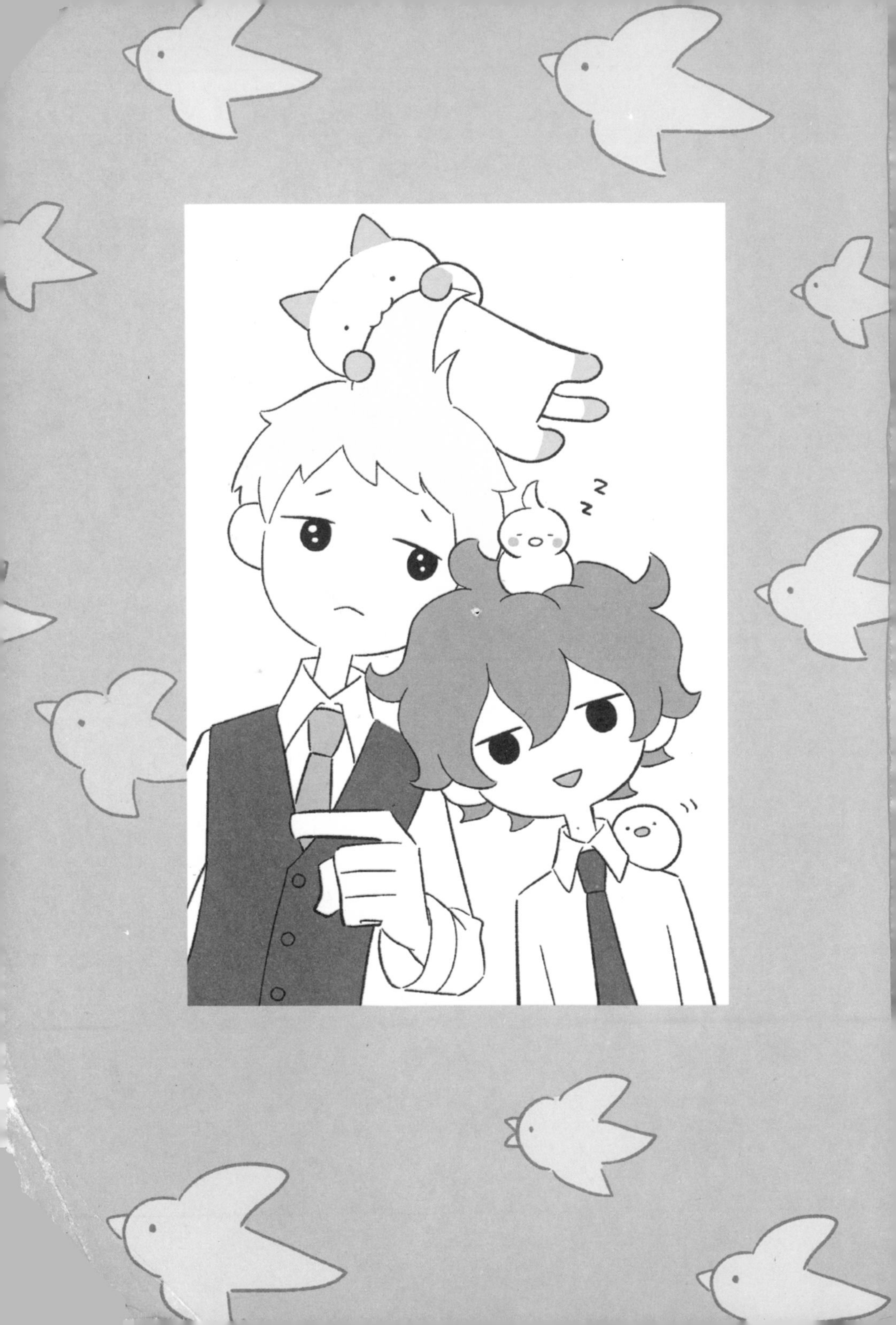

SEVEN SEAS ENTERTAINMENT PRESENTS

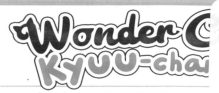

Wonder Cat Kyuu-chan

story and art by SASAMI NITORI

VOLUME 6

FUSHIGINEKO NO KYUU-CHAN VOL. 6
© SASAMI NITORI 2020 Printed in Japan
All rights reserved.
Original Japanese edition published by Star Seas Company.
English publishing rights arranged with Star Seas Company
through Kodansha Ltd., Tokyo.

Seven Seas press and purchase enquiries can be sent to Marketing Manager Lianne Sentar at press@gomanga.com. Information regarding the distribution and purchase of digital editions is available from Digital Manager CK Russell at digital@gomanga.com.

Seven Seas and the Seven Seas logo are trademarks of Seven Seas Entertainment. All rights reserved.

ISBN: 978-1-63858-390-5
Printed in Canada
First Printing: July 2022
10 9 8 7 6 5 4 3 2 1

TRANSLATION
Alethea & Athena Nibley

LETTERING
Roland Amago
Bambi Eloriaga-Amago

COVER DESIGN
H. Qi

SENIOR COPY EDITOR
Dawn Davis

SENIOR EDITOR
Peter Adrian Behravesh

PREPRESS TECHNICIAN
Melanie Ujimori

PRINT MANAGER
Rhiannon Rasmussen-Silverstein

PRODUCTION MANAGER
Lissa Pattillo

EDITOR-IN-CHIEF
Julie Davis

ASSOCIATE PUBLISHER
Adam Arnold

PUBLISHER
Jason DeAngelis

READING DIRECTIONS

This book reads from *right to left*, Japanese style. If this is your first time reading manga, you start reading from the top right panel on each page and take it from there. If you get lost, just follow the numbered diagram here. It may seem backwards at first, but you'll get the hang of it! Have fun!!

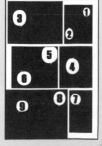